OTHER WHERE #1

MUDDY WATERS

SARA O. THOMPSON

CURIOSITY
QUILLS PRESS

A Division of **Whampa, LLC**

P.O. Box 2160

Reston, VA 20195

Tel/Fax: 800-998-2509

http://curiosityquills.com

Cover Art by Eugene Teplitsky

http://eugeneteplitsky.deviantart.com

ISBN 978-1-62007-847-1 (ebook)

ISBN 978-1-62007-851-8 (paperback)

Stephen Hawking Fears Rift-Related Doomsday, and He's Not Alone

Stephen Hawking bet Gordon Kane $100 that there is no such thing as paranormal phenomena. After losing that bet when the so-called "Rift" occurred late last year, Hawking lamented the event, saying it made physics less interesting. Now, in the preface to a new collection of essays and lectures called Humans and the Other, the famous theoretical physicist warns that the situation could one day be responsible for the destruction of the known universe.

Hawking is not the only scientist who thinks so. The theory of a Rift doomsday, where quantum disturbances create what is essentially a black hole that pulls in space and wipes out the universe, has been around for a while. However, scientists don't think it could happen anytime soon.

–By **Leslie Manning,** science writer for the New York Times, 2008

CHAPTER ONE

Someone told me once that if you have to *ask* whether you are going crazy, then you likely are *not*, in fact, losing your mind. I spent five years hoping that was true.

The thing is, I had finally gotten the litany of names right in my head, so it sounded beautiful. The names of all the women of my family.

Just how much time had I spent doing so? A thousand hours? Two thousand? More? Sometimes the list was the one fragile thing anchoring me to this world.

Time becomes a strange beast indeed when let loose from a clock.

It was this line of thinking I pursued, when on a tail end of a quick tap, the door to my room unlocked, then clicked open.

Nurse Tina, heavy of thigh and heavier of makeup, stood there with one of the boneheads. It was almost never the same bonehead. In five years, I rarely had the same one. I think the theory was the Reddick Witch is such a dangerous criminal, they'd best change up my handlers in case we have an "incident."

"Reddick? Somebody here to see you. Get on up," Tina said. "Come on, now."

I was flat on my back on the cool floor with my legs up the wall. I tipped my head to look at her, upside down. Tina doesn't take any shit from anybody, Human or otherwise.

"A visitor? Another magazine reporter?" I made air quotes around the word "magazine," still not deigning to move. Because why not?

Tina shook her head, over-inflated bleach-blond hair totally motionless. She's one of those southern women who think the higher their hair, the closer they are to Jesus. "Naw, we don't have no magazine reporters. Come on now, get up."

I took a while to get off the floor.

"How long has it been since you washed your hair?" Tina put a hand on her hip, a teasing smile showing her crooked teeth. She's not scared of me or anybody else for that matter. Granted, no one can do magic in the building, so she has little to fear, but that's beside the point.

"For your information, I washed it yesterday. As you know, I am without such luxuries as proper grooming equipment. What do you think this is? A Beverly Hills spa?" We both laughed. Gallows humor does a body good. I raked a hand through the tangled mess on my head, which, unless I was missing my mark, currently looked like I went through a carwash then fell asleep in a wind tunnel. It had grown way out and now fell not simply down past my shoulder blades but *out* past the ends of my shoulders. And, of course, I would not be so lucky as to inherit my mother's beautiful straight black hair. No, it had to be some other relative's crazy red spirals.

Derek the Bonehead brandished a pair of soft restraints, which I casually allowed to fasten on my wrists. Then he put on the restraint belt tethering us together. I allowed that too. Really, what was the point in struggling? Back when I fought every chance I got, I would buck and writhe and make it hard for them to get me to do whatever they wanted me to do.

Maybe I got smarter.

Maybe I just gave up.

Besides, I wanted to see this mystery visitor, even if he ended up trying to kill me, like the last one did.

Derek took a solid hold of my arm, and we marched forward. I'm fairly certain many of the hospital's boneheads must have been Werehounds, but it was never confirmed to me.

"Watch it, kid, you'll bruise the merchandise." I waggled my eyebrows. He scowled and let out a very low growl but held firm.

Just outside the door loitered a small cadre of boneheads.

"All this for lil ol' me?" I batted my lashes. They surrounded us, me and Derek in the ring of armed guards wrapped in protective gear.

As the herd shuffled down the hallway, I bombarded Tina with questions. "Who is it? What does he want? What does he look like? Is he tall, dark, and handsome?"

Tina laughed in spite of herself. "Girl, you are too much. I don't know. I ain't seen him. They just called and said bring you down. But he's got all kinds of papers on you, supposably." Even though she's one hundred percent Human, Nurse Tina can pin a water buffalo in point three seconds. Precise diction isn't part of her general repertoire though.

We arrived at the waiting room. Institutional-grade couches and coffee tables peppered the place, but the visitor sat at a low Formica table at the back wall. The sharp tang of disinfectant made my eyes water a little. When he stood, I was struck by how tall he was. A good bit over six feet. And attractive. Granted, my bar for "hot men" was set pretty low. After this long, I'd seen a couple of bare-naked asses, but trust me, at a place like Lakeland, those weren't the ones you wanted to see. This guy though... He reminded me a little bit of the Goth wannabe Witches at my high school back in the day. But he was *actually* cool.

His skin was pale and his blue-black hair shaggy but not unkempt. He wore dark jeans, a black t-shirt, and a deep gray leather jacket, all of it fitting like it was tailor-made to grace his body. A Dark Elf. Been a while since I'd seen one, even before I began my unfortunate incarceration at the Lakeland Psychiatric Hospital. Full Others work there, but Humans, Halfs, Knackers, and the rare Other are the only ones allowed to be patients. I sometimes wondered if Others have their own version of Lakeland on their side.

My mouth went dry and my palms clammy, as my mind began to wake up for the first time in five years.

A guard posted himself at the door. Derek guided me into a chair and fastened me to the bolt on the table.

The pale man looked at us.

"Is this she?"

"I'm Tessa Reddick, if that's what you're asking," I barked, much harsher than I wanted to. Besides my daily chats with Tina, I hadn't had a lot of practice in the social arts the last few years. He gave me a hard look.

Tina cleared her throat behind me and squeezed my arm hard—a message to shape up. People like Tina make or break you in a place like this. She could have had me in a drug-induced haze three feet thick in no time flat if she wanted to. "You all have a little talk." She pointed daggers at me with her brown eyes. "I'll be out in the hall. But I don't expect there to be any problems." I nodded my assent. "Your fifteen minutes starts now."

I shifted in the hard plastic chair. He sat rigidly across from me and pulled out a very shiny badge. "Special Agent Qyll Toutant. FBI. Supernormal Investigations." That voice. A little bit of a Welsh accent in a most pleasing timbre. The trademark silver eyes of his race.

My warm bits got a little warmer.

"Supernormal? Is that what they're calling them these days?" I tried to sound cavalier.

"It was deemed the least offensive term for the immigrants."

I snorted.

He folded his long-fingered hands on the table. "Miss Reddick, I shall not mince words. I understand you are a Witch and a rather gifted one at that. Also, you have a working understanding of Otherwhere and are a superior practitioner of Air Magic. Is that accurate?"

The answer hung in my throat. I'd worked hard trying to convince myself that Magic was bad, that it was the reason I was in this aesculapian prison and therefore not be mentioned. But it's like telling a fish not to swim. And now, this man, here, bringing it up like an everyday thing.

I leaned closer to him. "I want to know who you are and why you're here."

"I've told you who I am." His tone sharpened just a hair. "And I'm here because the FBI needs your help."

My jaw tightened. I kept my voice low, too, and stared him right in the eyes. "Yeah, I'm a Witch. I know all about the Rift. I know what goes bump in the night, *and* I can pull a rabbit out of a hat. I've been on death row, I've been declared mentally incompetent, and I've been subjected to all manner of bodily searches. I also cannot imagine what the FBI wants with me."

Which didn't stop me from being curious and terrified at the same time. I'd been at Lakeland for so long and had only the odd visitor come to gawk at the crazy killer Witch, like the damn rubberneckers at a circus freak show. Tina sends them packing, except the one time, the first time... when a hex mage blew himself up trying to curse *me* inside a heavily fortified anti-magic area. "I don't know any FBI agents. And I didn't think I warranted a federal case."

He inclined his head. "Can you tell me your mother's name?"

"No," I said automatically. He lifted an eyebrow in surprise. "Sorry. Old habits." You don't give names out easily if you know what's good for you. Too easy for something to summon you if it knows your true name. But I guess it didn't matter now. "Cerridwyn Reddick. She's dead. She died..." Heat bubbled in my chest at the thought. I fought down a grimace as my voice caught in my throat. "She died a few years ago."

"Yes. In a house fire that killed thirty-seven people. All women. All Witches. All your blood kin."

"Bullshit." I growled as anger kept rising unbidden in my eyes, and a hard lump swelled in my throat.

"A house fire you deny setting." His tone wasn't condemning.

"I didn't summon it." I slammed my fists on the table. "And I didn't set that fire," I said. Well, shouted, whatever. "We were getting ready for a High Sabbat... and, I still don't know what happened. *I don't remember*. It's all in the court documents, which I'm sure you have read."

He kept looking at me with those silvery eyes, his voice curiously calm. "And what do you know of the Rift?"

"Seriously? Screw you, jackass." I stood up, chains clanking, awkward in the restraints. "Tina! Come back. I'm done."

He remained silent, staring up at me.

We glared at each other for a long beat.

"For fuck's sake," I muttered, sliding back into the chair. "Ok. I'll play along." Placing my hands primly in front of me, I gave him my best a cheesy documentary voice. "Hello, I'm Tessa Reddick. I'm a Witch. My family is centuries old, maybe more. Before the Rift, people like me told everybody we were just really good at being Wiccans. More than a decade ago, the veil between the worlds just dropped. How curious! Now, the event itself is called "the Rift." The actual hole between the worlds is also commonly referred to as "the Rift." For example, "Before the Rift, I could not schlep my ass through the Rift."

"Creatures not from Earth, from the place we call now Otherwhere, come through the holes. Some of them on vacation! Look at them now, watching the fat lazy Humans like cows on a farm! Sometimes Humans go the other way into that world. Look at *them* now, getting lost over there and getting turned into god-knows-what! Big bads and big goods can't stay long on Earth because they're too powerful. We're all one big happy family now, except we're not. Go this way or that, we're all mad here."

By the time I got to the end of it, my voice was shaking and stone cold.

"Is that enough?"

Agent Toutant regarded me for a moment, then nodded. "It will suffice for now." He flipped open a file in front of him. "First, I'd like to talk about why we need your assistance. The FBI created the Supernormal Investigations unit seven years ago. We are a regional office covering the Mid-Atlantic and Upper South area of the United States. You have probably not heard of us. We are, as some say, under the radar. Our purpose is to investigate crimes in Earth involving Others or those who have learned magic. As well as the mostly Humans. Earth-born, I believe most call them."

"Mostly Human as in, say, Witches."

He nodded. "Precisely." He flipped through his papers. "To which end, your father? I'm sorry, I am not aware of his background."

"Neither am I. He was Human. That's all I know."

Toutant made a note.

"So by-the-book." He raised his head. "Oh, don't mind me. Document away. But just tell me first, where the hell were you and your little file when I was tried and locked up for something I didn't do?" My voice sounded strained and uneven.

He blinked. "There was an agent present at every legal proceeding. However, the evidence against you was great enough that at the time, we couldn't have done much. Laws have changed, and our counterevidence is much more plentiful now."

"Took you long enough."

"Be that as it may, SI deals in Other affairs as well as those of Original Other beings like Mordieri Primus, and Wrach Du. All the magical hierarchies from Hedge to Hex. The Weres, as well as Fulls, Jezebels, Bachuses, Totemics, among others. Those with learned magic via talisman or curse are also among our purview. Tell me, have you heard of Others' Little Helpers?"

I nodded. "One of them tried to see me several months ago. Wanted to interview me." The guy—Mark something—had nearly gotten through because Tina was off that day and the nurse in charge thought the kid really was my brother.

Toutant pointed to the paper between us. It was a screenshot of an Internet site. "They fancy themselves a watchdog group for individuals in your situation."

"What, in the loony bin? Yes, the editor has made rather a nuisance of himself. He writes me a *lot* of fan mail."

"Mr. Mark Tabler, correct?"

I went with a noncommittal nod. "He's been emailing for a while." What I mean by that is, he sends Tina emails, and sometimes she reads them to me, and we have a bit of a laugh. I'm not allowed access to the Internet, and I'm sure my old address is jammed with spam, so it's the best I can hope for.

"He's been busy. They believe you were framed, Miss Reddick," Qyll said quietly.

I looked up at him, waiting for the punchline. That didn't seem to be forthcoming. My heart rate quickened again. I wanted to shout, "I was! I *was* framed! I didn't do it!" But I'd spent my first year screaming that to everybody in shouting range, and all I got for my efforts were bigger doses of Attivan and Klonopin.

I swallowed hard instead.

It should go without saying my many months at Lakeland had been the most despairing in my life. I had zero proof I did not start the fire, and to hear someone—anyone—set themselves on my side fostered a tiny cautious hope.

"We believe them. Partly because you were tried by an exclusively Human court instead of a jury of your peers, and in the last five years, we at SI have been unable to touch you or your case. Blocked, as it were. I don't have time to go into details now, and many of them are above my pay grade. What we do know is that the evidence was circumstantial at best, and at worst, a carefully articulated frame-up.

"The Arcana put a curious lack of emphasis on the situation as well, even after the attempt on your life. We don't know why they turned a blind eye, but they did, and for the most part, they remain rather steadfast in the belief you are indeed guilty. While the details of your case remain bizarre and something the FBI plans to investigate further with your full cooperation, most importantly, we want you to join Supernormal Investigations. SI needs your expertise. And you need our protection. We have not been able to find an American Witch on this side who is of your caliber. Especially after those who may have been of help perished in the very house fire that you have been accused of starting."

He did not say any of this unkindly. And he smelled, I noticed, very nice—like the winter woods at midnight.

"Flattery will get you everywhere, my dear." My tone was grim.

I let it all percolate through my head. Freedom and a chance to figure it all out. I'd be crazy not to jump at this, right? (Ha—see what I did there? Crazy?)

"Ok, but what's in this for me? I'm not really interested in being someone's trained monkey. And I'm kind of out of the magic business."

"You mean besides clearing your name and learning the truth?"

Toutant flipped through the file. He laid out four eight-by-ten glossy photos that were mostly just masses of red and purple with brown streaks. I took them for snapshots of some kind of modern painting until I realized what I was looking at.

"What did that?" I gasped, looking at him in horror. His face remained placid.

"That, Miss Reddick, is what we need you for."

"What happened to those... oh my god... were those horses?" My gorge rose at the sight. I fought not to vomit my cafeteria Salisbury steak all over the table. He put the photos away. A few deep breaths through the nose settled me down a little bit.

"I can get you out of this hospital, released on your own recognizance, but ultimately under the protective wing of SI. We've pulled a few strings. Many strings, in fact. Someone above me, and my boss, in fact, really wants you working with us. In return, you will stay on with SI for a minimum of seven years and one day. During such time, you will have a job, a modest paycheck, and a secure place to live. We were also able to re-establish the shop you owned with your mother, including the apartment and its accompanying chattel. It will afford you a home and additional income, beyond what we are able to pay you, which isn't terribly much, I'm afraid. Although, you will have decent benefits should our arrangement work well and you stay on with the FBI. Perhaps you will also regain some of the social standing lost during your stay here. We even found your, erm, cat."

Dorcha! My mouth fell open. Just the thought of that ball of fur made my atrial mechanics stutter.

I stared at Agent Toutant for what felt like hours, waiting for him to dissolve into mist. Magic wasn't allowed in the hospital, strictly speaking, but some bored demi-god could have managed this as a practical joke if he really put his mind to it.

"Should SI decide to terminate your employment at any time before your 2,556 days are up, you may still enjoy the protection until your seven years are through. Should you decide to terminate the contract, our agreement will become null and void. In short, we will have no way to protect you."

I smirked. "Sounds like an offer I can't refuse, Godfather."

A quick puzzled look appeared on his face. Then recognition. "The film. Yes. I should think you would be quite open to this arrangement."

"So, I come out and work for you, you protect me. If you decide I'm not working out, and you fire me, I'm still safe. But if I decide I'm no FBI agent, I'm on my own?"

"This order has come down from the Assistant Director in Charge. I admit this is a peculiar plan of action, but I have been informed that more information than what I have shared is not available to me."

I looked out the window. Cleared my throat. Wondered if this was worth it.

He checked his watch and his manner became a little brisker. "The other item I'd like to discuss is linked. We have reason to believe you are currently being targeted by whomever made the previous attempts at eliminating your family. Finishing the job, so to speak. The sooner we remove you from this place the better."

"Oh? And how do you know that?"

"Miss Reddick, the FBI is not completely incompetent. While you may have been held out of our grasp during your trial, we have been keeping tabs on you here. There is a facility staff member who has arranged for the delivery of a weapon, the express purpose of which is to execute a certain Witch."

Witch. The word brought me up short. It sort of implied doing magic again. But did I want to? Look where it had gotten me. Maybe I should just let him shoot me, whoever it is. Lakeland's no party. Would death be that much worse?

I shook my head. "No. I'm not going with you. I don't want to get involved. I'm in deep enough, thanks very much. I just want to do my time, get out, and disappear."

Toutant's look sharpened considerably. "Miss Reddick, I know of no way to illustrate to you how important you are to our organization." His voiced dropped as he pinned me to my seat with his gaze. "I will speak as plainly as I can. You will die here. The odds are nearly one hundred percent likely that it will be today. Soon. Unless you come with me. Now."

I leaned forward and matched his tone. "No. I told you. No more magic. No more spells. It can't save me. It won't protect me. It didn't protect my family. Besides, I'm not afraid of dying."

He looked irritated, but also somehow empathetic. "No. I understand that. But Miss Reddick, I must inform you again that if you do not come with me, chances are, death may be the least of your worries. Not only that, I believe you are the one person who can help stop these murders. Further still, I believe you are also the one person who can help us stave off what's coming. There are indeed things worse than death, I assure you. I have seen it." He leaned on the table, gripping the edge.

"I do not mean to sound dramatic, Miss Reddick. I also do not know how else to convince you. There will be an attempt on your life today, and you will not survive it; and if you do, you will wish you had not."

It was as though the very air in the room congealed around me. The way he spoke, the way his eyes bore into mine. He was *not* kidding or lying or overstating.

I sat back down.

For half a heartbeat, we locked eyes.

Then I nodded.

"OK. I'll go." He appeared visibly relieved. "Besides"—I leaned toward him again, grinning—"I almost never say no to handsome strangers."

As we raced through the sun-bright streets, I pelted Qyll with questions.

"Where are we going? What else do you know about me? What's

going on? Where's Dorcha?"

He ignored me, and we drove in silence for perhaps fifteen minutes.

Finally, he said, "We learned someone on the hospital staff was going to make an attempt on your life today. Not by magical means this time, as you may have noticed. Most likely with a gun to your head. Or the heart. Thankfully, we also had some on the inside working with us."

"Who? Was it Tina?" It had to have been. Nobody else was close enough to have access.

He inclined his head. "Well-spotted. She is part of a small but diehard group that believes in your innocence. She has been biding her time, watching over you. And when she learned of this attempt, she called me. I'm taking you to your shop, but you must not go anywhere for several days." He looked at me. "It won't be safe."

My shop. My life. Even confined to my apartment, no more restraints or medications or people ignoring me and afraid of me because I came here ranting about being framed with magic. No more crappy hospital food or locks on the doors. I could have shoes with laces and drink bourbon and shoot a gun if I wanted. I don't typically shoot guns, but the point was that I *could*. Maybe I should get a gun just so I could shoot it.

"Wait, what about the Arcana?" The rising hope in me paused. "They assigned me a Watcher. They still think I did it."

"Ah." His eyebrow rose. "Your Otherwhere liaison. We freed you from Human imprisonment, but at the moment we have little jurisdiction over the Other half of your punishment. You will retain your Watcher for the time being. That might not be a bad thing, an extra pair of eyes on you if someone intends you harm. And as far and we can tell, you remain *persona non grata* with most of the supernormal community."

My Watcher, Gideon. White suits, white teeth, white-blond hair. Ice-blue eyes. He's exactly what you envision when you think of an Angel. The Judeo-Christian Dolce and Gabbana parole officer version of an Angel. Luckily for my composure, he wasn't allowed to just pop in at Lakeland; he had to schedule meetings via Tina.

I hissed through my teeth. "So whoever framed me was pretty

thorough. I knew it was too good to be true." I banged a palm on the dashboard. But still, it beat staying at Lakeland, especially given the assassination attempt I had apparently missed.

On the sidewalk, as we stopped on a light, a big group of Humans, maybe forty or fifty in all, stood swaying, wearing what looked like linen robes in shades of brown and green.

I rolled the window down to hear them chanting.

"What are they doing? Who are they?"

Without looking, Qyll hissed through his teeth, "Roll up the window. They are called 'the Fervor.' Roll up the window *now*."

No, seriously, that stick up his ass had to *go*! "They can't hurt us, Q. Look, they're slower than my over-medicated ex-neighbors at Lakeland. Who are they?"

"They claim to have reached a higher spiritual plane than everybody else. If you believe them, they are as close to what they call 'God' as it is possible for a born-Human to get. Without having died, of course. They speak ridiculous prophecy and all manner of gibberish. Roll up the window, Miss Reddick."

The people had shaved heads and blank eyes. As we sat waiting for the light, one of them looked directly at me then ambled out into the street toward the car, pointing and mumbling.

"Roll up the window," Qyll said, with this deliberate evenness you'd use with a toddler.

"What's she saying?" I leaned out toward the woman. The closer she got, the easier it was to see her pink-rimmed eyes were nearly colorless, as were her lips. Her mouth worked to say words I couldn't hear. She was death-pale, the skin on her face dry and flaky.

"Hey!" I screeched. Qyll used the electric window button. The woman's hand almost got caught, but she froze at the last minute, palms pressed on the glass, odd eyes burning holes into me. Her lifeless lips droned on, inaudible over the traffic and chanting. We set off, leaving her in the road, the cars behind us honking and swerving.

"Was that necessary?" I demanded.

"They say the Fervor is really an illness of the body as well as the mind." He glanced at me. "Those people don't live anymore, they don't sleep. They have left behind jobs, families, children, pets. They simply... walk away. A Fervor faithful has never been brought back to their normal state once they have been fully converted. They just chant their meaningless garbage in the streets, all as gaunt as you saw, because they rarely eat. Once in a while, they become violent," Qyll said, almost sadly. "It's best to stay as far from them as possible. No one is entirely sure how one becomes stricken. The recent research now points to a communicable state."

A couple more loitered on the sidewalk, shuffling along.

"What will happen to them?"

He sighed. "There are shelters. At best, they can be coaxed indoors during inclement weather, rather like cattle."

"How long has this been going on? The Fervor?"

"A few years, on this scale. They used to be small enough in number that their families would take care of them, thinking it was some sort of depression. Until they died of starvation or wandered into traffic and were hit by cars. These days, it's becoming a public health problem. There are so many of them and at some point, they began to, well—organize it too strong a word. Congregate? Like the group back there. They are taken to hospitals when they become too weak or badly injured."

He glanced out the window.

"Some say it's a reaction to the Rift. That when the Humans saw their reality dissolve, their beliefs dismantle, their religions crumble..." He paused. "They've seen the edge of the universe, and they've all gone totally mad."

"Before the Rift, the word 'ecumenical' referred to something that represented various Christian religions. Now we understand 'ecumenical' as meaning the Earth-bound religions, including Christianity, Islam, and Judaism. Although, we are finding that they have their roots in Other and Otherworldly traditions."

—**Dr. Jania Smith,** president of the Society for an Ecumenical Earth, in 2010

CHAPTER TWO

The months after the hospital were hard for reasons I hadn't even thought to be worried about. Special Agent in Charge Constance Pryam sent me to Quantico, Virginia, for a sort of a crash course in FBI field training. It was pretty much everything you've seen in movies or on TV about boot camp combined with graduate school, all crammed into six weeks. In other words, pure hell. But it was nice to be someplace where nobody really knew who I was.

Back home in Louisville, I was still getting accustomed to real life, which meant remembering how to run the Broom Closet. The shop had been shuttered when Lakeland called, left to collect dust and a couple of really late notices about water shut-off. Even though the FBI had gotten all the accounts back in good standing, with the power and water restored, there waited for me about three feet of grime and a couple pounds of cobwebs. Plus, all the normal grownup stuff like laundry and buying groceries. Not to mention Qyll, who occasionally checked in or stopped by, mostly to dump more paperwork or case files.

All of this was singularly worth it, because every morning when I woke up, I got to remember this was my own bed, and I was out of Lakeland—a free(ish) woman—and not yet accosted by an angry mob as I obediently stayed inside, ordered takeout, snuggled with Dorcha, binged on TV, and fielded a surprising number of shoppers at the Closet.

One of the first things I had done in those quiet few weeks was dig into an old suitcase for a purple bag that held my grimoire, a gift from Mama when I turned thirteen. The black leather cover featured the image of a crow worked in silver. The velvet bag had done a good job of warding off the tarnish. The pages were thick, creamy ivory, the kind that begs you to use your blackest ink and your very best handwriting. The first few sheets were covered in spells I had copied religiously from plain lined paper. Eventually, the spells got more sophisticated and the illustrations more elaborate.

What stayed constant for years was my special ritual for working in my grimoire. A cup of very hot lavender tea sweetened with honey. White candles. I wore a long white sundress, with a shawl if it was cold. I would send a prayer to the universe and wash my hands with salt water for purity. It made me feel like a grown-up Witch doing "real" magic. Bits of the ritual dropped off as I got older, but still a sense of reverence washed over me whenever I pulled my book out. This time, it also felt like seeing a long-lost friend.

The grimoire is a Witch's diary, spell book, experiment record, and guide—all in one. It is as personal as heartbeats, as breath, as skin. It's a Witch's whole life, from the time she comes into her powers until the time she is released into the Ether, to whatever comes next.

My own book of spells didn't yield much information yet. It was missing half a decade of practice and experience, and I wanted to start writing down everything that had happened in the last few years. But it would wait for another time. I needed to get back into the habit of using my grimoire, writing down all the events of the last few years, teasing out details that left me upset and crying. I wanted my book to be the best record of my life, and it meant being totally honest. After my family died, and many of their grimoires were destroyed, it was up to me to keep the history of what was left of the once-great Reddick clan.

Unfortunately, all good things come to an end. So did my quiet days.

Eventually, the old-fashioned scare tactics started up, presumably from those in the Other community still convinced of my guilt, or the

Humans who saw the shop has reopened. Notes tacked to trees around the shop and the apartment with burning arrows. A cauldron full of water with a Barbie doll Witch dangling over it, a charming little reminder of the dunking days for us Witches. Dead rodents on the windowsills and doormats. Not especially dangerous, just people not-so-politely telling me they knew I was back and they weren't too happy about it.

Which, in a knee-jerk reaction, made me question if opening my shop back up was anywhere in the ballpark of a good idea. Then again, I wouldn't be exactly embraced anywhere I went, and Qyll did get as much security on the place as he could. Not to mention, I had started putting up my own protection spells. So, no, I was mostly safe. Most of the time.

It was so strange, using magic again after so long without it—almost illicit. My hands remembered the motions; my voice remembered the words. But it was like putting on clothes I hadn't worn in decades or speaking a long-disused language. The first spell I did when I got home was to make ice for a drink, and it was days later before I felt like trying something again.

Not that I had had much time to re-hone those skills. The shoppers kept coming. I suspect that was from a little flyer circulated with envelopes full of mass-mailer coupons. A woman brought one in: GRAND RE-OPENING! CELEBRATE LOCAL MERCHANTS AT THE BROOM CLOSET! FINE PURVEYORS OF SPIRITUAL SUPPLIES—BOOKS, JEWELRY, STONES, AND MORE!

I asked Qyll, and he shrugged. "I didn't know about this, but if it was to make your store seem more legitimate, I think it succeeded? Looks like one of our interns' work. I'll have a word with the team that set up your shop." He glanced down at me with a crooked grin. "You do want me to thank them?"

One sunny morning in July found me in my shop doing inventory on a collection of moonstone and carnelian jewelry. The front bell jangled, and a young girl sauntered up to the counter. She looked about sixteen and wore a short green-and-blue plaid skirt and white polo top.

Over her arm was a purse that cost more than my (gently used) car. It all marked her as a student at a local girls' Catholic school. In the weeks I'd been free of Lakeland and back at my little shop, I'd seen several of her kind. They were curious and brazen, had a lot of money, and were uniformly annoying. They treated magic like a service they were entitled to, like a massage or a car wash, instead of a very dangerous gift they had not been given and thought they could just buy.

There always have been, always are, and always will be, THESE kind of girls. I spent a few years in a Catholic school myself. Mama always said Catholics are a Pope and a patriarch away from witchcraft anyway, so why not send me to St. Brigid?

"Welcome to the Broom Closet. Can I help you?" I tried to sound polite. I failed.

She pushed her messy blond hair behind her ears with expensively manicured fingers. A sly smile crept over her face, as if we were part of some secret together. "I need a spell." She whispered it as if it were a dirty word and we were at a slumber party.

My eyes narrowed, but I tried to keep my voice light. "I have lots of books on many new age and mystical subjects on those shelves. Have a look if you like."

"No!" She lowered her voice a little more as she leaned over the counter. "You're a *Witch*. A real one. I saw you in the papers."

I gave in and rolled my eyes. These kinds of kids have been coming in since my mom opened the shop. *Can you show me how to do magic? Can you give me a spell to get me a boyfriend? Can you make me lose weight?* More often than not, they just need a healthy dose of confidence or a few more hours of study time. Even before the Rift, there have always been strict laws among Others against performing magic for or on a Human, and post-Rift, there were even more and even stricter. The rules are sticky even if you have explicit consent and stickier still when the Human is underage. Mom was really good at saying just the right thing to convince them to go home and start lifting weights or using a different soap or whatever it was they *really* needed.

I, however, am not so subtle. Or patient.

"I don't teach. I don't need an apprentice. And I don't sell spells. Crystals are twenty-five percent off today and incense is buy-one-get-one-free." I turned my back on her and stomped over to a display case. *I don't need the Arcana or anyone else coming down on my ass. Again.*

"Please?" she whined. Even put her pretty hands in a prayer posture and stuck her glossy lower lip out in an exaggerated pout. Few things irritate me more than whiny, rich, blond bitches. (Nothing against any of those traits separately, just all together.)

"No." I set aside my inventory list, picked up a feather duster, and busied myself very aggressively cleaning a display of chakra crystals.

"But I can pay." She pulled a wad of cash from her expensive purse. So help me—a *wad* of cash. Judging by the purse and the big red SUV hybrid she had parked outside, that wasn't her babysitting money. "Come on. Just a *little* spell. I need to pass all my finals this semester, or I can't go to prom, and then Jacob Moore will take Hannah Liston instead of me."

Oh, she really burned my toast. I faced her and slowly walked over. "*Athena's tits*, kid, you're really asking for it. In my day, you worked for what you had. Including your grades. Kids didn't get money and fancy cars from their parents. I didn't even *go* to my high school prom. Are you kidding me, coming in here flashing your money like this is a fucking Turkish bazaar? Go home, Bambi, before somebody shoots your mother." I emphasized my words with the feather duster. "I told you. No spells." I stopped myself from swatting her in the face with the very same duster.

The doe-eyed begging look dissolved into enraged petulance as she folded her arms tightly. "How dare you talk to me like that? Fine. I'll just go tell the police that you did magic on me, but I didn't want you to. I'm a Human. And a *minor*." Whose smirk I *itched* to smack off her face with something much heavier than a cleaning implement.

"For the love of Odin, will you bugger off?" I came back out from behind the counter. "Just for argument's sake, you have zero proof. And you know what, Bambi? If I was going to do magic on you, I'd make you a nicer person. And *ugly*. Really. Stinking. Ugly." I got right in her overly made-up face and dropped my voice. "Do you even know how hard it is to undo an ugly spell? You don't, do you? Well, let me put it to you this way. I might do little jail time, but you? You *will* be hideous." I paused for a moment before whispering ominously, *"Forever."*

That did it. She positively quivered in horror.

"Look, its 9:00 a.m. Go on back to school, Bambi. I should call your principal and tell him you're truant. Do you know what 'truant' means?" I pointed at the door with the duster, my other fist clenched. She looked at me as if I'd slapped her, trying to think of some comeback, then slunk out, muttering self-righteously about the Witch bitch.

Like I'd never heard that one before.

I put on a relaxation CD and lit some calming incense.

Besides the people coming to the shop, people used to show up at our back doorstep all the time at the big house on St. James Court. Pretty young women desperate for love. Conmen with hearts of gold. Old ladies yearning for youth. But no matter what, there's a little rule most of us Witches live by. Don't do blood magic for anybody. You can do it for yourself, since you're the only one it would hurt, but even still...

This was tested once when I was a teenager, and my aunt Tamsin got herself in a bit of trouble. It was the middle of January, a foot of snow on the ground, bitter cold, and there was a knock. Dressed in a sequined evening gown and nothing else, Tamsin staggered into the foyer and fell at Mama and Auntie Vi's feet.

She had fled her home in New Orleans after a mobster's jealous wife paid to have a curse put on Tamsin. It wasn't just a killing curse. No, that would've been too quick. Slow, wretched poison that would take a good long while and a lot of pain to finish her off.

And it wasn't good magic. The wife employed the services of a shady Hedge Knacker, someone with such a small amount of innate talent to go with a wild kind of knacked, impure magic as to be incredibly dangerous. Knacker's magic is stolen, so it's muddled, their spells coming out twisted, wrong. It's like having bad baking soda. You know you're supposed to use it for the cookies, but you can't figure out why your cakes taste funny. Funny enough that you notice the strange, almost salty taste, and maybe, the batter didn't rise to where it should, but not bad enough that you won't eat it. You can train up the Hedge Witches, sure, but it's best to shut them down altogether. It's safer, really.

Now, we all knew Tamsin hadn't touched the mobster. The sin she might have been guilty of was being prettier and flirtier than the mobster's wife. But she was a nightclub singer, and it was kind of her job to be prettier and more flirtatious.

And my mother thought it was the coven's job to lend Tamsin a helping hand, so she and the others fought about it for a while. Violetta didn't want any part of a counter-spell for a shitty Hedge's hex. She told Tamsin she should've handled it herself. Vi wanted justice to come dispensed by someone else's hand and the Threefold Law to come down on someone else's house. Why—they grouched—not simply send Tamsin back to New Orleans and let one of the voodoo queens take care of it.

"No," said Tams, "the voodoo queens won't come near me. They know who the Reddicks are."

"Clearly, the stupid swamp Witch who put together this hot mess of a curse is unfamiliar with us," Violetta snarled. "It's against the laws of magic, is what it is."

When Mama tried to be reasonable, Tamsin and Violetta almost came to blows. Finally, Mama threw up her hands. "What do you want me to do, Vi? Call the police and tell them a shoddy Witch is killing people, and could they please arrest her and make her reverse her hex?"

But Tamsin was family, so in the end, she moved into the little bedroom at the end of the hall. Then the coven worked a complicated counter-hex, which I was forbidden to participate in.

They fasted and chanted and prayed and sprinkled salt for three days, the Hedge Knacker's efforts to stop us from completing the ritual notwithstanding. But Tamsin didn't get well.

One night, I helped Mama tend to her. "She'll turn into a wraith," Mama said as we closed the door behind us.

"A what?"

Mama shook her head, the dark braid around her head glimmering in the hall lamplight. "A wraith is... a soul that's been stripped of its self. In essence, the soul is destroyed and all that's left is the rage. It's like making an outline of a person then filling it with all the bad you can find." She looked at me with her luminous purple eyes. "Truly, a fate worse than death."

The counter-spell put the mobster's wife in a coma. It killed her husband *and* the woman he was really carrying on with, behind his wife's back, *and* the Hedge Knacker. The wife came out of the coma, but she wasn't right anymore. She died maybe six months later. Tamsin stayed sick with fever and lost the sight in her right eye. She lived out her days in the little room upstairs, rocking and singing to herself.

It's one of the most important laws of magic and a lesson some folks learn the hard way.

Since I'd reopened the Broom Closet, I had lots of customers, but I hadn't seen a single one of its regulars. The solitary Witches who practiced their own kinds of magic without covens. My family's old friends or those clients recommended to us. All gone. Plenty of casual shoppers, several gawkers, and kids like this girl; plus some online orders, because the Internet hadn't realized I was "that Witch who killed her family." Or maybe it had and wanted a souvenir? At any rate, I craved news from friends or allies, but they stayed quiet.

And so I waited, doing the adult-y things. Though that was just an excuse. In truth, I was scared.

The doorbell tinkled again.

"Look, honey, I don't mind you looking around but—" My hackles rose then settled down when I saw him.

That black hair, tips of slender pointed ears just poking out. Pewter t-shirt under a black leather jacket, even though it was the middle of summer and already beginning to swelter by 9:00 a.m. Dark jeans. Black boots. He looked like a willow tree. A sexy, moody willow tree.

"Oh. Qyll." Brilliant. Why can't I be a little more... *suave*? I hadn't seen him in more than a week. There had been a bunch of cold leads on the case he's been feeding me, so little need to chitchat as I'd gone over the files he gave me, with no fresh ideas. I ran a hand over the violent mop that was my hair, wishing I'd at least washed it before I came down in the morning. And why didn't I wear makeup when I was in the store? "I was just opening for the day."

He stood at the edge of a sunbeam, just out of the swirl of dust motes between a rack of velvet capes and a bookshelf that bore titles such as *The Green Goddess in You*, *Raising a Pagan Baby*, and *New Spells for the Modern Witch*.

"There's been another murder. Pryam is already at the scene. She believes it's connected to the other murders."

"Good morning to you too," I muttered, rounding the counter to put my feather duster away.

He watched me with those inscrutable silver eyes. "Will you come? I haven't time to waste. I was on my way there."

"Why can't you just use the phone like everybody else? You live in Earth now."

"It... wasn't necessary. Your shop is on the way from my home to the crime scene." His shrug was elegantly careless. "You can ride in my car." He waited for me to come along. Qyll, it should be said, as a Dark Elf, has sometimes startlingly Otherwhere-ish ways, such as his aversion to cell phones.

I sighed. "Let me get my things."

Qyll asked, "Will you be wearing that footwear?"

"What's wrong with my boots? I *love* these boots. These are my favorite footwear of all time. Got them at a rodeo." We both looked down at my cowgirl boots—deep red with a pattern of birds tooled into the leather.

He sort of smirked. Qyll does this sometimes. I think he thinks he's joking with me. But it comes out weird. It's okay. I'm no stranger to awkward moments myself, especially with menfolk.

"Let's go," I grumbled.

Qyll's car was parked outside, behind mine. I flipped the shop door sign over to read CLOSED and got in. Seatbelt—safety first. Window down. Seat back. "Let's do this."

Off we went.

"Why do you even drive? You can navigate Other, why not just slip through the Rift?"

"I rather enjoy automobiles," he said. I couldn't see his eyes behind his dark sunglasses. "And things are somewhat unsafe for Earthsiders, even those native to the other side. It isn't wise to walk the ways of the Other just now."

"You know, you never say anything about where you come from or what you're doing here. When did you come to Earth? Why?"

"I had always wanted to come to Earth. Well, when I learned it was a real place. We grew up thinking you are just as much legend as you us. In fact, one of our most beloved figures of folktale is Niall, ancestor to your St. Patrick."

I laughed. "We got Legolas. You got St. Patrick. And the FBI seemed like a good idea for something to do here? Why didn't you... go back home. Or, be an actor. A model. You could've been in the movies or something. Been famous." I leaned back in my seat, propping my arm on the console between us.

He shook his head. "My people are not performers. And I very much enjoy my work with the Bureau. Human crime is fascinating. But I do miss the old days."

"The old days?"

"I came across in your year 1946."

"What? Are you serious? Also, how old are you?"

"I came in search of information." Our car swung the car into traffic with expert ease. "Somehow, a Project Mogul balloon made its way into our realm. My father was asked to send someone to investigate, see if it was a war salvo."

I swiveled to face him. "You mean to tell me you came to Earth to investigate what started the alien conspiracy theory debate in Earth for oh, eighty-something years? You. Mr. Dark Elf Secret Agent Man. Mr.... Mr.... well, whatever."

Project Mogul, you may remember, was a 1940s-era U.S. military project designed to float microphones on unmanned balloons in an attempt to detect sound waves from Soviet atomic bomb testing. When one of the balloons crashed in the desert of Roswell, New Mexico, in July 1947, the military moved to conceal the true nature of the project and probably to stop the public outcry in Russia resulting from the U.S. government confirming it was spying on Russian bomb testing. The PR man released a statement saying it was just a weather balloon—no big deal.

"You may have read about Major Marcel?"

"Was he the one who went to the farm and picked up the debris?"

"Correct. Now, all the reports mention he was accompanied by a man in plainclothes."

"*You* were the man in plainclothes?" I slapped the console, grinning. "You are killing me right now! I used to watch all those alien conspiracy shows and stuff. I mean, we know now it was a spy balloon—but man! So, you were there?"

"The balloon we found on the Other side was indeed a Mogul spy apparatus, pushed through the ether into our world from yours. My father sent me in to find out if this was a sort of espionage or an act of war. And there *was* another balloon found on a ranch in New Mexico. But that rancher did indeed see something else that was not Human in origin."

"What did he see?"

"A sand scaler. Small sand spirits. Harmless, but they adore string for some reason. It had gotten caught in the balloon. It was nearly dead when we got to it. I wanted it sent it back to the sand, but too many people knew too many half-truths by then. I think that's why the UFO conspiracy began. We couldn't keep up with the rumors."

I burst into laughter. "This is great. I love hearing about you." In the times I had spent with him, he was usually quiet, all business.

He finally looked at me, my face reflected in his aviator sunnies. "There isn't much interesting to tell."

I snorted. "Patently untrue. Do Elves even commit crimes?"

He smiled a tiny bit. "Every race in the known and unknown universe commits crimes, Tessa. It's really a matter of who does the judging that makes the difference."

I nodded. "Very sage of you. So that's how you became Special Agent Toutant. How did—" And then, my phone rang. I fumbled with it so long, I thought it would end up going to voicemail. I was still getting used to the damnable thing. During my time at Lakeland, cell phone tech had advanced far beyond my old clamshell model.

"Is this Tessa Reddick?" I struggled to roll up the window to hear over the rush of traffic and wind.

"Uh, yes." I am always so leery of strangers calling me. I'm just positive it's bad news, like the Arcana calling to send me to the furthest evil reaches of Otherwhere. Now, I know they wouldn't call me on a Human phone, but stranger things have happened.

"I'm sorry to bother you. This is Dr. Charlie Bartley. I wondered if you had some time to talk? I have a few questions of a spiritual nature. I really need to speak to someone about this." He spoke softly and quickly.

I sighed. My mother and aunts used to get various flavors of these calls from time to time, especially right after the Rift, when everybody in America immediately went either totally Jesus-crazy or some variation of neo-pagan. "Mr. Bartley, I didn't know Jehovah's witnesses made phone calls these days, but I assure you, I have no need to find religion."

I know exactly where the religion is and mostly run in the other direction. It's not the God part that bugs me—it's His self-styled minions.

He laughed nervously. "Oh no, no. I'm not peddling anything. Listen, how about I pay you for your time, say 125 an hour? And after an hour, you can kick me out if you like."

Well. He had me over a barrel there. Money talks, people. That's why I have set up shop call forwarding, after all. In case someone urgently wanted to deposit a handy sum in the Closet register in my off hours. "You have a deal. Can you come by the shop later? About eleven-thirty?"

"Off Bardstown Road? I'll be there." He hung up quickly.

Qyll didn't seem to care about my conversation, so we sat in silence for the rest of the ride out to the northeastern suburbs, to an enclave of enormous modern mansions. I'm always surprised to see he is a good driver, despite the fact that he spent his whole life in Otherwhere lounging around on moonbeams and munching on evening primroses or whatever it is Dark Elves do.

As we turned into a driveway, police officers waved us through the gate. Up a slight hill stood a sleek chrome and glass palace. Caution tape fluttered in the summer breeze. Half the place looked like a giant had stomped on it.

On the way up toward the house, Qyll murmured, "I must caution you, the situation is rather gruesome."

"I can handle gruesome, Q."

"No, you can't. Everyone knows that." I blushed. In truth, while I had done well at Quantico, the report to Pryam included several warnings that I may be a liability where graphic violence is concerned. Which... well, I certainly hadn't been the one gunning for this gig in the first place. So the SI jack wagons could just stuff it.

Qyll turned to look at me, which is unnerving at the best of times. "Not to mention, this is... immediate, Agent Reddick. There are several victims, and as you can see, the place was ruined."

"Several? More than four?" I blurted. That's a lot for one murder scene in a town like Louisville, even post-Rift, when things went from weird to worse.

He nodded. "Seven, actually. It's a similar situation as the animals and the *bakemono* family. Wanton destruction, extremely messy, no suspects. And the bodies..." Qyll let out a breath. "We're fairly certain it was early this morning. UPS came to deliver a package and—ah, here we are."

Across the lawn, around the house, hung the deep purple-green haze that signaled dark magic. Like smoke after fireworks, it drifted, thick and menacing. Foggy shapes swam in and out of it—animotoids. Supernatural cockroaches.

In the foyer, we found Constance Pryam, Special Agent in Charge of Supernormal Investigations. She nodded to us, making her way around piles of rubble. Pryam could be forty, or she could be eighty. It's hard to tell. She's tall and wiry, like an Olympic sprinter. Her smooth skin, ink-black eyes, high cheekbones, and closely cropped hair make her appear otherworldly, like a supermodel from a country of warrior women, but the look in her eyes is sharp and wary.

"Reddick," she said, her tone crisp.

I mock-saluted. "Present, sir." She ignored me and motioned for us to follow.

"Your first real crime scene, Agent Reddick. Considering you got only the cliff notes version of FBI field training, I'm very eager to see how you do on your maiden voyage."

I swallowed hard and forced a grin.

The three of us went up the curving marble staircase to the second-floor. The purple vapor got thicker and more plentiful with every step. Animotoids crept in and out of my sight, devouring the black magical residue clinging pretty much everywhere.

Uneasiness settled into my limbs. The house was—had been—beautiful. Stylish and high-tech, it was something you'd see as the "after" on a home renovation show, all glass and brushed chrome and fancy gadgets. I paused at the top of the steps, looking down into the front hall. The door hadn't just been opened, it had exploded inward. Shards of wood were scattered everywhere. The remnants of a sophisticated home security system lay in a tangled mess halfway across the room. Anything glass had been reduced to sand. Dirt and mess everywhere. Forensics moved about, snapping pictures and taking samples.

Curiouser and curiouser.

The first thing I thought when we got to the upper hallway was: *I am surely going to toss my waffles. Right in front of Pryam. And Qyll. And the rest of the team.* The second thing was that someone had dreamed up, planned, and executed an amazingly complex black magic spell. Black magic leaves a distinctive trail, like a smudge on glass—this greenish-purple residue, thick and putrid, with a very particular scent. Like rotting corpses and raw fear. White magic has its telltale signs, too. And none of those were present.

The stench of blood and black magic was beyond overwhelming. And I've smelled some pretty foul things in my life—one of those stinky jungle flowers, Demon excrement, a rotten hellspawn. But this... it had become a living, prowling, snarling thing. Even though half the house had been smashed and burned to ashes, the fresh air and lingering smoke were no match for the metallic tang of Human exsanguination and plain old-fashioned evil.

I stepped into the hall behind Qyll and Pryam. What was left of the hall. My stomach contracted. I took some deep breaths through my mouth as nausea swelled from my tripes. Both knees began to wobble. *Keep it together, Reddick.*

At the far end, walls had been bashed out, the trees swaying beyond the hole. Ceilings dripped dead wiring. Stinking red fluids coated every surface. It was like the elevator scene from *The Shining*. On a scale of 10,000.

I took a breath through my mouth. And another. My eyes watered.

Qyll looked at me. "Are you all right? Are you going to vomit?"

His eyes met mine. Something like concern swam in his, but I was too nauseated to dwell on it. I swallowed hard and shook my head, waving at him dismissively.

"Just peachy."

It didn't help that one of the FBI office clerks took to calling me 'Easy Queasy' and reminding me, 'queasy does it.' I can't help that I have a sensitive inner ear. Or that I get easily motion sick and bad smells make me barf. Not my fault.

We kept going down the hall.

"The victims are in here." Pryam pointed to a sheet of plastic hanging between ragged edges of wall. She handed us disposable latex gloves and surgical masks, which we all donned.

The room was unlike anything I'd seen before. It was how I imagined a palace looked after a house party at Caligula's. Bodies were haphazardly flung around. Their clothes hung from an enormous crystal chandelier, swinging in the breeze from the hole in the outside wall. Under streaks of filth, bone and muscle peeked through, as though every last drop of blood had been drained, leaving only the pinkish tissue. Besides the viscera and blood, there looked to be dirt blotched on the walls and the bodies, along with Zeus knows what else.

Before I could make a whit of sense of the scene, the psychic assault started. It's different for all practitioners, but for me, walking into a space where this level of black magic has been performed so recently is like being locked in one of those iron maidens that's full of sharp knives dipped in battery acid, while extremely loud death metal music blares in my ear to an accompaniment of a million strobe lights. And I'm not that sensitive, even. People who have a real gift? If I was one of them, I'd be in a coma by now.

Closing my eyes, I reached for my necklace, a silver and moonstone triple goddess pendant. I imagined a bubble of warm light surrounding me, scented with chocolate chip cookies, the arrows of black energy bouncing harmlessly off it. After several moments, tension drained from me. My years of practice were serving me well. Just like riding a bike, it all comes right back.

When I opened my eyes again, I found Qyll staring intently at me.

"What do you know about the victims?" I managed to ask.

Pryam reappeared, her gaze like tempered steel. She's Human (well, Human-*ish*), but has an otherworldly way of looking at things. I mean that literally and figuratively. Very soon after meeting her, you start to notice Pryam doesn't pull any punches. "Someone with your talents could have done this."

"No. Nope. Wasn't me." I had no other way to say it. "I mean, I am certainly capable, if I really, really wanted to, but this," I gestured to the room, "would likely end my cushy job with SI *and* get me sent to the Otherwhere version of a concentration camp. And I'm kinda partial to this dimension. Who else? Demons could do this. Easily. Particularly savvy Werewolves? No. Perhaps a really pissed off Vamp. But the

Vamp... would have to have... drunk...." It dawned on me that what I thought was clothing hanging overhead was really skin.

Whole, intact suits of human skin.

I rushed into the hallway, ripping off the flimsy mask, and puked enthusiastically into a decorative ceramic vase that had somehow survived the onslaught. Several times.

Note to self: be sure to eat another breakfast. The first one isn't going to count.

When I returned, it was to Qyll saying, "We know it wasn't you. Just trying to make a list of the kind of people it would take to do this. We can't rule out magic by anyone these days."

"What do you mean?" I asked.

He glanced at Pryam then me. "SI was created to address just this. Strong magic in a realm where there has typically been very weak magic handled by inexperienced practitioners. But we've been noticing... Knackers, I believe people call them."

"We'll talk about this later, Agent Toutant. Right now, let's get moving," Pryam said.

Her gaze lingered on me for the exact amount of time it took for me to grow intensely uncomfortable.

"So, uh, whose house is this?" I asked, my voice thin. I wiped my wet eyes with the back of my hand. I have thrown up so many times in my life in so many situations it hardly bothers me anymore, except for being a little embarrassed to have done so in front of my boss and a coworker.

"Belongs to one of the vics. A Benjamin Koby." She consulted her e-tablet.

"What else?"

Pryam glared at me. "We don't have much time, Reddick. We'll deal with the metadata later. Forensics is chomping at the bit to get up here. What can you *see*?"

I nodded and drew in another deep breath, keeping my little bubble strong. The bubble is a trick I learned as a kid, when the other kids teased me for being weird, for being a Witch. What I do is relax and imagine this shell protecting me from all the bad juju and keeping all my good juju inside. The noise of the room faded until it was just me, thinking.

I approached one of the bodies. Without skin, their eyes and teeth were totally exposed. Eyeballs staring at nothing. Rigor mortis was well past. They looked like plates in an anatomy textbook. I tried to think of that. Pretend I was looking at *Gray's Anatomy*.

"Were they wearing wigs?" One of the women had a bright purple nylon tangle beside her head.

"There are a couple around, but we don't know who had them on. I'm emailing you some photos of vics now. Pre-murder."

I went to stand under the chandelier, trying to keep my breath steady. A photographer finished up her work, looking green about the gills as she hurried out of the room. "What about these?"

"We brought one down. It's over there." Qyll pointed to a table by the window. I forced myself to stay calm and think about our art class in high school. The drawing teacher told us to think in terms of lines, shapes, negative space. Don't think of it as a truck, think of it as a series of vertical and horizontal lines and the spaces around them. Don't think of it as a naked person, think of it as a series of curved spaces. Don't think of them as skinless Human beings...

This is how I approached the specimen on the table. It was as though the inside had busted through the skin, a little bit like the front door had busted into the house. A jagged rip cleaved the dermis from forehead to groin.

"It's like... the insides... came out of a suit of skin. What on earth?"

"It's a mystery," Qyll said drily. "Oh wait, what is it we pay you for again?"

"Look, I'm just thinking out loud," I shot back. "You don't have to be an asshat about it."

I walked around the table, thankful for the breeze wafting in through the gaping wall, and concentrated harder. Seeking, probing. The flashes in my mind coalesced into a lightning storm. A tremendous heat swelled around me.

Finally, I said, "Definitely blood magic. Very powerful. Very dark.

But there's an element of chaos here. Like, something went wrong, maybe? Someone was angry. Even if the skin was intact, which would suggest the killer took his time, the motivation was pure anger."

Pryam snorted. "What a shock. Toutant, stay here. I'm going to see about these footprints." Her heels squished on bloody carpet.

I concentrated again. Images swam before me. I'm not a strong Sensitive, but I can manage a sneak peek. This time, I caught a glimpse of some people milling around, sipping from martini glasses and laughing. Then one of them screaming and running for their life, but what threat set them off, I had no idea. "For blood magic, you have to have some of the, well... victim's blood. Obviously. Occasionally, hair works or other parts of the body, such as bones or teeth." Qyll frowned.

I picked my way through the room, nudging things aside with the toe of my red cowboy boot. "There's no summoning circle here that I can see, no marks of a source of power. I mean, it could be drowned out by all the blood. But smart money says, the killer had to be a puppet. A hired thug on borrowed power, controlled from somewhere else."

I have a tendency to over-explain to him, which he has never commented on, but often I get the sense he's patiently waiting for me to shut up.

So I kept on. "This looks like pretty unusual magic, some old Earth juju. I don't know much about it, except a few lessons on, DON'T DO OLD BLOOD MAGIC UNLESS YOU ABSOLUTELY HAVE TO. You can do little bits in certain circumstances, but you really should stay away, if you can help it."

"We haven't had much experience with blood magic in the time SI has been organized," Qyll said. "I can make an inquiry with our archives department."

I sighed. "Well, just by the very nature of the violence... You can't do this kind of crap in a post-Rift world without conjuring some serious power. This? It's not only illegal, it's crazy-dangerous because it's usually people who don't know what the hell they're doing. But I will know more once I understand who these people are. Or, were."

The look on Qyll's face stoppered my babbling mouth.

Things since the Rift have been odd, to say the least. For reasons no one can yet explain very well, the barrier between our world—what's now referred to collectively as Earth—and Otherwhere got thin.

Real thin.

So wispy, in some places it vanished altogether. Otherwhere is the place you might have known as "the spirit world" or "faerie." Sometimes, it's Heaven or Hell. Hades, Valhalla, Takama-ga-hara, the Summerlands. It has a lot of names depending on who's doing the talking. There are rules about what can and can't happen when the worlds and their various inhabitants intersect. That's where the FBI Supernormal Investigations Department comes in. On the Earth side, anyway.

"Is there a weapon? A non-magical one?" I peered around at the detritus.

Qyll shook his head. "Not one we can find. Nor can we locate the source of the damage to the building. It obviously had to have been something big. Like a Siberian snow troll. Or a..." He groped for words. "Bulldozer. A crane, perhaps, but there are no tire markings in the garden to support that theory." He pointed. "These three are Human. The other four worked for Antaura. Bacchus and Jezebel Demons. None of them alone would have been strong enough to inflict this kind of structural damage. Or cause this type of carnage. And none are typically associated with murder. They're more the type to get drunk and have a weeklong orgy."

All I could manage was, "Shit." Antaura, AKA the Red Queen, owns a famous—or infamous, depending on who you ask—local hotspot that straddles the Earth and Otherwhere. Called Queen of Hearts, it caters to, well, *anybody* from here to the end of Otherwhere. Rumor has it, it procures for you whatever you want, be it heroin, gourmet *foie gras*, or a threesome with a couple of randy satyrs. You can have all three, but that's extra. Of course, a bunch of Bacchus and Jezebel Demons would be in her employ. I can see them hanging out in her clubs, encouraging people to guzzle their fill or get down to the sexy times—basically indulge any and all physical desires.

In the years after the Rift, the Red Queen had set up shop half in half out of Earth and put order to a certain breed of criminal chaos in the entire southeastern U.S. She isn't allowed to perform rituals or do magic on anybody in Earth. But she hires low-level Demons and Humans who have, shall we say, flexible morals, to do it for her, and in turn, keeps them in line—out of Human jails and off everybody's radar. I heard she started in Atlanta then moved her operation to Louisville and manages her people from here. Bully for us.

"What about the rest?" I wandered the room, trying not get distracted by the stench. It really was enormous.

"We have an accountant—married—and a housewife with a couple of kids. A seminary student. And the Demons. No connection we can find yet, besides the Demons working for the Queen," Qyll said. "We found this, but have no way of knowing if it's from the victims. Someone found it on the floor in the hall."

It was a torn and bloodied business card for the Church of the Earth, Gardener Dr. Isaiah West, Head Pastor. "Could be from the seminary student. Is this your connection? I mean, Bacchuses in a church led by a self-proclaimed Prophet is odd, but you know what they say…"

"They're right." Qyll prodded a chunk of a god-knows-what with a pencil. "The truth is stranger than fiction."

While the Red Queen was busy putting a scaly fist to a vast company of Human and Otherwhere drifters, a slew of new churches popped up like mushrooms after a spring rain. Religions began to fuse together and follow a set of principles set forth by an international conglomerate called Terram Divina.

The scariest of these was Church of the Earth, headed by a man calling himself the New Prophet. West was born in Texas to a cattle rancher and a schoolteacher. His birth certificate says his name is "Lawrence Gerald Grosh." He changed it to Isaiah since the Christian Bible takes its stance on monotheism in the book of Isaiah, and West because one of the signs of the Apocalypse is supposed to be the sun rising in the west. I've seen him on television. He's a slippery blend of attractive and charismatic that makes thinking people afraid.

He started his megachurch in the 1980s, and by the time the Rift happened, he was ready. His followers claimed he performed miracles. His sermons gathered thousands in person and millions on TV or streaming online. Eventually, he declared himself the New Prophet, chosen by the One True God to deliver believers to Heaven and escape Armageddon.

West's crop is into God in a creepily hardcore evangelical way. They preach that the end times had begun and the Book of Revelation is being played out before our eyes. They are also really into the Earth and how it's God's gift to Humans and stuff like that. Most of the churches have trees or flowers in their logos. Often, the liberal-minded sorts refer to the more zealous followers of Terram Divinia as "treevangelicals."

"Can you tell me more about the particular spell? How did they do this?" Qyll waved a hand toward the bodies.

I shook my head. "If I even thought about doing this, man... it's not good. This is pretty black. I can look in my books and get back to you. You know I can't mess around much with black magic." The pleading in my voice irritated me, but I couldn't help it. If the Arcana found out I was so much as researching it in depth, I was in for seven worlds of hurt.

"Then we're at a standstill," Qyll said, frustration coloring his words.

"Okay, okay!" I put my hands up in defense. "I'll see what I can do. Who put iron in your Wheaties?" He glowered at me and turned to stomp off, but ended up colliding with Pryam.

There had been a couple of cases of strange deaths before, which was of course how I ended up on Team Supernormal in the first place. Though nothing had happened since my release from Lakeland, this was the biggest one yet, and nobody wanted it to get any worse. Last year was a family of Japanese *bakemono*, harmless shapeshifter spirits, then a bunch of show horses at a farm in Goshen, the pictures I had seen when Qyll came to spring me from Lakeland. A few other random events that had some things in common. And now this. It was too much to be coincidence but not enough to figure out who was behind it.

Pryam said, "The footprints start at the edge of the driveway by the east flowerbeds. They come into the house and up here. Then, they lead back out to the patch and disappear. No trace of mud anywhere else. No prints in the yard or garden, the driveway, the street, or around the pool. It's been dry the last month, so it would be obvious."

She drew herself straight. "Toutant, go talk to this preacher, West. I'll handle the Red Queen."

"What about me?" I protested.

"Correct me if I'm wrong, but you haven't gotten quite the hero's welcome from your old friends, have you?" I took a heated breath to defend myself, but she kept going. "Stand down, Reddick. I'm not benching you, just sit out this inning."

I sighed. "Fine. I've got to get out of here anyway. I'm going to barf again."

On the way home, Qyll took the side streets instead of the interstate, with the windows down.

I'll admit, I'm no Nancy Drew. So I tend to just ask a bunch of questions I have seen TV detectives ask.

"Who would care about that specific party? Why? They were nobodies, really. Ben Koby had some money, right? But he wasn't powerful. None of the others were, either. Humans and run-of-the-mill Demons. So why bother with them? Bacchuses and Jezebels really rank more in the nuisance arena than the public threat."

"A nice summary, rookie."

I glanced over. I still couldn't tell if or when he was being patronizing. "So how'd I do on my first job?"

"Rather well. We never experience the physical manifestations that cause such an upset in your body. But you appear to have powered through them."

"You're not saying barfing is a uniquely Human affair, are you? Out of like fully sentient creatures?"

We lapsed into silence as I started cataloguing my Otherwhere experiences in my head to refute his point.

That lasted me until we got to the shop, and I got out of the car, with no satisfactory example to hand. "Bye. Call me if there's any news?" I said, absently.

As I pushed the door open, I was still so lost in thought, I barely noticed my cozy little Broom Closet had been entirely replaced. Not just things moved around. The whole room beyond the door was gone. Despite it being later in the day and sunny outside, I was enveloped by chill darkness and the weird light of blue flames. My shelves and racks were gone in favor of a huge roaring fireplace and a million velvet cushions on the floor. The aroma of brimstone laced the air.

Someone had replaced my shop with a pocket of Otherwhere. Normally, it's not terribly hard for experienced practitioners to open a slit in the ethereal veil and slide something in. Sort of an "if the Mohammed won't come to the mountain, the mountain will come to Mohammed." But due to my pariah status in the magical community, SI had ponied up for extensive security measures. It should have been *hard* for anyone to do this. Not only that, this was rude.

"Dammit. You're not supposed to be here, whoever you are." I made a mental note to have SI put stronger protective sigils and spells on the place ASAP.

A pair of figures emerged, nearly identical female Demons in gauzy white dresses. They had beautiful ebony skin and from their torrents of black hair, two curved black horns poked out. One spoke, her voice like poison-laced bells. "Her ladyship bids you welcome and requests the honor of your presence." They smiled in unison, showing pointed teeth, and bowed, sweeping their hands toward the fireplace. I could see the outline of a large throne.

The slender person seated before the fire was clearly a woman, veiled from head to toe in red fabric. She wore long red leather gloves. It was hard to tell because she was sitting, but I estimated her height at... pretty damn tall.

"Madame Reddick! Welcome home, honey," she said. "May I formally introduce myself? Some call me the Red Queen of the Abyzou, but for you, Antaura will do just fine." She stood and came toward me, unveiling as she did. She was (obviously) taller than most Humans, probably a hair under eight feet. Tiny shimmering red scales made up her skin. A sheet of cornsilk-white hair fell to her waist and set off her blazing emerald eyes with no whites.

When she smiled, I fought the urge to recoil at her teeth. "I trust you know of me, as I know of you. I would like to, as the Humans say, make a deal." She laughed gaily and snapped her fingers. A large comfy-looking chair appeared. She didn't so much offer it to me as pushed me into it before sitting back down on her throne.

Rumors about the Red Queen abounded. That she had been Human once and made a bargain with some Otherworldly creature. That she was the *original* Original Vampire in Otherwhere, mother to all vampires. That she was something very ancient from before the world formed, like Tolkien's Balrog. Before the Rift, she had hidden in plain sight, costumed as a businessman who built and lost fortunes with the carefree attitude of the very rich. After the Rift, she came clean (ha!) and now does business as herself. She's well-known for saying outrageous things but also for being a shrewd entrepreneur and an astute politician.

"I charge one-fifty per hour, your highness," I said.

Antaura laughed again. "I heard you had a keen sense of humor!"

I crossed my arms and glared at her.

After a long look, her laughter faded. "Let me be plain. I want you to stop helping the Dark Elf and the black Human."

"Black Human?" I mocked shock. "Oh, maybe you don't know? They call them African Americans now."

She shrugged. "I am many things. Perhaps I am also racist. In any event, the business at the mansion, the deaths, I am disinclined for your Human friends to know more." She laid red-gloved hands on the arms of her throne. "You see, Miss Reddick, I would like to deal with this in my own way. Those in my employ are none of FBI's concern." Her accent was of someone who didn't speak English as a first language. Or second. She sounded sort of Middle Eastern by way of Argentina and Ireland as spoken by a snake, if I had to nail it down.

"They're coming to talk to you. You're on Pryam's 'to-do' list."

She shrugged and smiled, showing those ghastly teeth. "The Lady Pryam and I will not speak. She should know as much by now."

"What about the Arcana? Shouldn't *they* be handling the Demons? And letting SI work on the Humans and Others?"

She barked a laugh, a rocky dangerous sound. "There is no need. They are my people. It's not necessary for Humans to be involved, my little Witch. And the Arcana is more than happy to let me, how would you say it, take care of my own. We will take appropriate steps. I should have been made aware of the... potential for transgression, before it became a problem." She turned her head briefly toward the horned woman to her left, who shook her head. "Those responsible for not bringing it to my attention will be dealt with, I assure you."

"What about the Humans? You don't give a fig about them."

"As I said, this unfortunate event is my provenance, Madame Reddick."

Damn Cheshire Cat double-speaker.

This is one of the (many) problems with post-Rift life. Beings from the Otherwhere show up and want to meddle in the affairs of Humans or Others. Sometimes just for fun, sometimes because Humans are way easier to control. The Arcana was supposed to negotiate with beings like Antaura since she's pure Otherwhere. She has her irons in a lot of fires, and the Arcana is sort of the Otherwhere version of the SI. But as I have learned over the years, the Arcana is just never there when you need them and often there when you don't, and people like her somehow always feel they are outside the law.

"So you want me to tell Qyll I'm not going to help them? It's too late, I've already started. And I *will* get to the bottom of this."

Bluffing—it'll get you everywhere!

Antaura held up her hand again. "Yes, yes. We know." She waved her fingers. A largish bag appeared on the floor in front of me. A bagful of money. Full. Of. *Money*. American dollars, by the looks of it. Hot off the presses. I had a shop and a modest paycheck, but I was definitely cash poor.

Her tone was light, but there was no mistaking her intent. "Trust me, young Tessa Reddick. It will be better if you stay out of this. I have more experience in these situations."

And that pissed me off. I didn't know those people who'd died, but I was willing to bet a birch tree they didn't deserve to die in such a hideous way. I stood up, hand on my hip. "You show up here and take over *my* shop to threaten me not to do *my* job? My legal Earthling job that keeps me out of the kind of trouble I have definitely been in and would like to stay out of? Who do you think you are, lady? Yeah, yeah, you have some tricks up your sleeve. But I can cut a hole in the veil too." (Actually, I wasn't very good at it, but how would she know?) "How would you like it if I showed up in *your* living room and pushed you around?" I suddenly realized I'd been getting closer to the Red Queen—all up in her grill, as the kids say.

She hissed at me, and the handmaidens in white moved forward to block their mistress. Each of the horned women had four hands, and I was now faced with eight fearsome-looking swords. Their horns grew more pronounced, and their eyes darkened until no whites showed. Pointed white teeth shifted into long black fangs.

I backed into a defensive position, but I knew they weren't going to hurt me. Not here. This was just the Queen flexing her muscles for a rival.

Finally, she said, "Mohini. Vishna. Be still."

The sound that came from the Queen now was harder and colder. She pointed a leather-gloved finger at me. Her crazy-green eyes flashed. "Let me say it again. This doesn't concern you, Witch. I had so hoped you would be more careful around me." She paused, thoughtful. "Odd, your allegiance to these people. Would you like to be paid in another fashion?"

She waved a hand, and the bag became a comically large treasure chest of gold and silver pieces. I shook my head.

Again, she waved, and the bag turned into a cartoonish pile of food and drink—a whole roasted turkey, silver bowls of fruit, trays of olives, some enormous cakes. Carafes of wine and kegs of something. It was as if a medieval palace had catered my meals for the next twenty years. I shook my head.

"Perhaps this is more to your liking?"

The food dissolved then coalesced into a familiar form. Without thinking, I shouted, "NO." There was no mistaking the cut of those cheekbones, shaggy dark hair, luminous silver eyes. *Where the hell did that come from?*

She laughed. "Very well." She leaned forward just a hair. "Perhaps you would like to know something about... the fire?" Her grin was wicked.

I might as well have been sucker-punched.

Fury pounded in my chest. "What do you know about the fire?" My voice was barely above a whisper.

She leaned back and waited.

Mama's voice flooded my head. *"Don't make deals with Demons. And never play in, on, or around the gates of hell."*

I gritted my teeth and stared her down. Whatever the Red Queen claimed to know, someone else would too. Someone I could barter with.

"Surely you don't think you can keep going on by yourself in this post-Rift world, dear one? You need more power. Think of all you could do with the might of the House of Abyzou behind you." The Queen got up from her throne and stepped over to me, through the remains of the faux-Elf fading into the flickering shadows. She stood before me, her head swaying like a cobra ready to strike. "We would go so far together. Your singular talent. My influence."

I shook my head hard. "No chance, Red. Hard pass. I'm a solitary Witch these days. And now, I bid you adieu." I shoved my palm toward her, a reflexive motion that sent my will focused right at her. "I banish you in the name of the triple goddess! Maiden, mother, crone, I invoke thee! Be gone!" I repeated it three times, using my laser-beam will to force her out. And just like that, the darkness retreated like water down a drain. Sometimes, when the magical rug is pulled out from under you so quickly like that, it gives the sense of vertigo. So, as the remnants of Otherwhere dispelled and my shop reemerged, I promptly threw up on a stack of clearance-priced wolf t-shirts. Or rather, tried to throw up. My stomach was already spectacularly empty.

Clearly, she'd thought I was going to go along with her plan so hadn't put up much effort into sticking around. I stood shaking a little bit, leaning on the counter by the register. My heart beat so loudly, it knocked in my chest. Then, I realized someone was at the door.

A man peered through. "Miss Reddick? It's Charlie Bartley. May I come in?"

The most ruthlesse of all ye hunters; he shall come forth at times of need and slaye ye Wytches. In all ye corners of the Earthe, he shall seeketh, and suffer none to live. He shall enter your house seen but not known. See ye Wytch-fynder General and despair.

—from the grimoire of **Hilda of Whitby,** 625 A.D.

CHAPTER THREE

C**harlie perched at the little table where I do tarot readings** sometimes, his gaze darting around. I made us tea and found a packet of cookies in the back, hoping a snack might put him at ease. And I was starving. He was the kind of man my grandmother would have called handsome. He seriously looked like he walked off the pages of a J.Crew catalogue: neatly pressed khakis, equally neatly pressed navy button down, and a blue-and-white striped tie with a little gold cross tie tack. Hair slightly gray at the temples, but thick and nicely combed.

After some chitchat and his life story about being a dentist, I finally asked, "So. What I can help you with?" I popped a cookie in my mouth. Happily, they weren't too stale.

"Well, Miss Reddick, I've been married to my wife for thirty years. I'd like to say I know where she goes, what she does, what she thinks. She's *doing* something."

I waited and finished chewing. "Doing what?"

"How do you young ones say it? Another man?" He sighed. "Maybe? I don't know."

I nodded slowly. "And you're here because…?"

"My wife disappears into the conservatory for days sometimes and comes back filthy. Absolutely filthy."

"Your conservatory?"

He blinked. "Why yes. It's not technically ours, but well, we are very interested in botany. We are on the Botanica board. Several buildings are being put up to house various plants. The botanical garden won't open to the public for a few more years, but she loves to go there."

"Oh, right. Conservatory. Like in *Clue*."

"Excuse me?"

"Never mind. Go on."

"She's started spending more and more time there. And she's put up butcher paper on the windows. No one can see in anymore. Construction is temporarily on hold, there've been some financial backer dropouts, so it's at a standstill. And she has a huge stack of old books. In her study, there are all these books! Old, old books, and they're in languages I don't understand."

"Nothing says, 'I'm having freaky, rough forest sex' like dirty clothes and books," I said.

"She's acting differently," he insisted. "Secretive."

I felt a little sorry for the guy. "Okay, why come to me, though? I just sell herbs. Why not go to the police? Or a private investigator?"

He took a piece of paper from his pocket and handed it to me. It was that stupid little coupon from the mass mailer envelopes.

"This was on the kitchen table."

I considered the situation.

"I've been so busy at work, and I thought she was happy, volunteering at church and doing things with her friends. The police can't help me. I have no proof she's done anything illegal. She's not missing or anything, and I don't have evidence of any kind of crime."

"All right, good, but you still haven't answered my question. Why me? What about a private eye? Or you? Why don't you follow her yourself?"

He winced. "Miss Reddick, not only am I extremely busy, I'm a terrible liar. If she caught me, I'd panic and tell her the truth. I don't want her to know I think something is wrong. This has to be secret. If word got out at all I was looking at my wife that way, it would be bad. She's well known in the community, and I just... I don't want that.

"And this is... Look, Ms. Reddick, she isn't herself anymore, and it feels otherworldly. I saw you on the news, back when you were on trial."

I started to interrupt, but he held up a hand.

"I never thought you did those horrible things." His earnest grandfather-face softened. "If I'd had kids, maybe one of them would have been like you. Or a granddaughter? I would have loved to have a granddaughter."

I honest to gods thought he was going to start crying. I busied myself with pouring more tea and scooping too much sugar into it.

Mama did a little of this work when I was young—investigations and the like. But it was low-key stuff. Witches whose men were sneaking out with Vamps, Weres whose families feared they were going vegetarian. This was a first for me and obviously totally different from working with SI. A solely Human case. And a pretty vanilla one, at that. Maybe this would help me rebuild my cred.

"Please, Miss Reddick." He pulled a checkbook out of his pocket and began to write out a check. I almost jumped in his lap—cash was my friend these days. "I just need you to tell me if what she's doing is dangerous. Oh god, what if she's making some drugs? Or... or, jests aside," he swallowed hard, "actually cheating on me? After so many years."

"What does she say about where she's been or what she's doing? Why do books mean she's having an affair?"

"Sometimes, she says she's working on cultivating a new orchid species in the conservatory and doesn't want me to interrupt her delicate work. The old books are supposed to be more informative. I don't believe her. I don't. I've known her long enough to know when she's... Well, I know she isn't being truthful. I *know* in my heart something is wrong." He slid the check over to me. I almost gagged on all the zeroes. The second time that day someone had thrown money at me. This time, I intended to keep it.

He was looking at me with absolute despair, wringing his hands. Like I was his last hope. I hate it when people do that. He seemed so nice, like someone's kind uncle or father, and having never had any uncles or known my father, I wanted to help this one.

I learned a little more about him as we talked. Dr. Bartley was close to retiring. He wanted to spend his golden years with his wife, happily touring lighthouses of the world and adding to his model train collection. And of course, the plants. They loved their plants. No kids, no pets, no family to speak of. A perfectly ordinary, self-sufficient couple.

I picked up the check and folded it neatly in half. "I will call you to touch base." He shrugged. "I'll use my discretion." I found a scrap of paper. "This is my cell number. You can call me anytime." I passed it to him. "All work is completely confidential, though not guaranteed. I'll need a list of places she might go."

He dutifully scribbled out some things. "And include on there how I reach you."

He nodded. "Of course. Here. This is the address of the conservatory. And this is my cell."

"I won't call unless it's absolutely necessary, but you should be ready for contact whenever I need it." He bobbed his head again, permanently and heartbreakingly cowed.

"Ann wouldn't pick up that phone anyway. She has her own cell phone."

"And is that her name?"

"Ann. Yes. Ann Bartley."

"Okay. So, the conservatory. Where else can I find her?"

"She doesn't work, but she does a lot of charity things. And she's involved in several groups at church. She's chairman of the board for Botanica. She's always raising money, scouting donors, looking at plans. I'm usually at work most of the day and late into the evening. And here's our address." I took a second scrap of paper.

As I showed him out, Charlie said, "I just want to know she's safe."

I nodded.

I hadn't had any customers, so I closed up early.

After I locked the store doors, I made my way upstairs to the second-floor apartment. It's super convenient and saves tons on gas money for my broomstick. Ha.

I kicked off my red cowboy boots and called, "Honey, I'm home."

Dorcha barreled around the corner from the bedroom and rammed my hand with her head, her purr like a motorboat. "Hey girl." I scratched behind her ears. I think she's afraid I'll disappear again.

Dorcha isn't a regular cat. First of all, she can appear to non-Others like a plain little black housecat. But to me, and those like me, she shows her real form: a sleek, oversized panther, black with dark gray markings, impressive white fangs, the whole shebang. A midnight saber-toothed tiger. Years ago, I came into my bedroom one night and found her sleeping on the duvet as if she owned the place. Terrified, I cast a quick protective spell, but she just rolled over and showed me her belly, her feline face inviting a rub. So I gave her a raw steak I happened to have, and we've been besties ever since. I'm certain she came from Otherwhere and just liked it so much, she stayed.

She even stayed while I was at Lakeland. But not here. At least, I don't think it was here. She hasn't offered that up to me yet. I get the sense she feels bad or guilty about something, but if it's for the silly reason that she went back to just across the border in Otherwhere to wait me out, I have no idea. Qyll and co. found her sniffing around the back door once they started putting the shop back in order.

After she'd had her fill of scratches, Dorcha disappeared out the window. No clue where she goes at night, but if she's anything like a normal cat, she's got another family somewhere who thinks she's theirs and calls her Blackie.

I had just settled into the couch with a Woodford Reserve (something they do NOT have at Lakeland) and a trashy true crime novel when there was an almighty bang on the back door.

"What *now*?"

"Yoooohoooo!" A singsong voice called.

As if the day could get any weirder.

I took a huge gulp of my bourbon and trudged to the door. On the second-floor deck dawdled Gideon, his trademark white suit in attendance. When he saw me, he flashed that ridiculously brilliant smile of his and waved, as patently affable as a world's most dapper loan shark.

I muttered the spell to unlock the door and let him in.

As he stepped delicately into my kitchen, I was painfully aware of how Earthly and mundane the place was to his non-Earthly glamor.

Before I could speak, he pushed by. "Tessa, *darling*, I won't waste time. You've only been out of your jail for a *month*, and here you are, back to being a very bad girl." He—for lack of a better word—*sashayed* past me and into the living room where he waved a hand and sat delicately in the white white WHITE chair he conjured on the spot. "Come. Sit. *Talk* to your Watcher."

Gideon is a Malakim, sort of a lower-caste, messenger Angel—and yes, my Watcher.

Once I was assumed to have broken the laws of both Earth and Otherwhere, I became subject to certain punishments. As I was convicted by the Human court of not only mass murder but also declared criminally insane, I was placed at Lakeland. And was assigned a Watcher: the Other equivalent of a parole officer. Gideon took up the post last year when the previous Watcher retired, and has taken it on himself to be a royal pain in my ass. Twice he showed up at Lakeland during my interviews for potential release, shaking his head sadly from just behind the moderator's chair.

Needless to say, I was not, in fact, released.

I flopped down on the couch again and pointedly picked up my book. If I ignored him, he might go away.

"We heard there was a *teeny* bit of magic recently that killed a *few* humans and demons, and it is just *so odd* you are out of jail and now this happens. I *know* I don't need to remind you that as a dweller of *both sides* of the Rift, you are subject to the laws of Earth *and* Otherwhere, pursuant to the fourth and fifth articles of our regulations governing the use of magic against Humans in the Human realm. *Again*, that is."

The sad part is, he's right. And yes, I know it's stupid. When it comes to making laws and guidelines in a post-Rift world, we're putting the 'moron' back in oxymoron.

"Are you kidding me?" I couldn't keep the pure incredulousness out of my voice. "Yeah, kinda familiar with the laws, Gideon. But those murders are part of a larger case. I was in the hospital—jail, as you call it—when the others happened. Why on Goddess' green earth would I pull a stunt like that and get into trouble again?"

After the Rift, both sides scrambled to put something that looks like law and order into place around the resulting chaos. Otherwhere might look like bedlam to a Human—all fun-house mirrors and weird creatures running amok—but there are, in fact, sets of rules they live by. Strange, contradictory, sometimes unfathomable rules, but there you are nonetheless. The Arcana supposedly serves as judge, jury, and executioner for the misuses of magic by Others. And the odd Earth-born Other. Such as, say, me.

He didn't say anything.

"You think I did it? Doesn't your boss see and know everything?"

Gideon pouted. "You know that's not how this works. I'm not privy to that." Though from the part of Otherwhere most Humans call Heaven, Gideon's too low on the totem pole to have gotten very close to the big guy upstairs. The purest being in all the universes doesn't concern itself with Earth. "Besides, I don't *know* if you did it. I just *suspect* it, say, so you could take over as the most powerful Witch in Earth. I mean, perfectly understandable. No one would *blame* you, really."

"Yeah, well, then you need to get your facts straight. I had nothing to do with any murders. Not the one last night. Not the ones from five years ago. So get your feathery white butt and impossibly well-moisturized skin out of here and let me relax. Surely you have other people to torment?"

I glared at him while he smirked at me.

"Can you prove your whereabouts last evening?" He looked smug.

I thought about it for a minute. "I was here. I'm always here. Or downstairs. Dorcha can tell you. She was... crap. Out hunting."

Gideon's smug got smugger. He stood. "Don't *worry*, pet. I'm not turning you in. *Yet*. You're right, I don't know for sure. I wanted you to know I'm just, as they say, *watching*."

I stood and pointed a finger at him. "You are a sanctimonious jerk, you know that? You're supposed to be *good*. One of the good guys. I didn't have anything to do with that fire. Why won't anybody look into that?"

"You were tried, my dear, and found guilty. There was absolutely *zero* evidence anyone else had *anything* to do with it."

"No one Human, you mean? The Arcana didn't try me!"

"It really wasn't necessary, was it?"

I literally smacked my forehead with my palm, squeezing my eyes closed. "I was shipped off to a Human hospital for mentally ill. Crazy people. Because when you are found guilty of killing that many women, you are clearly *not* of sound mind. I got out because somebody realized the truth."

The look in Gideon's ice-blue eyes was hard to read. Malakim's default setting is justice, and he truly believed I had killed my family and was now about to get up to more evil shenanigans.

"Just step carefully," he said softly. "Carefully indeed." He vanished, leaving me spitting curses at vacant air.

**AREA WOMAN DECLARED MENTALLY INCOMPETENT
TO STAND TRIAL—AP, LOUISVILLE**

*Late on Wednesday afternoon, federal judge
Krishna Tibbs ruled that Tessa Reddick is
not mentally competent to stand trial.
Reddick, 31, allegedly started the fire at
her family's ancestral home on St. James
Court on June 8th. The fire left thirty-
seven women dead, including Reddick's
mother. The other victims were reported to
be Reddick's aunts, cousins, and other
female relatives.*

CHAPTER FOUR

In the morning, I awoke still thinking about the fire. I had made a few calls, sent out a few owls. I'd heard nothing. Not even a solid, "eff you, Reddick." I think that's worse, when your friends won't even tell you off, that's how pissed they are. I had been going down a list of people to talk to, and as the names dwindled so did my hope of learning anything from a trusted source.

While adjusting a wind chime in the corner of the shop, I heard water running in the little half-bathroom under the stairs. Odd, since I was kind of alone. I rushed in to see the sink filling up with dirty brown water, despite there being no plug in the drain and the taps firmly turned off.

I flipped the light switch and peered into the basin. Swimming in figure-eights was a tiny catfish. It came to the surface, its slimy whiskers fanning out beside its wide mouth. A trail of bubbles descended, hovering over the murk.

As the bubbles popped, words whispered from them: WELCOME HOME, HUSHPUPPY.

I smiled. The catfish slapped its tail in the water, then the whole mess slid down the drain, and in a moment, it was dry and empty.

"Tell him I'm on my way!" I shouted after the phantom fish.

Finally. A message from a friend.

For as long as I could remember, Papa Myrtle lived by the river in the west end, past Portland, in a funny old hut up on stilts. He remembers the Great Flood of 1937, the race riots in 1969, and the tornado in 1974. When I was little, Mama would take me to see the Nickers: Papa Myrtle and his gaggle of children who loved to leap off the dock into the river. Although Mama forced me to be a good swimmer, Witches don't love water—some kind of ingrained leftover from the days of the witch trials—so I sat in the shade on the banks and watched them frolic.

Nickers can usually be found any place there's a river and a couple of months' worth of warm weather. They're low-level magic users, mostly limited to being able to breathe underwater and talk with fish. Papa Myrtle came to Kentucky from Louisiana, but a huge chunk of his family was wiped out after Hurricane Katrina. My Aunt Tilly called Nickers the stewards of the rivers, the caretakers of all the slimy swimming critters.

It took me near an hour to find the place again; it's been two decades. The Nickers keep to themselves, living and working apart from pretty much everybody. Most Nickers I've heard of make their home in the Deep South bayous and rivers, having descended from German immigrants.

I parked in the weedy yard and climbed to the door. The house was a house in the loosest sense of the word—four walls, a floor, a roof, and it sheltered those inside from some of the elements, but that's about it. Things hadn't changed much since the last time I'd been there.

My knock was answered by a little girl of perhaps five. She had a wide mouth, huge pale eyes, and lank hair. Tiny gills lined her skinny neck. "Maya, come away from that door," a woman commanded. She appeared behind the girl—her taller, older version.

"Josie? Is that you?" I shaded my eyes with a hand to get a better look.

Her eyes narrowed. "Shit. *Shit*. What the devil are you doing here? Go away. He's not home." She tried to slam the door on me, but I was too quick. Josie and I are about the same age. She was one of the children playing in the river when we were small.

"He sent for me, Josie. Do *you* want to go tell him you sent me away? Because I don't think he'd like that." Nickers are clannish and aloof, and when pushed, they have terrible tempers.

Josie pursed her lips and opened the door. Little Maya stared, wide-eyed. I stepped into the warm gloom.

"Papa!" Without taking her eyes off me, Josie yelled "She's here." She kept muttering under her breath while Maya watched with interest.

We stood glaring at each other for long moments until the familiar shuffle-shuffle-*thump*, shuffle-shuffle-*thump* neared from down the hall. Papa Myrtle and his ancient walking stick appeared, his catfish-like face breaking into a toothless grin. "As I live and breathe," he wheezed. "Hushpuppy. Come on, girl, give ol' Papa a hug."

I crossed the room in two short steps and leaned down to embrace his rounded shoulders. He patted my back with a plump hand, the webbing between the fingers damp. "Go on, sit yourself down now. Josie, where yo manners? You get some iced tea for our guest." At the first protesting noises she made, he gave her a sharp look and stamped the walking stick against the wooden floor. "Who raised you, girl? This is an old friend. Git, now. Scoot. Maya, g'on, help your mama."

I sat on the edge of the couch, the plastic covering crackling under my weight. Papa Myrtle settled into a rocking chair that had to have been two hundred years old. His bulging eyes were cloudy with age behind a pair of round spectacles. The flattened nose, bald head, and gills gave him the appearance of a strange old frog.

"Don't mind Josie." He waved a crooked paw at me. "She's just scared. They all are. I'm too old to be scared." His laugh was a croak.

"I didn't do it, Papa. I swear," I blurted. My old friend Papa Myrtle, letting me in. Treating me like I wasn't a leper. It was a relief I could barely find words for.

He put up a hand, the palm pale and smooth. "I know you didn't. I've known your family for a long, long time, and I don't bother much with rumors." He looked at me carefully. I knew, despite his failing vision, he could see me just fine. "Josie's right, you're putting us in danger being here, but it ain't all your fault. I reckon somebody is going to come looking for you sooner rather than later. And I 'spect you don't have a friend to turn to now."

"Everyone thinks I did it, don't they?" I try not to ask questions I don't already know the answers to, but this one sort of slipped out.

Papa Myrtle shrugged and sat back. "Hard to blame 'em. Sure do look like you killed an entire coven of your own kind and kin."

I frowned. "Then, why do you believe me?"

For a long time, he was quiet, looking toward the window. Thoughtfully, he said, "Your mama was a good friend. A good friend to me and mine, and Nickers don't forget friendship. I can't do much for'n you, but I got something. Look in that box yonder. Go on, go get it."

On a rickety bookshelf, there sat a wooden box the size of a loaf of bread, carved with a pair of koi. I sat back down on the couch. Inside, there was an envelope with my name written on it in my mother's unmistakable hand. Shaking, I tore into it and tilted the contents onto the coffee table. It was a big round locket, silver with a carved moonstone face set in front. I stared at it dumbly, trying to remember it. Then, I tried to pry it open, but no luck.

"Okay, what gives?"

"I was hoping you'd know." Papa Myrtle chuckled. "She sent it to me years ago. Said to give it to you when the time comes. Said I'd know. Thought this was it." He sat back and rocked gently.

I rubbed some of the tarnish off with my finger. It wasn't familiar in the least. My mother wore jewelry, of course, and preferred it to the protective tattoos I had chosen. She liked sterling silver and rose gold, moonstones and amethysts. She was hardly ever without a couple of necklaces and bracelets, and a pair of moonstone earrings dangling from her lobes. But I would remember a locket with a face on it. I know I would...

"What is it?" I kept trying to pry it open six ways to Sunday. "Where did it come from?"

He just rocked a little in the chair, a hint of smile on his fat face.

"So this is it? You called me out here to give me an old necklace?" I regretted it the instant the words left my lips. It wasn't polite, first of all, and second, this was an alliance I could not afford to lose. But Papa Myrtle didn't even raise an eyebrow.

Josie returned with a tray of glasses, a pitcher of tea, and a bowl of cut lemons. Maya followed her, carefully carrying a chipped plate of cookies, which she offered me shyly.

"Did you make these?" I asked, glad to be distracted from my anger. Without taking her eyes off my shoes, she nodded. "They look yummy." I took a bite and swallowed. Too much sugar for me, but I said, "And they *are* yummy. Thank you." She grinned and set the plate on the table, then scurried to stand by her mother, occasionally daring a smile.

Josie didn't sit, just stood rigid and scowling, her arms folded across her chest.

"Sometimes you just have to put things back for a while, until the meaning becomes clear," Papa Myrtle said, stirring sugar into his glass. "But then again, maybe it's just a pretty thing she wanted you to have."

"Daddy, that tea's already got sweetening in it. You're going to make yourself sick." Josie said it in a way that let me know it was a common thing between her and her father.

Papa Myrtle waved a dismissing hand and kept looking at me. "I wish I could offer you more, Hushpuppy, but my debt to your mama has been paid off. And I wish you the best. I'm sorry, child. I truly am."

I knew what he meant: "We can't protect you, and we can't help you." But I thought he wanted to, and he would have, if he could.

We drank our tea, the only sounds the clinking ice and the rattle of cicadas outside.

"We done heard about you gettin' set free, but we had some family business to attend to in Louisiana." He took off his glasses and began to polish them with his t-shirt. "My cousin passed, and we were down to the funeral."

I nodded, more than a little relieved that at least they weren't ignoring me exactly on purpose. Maybe that's where everyone else was—on summer vacation.

"We won't be seeing you for a while again, Hushpuppy. Setting off back for New Orleans soon, be closer to our roots. So you take care now." Papa Myrtle struggled to stand. His hand was clammy on my arm. "You'll be all right, I reckon."

"Oh, sure. No friends, but I'll be fine."

"Let an old man give you some advice, child." He wheezed a little closer to me. "Sometimes it don't do no good to look back too much. You'll trip on the future." He broke into a toothy grin that dissolved into a hacking laugh.

We hugged.

"Bye, Josie. Nice to meet you, Maya." The little girl beamed and waved. Her mother continued to scowl, but it softened a hair.

"Tessa." Josie grabbed my hand. In a low voice, she said, "You take care, you hear?" I nodded.

With that, I went back out into the yard, the sun too bright after my time in the dim shack. As I pulled away, I saw Maya waving from the window, Josie standing behind her with a look of sadness and resignation on her face.

So, my mother gave a locket to an old friend to keep for me. It didn't seem very special, except it had maybe been hers even for a few minutes. Did it have something to do with her death? It didn't feel like it, if I was being honest about it. It just felt like something my mother would do for some quirky reason. Like the time she came and got me out of school in the fourth grade just to go to the zoo on a Tuesday afternoon. That's Mama.

I looked at the locket. It was one of the only things I had that was *hers*. I should have been more grateful to Papa Myrtle.

By the time I hit the expressway, I could barely see the road for all the tears and snot. I was full-on bawling, missing my mom and family and my friends, feeling alone and very sorry for myself. I got home, stared at the locket for a long while. I fastened the clasp around my neck, the metal warm against my sternum. Then, I poured a large quantity of bourbon before sliding *Practical Magic* into the DVD player. I fell asleep on the couch and dreamed of frogs with big smiles leaping into the river.

I woke up at dusk, thirsty and cramped. After a hot shower and a big glass of cold water, I went into my library. Research on several topics was on the agenda—Charlie Bartley's case, my mysterious murders, and maybe something about my mother.

I spent most of my life living with my mother, a gaggle of aunts, assorted cousins, and relations in a giant Victorian house on St. James Court. They were into all manner of things. One aunt wrote books on the occult. One was a potter and ceramics artist specializing in items for the Craft such as altar patens, candleholders, and sculptures of gods and goddesses. A cousin was a veterinarian. My mother was, among other things, a seamstress. Her workshop was in the apartment I now inhabited, where she made elaborate costumes and robes, wedding dresses and bespoke suits, all under the watchful gaze of her prized Brigid statue. When the downstairs tenant retired from the shoe sales business, she bought the building and opened The Broom Closet with some of the aunts, when I was about nine years old. She then ended up running the whole thing when the others lost interest. I lived in the big house until I was in my early twenties and eager for a bit of freedom. Mind you, the farthest I would go was the apartment over the shop when Mama got too busy to sew.

Soon after, she moved all those books and things to my apartment. I took over the smaller of the two bedrooms, and we made the master into a library and magical item storage area. I always assumed it was just because we ran out of room in the house.

Thanks to my family, I have what I suspect is one of the best collections on the Craft and the occult in the world, and I'm not just saying that. I have some really weird things—a spell etched on the femur of a female Druid, books written on various animal skins (including Human), grimoires from the last dozen generations of Reddick women, a bunch of shotguns that shoot things such as holy water bullets, salt pellets, and silver arrows. There's even a glass eye from a Pope. It's a lot better than the internet, but it's spectacularly disorganized; a lot of it still in old unmarked trunks or grubby wooden boxes. I haven't been through the tenth of it all; if I'm to believe myself, an inventory is totally on the agenda.

After three hours of digging through dusty books and talking to the ghosts, I was done. I would have to ask the oracle at Google for some more information, but that could wait. Besides, I was ready to get out and about.

Time to do a little old-school recon.

The Three Libras is a bar in Smoketown on a nondescript street. It's owned and run by a trio of sisters, Nona, Deci, and Morticia. They don't advertise, they don't have specials. They will never serve microbrew or put a jukebox in. They don't accept credit cards, debit cards, or blood money.

I parked the Camry at the curb, got out, and pulled up the hood of my cloak. Its deep indigo velvet is lined with fine soft wool, with all sorts of pockets sewn in. A silver aspen leaf clasp holds it fastened. It's the sort of thing that keeps you cool in warm weather and warm in the cold. Like magic. It's the perfect thing to wear to a place like Three Libras. Although it is possible the overall effect got ruined by my beloved red cowboy boots.

I took a deep breath before sauntering up to the guy at the door. On giving me a close once-over, the bouncer nodded me in, past the long line. He didn't look familiar, but I slipped him some of Charlie Bartley's money as I passed. Most of the guys at the door have some notion who's Human and Other and who's looking for trouble. It never hurts to grease a palm, just in case.

The place hadn't changed much. Not that it ever did... It's always been dark, but for candles burning on all the flat surfaces and a couple of well-tended fires. No matter what time of year it is, Three Libras is always the same sixty degrees, which is why my cloak came in handy. The bar is a combination hideout, hangout, and refuge for the things that come through the Rift and want a taste of home. Or for those of us on this side, with Otherwhere-ish tendencies. It's generally a good place to go for information and creature-watching.

I edged to the bar, happy to see Nona working.

She swept over, her brown eyes wide. "As I live and breathe." Her long nails were a beautiful indigo, as was her lipstick. "Morty said you were coming, but I hardly ever listen to her these days." Uncertainty played on her features like a water bug on a still pond. "My goodness. Well."

"Hi, Nona. Can I get a Woodford, please? Neat."

Her hospitality subroutine kicked in, and she smiled widely. "Coming right up." Her long blond hair swayed as she glided off. Always the height of fashion, that one.

I assumed she wasn't sure which side of the game I was on, whether she should ally with me or stay out of it altogether. Nona isn't the one who makes these decisions, it's Morticia. Morty is rarely seen at the bar. She scares the customers.

Begrudgingly not kicked out on the street, I took my drink to a corner of the polished wood bartop, the perfect spot to peer out from under my hood.

You won't find any electricity here (hence the candles and kerosene lamps), because it's too easy for someone (or something) to use it as a weapon or travel along it as if on a paranormal highway. Music often comes by way of an old wind-up player piano, or the occasional impromptu jam performance. The walls are coated in sigils meant to tamp down magical energies. Makes it hard to cast a spell or hulk out on anyone in here.

From my vantage point, I could see most of the room. Relief skittered through my chest when I didn't notice anyone I knew.

But that feeling was short-lived.

"*I didn't hear that. I can't believe they let her out!*"

"*My grandmother said they had it coming; it's a wonder she got to them first and not somebody else.*"

"*Can you imagine? Offing your whole family? I mean, I hate my cousin Demarcus, but I'm not going to kill him, you know what I'm saying?*"

"*What on earth is she doing here, anyway? Isn't there a price on her head?*"

Zeus's balls.

I concentrated on the bourbon.

You know how you can tell when someone is watching you? Like, more than idly. I got that feeling about twenty minutes later.

I turned around, hackles up and ready to fight, and came nose to nose with a rumpled little man.

"Reddick," he wheezed, his wet gaze lapping at me. "Long time no see." He patted me clumsily on the back.

"Victor Funar. What's shaking?" He clambered up on the stool next to me and signaled to Nona.

She brought a dusty bottle, with no label, from somewhere and poured a tumbler full of a deep amber liquid. She glanced at me again, still trying to work out how she felt.

"I don't know how you still drink that swill," I said to Victor, shaking my head.

"It's not real *palinka*, but she does try," he grumbled, gesturing to the retreating Nona. After seven centuries, he still hadn't bothered to lose the thick Hungarian accent. "What I wouldn't give for real thing. My papa used to make it in our barn when I was a boy. This," he gestured at the glass and made a rude noise. "Muddy piss water. But," he sighed, "is the best I can do."

When Victor was a boy, there was no America. They thought the Earth was flat, and there were dragons at the edge of the map. Eastern Europe was vastly different than it is now, and in his lifetime, has included places like Byzantium and the Holy Roman Empire. He was turned into a Vampire in his late twenties, before dental hygiene, skin care, or fortified milk.

After the Rift, when cultural trade began to pick up steam, some of the beings from Otherwhere got quite a kick out of seeing how their kind was represented in Human books and movies. The Trolls were pleased to be upgraded to slightly smarter and better-looking versions of themselves. The Elves were miffed at being cast as a laissez-faire race of pointy-eared supermodels. Vampires are likely still incensed about the mess Hollywood made of their history, and a particularly pejorative term among them is "Sparkles."

We sat in silence for a while.

"I miss anything while I was gone?"

Victor shrugged. "Some murders with Humans and Others. There was some fear for a while. People think you did it."

I groaned. "I know. Should I be worried?"

He shrugged his lopsided shoulders again. "Some people still think you called something from the deep to kill your family. Then you did other murders by casting a spells or something from your jail."

I had to laugh at that. People were giving me way too much credit. "You don't seem bothered by me. Why is that?"

Victor shook his head. He cast a glance around, as though fearing an eavesdropper. "I don't believe you did anything. Besides, they killed a shapeshifter family, a couple of lesser demons, some cows, maybe? I don't bother with such things, but I know you wouldn't kill a family like that. Especially a family of Others with little children."

Interesting. There had clearly been some talk through the Other grapevine but not enough to work him up. Granted, Victor was an anomaly, even in Otherwhere. He was Turned—a Human who had been bitten by a Vampire—and he had managed to survive so long largely because he never wanted power or wealth. No, for him it was enough to mosey along, staying out of everybody's way, drinking his *palinka* and trawling for porn on the internet. Oh yeah, he's old, but he's pretty up on naked girls. He's a connoisseur, seeing as how he's seen practically every kind of pornography known to man. Ignorance is bliss, and Victor is a case study on willful ignorance. Most of the time.

Whenever I see those movies where the Vampire is super-hot and played by a teenage boy, I laugh and think of poor old Victor. Born to a family of rope-makers, in what is now Hungary, he was turned by a Vampire drunk on Faerie blood at one of the Vamp high feast days. Victor told me the Vamp thought he was Natalia, Victor's younger sister, and turned him instead. Boy, was that Vamp mad when he sobered up and discovered he had lumpy, stinky male Victor instead of the much younger, much blonder, and much less pockmarked female Natalia. I imagine he got as far from Hungary as he could, which in those days, was probably like ten miles. Currently, Victor was a world-renowned scholar and teacher of Eastern European history and folklore.

"It's nice to not have you treat me like a leper," I said. The twisted little man blushed, his gnarled cheeks reddening in the dim light.

"I knew your *nagymama*, Lydia. Beautiful woman. I don't believe you would do this terrible thing to them."

"When did you meet my great-grandmother?" I hadn't heard that story.

He waved a hand dismissively. "A long time ago. It was the Belle Epoch. It's nothing. Look, it's nice to see you again, Reddick. Excuse me, I see a Whisper Demon who owes me money. Be careful, yes?" He patted my arm then slid off the stool and shuffled into the gloom.

An accordion band began to warm up in the corner. Great. Of all the nights to get out of the house, I had to do it on Squeezebox Sally and the Magic Accordi-orchestra night.

"As I live and breathe. If it isn't Glinda, the good witch of the east end." Someone slapped the bar and plopped onto the stool next to me. "I heard they let you out of Oz! Woo hoo, right?"

Mark Tabler, erstwhile champion of mine. I groaned inwardly.

"Will you shush? How did you get in here?" I hissed. "I told you when you tried to weasel your way into Lakeland, I don't want to talk to you."

With his rumpled dark hair, over-large ears, and gawky limbs, the kid looked much younger than his twenty-four years. Raised on a steady diet of cheap science fiction and fantasy e-books, social media, and the Syfy network, Mark was trying to be the Next Big Thing in supernormal news. His website, the Southern Supernormal Explorer, was a haven for those really into Other culture and taking the field for Others' rights.

He put a hand on his chest in mock hurt. "Is that any way to thank me? As founder and president of Others' Little Helpers, I have connections. A lot has changed since you were last out here in the real world." He turned to a woman beside him waiting for a drink—a young

Latina in extremely tight leathers that had her boobs locked and loaded to within an inch of their lives. She sported a tattoo of a bat around her navel. More ink decorated her arms, mostly pieces that declared she was Human but open to being fed on by pretty much anything with teeth. Given the marks on her neck and arms, it seemed she was popular.

"Hey there." He grinned. She hissed at him and flounced off.

"Can't win 'em all," Mark said cheerfully.

Nona appeared again. "You're quite the belle of the ball." She winked at me.

"Mountain Dew and Red Bull, barkeep," Mark said.

"I told you. I'm not talking to you," He really was an embarrassment and a half.

"How about I ask yes or no questions, and you just nod or shake your head?" He pulled a tablet out of his nerd bag. Ever notice how nerds always have bags? Usually, they're of the crossbody satchel variety and full of their nerdy toys. Then again, I guess I don't have room to talk, because I have a Witch bag, but Witches are cooler than Nerds, right? Right?

I took a swig and pulled my hood a little farther forward, so I couldn't see him at all.

"Come on, humor me." Mark nudged me with an elbow. I resisted the urge to shove him off his barstool. "Besides, I'm pretty sure you don't have many friends around here." He said it softly, like he knew I'd been getting an epic cold shoulder.

I turned to give him a good hard glare. "What the hell do you know about it?"

He gave a casual shrug. "Just... that a lot of people are talking."

"Yeah? About what?" I demanded.

"About how they think you did it. Or didn't. I don't, obviously, but I have a theory that a lot of your old pals have vanished into the woodwork. That you're kind of the opposite of popular these days." He looked closely at me with kind eyes. "Am I getting warm?"

I didn't say anything, but of course he actually was.

"Hey." He put a hand on my arm. "It'll work out in the end. I'll help you. And the FBI seems pretty keen on you, yeah?"

We sat there for a few minutes, listening to the accordions—the low-born wheezy bellows of nineteenth-century dance halls. In a terrible pun-filled irony, they were doing a cover of Wang Chung's *Dance Hall Days*.

"I'd like to invite you to one of our meetings. For my group. Others' Little Helpers?" Mark said, his forced casualness endearing him to me. Just a wee bit.

"Why? Is it show-and-tell day?"

"No. It's just that I... I mean we, we in the group feel like we helped get you free. And we'd like to say how glad we are that you are. Free, that is."

For a split second, I was thrown backward in time to my junior year in high school. I was at Taco Bell with Vail Paquane. We were guzzling Pepsi and laughing, I forgot about what. But I won't forget him. My first love. My first real boyfriend. Technically, my last real boyfriend, too. He was so sweet. Until the day my mother caught him preparing to perform a ritual that would have killed me and blasted him to Kingdom Come. Vail never knew what hit him.

And here was Mark, being sweet.

I just wanted to run.

People aren't nice to you unless they want something.

Or they're nice to you as a prelude to your death.

"I suppose you all want me to thank you so very kindly for springing me from my unfortunate incarceration?" Bitterness shaped my words.

I don't think either of us noticed the man who stomped up to the bar until he was reaching over the seat to grab me.

"You! You sold out your own people!" he blared in my face. He had me by the shoulders, three feet off the ground, and was shaking me like a ragdoll. My glass smashed on the floor. The guy had to have been six feet tall if he was an inch—albino and thickly muscled. Suddenly, people had gathered and were shouting things and throwing beer. The accordions stopped their honking. "You killed them! All of them!"

The next few minutes were a flurry of activity. You can't really do magic in the Three Libras, but there's nothing preventing bodily harm, wild haymakers, or flying malt brew. A stocky man with long tangled mane came up behind the albino. The noise grew to a harsh roar. My brain had been so vigorously scrambled, I couldn't have reacted even if I'd wanted to. The stocky man sank a swift kick in my captor's kidneys, and he let me drop like a sack of potatoes onto the floor.

Immediately, Mark shoved his way to my side and helped me up.

"You jackwagons!" I hollered over the din. "You cannot possibly still believe I killed my *family*, you morons! I've been released! By the ever-loving *FBI*! Doesn't that mean *anything* to you?"

Nona wrung her hands, waving another bouncer over.

"Come on, Tessa. Let's go." Mark pulled me toward the door. The stocky bouncer took my other arm and led us out. Behind us, the bar descended into a brawl.

Outside, the air lightened, and I sucked in a breath.

"Look, I don't have an opinion about you one way or the other," the thick lion-haired man said. "For what it's worth, I know you didn't cause that ruckus in there, but I think you'd better watch out. Nona will talk to Morty and Deci, but maybe give it a couple of weeks?" He did seem apologetic.

"Your drinks are crappy anyway," I muttered and stalked off toward my car.

"Hey, Tessa, wait," Mark said. I didn't stop. I charged toward the Camry and flung myself in the driver's seat.

"Stop!" Mark grabbed the door and held it open.

Not taking my eyes off him, I put the key in the ignition and put the car in reverse. He yelped in protest, but let go. As I pulled the door to, he shouted, "Be careful, Tessa. They're coming after you."

Researchers at the Karolinksa Institute in Sweden remain puzzled as to the inability of Human-Other embryos to be brought to term in either species, or in lab-controlled environments. So-called "hybridization" research continues.

—News item from the **Max Planck Demographics and Research Newsletter**

CHAPTER FIVE

I **emphatically wasn't ready to go home after that, yet clearly** unwelcome anywhere there were people, so I made some inquiries via my cell phone's GPS system. Within moments, I was heading toward the future site of the Louisville Botanical Society's conservatory.

River Road was deserted, and I knew the curves pretty well. Thank all the tiny gods for full moons. I mashed the gas.

I turned south onto Frankfort then east up an unpaved road. The area was silent but for the rustle of dead leaves and the occasional car. It was quite a drive back into the bluffs. I parked near some bulldozers. The glass fairly glowed in the light.

The spell I needed was an oldie but a goodie. It amazed me, how quickly it was coming back. Scared me a little, too, since I'd thought for so long I'd never want to do magic again.

I held up my hand, palm out toward the woods, and whispered, "Magic leaves a magic trail, through fog and wind and icy hail. Make this one strong so I might see, the magic hiding here from me." Yes, it's corny, but that's how it works—you build your own spells because they're more powerful that way, and I built that one when I was about ten so rhyming was *super* important.

It pleased me to see a pale lavender path through the trees begin to lighten, softly at first, then brighter. My gut tightened. The moon was helpful, but I didn't want to take any chances. I took out my compact LED flashlight, so I didn't end up head-down in a sinkhole or knee-deep in a pond. The trail led back away from the main greenhouses, through the woods between them and the river, for perhaps a half a mile or more. I don't know, I'm not good with distances. Certain I was making an enormous racket, crunching through the woods, I did a little noise reduction charm on my feet. "Mousy feet, so mousy mousy, let me go quiet 'round this housey." (Don't judge. I was perhaps seven when I wrote that one and we lived in a really old place with creaky floorboards. I needed a way to have a brownie at one a.m. if I wanted it without waking up the whole house.)

Eventually, in a clearing on the far end of the glass buildings, I found it.

It was like someone had toilet-papered the trees and the huge greenhouse structure with magic. It hung in thick swags from the branches and coated the ground like sheer green-purple snow. But it took on a distinctly green sheen that deepened the closer I got to the clearing. It meant one thing: dark magic. Very dark. And by the looks of it, done here often in the last few months.

Magic, at its simplest, is focused energy. When energy touches something, it changes it—the trees, skin, water, whatever. People who are really good at it can focus this energy and manipulate it with laser-sharp accuracy. As with anything, some folks are better at certain kinds of magic than others. Elves, for instance, are good with air. Incidentally, we Reddicks are also masters of the air. Nickers, like Papa Myrtle, are expert water-crafters. One of the hallmarks of dark magic is that it doesn't dissipate easily. The bad juju does its job, but then it just sticks around and rots, for lack of a better description. It's like plastic in a landfill; it gets used and just never goes away. The remnants of light magic burn off like fog in the sun.

Something drew my attention to the trees. It kept itself just out of my line of sight, but if I didn't try to look at it, I could make out dim shapes. A tiny wave of relief washed over me when I realized they were just Animotoids, feeding on this old, dead black magic. They're not very smart, but they are harmless and startle easily.

Even with the Animotoids' efforts to consume all the leftover magic, my skin crawled as I walked into the circle. My tattoos aren't just decorative or to piss off a parent. (Not that Mama Reddick minded at all.) I have seven, and they're all imbued with protection, the way defensive house spells keep the inhabitants safe. Besides the pentacle and triskelion, I have an Irish cross on my left shoulder, a triple moon on the right, a Heka hieroglyph on my lower back, and the Buddhist *sanko* and West African *nyame dua* on my right and left ankles respectively. Evil is evil in any religion and on either side of the Rift.

I nosed around the conservatory grounds. The leaves and sticks had been cleared away and the dirt swept smooth. Lines snaked, carved in the earth, but not in any pattern I could discern—lacking perspective. I turned the doorknob; it was, of course, locked. I tried a simple unlocking spell and was surprised when the greenhouse bit back. Someone had set up the magical equivalent of an electric fence. I didn't try anything else to get in, for fear it might trip some kind of an alarm. I would wait and learn more before I went busting through.

Near the back edge against a tree trunk, a sheet of plastic rustled in the breeze. I crept over and peeled away one corner. Underneath, was a big smooth block, cool and clammy to the touch, like the forehead of a sick person.

On closer inspection with my LED, I saw the plastic covered a huge cube of reddish clay. I smelled my palm to confirm it, inhaling the telltale scent of earth. The plastic featured a label proclaiming this was Sedona Red Clay, by way of Spot's Art Shop. "Curiouser and curiouser," I muttered, scraping some of the thick earth into a little in-case jar I carry in one of my cloak pockets.

Tucked under the plastic was something else—a piece of paper with ragged edges and writing I couldn't see in the dim yard. Carefully, I teased it out and stepping behind a substantial oak tree, turned the flashlight toward it. The tree should block anyone from the road or building site from seeing me.

The page was clearly ancient, with mystifying markings. For starters, the diagram featured several pentagrams with circles in them, and a curved line in the middle and two sets of arrows around the edge, one clockwise and one widdershins. More markings dotted the edge of the circle. A couple of figures and paragraphs of writing scribbled all over the page, too small to read. A vaguely humanoid figure was drawn under the central line. Four triangles pointed toward the center of the circle. There were other runes and markings I couldn't see very well. Others I could, but didn't recognize. Some were protective sigils, a few were banishing runes that would probably have been used for controlling an entity. But what where they doing here? And together?

"What's *this*?" a smooth voice inquired. "Knee-deep in dark magic in the middle of the night, are we?"

I readied a spell as I pushed my back against the tree. How the *hell* did I let myself get so distracted?

"Cherubim know the divine secrets above all, while Seraphim excel in that which is greatest of all, namely in being united with God himself."

—Saint Thomas Aquinas

CHAPTER SIX

Fortunately, it was only Gideon. "Fortunately" being a relative term.

"Shush, you bleached-out, self-important idiot!" I hissed. He was leaning against a tree. Glowing. Because Celestials just can't resist showing off. I stomped over and gave his shoulder a little shove.

Gideon put his hands on his hips. "Now is that any way to behave toward your *Watcher*? Especially one who's going to put you in a maximum security Otherwhere lockup guarded by *hell trolls* as soon as I prove you're behind this?" He waggled his manicured fingers at the clearing. "Whatever *this* is. Looks like trouble."

"What are you even doing here? I just saw you yesterday." He smirked. "Look, it's not what you think. There was a fight at the bar and... Oh here." I pulled out the page I'd been looking at.

Gideon's eyebrows rose so high, they nearly hit the back of his head. "And she hands me a receipt for her wrongdoing! The proof!" He waved it around like a prosecuting attorney in a based-on-real-events movie.

"Be careful!" I screeched. "I don't know what that is!"

"*I* do." He stopped waving it so vigorously.

"Oh, you do?" I demanded.

"It's obvious what it is."

I crossed my arms. "Go on."

"It's an ancient document," he said grandly. "Well, a copy of one."

"And it does what, exactly?"

"It's evil, I can tell that much. That's a symbol for evil right there. And here's another one. Oh, and one more."

I grabbed the paper carefully and stowed it in my cloak before he could react. "You have no idea. I told you. I just found it. Just give me time to figure this out, okay?" Gideon was sort of a narcissistic prick, but most of the time, he could be reasoned with. He wasn't bad at his job, exactly. I guess it's not his fault he can't stand me.

"Well..." Gideon made a show of sighing and rolling his eyes. "*Okay*. You have seven days. I haven't met my quota for this month and just between you and me—" He leaned in closely and stage-whispered, "I have money riding on this."

Poof. He was gone.

By the time I got home, it was near three a.m. Dorcha was sitting in the living room in front of the door like a sphinx—head up and staring. When I came in, she bounded up, knocking me over.

"Mmmmphh, get offa me, you beast!" I huffed through a mouthful of silky black fur. She gave me another hard bonk in the chest with her head and trotted off, clearly assured of my alive-ness and now ready for her nightly excursions.

I wasn't even close to tired, so I put my cowboy boots by the door, changed into comfy clothes, and made some coffee. Then went back into the library to continue where I'd left off, bringing with me the little container of clay.

My library is the master bedroom of the apartment. Mom and I had installed floor-to-ceiling shelves and cabinets. A big heavy table sits in the center, along with a squashy armchair and a couple of lamps. One wall is books I inherited from my family. All my surviving grimoires and books of shadow are there, dating back centuries. Some of them I can't read since I'm not up on my Latin or old English or high German.

I settled in for a browse.

Luckily, some of my ancestors enchanted their books of shadow, which, while being a super-neat trick, is also incredibly handy. I started with great-great-auntie Sheridan, who is almost always the most helpful.

Her book of shadows is huge. Probably, a thousand parchment pages all covered in her elegant script and vivid illustrations. This is one of the reasons I love Auntie Sheridan's book—because it's so pretty. The book itself is green leather with the face of a green man worked in the cover, his mischievous features poking out from a pile of oak leaves. Another reason is, she was so meticulous in her detail.

I undid the latch and opened the book.

A fine mist leaked from the binding, swirling and drifting until it finally coalesced into a woman in Victorian garb, bustle and elaborate hairdo included. She stood about two feet high and was rendered in shades of gray and white.

"Tessa, my darling! It's been too long!" She always says that. I don't think enchanted books have much sense of time.

"Hello, Auntie. How are you?"

She sighed, patting her ornate coif. "I simply must get these spells right or mother will be quite cross." The book's spirit will create sort of a composite personality of its owner over time. Auntie lived to be almost one hundred, so she had a lot of time with this tome. It had soaked up an extremely accurate version of my ancestor. "I haven't much time, dear, so tell me, to what do I owe the pleasure of your visit?"

I quickly got her up to date on the situation, leaving out some of the more anachronistic details. These book spirits were sort of stuck in the time they were created, so Sheridan didn't understand things like computers or the internet.

Then, I held up the page from the conservatory.

"That symbol upon your paper there is a hamsa." I knew that. I have a tattoo of one. A hamsa looks like a hand with an eye in the palm. "It's a protection sigil." She frowned. "This is ancient Hebrew, and I believe it's a diagram for calling forth a spirit of some sort. I cannot tell if it's evil or not. Now, I don't know Hebrew very well. Hold it closer, would you?" I did. "Hmm..." She made a squeal of discovery. "I wonder if someone has unearthed a Book of Creation."

"A Book of Creation," I scribbled it down on a notepad. "Never heard of it."

"Legend has it, they were the first books, scrolls really, written by the first holy men. They were reported to have unlocked the... well, ultimate secrets of life, and these books described various rituals to do with the very creation of life or destruction of death. Only the most trusted holy men, those pure of intention and clean in spirit, could produce or use them. At some point, it was decided Humans shouldn't wield such power. Various religious factions banded together to have them outlawed and declare their contents dark magic. All the books were said to have been destroyed, but of course, there are always copies of such things floating about where one least expects."

"What exactly was in them?"

"An excellent question. Supposedly all manner of rituals, incantations, hexes, and curses. Spells to call Demons and bind them. To banish Angels. To give or take magic. Hard to say, exactly. It's nearly all rumor and legend, to be sure. None of us could ever find one. We did think we came across a few pages here and there. Let me show you."

The book flipped itself to a point near the end.

"I believe the pages from which I copied this are from a Book of Creation dating around perhaps two thousand years ago. I saw it in the private collection of an archaeologist in Nepal. He said he found it in a cave near the sea in India."

The page had a similar diagram to the one from Mark's book. But it appeared simpler somehow. Not as many sigils.

"That symbol means 'earth'," Sheridan said. "And that one means 'fire.' I don't know much else. Oh, I *am* sorry, dear."

"Auntie, what are you talking about! You were such help. Oh, are there any spells I should have handy if I wanted to maybe stop a ritual like this?"

She frowned slightly. "I would say some sort of water-courting spell would be helpful, if fire and earth are on that chart. Not wind. Earth, of course, you can fight earth with earth. That is all that is coming to mind right now."

I scribbled some notes. "Auntie Sheridan, thank you so much!"

The little figure on the table beamed her misty gray smile. "It is always my pleasure, darling. Do be careful, and let me know how you come out in the end, won't you?" She blew me a kiss and dissolved back into the page.

Spells. Now I had to write some spells. But not at half past five in the morning. I finally hit a wall of sleepiness, so I tidied up and wrote a to-do list.

Satisfied, I took my yawning self to bed. Dorcha, back from her nightly wanderings, rolled over in her sleep and made a contented sleepy kitty snort in my face.

We were here from out of town, and wanted to check out the local Other scene. The Queen of Hearts did not disappoint! Our party was treated to attractive and attentive staff, an elegant yet discreet environment, and gourmet food. After an enchanting meal (always order the house special—ours was assorted pickled livers, raw green peppers and onions, and the filet of soul. Mouthwatering!!!!), the house troupe performed a lively and inventive floor show, complete with Demon burlesque and a (simulated!) disembowelment. Our bill came to fourteen lies and half a broken heart, including gratuity. We'll definitely be back. Four stars!

—Yelp reviewer **JezziBelle666**

CHAPTER SEVEN

The phone woke me earlier than I would have liked. Without checking who it was, I growled in a sleep-scratchy voice, "I'm wearing a silk nightie and no panties. Talk dirty to me."

After a silence, Qyll wryly obeyed. "The crime scenes are all filthy. Is that dirty enough?"

I rolled over on my stomach, grinning. "Look at you, with your Human sense of humor. Why are you calling so early? And don't you, like, hate phones?"

"Tessa, it's eleven a.m. That isn't early. And it turns out the Human victims from the Koby house do have something in common—they are all members of the Church of the Earth."

"Ohhhh... treevangelists, huh?"

"Yes. And the others are indeed Bacchus and Jezebel Demons. All, incidentally, completely undocumented."

"So if there's an investigation into Antaura, she can be brought up on charges of employing illegals in Earth?"

"Certainly seems that way, yes. But I'm not sure that's enough of a motive for her to make this big of a mess. It's not her style."

"Maybe." I had crawled out of bed and wandered toward the living room, yawning.

"I've emailed you the victims' names."

"Swell. I'll look at them in a minute."

I heard him sigh. In a low voice, he said, "McReynolds is here, and she's on the warpath. She came in spitting fire because the local police let it leak that the crime scenes were muddy so the papers are all talking up the "Mudman Murders." And of course, we're nicely in the dark. Mind you, if you listen to her, it wasn't magic that killed those people. Couldn't have been."

McReynolds. The thorn in the side of the SI. I hadn't had the pleasure of meeting her, but boy, I'd heard stories.

"Oh?" I snapped to. "And how does she come to such a conclusion?"

"Says there's been a serial killer working the southeast for the last ten years who skins vics." He sounded uncharacteristically irritated. Qyll keeps his cool like no one I've seen before. "Yet, she seems to possess exactly zero understanding of a serial killer's M.O. How does she account for the inconsistency in the number of victims? For things like the destruction and mess? How, exactly, is our killer *finding* or choosing victims?"

"Qyll, you need to go to Pryam and get her to take this to a higher up. McReynolds can't do this. An Assistant Director in Charge or not, she *cannot*. It's... it's... illegal! Right? Even *I* know post-Rift law requires the department heads—"

"Tessa." His voice, smooth even in irritation, stopped and calmed me.

"What?"

"I know. The bottom line is this: we need to get this case figured out sooner rather than later. I tried to question West about the card. He won't talk to me because I'm very obviously Other. Pryam is getting the permissions to bring him in for questioning. And she's had no luck with Antaura."

"Surprise, surprise." I flopped down on the couch. "She paid me a little visit yesterday. Made a big show of how powerful she is. That reminds me, you guys need to beef up my security protocols. Because trés rude!"

"My apologies for..." Qyll cleared his throat. "Right. Pryam just messaged. She wants you to go butter up West. If he won't talk to you, we'll escalate. For now, she's having a little trouble justifying dragging him in. Insufficient evidence to tie him to the case. Those business cards of his, they're a dime a dozen."

"Oh great. Send the new girl in with the scary zealot man."

"I've no doubt in your abilities on that front, Agent Reddick."

I snorted, "You're killing me here, partner," and felt more than heard him smile on the other end.

"I must go. I hear the stomping of little mudtroll feet."

"Margie McReynolds, eh? You do that. I'll see how far I can get with West. Call you later?"

I turned on my computer to indeed find the email from Qyll, a mishmash of information on the Koby victims. Paul Courtland. Cara Courtland. Husband and wife, he an accountant, she a secretary. Dana Sykes, a retired schoolteacher. Gislette Ghyslain and Porphyria (no last name), both Jezebel demons. Besides Koby, Dularc Johnson was also a Bacchus Demon. He was listed as having no permanent employment, immigrated to Earth two months ago.

After coffee, a shower, and clean clothes, I put a sign on the shop door saying, "CLOSED UNTIL THE NEW MOON." I figured with Bartley's money, I could shutter the place for a couple of days and not worry too much about keeping the lights on.

Next item on the ever-growing agenda: a trip to see Gardener West. I had hoped to look into my own case and you know, maybe clear my name, but that would have to wait. I guess my history wasn't going anywhere. After five years, a few days wasn't going to make a huge difference.

I do try to stay out of news and politics, unless it deals with Others' rights or something. Isaiah West stands out as the figurehead for a huge organization that wants to send Others back to their homelands and keep them there. Rebuild the veil or at least get some border guards to keep out the unwanted. Even the naturalized and documented citizens of Earth like Qyll. Even the ones *born* here. West found himself in a little quandary when it came to Angels in that they're on the list of deportees, although apparently welcomed in his church while they're here. To a point. West says that Satan disguises himself as an Angel of light and quotes the Bible with a silver tongue. So really, every Other's a suspect.

And here I was, wading into enemy territory.

The Louisville branch of Church of the Earth nestled in the eastern suburbs near I64. The place was huge. Ironically, it looked like a spaceship. There is a reason they call these places "megachurches." The black glass windows and burnished copper roof glinted in the early afternoon sun. The parking lot was a ridiculous size. You could fit six or seven naval aircraft carriers in it and have room for a good part of the Grand Canyon. For a church named for the Earth, there wasn't much of it to be seen after the asphalt ocean had been put down.

Outside, a group of Fervor loitered in a loose glob, staring at the building, a security guard keeping a wary eye out.

Steeling myself with a deep breath, I ducked through the doors into the cool interior.

"Ma'am? This way." I didn't get two steps in before they stopped me.

I held up my FBI creds to the guard. "Agent Tessa Reddick." (I still wasn't used to the coolness factor.) "I'm here to talk to Gardener West."

The guy was short and bald, but had an enthusiastic goatee. "You're not going anywhere until you're cleared."

Another guard ushered me through a metal detector. When it lit up like a Christmas tree, he got on his walkie-talkie. "We have a code red here, Greg. CODE RED."

I crossed my arms. "How did you know my nickname is Code Red?"

"I'll need you to remove your bag and stand here." Bald Goat pointed to a seal of Solomon painted on the carpet. I snorted.

"Cute. Real cute." I obeyed, for expediency's sake.

"No speaking until you've been processed, ma'am." So we waited for Greg.

Inside, the place looked like a brightly lit shopping mall, with escalators, a coffee shop, and a huge welcome desk. There was a giant waterfall cascading from the second-floor into a pool with actual fish. People milled around, talked. Some trotted along, purposefully.

Posters advertised meetings and events. Huge screens up on the walls played what appeared to be taped services and appearances. There he was, Gardener West in technicolor hi-def.

On a smaller screen to my right, the volume was up, so I actually got to hear the fearless leader. He was preaching fervently, a headset mic blaring his voice to the gathered flock. "Thank *God* for the hurricanes on the East Coast! Thank *God* for the two thousand dead Mosquitoes and Fangs now fertilizing the ground over there. Two thousand so-called 'Vampires,' those Mosquitoes! And Fangers, nasty 'werewolves.' This is how the Lord deals with His enemies. And, folks, the Lord has got Himself some enemies, doesn't He?" The crowd roared.

"And let us not forget Others. Filthy Others. Filthy, disgusting Others!" The crowd went nuts. "And the Lord said to Satan, 'From where have you come?' Do you know what he said, brothers and sisters? Satan answered the Lord, 'From going to and fro on the Earth, and from walking up and down on it.' That, my friends, is what faces us today." He preached with an intensity at once frightening and charismatic.

Earthers are fond of referring to Vampires as "Mosquitoes" and Weres as "Fangers." It's the post-Rift equivalent of calling a gay person a "fag" or someone with a mental disability a "retard." Yep, I was certainly in the right place.

The strangest part about setting foot in here was what I felt. Rather, what I *didn't* feel. Sure, I felt all kinds of revulsion and horror, and I was nervous as hell. The thing is, with most places of worship, whether on this side of the Rift or the other, I feel *something*. It could be anywhere from a temple to praise a sun god or a humble Protestant chapel. As long as people connect with a supernormal being, there's *something*. A signal that a powerful being is present—in the minds of the congregants, anyway. When you call something from Otherwhere, some part of it is bound to come. Theoretically, any church where the congregation believes in a god literally *is* calling that god, who responds by being present in some way. It's just how things work.

I'll let you in on a little secret. What most people either don't know or won't accept even in the face of stark screaming reality, is whatever they call "god" is the same god everybody else calls god. Really. Everybody is right when it comes to that part. God is a Celestial—the biggest, strongest one—and lives in a part of Otherwhere that is so far away from Earth, I don't even know how to explain it. "Heaven" and "Hell" are real; they're just more really far-away parts of the Otherwhere. Satan is real (sort of, it's a long story), he's just in the opposite far-away part.

In order to keep the peace, there can't be an imbalance. You can't have too much good or too much evil in Earth. Humans (and a bunch of Others) wouldn't survive. There'd be just too much power. Sort of like standing on the Sun while surrounded by ten thousand nuclear bomb detonations.

Way back in the day, the Powers That Be put a series of protections in place to keep Humanity safe because Humans can't stand to be in the literal presence of the beings we refer to as God and Satan (I'm speaking in really loose terms here). So the big cheeses delegate to their trusted advisors who delegate to their governors and on down the line. At some point, you reach the ones who can navigate boundaries more easily, by being less absolute, and not upset the balance. The further down the chain you go, the less pure good or evil they retain, and the easier it is for them to cross the Rift into Earth.

You'd have to punch a pretty big hole to get the really powerful entities through. A lot of folks think the Rift was the breaking of one of the protections. Neither side is claiming it, though.

So for now, we'll just call it *complicated*.

To get back to my original point, I felt *nothing* especially holy or powerful in the atrium of the Church of the Earth.

"Can I help you?" An elderly woman whose nametag read DARLENE JONES stood in front of me, blinking through thick glasses like a particularly curious owl.

"I'm here to see Gardener West, please."

"I said, no talking." The metal detector guard snapped.

Darlene eyed me cautiously. "Does she have an appointment?"

"I'm FBI."

"I said, shut it, *Witch*."

I turned to face the man. "Look, *Wayne*." I jammed my hands on my hips. "I can see by your beer gut if I so much as skipped away, you wouldn't be able to keep up with me. Also, your gun hasn't seen much use, the safety is on, and I'm willing to bet you're a terrible shot. Plus, caffeine makes your hands shake, *Wayne*." I pointed to the half-full Mountain Dew bottle on the counter. "I showed you not only my credentials but a certain degree of social courtesy since I have been in your presence. I have seen neither from you, *Wayne*. I get it. You want to protect your prophet. But if you impair my investigation in any way, shape, or form, I am legally authorized to use *appropriate* force to remove that impediment. Now, I'm still kind of new at this, so maybe I'm not exactly sure what *appropriate* is in this case, *Wayne*. You might end up in a serious headlock and who knows how much pressure you can take. You look like you're on the verge of an embolism anyway, so let's just agree to let me do my job, okay?"

Every time I sneered his name, his face got a shade purpler. His maw gawped open, no doubt to let me have it.

Luckily for us all, Greg appeared. (Greg, according to his nametag.)

"I've got it, Wayne. Darlene, thanks. Right this way, ma'am." The man reached out as if to grab my arm then appeared to rethink that decision, probably from the expression on my face. One does not simply *grab* a Witch.

I gave Wayne one last glare then found myself in an office under the escalator, seated at a desk with a pile of forms. One asked after my "heritage," which meant, "Which OTHER are you?" One asked for any convictions of crimes against Humans. My address, my height, weight.

"Excuse me, Greg," I said. "I'm just here to speak with Dr. West. I'm not applying to be a member of your congregation. I feel these forms are an invasion of my rights as an American citizen."

"It's a safety precaution, ma'am."

"Right. Well, I was really hoping to see him today. If I fill all this out, we'll be here a long time."

He rolled his eyes. "Just fill in the blanks, ma'am."

I whispered a quick spell that filled out every last line. And every last word was gibberish. I handed the papers to Greg.

"That was fast."

I smirked. "I'm quick with a pen." Then I got up.

"Hey, you're not going anywhere yet," he huffed.

A female security guard trotted in. She had a poufy bottle-black hairdo, long red nails, and a disingenuous smile. I was losing my patience fast.

Greg left. Poufy said, "Now, honey, I just need all your weapons." She snapped on blue latex gloves with a business-like *thwap*.

"My what?"

"Weapons. No guns, wands, staves, swords, knives, bolines, athames, spears, or clubs. No potions, powders, pills, herbs, or bottled substances of any kind, including prescriptions from an Earthside doctor. No spell sheets, grimoires, books of shadow. No familiars, homunculi, crystals, broomsticks, cauldrons, or other heretofore unnamed magical objects. Should you spellspeak, chant, incant, or recite anything that may cause harm to any Human within the premises, we are authorized to shoot to kill." I hoped my little form-filling spell didn't count.

With that, she began to pat me down.

"HEY." I backed up. "You don't get to do that. Are you people insane?" My cheeks flamed. "You're violating, oh, I don't know, THE ENTIRE FUCKING CONSTITUTION!"

She smiled again and kept patting. "Oh honey, if you think you're going to see Gardener West on these private premises without being certified secure, you have another think coming. Now come on, I haven't got all day. If you want to leave, you can. But you're not getting past me to see him until you've been inspected."

Just play by their rules, I said to myself. Repeatedly.

Poufy asked me to take my wallet out of my bag, which I did, grudgingly. She fished out my driver's license, read it carefully, looked at me, and put it back. She kept my cell phone, but I managed to lock it before she snatched it from me. Then she left me fuming in the little office. After what seemed like a million years, Greg appeared and gestured for me to follow him.

We headed up the escalator. Banners hung from the ceiling with slick marketing photos of trees and mountains. One read, "Find God's place for you on this Earth." Another proclaimed, "Of the Earth, by the Earth, For the Earth." The church had come under a lot of fire for its stance on Others. So much pre-Rift Christian dogma was misogynistic, homophobic, racist, and plain pro-Old Testament Bible: women didn't work, men had final say in everything, God hated gays, and so on.

Post-Rift was a different story. Churches like this, whose congregations called themselves "Earthers," are built on the idea that Humans alone are God's chosen people, and that magic, when not performed by specific prophets (read: Jesus), is a perversion of nature. Post-Rift, the whole resurrection story (even though, hellloooo, Jesus was an original badass magician) sort of took a backseat to the passages about not suffering Witches to live and so forth. They've stopped calling their leaders 'Reverend' or 'Pastor' and have taken to referring to them as 'Gardeners' or, I've heard sometimes, 'Father Farmer,' for tending the garden of Earth or something like that.

Hell, I can't keep up with it all.

"How long have you been a security guard, Greg?" I asked as we went down a hall. He ignored me. "Seems like a big job, guarding a whole prophet."

We approached a set of double doors, flanked by more security guards, but they were in much better shape than Greg. Also, they were much more heavily armed.

"This is the one." Greg shoved a thumb in my direction. The man on the right nodded and opened the door.

As I walked through, toward the inner sanctum, I heard people talking loudly. A man sounding firm, and a woman, upset.

"This isn't good for the church," he said.

"We know! They've gone too far this time. I don't think we can stop them."

"Well, you'd better stop them. I don't know how they're doing this, but it could ruin *everything* I've built here. I can't take that chance and you better step in line."

Some garbled mumbling, then "...thinks it's our duty to protect Earth, just like you said, at any cost. They're going after... one at a time. I... I'm afraid, Gardener. She won't listen to reason. You have to put a stop to this."

"I never said..." (Mumbling) "Like any good gardener, I will trim away any branch which does not bear me fruit, but I will pray on it. The Lord will give me guidance."

"Gardener West, people are dying! Even though some are... (mumbling)... The commandments say—" The voice crossed into desperate.

"Shhhh. Shhh. This is different. I'll figure something out."

Greg finally pushed past me to pound on the inner office door. It opened, and Gardener West and a young woman stepped out. A little Pele Demon, with the reddish skin and filed-down nubbins where usually there would be black horns like ebony antelope spikes. Some Demons choose to clip their horns as a sign of renouncing their "sinfulness." She had obviously been crying, and held a wad of white tissue in one hand. She was so small, I wondered if she shopped in the junior Demons department.

"Thank you, Gardener," she mumbled, glaring at me as she passed. He patted her shoulder and turned to me.

"Ah, you must be Tessa."

"Agent Reddick, sir."

He smiled coldly. "Come in."

"I'll be right out here, Gardener," Greg emphasized with a glare. "Just in case."

"Treesus Christ." I threw my hands up. "You are the most bigoted, ignorant bunch of jack wagons I've ever met. You're making the Ku Klux Klan look like Bert and Ernie!"

"Listen here, missy—" Greg hoisted his pants up a little higher, his piggy face reddening.

Gardener West put up his hand, and the man was immediately calmed. "Go on about your business, my good man. I am well. Thank you for your service." Greg nodded and turned on his heel.

West faced me. He was perhaps late forties-early fifties, with gleaming blond hair and intense brown eyes. He wore a tunic and pants of dark green linen and a heavy gold cross, etched with leaves, around his neck.

We stared at each other for a while. I was waiting until he got uncomfortable. He just stood there and watched me, as if he had nothing else to do all day. So then *I* got uncomfortable, but he broke the silence.

"I am sorry you feel you've encountered injustice within our garden." His voice was like one of those huge wind chimes with the low, low pitch. "We can't be too careful though."

"I'm just here to ask some questions."

He motioned me inside his office, a graceful movement, like a jungle cat on its home turf. The room was done in the same spring grass and earth tones as the rest of the church. Dominating it was a huge desk made of a solid piece of natural wood. A little fountain burbled contentedly on it. "Sit."

I sat.

"So. You are a Witch. Normally, I would say I harbor no hatred for you. That you are a child of the one true God, born on this beautiful Earth. That no harm will come to you while you are here." His gazed pierced me. "But you are a cold-blooded killer. And I can barely abide your presence."

He gazed out the window. I didn't know what I was supposed to say. I hadn't been prepared for that.

He stood back up and came around the desk toward me, bottomless brown eyes meeting mine. All my tattoos went nuts. My skin vibrated and burned. It was as though I'd walked into a den of hungry Original Vampires. I hissed inwardly, kicking myself six ways to Sunday. *Why oh why had I waltzed in here without any backup? And what the hell did I have left that I could use for protection besides spells?*

"In the name of dearly departed Cara Courtland, I command thee." His voice was an invitation to drop into a warm, cozy bed with flannel sheets. He took my left shoulder gently and put the palm of his right hand on my forehead, barely touching me, and murmured, "In the name of all the angels in Heaven, I command thee."

His voice was like a siren call. My vision swam, and suddenly, I wanted to do whatever he said. Whatever he wanted me to do. In that moment, had he asked me to strip and have wild sex on the raw wood desk, I would have done it. Had he asked me to shave my head and become a treevangelist, I would have done it. But my tats kept trying to rip themselves off me, which is never a good sign.

I realized what he was doing and jerked back, West's expression indignant.

"Your magic voice won't work on me, buster!" I squirmed out of the chair and his grip.

He stepped back. "I was praying over you, Tessa. Your soul can still be saved." He reached out for me again, and I slapped his hands away, glaring. By the look on his well-moisturized face, that did not happen often.

"You're assaulting a federal agent, buddy. So I suggest you sit down and start answering my questions."

He looked confused.

"Sit down." I pointed to his desk chair. "So *I'm* not allowed to spellspeak, but *you* can? Is that how this works?"

He didn't look like he was going to do it, but he finally walked around the desk without his eyes leaving my face and sat warily. "It wasn't a spell. It was a prayer. Besides, you're in my garden now. You play by my rules."

"Oh yeah? Well I have a couple rules of my own. First, don't try to exorcise me. Second, just answer my questions, and I'll be out of your hair."

West stared, then nodded. Once.

I lowered myself onto the edge of my chair. "Not that it's relevant, but I didn't kill Cara Courtland. Or her crew. I haven't killed anybody. Ever."

"Why should I believe you?" Though he was no longer "praying" over me, I still wanted to dive into his voice. It was a struggle to stay on top of things, although my vision had cleared. He was seriously rivaling some Others in his ability to control via his voice. Did he have some powers of his own? Oh, the irony if that were true.

"Let's start with motive. *I* am here to question *you*. Besides, why would I kill a couple of useless Demons and some treevangelists? What reason could I *possibly* have that is actually logical?"

He frowned slowly and deeply. "You are insane. You are a... you..."

I raised my eyebrows.

"Well, you're the only one who could... right?"

"How flattering. But no. Not even remotely." I held up a hand. "Here's the truth: now that the veil is gone, so much magic shit is flying around, you don't even know. Is that all you've got?"

He looked at me coolly. "You're trying to make a statement about our church community. Kill our people like it's nothing. And your own. You don't value life."

I rolled my eyes. "And why did I kill the Demons? My own kind, as you say." Then I sat, letting the silence stretch.

Through his deep frown, he said, "What questions do you have?"

"About your congregants. Specifically, the ones found skinned last weekend."

"My forest—"

"You call them your *forest*?" I couldn't hold back. It sounded ridiculous.

Irritation grew on his face. "Ask your *pertinent* questions."

"Okay, as you know, some of your... trees?... were killed early Saturday morning. They were in the home of a Bacchus Demon and in the company of a Demon or three. Do you know who would've done that? Why they were there in the first place? Together?" I didn't have my phone, so couldn't show him pictures or remember all their names.

"I believe those present were part of a Bible study and program that offers hope and encouragement for people to leave the Other lifestyle."

My mouth dropped open. "What the hell are you talking about?"

He explained patiently. "Sometimes the one true God's creatures stray from the path. They choose to do magic or give in to their base nature, for example. Or mingle with species different from the ones they were meant for. Our outreach program gently draws them into the garden. So they may live a Christlike life on Earth and be reaped in accordance with the one true God's will."

After that comment, it was easier to shrug off whatever mysterious hold he had on me. *Focus, Reddick.*

"And you think that's what they were doing?"

"I don't know. It's troubling my soul. Cara and the others have been taking matters of this nature into their own hands. Getting a little bit radical, you might say. One of the girls in Cara's group is a Reform Demon. Her name is Heather. She's here today, leading the support group for Others wishing to join our forest. She and Cara were very close. They were all good people. Even the Demons. I met them, they were truly trying to let go of their wicked ways."

"A Reform Demon?"

"People of Otherwhere who have come to Earth and no longer wish to participate in the Other lifestyle. This young woman used to do wicked, horrible things. Now, she's a regular member of our church. She's overcome a lot of adversity, and we've welcomed her. Talk to Heather. She might be able to help you. Much more than I can."

My mind was officially blown to bits, so I simply sat.

Finally, West said, "In no way am I connected to the murders of those poor people. Nor do I have an idea of anyone who is. I swear that on the one true God."

I nodded my recognition of his honesty. He was a lot of things, but he was telling the truth in that moment. That, and *he*, at least, genuinely bought his own bullshit.

West stood up and went to the window, hands clasped behind his back. The late afternoon sun played on his face. He said almost sadly, "Whoever is not with us is against us."

A long pause.

"Babylon is falling, Tessa. And there's nothing you can do to stop it." He stood for a while longer then wordlessly went to the door.

Greg had returned and hovered just outside it. West didn't say a word to me, but to his little lapdog, he said, "She's ready to leave."

Halfway down the hall, a figure turned the corner toward us. The Pele Demon again, tears dried and a determined look on her face. "I'll take it from here, Greg."

The puffy guard hemmed and hawed for a minute before he let her over. Then he smirked and walked off muttering something about nothing so zealous as a convert.

I was frog-marched along another hallway and down a back staircase. She was surprisingly strong for someone so small. In heavily accented English, she said, "I heard you in there and don't know who you are, but you're not a Christian and not an Earther, and you need to tell me right now who you *are*. And why you want to snoop around a Revelation Bible study." She stopped on a landing and pushed my shoulder against the wall with rough force. Her strong floral perfume just losing out to the telltale undernote of brimstone.

The frown between her red eyes deepened when I took a second to catch a breath. "Who are you?"

"Who are *you*?" I snarled.

"Heather Mumford."

"Is that your real name?" I knew it wasn't. There are no Mr. and Mrs. Mumford somewhere in Hell, hoping daughter Heather stops by for Sunday dinner. She could speak English, but it was tough for her Demon physiology to make the soft rolling sounds of our language versus the loud barks and complicated glottals of her own.

Her nostrils flared, and she growled at me.

"Well, how about you let go of me and we'll talk?" I finally said. After a very long moment, her face relaxed, but her hand did not. I put my hands up in a surrendering gesture. "Isn't there a coffee shop downstairs? My treat." The last thing I wanted was for Heather to alert the world I was here. I had no weapons. No friends. No phone.

She exhaled hard through her nose. "Come on." She led the way down the stairs. We emerged on the first floor by the café. I got a coffee and she, a hot chocolate. We picked the shadowiest spot, which wasn't very shadowy but was sort of behind a plant. A guy had set up in the corner and was earnestly strumming a guitar, singing what I assume was Earther soft pop music.

As soon as we sat, she barked, "Talk."

"Pretty tough attitude from a girl with a mug of cocoa in front of her," I shot back. She glared at me. (Note to self: *work on your delivery and mind your tone.*) "Ok. I'm Tessa Reddick. With the FBI. I'm working on the murder investigation of some members of this church as well as some Demons."

Heather pursed her lips. "I know who you are. Everybody knows who you are. I know the group that was killed, too."

"How do you know these people?" I asked, wishing they hadn't taken my notebook and pen.

"Bible study. Well, it started out as Bible study. Then she kind of…"

"Who?"

"Cara, mostly. Cara Courtland. She started the group. She was obsessed with all these questions. We studied the Book of Revelation this time. We did Exodus last time, but Gardener West says we should be very familiar with Revelation. A bunch of the group has gone to the Baptist seminary, back before they found this forest. We started talking about Hebrew influence on the compilation of the Bible, and one thing led to another, and Cara started bringing different Bibles and some books with strange things in them."

"Wait, I thought you people believed in the one true Bible or something?"

Heather shifted in her seat then nodded. "Pre-Rift, Christian meant something different than now. Now, we have to think about fighting in the coming war. We have to use all the weapons at our disposal."

I tried hard not to roll my eyes. "The war."

"Between good and evil. The age-old story, right? But now, it's really coming. It's at our doorstep. The signs are all here. That's part of what this church teaches."

"Heather, you're enlisting to fight your *family*. Demons. You are. A. Demon. These people?" I waved to the Church. "Want to kill all your family."

It was like darts pinging harmlessly off a steel board. She didn't appear to register any of it.

"We are all born sinful. It's only when we reject our sin that we can be fully embraced by the one true God, Tessa. I have repented for my wicked ways. That's all in the past. I haven't had contact with my old life in six or seven years."

I felt like I was just starting to fall down the rabbit hole. "Okay, one thing at a time. Back to this study group."

"Cara started saying she thinks we can create an army to defend us against the beings from the Other side." Heather's voice lowered as Mr. God Guitar fervently sung about being plucked from the garden of the one true God. "She found these books and started talking about being the hand of justice. About being an Earthly army for the one true God."

"And what would that entail, exactly?"

She shrugged. "She kept talking about building an army. She wanted all the members of the Bible study to bring as many new people in as we could. Fortify the ranks."

I'm not very familiar with the communication style of Pele Demons, but I had a feeling that she wasn't quite spilling everything.

"The group must have been pretty big then?"

Heather nodded. "At one point we had about fifty people. But that's when I dropped out."

"Go on." I forced myself to smile winsomely.

"We're only supposed to invite people to Bible study who we can bring into the forest. That's how I got here." At the look on my face, she explained, "The forest. We are all trees on God's Earth, to bloom where we are planted. West is our Gardener. He keeps us from harm and fertilizes us, prunes and trims us."

I choked on my coffee. Probably a good thing since it stopped me from saying something about isolating you from your people and dumping shit on you while cutting out parts of you that make you *you*.

"Okay. So, bring people in…"

She nodded. "After she got me involved, Cara started seeking out places we wouldn't normally go to, bars and stuff, to find people. She thought it'd be a test of faith if we could get Mosquitoes… uh, sorry, Vampires and Others to become saved. I won't lie. It was getting really insane. But I had just started dating a little, and my job… Well, anyway, they started getting together to think of new ways to get people in. They even," her voice was barely audible, "went to that club downtown, in disguise, to try to pull in the Otherwhere crowd." Her face was a mix of incredulousness and shame.

It was like hearing a Jew talk about how much she loves being a member of the Nazi party.

But that would explain why Cara Courtland had been wearing a purple wig when she was murdered.

"Heather, do you know anything about how Cara and the others died?"

She looked fearful. "No! I dropped out of the group several months ago. And Cara and I haven't talked in a while. Well, before she died, that is."

"So, why did you drop out, again? Sounds like it ended up in a bit of a tiff?"

"Besides there being too many people and not enough studying scripture?" She glanced away, shamefacedly, then back. "It was just too tempting. I'm not into that anymore. I've renounced my sins, I've picked up the cross of wood, and I am making my way by the light of the one true God. Magic is evil. I was born evil. So were you. The way to Heaven is through Jesus and his prophets like Gardener West, and Others haven't accepted Jesus as their one true Lord and Savior. I don't hate you, and I don't hate them. But I hate your sins. I don't wish you harm though," she added quickly. "Not like Cara and them do. Did."

The crazy thing was, she was just regurgitating what her church had taught her. Greg was right. There's really no zealot like a convert.

Heather sipped her drink and ran a hand over the stumps of her horns—a sad, self-conscious gesture. "Look, I really don't know much more. Do you have to take me in for a statement or something?"

"Nope. Just one more thing. You've mentioned an army. Who were they going to go after? I mean, was this a car bomb situation or an organized attack?"

Heather pursed her lips. "They wanted to go after that... Demon or whatever she is who runs that club by the river."

"The Red Queen?"

She nodded. I took a sip of my coffee and thought for a moment.

"There's something else. They were practicing something."

"Practicing what?" I pushed.

Her voice barely a whisper, she said, "They were trying to summon Angels to fight for them." My mouth dropped open. I'd had to have heard her wrong.

"Dana Sykes, one of the ones who was killed, she kept inviting me to come back, saying something big was coming and I would want to be part of it. But I didn't want to. Like I said, I'm trying to stay true to Gardener West and his guidance. There's no place for me among the tortured now. Look, I know you're an unbeliever. But the end times are coming. Haven't you read about this? A Seal has been broken. The Church was brought to its knees."

I stared, soon making Heather uncomfortable with my sharpened interest. "I really need to go, okay? My class starts in a few minutes."

"Wait, what do you mean, a Seal has been broken?"

"I don't know. I'm sorry. Just, please. Go."

"Okay, but I'm going to give you my phone number. You can call me if you want to share anything else. Can you give me a list of any other people who might have been in the Bible study or connected in some way?"

Heather nodded. "Yes, all right. I'll call you later."

"Hey, Heather?" A man walked over to us, a cup in hand. "You ready?"

She looked up at him, her eyes wide in alarm. "Yes. Hi, Curt. I'm coming."

The man glanced at me with that insipid treevangelist smile. "Who's this?" Without my answer, he stuck out a hand. "Curt Gordon. Nice to meet you. You coming to the group session with us?"

Heather rose quickly and motioned for me to follow. "Nope. She's not really cut out for us, it seems. Let me walk you out. Be right back, Curt!" She dragged me away toward the security office.

"You have got to stop grabbing my arm like that," I hissed, yanking out of her grip.

"Just go. I'm busy. And I don't need anyone asking too many questions." And Heather was gone.

After a tense visit with Poufy to retrieve my stuff, she proceeded to practically shove me out. She escorted me to the door and waited until I was well out of the building before she turned away.

Ann Bartley was still MIA. A bible study had gone rogue. A Witch running about in an Earther church. What was the world coming to?

"Have you or a loved one suffered harassment, racism, or prejudice due to your Humanity or Otherhood? Call 1-866-357-9652 to get the help you deserve. You may qualify for compensation in the currency of your choice."

—Advertisement for **Barry, Barry, and Q Shokth Collaborative Legal Services**

CHAPTER EIGHT

Wanting to accomplish at least one thing this afternoon, I headed out to check about that sample of clay I'd gotten at the conservatory. Luckily, Spot's Art Shop is close to the Broom Closet. It would have been the nearest supply store for someone in the east end, if you didn't count ordering online.

Inside, the Saturday crowds were out in force, and there seemed to be only one person working. The customers were all children and their harried mothers. Art instruction over the summer vacation was all the rage among the helicopter parent set.

I browsed for a while among cluttered shelves and stacks. It smelled like my elementary school art room—chalk and tempera paint. I liked art, but my grade school art teacher, Mrs. Pollan, always said, "Halloween is over, Tessa. You need to stop drawing witches and black cats."

Tiring of waiting, I conjured up a little nudge to get the kids and their parents out of the store.

"Moooom, I'm huuuuungry."

"When's lunch?"

"I WANT A COOKIE!"

Funny how a spell that changes the scent to something less art room and more bakery can do that.

Mothers hustled their suddenly-starving offspring into minivans and SUVs bound for Panera or Nancy's Bagels. Finally, it was just me and the clerk, a gangly young fellow with an unfortunate presentation of acne, a concert t-shirt obviously older than he was, and a tag that had JARED on it.

I whipped out my FBI creds, even though this wasn't official FBI business. But sue me, I was in a hurry. "I need to ask you some questions."

Jared ran a hand through lank, greasy hair and bobbed his head, a petrified look on his face.

I placed my little in-case container on the counter. "Someone bought a large amount of this clay from this store recently. Think hard."

"Sorry. I don't know, okay? I just work here to pay for school."

I nodded patiently. "I don't care what they were going to use it for." Jared backed up against the shelves behind him, knocking off little wooden poseable figures.

We stared at each other. He cracked first.

"She maybe had weird hair? It was blue, like a wig. She came in to place an order, but we couldn't fill it. I told her to order online because we don't place orders for anything over five thousand pounds."

"This woman ordered five *thousand* pounds of clay?"

Jared nodded. He kept glancing around as if someone was watching us. "Six, actually. She said she was making a really big, um, sculpture? And she wanted a whole bunch of clay all at once?" His voice cracked. Goddess bless him, he was terrified.

My mind reeled. "And she wouldn't order online?"

He shook his head. "She said she would only pay cash." Ah. Paying cash to a local place meant no credit card trail.

"How old was she?"

He shook his head. "Older than you, I think."

I almost laughed. I had forgotten how, when you're young, it's so hard to tell how old people are when they're older than you. Everybody is either a baby or ancient.

I pondered all this. "Why are you so skittish? You're not in trouble."

A fast breath escaped his thin lips. "Because she came in after that and told me she'd... she said something bad would happen to me if I told anyone she had been here?" He kept making everything a question.

I snorted. "Don't worry, kid. Nothing bad's going to happen to you." He looked slightly less petrified. I took a green permanent marker from the jar on the counter and uncapped it. "Gimme your hand." I held my own out. "Come on, I haven't got all day." He put his shaking palm in mine. I drew a neat green pentacle and charmed it with a little protective spell. Now, if anybody come after poor Jared, or his household, he would be fine. "When you get home tonight, you put a line of salt across all your doors and windows. That will keep you safe. No worries."

His relief was visible. "You're a Witch."

I shrugged modestly. "At your service. Did she say anything about what she was going to do with the clay?" He shook his head. "Okay, well, how did she pick it up?"

Jared's face screwed up in thought. "Um, she had it delivered? But I don't know where to."

I was losing patience. "Can you look it up, please?"

He went to the computer on the counter and started clacking on the keyboard, his eyebrows drawing closer and closer. Finally, he said, "It's a Louisville address." He wrote it down on a piece of receipt paper and handed it to me. "We had to get a special large truck from Home Depot."

"Thank you, Jared. You've been very helpful."

In the car, I looked down at the address. "I'll be damned," I breathed. It was the conservatory site.

On my way home, I found myself turning left and following a familiar winding road to a bungalow nestled at the back of a neighborhood. An unassuming little house painted tan, with black shutters. I parked across the street and a few houses down and sat.

The house hadn't changed one bit. I wondered if the occupants had. Only one way to find out.

The door opened before my knuckles even touched the wood.

"Tessa Reddick." Same smirk. Same smoldering eyes. Same velvet caftan that was simultaneously too revealing and too covered up.

"Bathsheba."

She stood with a hand on her hip. "They've released you into the wild, I see. I'd heard a rumor, but you can't believe everything you hear."

I nodded. Bathsheba Paquane. My ex-boyfriend's mother harbored no tender feelings for me. Not then, not now. It was all very romantic, see. Very Romeo and Juliet.

"Look, I'm not staying long. I just need some information."

Her thin eyebrows arched. "From me? I can't imagine what you think I would tell you."

I rolled my eyes. "Your family motto is practically, 'Keep your friends close and your enemies closer.' You can tell me a lot."

Bathsheba drew a deep breath in her nose then gave a curt nod. "Touché, dear." She swept aside and wordlessly bid me to enter. "Have a seat, if you like." She picked one of the ultra-modern leather couches in the front room. The house looked small from the outside, but like a famous police callbox from British TV, it's bigger on the inside thanks to Bathsheba and Balthazar, her esteemed husband. I sat across from her, noting she did not offer me any of the customary hospitality our kind is known for.

"I was framed."

She said nothing. The look on her face was inscrutable.

"I was framed, and I think you know that, and I think you know who did the honors."

Being there, in that house, was an assault of memories. So many years ago, her beautiful son Vail and I had been... young. Young and in love. Well, I had been in love. He had been under direct orders to destroy me. "You tried to kill us once. You must have tried to help finish us off."

She tilted her head back, blue-black hair shimmering on her shoulders, and let out a hearty laugh. "You went to ground, and now, the enemy has left you no ground to go to. I can't tell you how delightful this is. I really can't. I wish Balthazar was here to see this."

"Look, whatever happened between you and your husband and my mother is ancient history. *I* never did anything to you."

Her face hardened in the space of half a second, and the sound she made was uncomfortably close to a hiss. "Watch where you tread, Tessa. If you can say you or your family haven't harmed a twig in my family tree, then you may speak as you wish, but you can no more say that than I can. I still revile you with the fire of a thousand burning suns."

"Bathsheba, can you sit here and tell me you wouldn't have done the same thing? You wouldn't have defended your son?"

She paled. I kept talking.

"Can you honestly tell me you wouldn't have taken bullets for Vail? Or swords? Or ten thousand burnings at the stake? Well? He was going to kill me."

"He wasn't—" she started then snapped her mouth shut and simply glared at me.

"He wasn't what?"

I didn't think it was possible for her face to harbor more full-on hate.

I was wrong.

Maybe, I'd made a mistake coming here. Not the smartest thing I've done all day.

"Listen, I'm calling on whatever shred of honor you have left and whatever loyalty our families ever had to each other over the last, what, five thousand years? Tell me what you know, and I'll go. It will be the last time I come to you. I swear on my mother."

She pursed her lips. On her lovely face played out her warring desires: kill me. Not kill me. Was there a point in either, now that her son was dead? Was I worth the wrath of Arcana? Finally, she said, "Very well. None of my House went after your family that night. I swear on my son." Her eyes glittered.

Thus, our bindings were made.

"But something is after you, yes. It's not a Witch. Not a Human.

What it is, I cannot say for certain, but I will tell you this. It walks toward you always. It will walk until it finds you. It might send scouts to prepare the way. But wherever you go, on this side or that, it will come for you. You are like a beacon to it in the dark universe. And however much I hate you? It hates you more."

"How do you know that?"

She leaned in, her purple eyes hard. "Everybody knows it. But everybody thinks you killed your family, too."

I sat on that for a second, looking around the living room for want of something better to do. Antiques from the last five hundred years nestled against newer pieces, the same as it had always been. The Paquanes had clung to their French heritage with tenacity. They had been in the States for dozens of generations, but they all still spoke French like a bunch of ex-pats.

Bathsheba purred, "I would think you would be on your way. I choose for the moment not to harm you, but I can't say the rest of my family will hold off. In fact, I might change my mind yet."

I cursed myself all the way home. How dumb could I get? Waltzing into the home of the high priestess and her consort from an old and revered coven of Gallic Witches was about as savvy as wearing a meat dress to a shark's pool party. Yet, it did land me a clue. A clue, whose source I couldn't trust as far as I could throw it. I snorted. Details.

When I got home, I immediately locked all the doors, the windows, and battened down the place tighter than Fort Knox on high alert. Though (probably) ultimately useless, it made me feel better.

My home clothes felt especially luxurious despite being a pair of musty yoga pants and a t-shirt that fit in a way that suggested I get back into my running routine sooner rather than later. Water was boiling and marinara sauce was simmering when I heard Dorcha on the back porch. I went to open the door for her, and she backed away from me, baring her impressive teeth. Her tail switched madly, and her hackles were up.

She went to the top of the steps and gave me a look, the one that meant I had to follow. Barefoot, I padded out into the dim evening. "What is it, girl?"

Dorcha let out a low growl.

In the shadow next to my Camry's driver side door stood a figure. I couldn't make out who it was. "Nice night to be out, isn't it?"

No answer.

On instinct, I fired off a mild stunning spell that hit it square in the chest. Nothing happened.

Dorcha circled the car and the figure.

I edged closer. Dorcha growled and moved into a defensive crouch. "You're trespassing, friend."

In the little bit of streetlight we had, the figure—it looked female, about my height with similar long hair—didn't move.

"Hey. Get out of here, or I'll let loose with something stronger." Which, after you've already been hit dead-on in the chest, is pretty heavy.

No cigar.

I got a stick and crept up to the car. Stretching my arm out, I poked the thing. Where my spell had hit, the stick sank in like a knife in butter.

It was a mud figure. One bearing an eerie similarity to yours truly. The mud-me had a (now) semi-melted mud-knife sticking out of her chest, just beside the scorch mark where my spell hit. Not only that, the car was smeared with mud, from fender to fender.

"Oh. *Hell.* No." My fear quickly curdled into fury. I slammed the stick down. Snarling and shaking with adrenaline, I aimed both hands and forced a ball of white-hot anger at the mud. It burst into a pile of ash.

I whirled around. "You nasty coward! You think you can scare me with your little mud pies?" I screamed. I stalked down the driveway past the shop toward the street, shooting little blasting spells at the crooked asphalt. With each mini explosion, a rain of driveway bits clattered back down. I probably wasn't the neighborhood favorite at that point, but what else was new?

"You're messing with the wrong Witch, buster. I will find you, and I will make you pay, dammit! You dirt-slinging, mud-whapping asshat! I am going to come down on your muddy ass like a rain of fire! So help me, I will invent very painful ways to punish you. VERY. PAINFUL!"

Dorcha skulked off into the darkness, searching around the house, checking to see if anyone was still there. I kept up my hollering for several minutes, until I went a little bit hoarse.

She returned pacified, if not relaxed, and sat beside the apartment door, waiting for me to finish my rant.

Tirade complete, I stomped back up the steps to my home.

"I cannot believe that! My car! Did you see my car?" We were inside again. Dorcha groomed herself on the floor, and I paced the living room. "Mother of fuck. Dammit. Dammit, dammit, *dammit*." I randomly smacked my palm into a wall or doorframe, which only served to hurt my hand.

At last, I sank into the couch, shaking. Since I'd been out of the joint, I hadn't felt the warm fuzzies from any of my old friends. Fine. But no one had ever come right up on my turf and done something like this. Something as overtly threatening as the mud sculpture. It made me mad and scared then even madder *because* I was scared and knew it was stupid to be scared. This was a cowardly act of aggression. A taunt. Whoever did it was telling me, 'Hey, we can get this close to you! Ha!'

The pots simmered over on the stove, steam and sauce hissing into the burners. I leapt up, snatching some paper towels, trying to corral the mess, cursing and swearing. In the end, I called Papa John's for a large pepperoni and olive and double-checked all my protection wards.

Later, as I sat digesting my dinner and nursing a bit of bourbon, something caught my eye. The paper I'd snagged from the conservatory peeked from a pocket of my cloak, flung over the back of a chair. I pulled it out. It was still a photocopy of a page with ragged edges, ink pen marking it all over—scrawled translations and diagrams over the diagrams.

I stared at the danged thing until my head hurt. With no other ideas coming to me, I sat down with my computer and started searching.

OLD BOOKS

ANTIQUE BOOKS

RITUAL BOOKS

WHAT THE HELL DOES THIS PAPER SAY????

ANCIENT RITES

TRANSLATIONS OF DIAGRAMS

I racked my brain for better search words then just kept punching in words in random order until I hit on something that made me smack my head. A rare book dealer in the Highlands. Why hadn't I thought of this before?

The website said they were open Tuesday through Saturday. I planned a visit then went outside and spent the next hour magicking mud off my car and cursing everything I could think of.

Angela Dodson: *John, there is no seventeenth act in Corinthians.*

John Constantine: *Corinthians goes to twenty-one acts in the Bible in Hell.*

Angela Dodson: *They have Bibles in Hell?*

John Constantine: *Paints a different view of Revelations. Says the world will not end by God's hand, but be reborn in the embrace of the damned. Though if you ask me, fire's fire.*

—From **Constantine**, 2005, directed by Francis Lawrence, starring Keanu Reeves

CHAPTER NINE

Tomas Antiquis' books were on Bardstown Road, between a head shop and a coffee place. I stopped by the latter first to get some breakfast, locally roasted Arabica and an everything bagel with cream cheese. Then, I headed next door.

The gold lettering on the glass read:

Rev. Dr. James H. Patterson, VI, Esq.

Rare, Vintage, and Antiquarian Books

Open M-F 10-4 and by Appointment

The place looked a little like an episode of one of those shows about hoarders. I wondered how the guy ever found anything in here.

A bell on the door signaled my arrival.

"Greetings and salutations," a voice said.

"Hello?"

A tall, stout, balding man in a ratty tweed jacket and jeans. "You're my ten o'clock?"

"Um... no. I just stopped in. I have some questions."

"I see." His tone frosted over. "May I ask you to step outside with your refreshments?" He was staring pointedly at my cup and bagel. "I can't risk contaminating my investments."

I stood outside munching and slurping, acutely aware of Dr. Mr. Rev. Patterson glaring at me from behind a stack of books by the window, arms folded tightly.

Finally, I swallowed the last of it and dropped the garbage in a nearby can. Wiping my hands on my jeans, I saw a sign in the window that I hadn't noticed before:

ABSOLUTELY _NO_ FOOD OR DRINK PERMITTED ON PREMISES. NO EXCEPTIONS.

THANK YOU,

MGMT.

Whoops.

Back inside, I said, "I'm Tessa Reddick. I'm hoping you could help me with this." I pulled out the sheet I'd found at the conservatory.

He took the paper and looked at me closely. "And you're... a Witch?"

I nodded, tensing.

He waved a hand. "I'm not prejudiced, mind you. I just like to know. Come. Let's sit." He seemed to have forgiven the prior misstep with my morning repast.

We parked ourselves in ancient velveteen chairs in front of a cold fireplace flanked by more shelves of books in what was once a dining room.

Patterson stared at the page for a while then said, "I recognize this. It looks like it came from a book I sold to a local woman just a few weeks ago. An unusual request, but there you have it. Perhaps you're looking for something similar?" His tone was hopeful.

"Do you remember her name?"

"I don't. I confess I'm surprised I remember that much. I have a rather poor memory for names. It was probably the surgery." He said the last part with the nonchalance that begs the listener to ask for more. I did not indulge him. I didn't have time, and people like that get on my last nerve.

"Would you recognize her face?"

"Perhaps."

I showed him a photo on my phone, which he mulled over before shrugging. "I think that's her, but her hair was different." He looked closer. "Wait, yes. Yes, that's the woman. That fair porcelain skin and petite appearance. Laura? Cora? Something?"

"Close." I retracted my phone. "Cara. Cara Courtland."

"Ah! Yes. Lovely lady. I wish she could have stayed longer to chat. I am not terribly knowledgeable in the realm of the ancient religious mystics and the like."

"This is an ancient religious text?"

He nodded. "Indeed. A part of a mystical book, either a Gnostic or Kabbalistic text, but likely a copy of a copy of a copy. Such tomes have been something of a holy grail for most literature scholars and book enthusiasts such as myself for centuries. I hadn't had a good reason to search until now, of course."

"How did she pay?"

"Cash."

"How much?" This was getting tedious.

His manner turned haughty. "I'm not at liberty to say, my dear. That's confidential."

"I do understand. However, I can have a warrant drawn up to search the place, including your records. Wouldn't this be simpler?"

"You're a police officer?"

I got out my FBI credentials, and he blanched.

"Am I in some kind of trouble?" His tune changed completely. The way he pulled at his collar made me wonder what he thought I was here to talk about, but I didn't have time to play cat and mouse.

"Not yet. I simply need answers. How much?"

His lips thinned. "Eighty."

"Eighty what? Pesos? Lira? Guineas?"

"Thousand. Dollars. Eighty thousand dollars."

My mouth dropped open. Literally. I couldn't help it. That was one huge hunk of cash. As far as I knew, Cara Courtland didn't have that kind of money just lying around. Where on Earth would it have come from? Unless she had a private donor. Maybe they'd pooled all their mattress change? "Okay, tell me more about the book."

"Let me retrieve my laptop, and I will be able to offer more information on this particular tome. I will also lock the doors so we are not disturbed." He swanned out of the room.

I got up and looked at the shelves, stacks, and piles. I was surrounded by what appeared to be biographies of people I'd never heard of. *Addams Historie of the Lady Valencia Theodosia Juniper Cornwall, Duchess of Elarnyae. My Life as a Sea Slug: Artimour Hounden, Oceanographic Biologist.* And *Lesser Japanese Empresses.*

Patterson returned, but froze when he saw me standing. "Did you touch anything?"

"Not with my hands. My eyes are a different story."

He made an irritated noise and sat back down with his Macbook Pro.

"I'd been hunting for that book for more than a year. Traveled fairly widely, actually. The Mistress Courtland emailed me asking for titles on ancient Gnosticism, Kabbalism, or early Jewish mysticism, specifically the ritual of the *Sefer Yetzirah* or the corresponding Gnostic ritual. Forgive me, my memory is so poor after the surgery." I didn't bite, so he went on. "I searched, found a few interesting items, but not what she was looking for. Then I just... came across it."

"Where?"

"Ukraine. I speak fluent Russian, so it was no struggle to tap my contact there. A bookseller like myself, with a large shop outside of Odessa."

"Small world. Okay, tell me everything you know about the book itself."

"The *Sefer Yetzirah*, as I understand it, was a ritual performed by early Jewish mystics. These 'books of creation' would have featured such things as being able to say, leave one's body for a time. Or how to summon an Angel. A large faction of the rare book community has always considered such editions a myth. A novelty, at best. Something made as entertainment for nobility. I'm of the opposite camp. I've always thought such books were at one time available. But not something I might see in my lifetime, mind you. They are sometimes referenced in other texts, but nobody has ever been able to *find* a real one. As I mentioned, the one I sold is likely a very good replica of an older work. Otherwise, I can't imagine it would be in a private collection."

"You landed it from a private dealer?"

Patterson shook his head. "The bookshop owner bought it with a large lot from an estate sale perhaps ten years ago. She had just gotten around to going through the stash, which is how I got my hands on it.

I was rather lucky in that respect. By rights, I suppose, there are museums that would have liked it, but—" He shrugged. "I'm a sucker for a damsel in distress." He glanced at me then back at the computer screen. "I'm looking at this and seeing many things I recognize, but also much I don't. These symbols are the Tetragrammatron, there's a hamsa, and a pentacle. An ourobouros."

"So you can't read the books, you just find them?"

His cheeks colored, as he seemed to take umbrage. "I can't possibly read everything that comes across my desk. After the *surgery*, I also became a rather slow reader. I simply locate the buyer's desires, in most cases. I have passable French and Latin and am fluent, of course, in English, Russian, with a smattering of Bulgarian."

I smiled to put him at ease. "Which absolutely makes sense. Now, Cara Courtland asked you to find her materials on Gnostic and Jewish mysticism. What made you think you hit the bull's-eye?"

Patterson waved a dismissive hand. "I'm sure I don't know, madam. But when I texted photographs to her, she was pleased. She took it, and she paid. That's it."

I was missing something, and I didn't know what it was. Some question I wasn't asking.

"Was she acting oddly? Doing anything strange?"

He shook his head. "Not that I recall, no."

Cara had been there. Bought a book. And somehow, a copy of a page had found its way to the future home of the Louisville Botanical Gardens.

I frowned, working it out in my mind. "This might come out of the left field, but if someone said, 'The Seal has been broken. The church was broken.' What would they be talking about?"

Peterson spread his hands. "Eschatology. Revelation. Armageddon. Ragnarok. It is a widespread theory that there are signs of the End of Days."

"Like the Four Horsemen?"

He smiled. "Yes, exactly. They are one of those signs. The idea behind the particular notion you mention is the Christian Church was a protection against the Antichrist. A seal, if you will. In the last few years, as the Church of the Earth has grown from the ashes of various Judeo-Christian religions, many have theorized this is a sign that the second coming of Jesus is nigh."

"Uh huh. How nigh?"

"No one knows. There are other Seals, which may or may not have been broken, depending on whom you ask." He looked as if he was about to launch into a very long monologue on the subject.

At which point, I was saved by a knock on the front door.

"Apparently, my ten o'clock is coming in." He looked at his watch. "Forty-five minutes late. I'm sorry. I'm happy to answer any additional questions later. Here's my card."

I walked as slowly as I could back to the front door, wanting to soak up any little detail I could find. But nothing particularly enlightening came to mind, other than, *next time, ask him about the damn surgery, m'kay?*

**237.110 License to carry
concealed deadly weapon**

*The Department of Kentucky State Police
is authorized to issue and renew licenses
to carry concealed firearms or other
deadly weapons including magic,
spellspeaking, talismans, totems,
potions, enchantments, familiars, or a
combination thereof, to persons qualified
as provided in this section.*

CHAPTER TEN

I **got a Diet Coke and some cold pizza from the fridge and took** them to my library. After setting the radio to an old-school jazz station, I pulled out some really ancient books I hadn't looked at in ages. My conversation with Patterson had gotten me thinking. I confess I hadn't read every single title I owned, and there had to be a wealth of information I was missing out on for no good reason.

For the millionth time, I wished for my mother's grimoire. Or any of the grimoires lost to the damn flames. Hestia's or Millibeth's would have been good, or any of the older cousins'.

I located the grimoire of a cousin four times removed. Her name was Darah, and she'd lived in various parts of Eastern Europe for decades. Considering Petersen's Odessa haul, this was as good a starting place as any.

Darah's spirit was faint. She hadn't spent as much time as Auntie Sheridan working on the book. She also spoke English with such a thick accent that it was hard to understand her. But she did understand me if I used small, simple words.

"Sefer Yetzirah. Tell me."

Darah looked surprised. She jabbered on for a moment, before I held up my hand. I pointed to my eyes, then to the book. "Show me?"

The pages whirred as she flipped through them at lightning speed. They came to rest on an elaborate drawing on two pages. It was like a crude comic-book-version of the fragment I had, but there were little annotations all over. Darah pointed at a tiny drawing of a person. I put my copied page down on the right, while Darah stood on the left near a heading that read .גולם In fact, the closer I looked, the more words I could see in the same script.

"It's a spell?" I asked. She nodded vigorously. Then, she walked a few steps and pointed again, this time to a little figure with long side locks and a long tunic, standing outside (you could tell by the trees and a poorly drawn cow). Squiggles were coming out of its hands in a universal sign. Ah.

"So, magic happens?" I consulted my page. Indeed, similar pictograms were there. "Go on."

In the next part, the tiny figure was zapping a blob of what I thought might be a mound with lightning. The cow looked alarmed.

From there, the page diverged into two halves. There was a circle with two arrows—one white, one black—pointing into it. On the white side of the circle, it looked like an angel (wings, halo, sword) fighting an angry horde (Prussian hats, one with a Pope's mitre). The other side clearly depicted a demon (horns, tail) slaughtering innocents (babies, women).

Darah looked at me, worried. She indicated the demon side and shook her head vigorously, muttering. Then she patted the angel and smiled, breathing an exaggerated sigh of relief.

This was the strangest game of charades ever.

I frowned. Darah looked expectant.

She burbled in her thick accent again, pointing and gesturing. Finally, she said something that sounded a lot like, "Goolam!"

"A goolam?" I repeated. Darah clapped. "Goolam? What the hell is a..." I smacked a palm on the table, leapt up, and shouted, "GOLEM! IT'S A SPELL TO MAKE A GOLEM!!" Dorcha snerked out of sleep on the floor, hackles up.

I didn't know a lot about it, but I was pretty certain Golems were supposed to be defenders of the Jews. More or less the way I recalled, you make them out of dirt, do this ritual, then the thing defends you against all who wish you harm.

I grabbed my laptop and started to enter words into the search box while gesturing to Darah.

She stood on a figure on my page and stamped her foot on something I had missed before. Two little lines sprang out of its head. One line led to a face that smiled beatifically. On the other, the face was angry-looking.

I puzzled over this.

"I don't think I get it." I shook my head.

Darah touched her head and chest then poked the angel. She looked at me hopefully. Then, screwed her face into a mask of anger and made the same head-chest gesture before pointing to the demon.

"Your head and chest... go into the golem? Your heart?" She made the same movements again, patiently, certain I would work it out.

"What you think and feel matters? Intentions? Uh... meaning?" She nodded and clasped her hands together.

That was interesting. So, whatever your true intention was, be it good or evil, it colored the thing that showed up to fight for you in a golem's armor.

Cara Courtland was playing her own little version of God. Then, something dawned on me. If she was truly doing this spell, the golem spell, she was likely sacrificing a piece of her own soul *every time*. Powerful magicians or Witches learn to pay for spells in other ways that don't hurt, but newbies? They don't know any better, and the only currency they have to trade in is their own blood and souls. I'd heard of people paying with their firstborn children or a parent, even. It's horrific.

I continued to page through Darah's book. Seems she had been to Otherwhere a few times and tried to make maps of the terrain. There were drawings of forests with elvish faces peeking out and a bizarre castle that featured a cat's open mouth as the gate.

After the Rift happened, low-level Others—those closer to Humans—were pretty much free to come and go as they chose. Humans, likewise, although that happens so infrequently and with such disastrous consequences, it's the punchline to lots of jokes. How many Humans does it take to change a lightbulb in Otherwhere? Two. One to change the lightbulb and one to buy a new house with a new lightbulb. The joke is that the first one vanishes because Humans can't get around Otherwhere. Or something. But it's rather easy for Others to get around Earth because it's so linear.

There are a fair number of Others in Earth. At some point after the Rift, most governments gave up on trying to keep them out and just folded Others into their Human immigration policies. As such, Others have to comply with the laws regarding establishing themselves in Earth. Like Qyll, they work, and they sometimes bring their families here. They, essentially like all immigrants anywhere, are seeking a better life. They file for residency status; they pay taxes. They can be a lot like regular Humans, in fact. Of course, there are some who come here to do bad things like the full-blooded Vampires who come to feed on Humans or change them into New Vamps, or Faeries out to enchant other creatures into slavery. I should talk. Witches came out of Otherwhere centuries ago and stayed in hiding until the Rift. From what I hear, very few are left on that side.

I didn't have much experience wandering around Otherwhere. My mother, by all accounts, had been something of an explorer long before the Rift. She negotiated with Other empires, bought and sold, and, according to one story, occasionally vacationed in various bits of the Other realm. Largely, it's because our coven is so old; she was just part of the ongoing legacy. I went in a few times, when I was very small, but I don't remember much, just snippets. A forest of upside-down trees, carriages pulled by birds, a carousel with real animals. By the time I was old enough to ask, she said it was dangerous and relegated me to lectures rather than practical experience. Like an astronaut who knows a lot about Mars and has maybe been to the Moon but no farther.

The creatures that come to Earth from Otherwhere are pretty low on the cosmic totem pole. The Red Queen is about as big and bad as you get around here and don't tell her I said this, but Earth is really lucky she's not driven to do more harm than she already does. She could really fuck some shit up if she put her mind to it.

My point—and I do have one—is that it's hard to get something *really* evil or good to come out of its cozy nest in Otherwhere. Not for long, anyway. It's too difficult for them to sustain for any length of time. Back to my analogy from earlier: Humans can't breathe pure oxygen. Evil things can't stand too much good. Good things can't stand too much evil. The Earth is like a scuba tank. It's mixed up enough in here that only the beings in the sort of nebulous in-between can survive.

WASHINGTON, D.C. March 23, 2001

(Reuters)—*Groups calling themselves "Others" seek asylum in the U.S. and Canada, and could pursue international arbitration to gain it, their spokesperson said on Wednesday, a week after appearances around the world.*

A North American-European-PanAsian consortium said it had been blindsided by the appearance of the Others and has scrambled to enact treaties and laws meant to handle these immigrants from the so-called "Otherwhere."

CHAPTER ELEVEN

Bright and early the next morning, I got online to look for someone who could help with my golem problem. Turned out, there was a guru type person in Louisville. Fancy that.

Professor Johan March, I learned, had once taught Jewish studies at American University and now wrote books from a condo by the river, not far from the Queen of Hearts. His website said he also enjoyed playing jazz trumpet and cycling. I called the contact number listed *and* sent an email, noting the urgency of my requests. About two hours later, he rang back to arrange a visit.

Which brought me to my next stop—a modern glass high-rise glimmering weakly in the noontime sun. The unit was on the fourteenth floor. A scruffy man in house slippers answered.

"Tessa?"

"Hi, yeah." We shook hands. "Thanks for seeing me on such short notice."

"Come in, come in." He waved me into the condo and down the hall. "Sorry it's such a mess in here." He was cheerful and affable, and I was immediately at ease.

His office was full of books and papers and framed art stacked against a wall. A behemoth of a desk almost entirely blocked the bottom of the enormous windows that overlooked the river. There was an armchair that had seen better days and a battered lamp. The Prof himself was a tall skinny man with a tangled graying beard and friendly brown eyes behind half-moon glasses. It was over these glasses he peered at me as he pushed a pile of books off a chair.

"I'm uh... with the FBI," I said. "But this is technically off the record."

He pulled out a book from the stack recently displaced from my chair. Thumbing through it, he studied me between page turns. "You're not Jewish."

I grinned. "Nope. Not even a little."

He made a dismissive gesture. "Everyone is a *little* Jewish. What is it that I can help you with?"

"Here. I need to know what this is." He set his book aside and took the sheet.

His face lit up as he studied it. "This is gorgeous. You know, people are very interested in spirituality these days. After the Rift, well, what do you expect? Bad things happen and people want answers; it's human nature, right? Now, golems. That's a fascinating subject."

"It *is* golems?"

He gestured at the paper with a look of surprise, as though I should have known. "This? It's basically a recipe for a golem. Like, it's from a Kabbalah cookbook." He peered closer. "Huh. Well, there are Gnostic symbols here." He flipped the paper upside down. "Coptic, maybe? Anyway, definitely golem. Enchanted figures created to defend someone. You know this, yes? Legend tells of Jewish mystics who could animate the clay of the earth. In the sixteenth century, the rabbi of Prague created a golem to defend the Jews from the Catholic Pope. This paper describes a ritual for bringing a golem to life." He gazed at the fine markings. "There's some stuff on here I don't recognize, but most of it, yes, it's a golem. I'd bet my last doughnut on it."

The wheels began to click in my head. "So it's possible to raise a golem?"

He paused in his book-thumbing and looked over the glasses again. "Oh yes. Any idiot can raise a golem, but," he raised a finger and smiled, "it takes a special *kind* of idiot to use it right."

I laughed. "So idiots make golems?"

Professor March nodded vigorously and laughed too. "Actually, you didn't used to be able to. I mean, you could then you couldn't. The ancients dabbled in it. The ancient Jewish mystics, the Kabbalists, the Gnostics, and probably the Greeks and the Chinese, but then the power was taken away for a long time. But the magic now, after the Rift, it's all over the place. It's like a live wire, shooting charge everywhere." He waved his long arms around in demonstration. "Even I wouldn't try to raise a golem. And I'm pretty much an expert. That's why you contacted me, right? A rabbi might be able to, easier than me. It's very dangerous. You know this. Black magic. Very unstable on this plane."

He put down the page and picked up another book, talking as he leafed through. "To some, it seems like things are going off the rails." He found a page. "Ah. Here we go. First, those doing the ritual will cleanse themselves, spirit and body. The soil they use should be undisturbed." March looked up. "The ritualists used to go to the middle of deep forest, a little-deserted island, maybe, on a lake. To the outskirts of a town. Then there's a ritual and a spell, and they make a statue. The key here," he showed me the book, "is the *shem*. You write the names of God on the paper and put it in the golem's mouth. Then another spell, and it lets you command the golem."

He stopped and a look of intense concentration clouded his face. "What do you need a golem for?"

"Athena's tits, no. No. Not me. But there was some clay; there were people. I'm putting it all together."

His eyes went wide, and he ran a hand through his white hair, which gave him the look of a very curious and intellectual dandelion.

"People, eh? The stories say golems were made to defend the Jews against various forces—Christian popes, Nazis, etcetera. This paper—where did it come from?"

"A colleague found this photocopy in a field. The original is a rare book, a *Sefer Yetzirah*? Sorry if I mispronounced it."

It was as though I'd told a kid he could have all the Baskin Robbins ice cream, right now. "A Book of Creation. Do you know what those are? Do you have it? Can I see it?"

"I don't have it, no. It's... well, it's complicated. But I know *of* them."

He seemed disappointed while trying to maintain what was left of his professional veneer. "Those were rumored to be manuals for early Kabbalists as they borrowed them from the Gnostics. If anything would, *they* would have such things as how to raise a golem. This is a miracle, if this page is from that book. But, if it got in the wrong hands?" He made a frightened sound. "I can't imagine." He tapped the page. "Dangerous stuff, this. The golem can grow uncontrollable. It can run rampant. *Sentience* isn't out of the question."

I laughed uneasily. "I guess anything is possible."

A serious look settled on his face. "You don't understand. That is what man is. God created Adam from the mud and blew the breath of life into him. And Adam got out of control."

Oh. *Shit.* Cara Courtland.

My horror must have filtered through.

"Are you all right? You look a little unwell."

I nodded. "Yeah, I'm just... some stuff is now making sense."

March considered me closely for another moment then backed off. "As I have said, in my professional opinion, it is some kind of ritual to raise a golem. These symbols here are the Tetragrammatron, and that's a protective sign." He began to sort of mumble excitedly, as though he'd forgotten I was in the room. "But this isn't like what I thought it would be. *I think*...this is saying you'll call a Demon to possess the golem. An evil spirit of some sort. Not a protective one. How strange. Who would want that?" His face fluctuated between thrilled and terrified. "Oh, this is a find."

I blinked stupidly at him. I really hadn't prepared for an existential theology debate, so I was glad there was a knock at the condo door.

After several long seconds, March looked up. "Probably UPS. I'm expecting a delivery of books. Please excuse me." He put the page down, got up, and stepped out of the office. He had to navigate some tall stacks of boxes and with his long skinny limbs, he looked like a pale grasshopper.

I took the paper he'd dropped and folded it up, tucking it into my bag. Then I picked up his reference hardback. As I flipped through, my phone vibrated in my pocket. It was a local number, but one I didn't immediately recognize, so I let it go to voicemail.

I'd heard a little of golems. Figures of clay animated by people's prayers or something. But I had never heard of anyone trying to make one happen. Let alone *Humans*. Humans doing magic is rarely successful, to be blunt about it. You have to have a certain amount of innate talent and cultivate it to Hell and back. You don't just get up and say, "Today I will do magic." Or, more specifically, "Today I will do magic successfully." It can happen, don't get me wrong, sometimes because people get really lucky or some Other being is around to give them a hand. But your Average Joe and Mary Jane Smith typically do not pull off elaborate spells such as animating dirt to do their bidding. Of course, I could have been off base. But I didn't think so.

A strangled sound and a loud thump drew my attention. Then, more thumps and a muffled cry.

"Professor March? Are you all right?" I got up and went down the hall.

Just inside the front door, my host was struggling with another, bigger man. The fellow had an arm wrapped around March's neck in a strange hug, choking him.

"Hey!"

The assailant dropped the professor onto the floor.

"Holy shit!" I yelped, backing into a side table. The thing turned its crude face and lumbered after me over the creaking parquet. It took a nanosecond to realize I was being chased by a golem.

I seek refuge with the Lord of the Dawn From the mischief of created things; From the mischief of Darkness as it overspreads; From the mischief of those who practice secret arts; And from the mischief of the envious one as he practices envy. **(Quran 113:1-5)**

CHAPTER TWELVE

sprinted down the hall to get my bag, thanking all the tiny gods that I'd long ago started keeping Elisha salt inside—salt consecrated by the holy men from all the major world religions. I slammed the office door behind me and locked it.

Somehow that made sense, to lock the damn door. Right.

Scrabbling at the zipper, I looked over my shoulder. The knob jiggled and something whumped against the wooden frame. The silence after that felt threatening. I yanked out the salt and began to pour when I realized something was coming into the room—from *under* the door.

Fluid mud inched through the narrow gap between the hardwood and the door. I stood frozen, salt in hand, struck by horrified fascination. The pool grew yet contained itself in a neat circle. Finally, my brain kicked into gear, and I poured the salt in a thin arc around the quickly spreading edge. Where it touched the salt, the mud pulled back like it had been burned and hissed.

Working fast, I finished pouring it in a half-circle in front of the doorway.

"Tessa? Are you in there?" March rasped from the hall.

"Get me some salt! As much as you can!"

To my continued horror, the mud began to take shape, feet first. It was like watching a sculpture grow from its shoes up in fast-forward. The legs formed next. My hand shot out and unlocked then opened the door. There was just enough space to swing it past the growing mudman.

Professor March rushed over, carrying a huge box of kosher salt, two smaller cylinders of iodized salt, and a little shaker shaped like a trumpet. His eyes were huge and fearful.

In the study, the torso had formed and arms began to flow from the shoulders. A powerful reek filled my nose—newly-churned soil and rotted decay.

Taking a breath, I leapt into the hall, narrowly missing the thing's arm as it swung at me, and grabbed the box of salt from the professor. By the time I'd gotten half the box poured, including my Elisha salt, the golem's head rotated to take us in.

It stepped backward to the doorway, its head now facing the wrong way. Then its whole body sort of shivered around, righting itself. Huge, with no neck, and the barest suggestion of hands and face, other than baleful holes for eyes and gaping mouth.

The last of the salt poured, I hastily called the circle and a column of energy sprang up, the faint trace of burnt ozone crackling in the air.

The golem's foot touched the salt ring, and it made a wet sizzle. The beast let out a noise that likely meant it was in pain. Or pissed off. It kept bouncing against the confinement of the circle like a remote control car stuck on forward, neatly trapped in a sodium chloride cage, and getting angrier by the moment.

March stood, holding his trumpet saltshaker, panting, muttering.

"How do I kill it?" I screamed.

My voice prodded him out of his paralysis. "Get... get the *shem*," he stammered. "It should be in its mouth."

"It's mouth? I'm supposed to reach in its god-blessed *mouth*?"

The mud figure was pounding on the walls of the circle cage. "Is it secure in there?" March pointed at the intruder.

"Yeah, for now. But I can't keep it locked up forever." It was my stored magical energy and all that salt stopping the golem from drowning us in mud or tearing us to pieces or whatever it was going to do. The spell I cast was a solid one, drawing on the energy from the nearby river, but again, I couldn't do it all day. "Can we slow it down? If I let it out, can we delay it long enough to get the *shem* out?"

March nodded. "Water. Water will dissolve some of it. I think. I mean, theoretically, right? I've not tried this, of course. There's some debate about the rationale—"

"GET A BUCKET."

The golem pounded on the magical walls. It was tall, perhaps a shade over seven feet, and stocky. Whoever had sculpted it hadn't bothered to make clothes, just the formation of limbs and a head. No nose. No neck. Legs and arms ended in squared-off feet and hands with no fingers or toes. Despite the rudimentary features, the thing was still scary as all get out.

As I waited for the bucket and a chance to stick my hand in the monster's maw, exhaustion began to creep over me. It was as though I had not slept my whole life. Since I was not prepared for this, my own energy drained quickly and my water-energy skills were rusty. It would have killed a more inexperienced practitioner already. But we do what we can on the fly. I would've been okay if I hadn't nearly lost consciousness and my head hadn't hit the wooden floor with a painful crack.

"Tessa! Tessa, can you hear me?" With my now-blurry vision, I saw Professor March's wool-slippered feet. He knelt beside me. "What should I do?"

Before I could answer, he was knocked violently to the side, breath *whuffing* out of him as his body slid into the couch. The mud monster had broken through the magical force field when my guard was down.

Panting, I rolled onto my back and found the golem leering down at me, its ragged mouth hole gaping. "Hey," I said weakly. "You got some dirt on your face."

It leaned over and picked me up by my shoulders, holding me at eye level as it opened its mouth to roar. I tried what girls are supposed to do in those situations and kicked it in the crotch with my trusty red cowboy boots. Instead of causing any real damage, the pointed tip of my right boot sunk right into the thing's blank man-parts region.

Spell time, even though I had barely enough energy to keep my eyelids open. "I am Papillion, winged *brise* and light, release me now, without *le souci*." (From my high school years. French words are fun to say.)

I slipped out of its grip and floated backward to the floor like a feather in a breeze, near-comically confusing the golem, even as March stirred from his crumpled ball state near the baseboards, moaning. The golem must've figured it out, bellowed, and came galumphing toward me.

Damn. It.

My whole body ached. Bones, muscles, even eyebrows throbbed with every heartbeat. I gathered the last of my fortitude and scooted sideways. The thing swung at me but missed, its fist pounding the floor and dissolving, before reforming almost instantly. I grabbed the professor's big green plastic bucket of water and snagged the little saltshaker he dropped and the last of my Elisha salt. Skittering farther into the living room, I managed to toss all the salt in, hoping enough grains would seep into the water, and said a little charming spell, just to give it some fortitude. The golem did its "don't turn around, just morph yourself the other way" trick and headed my way again.

This time, I was ready.

I heaved the water out of the bucket and at the mudman. Even though I didn't throw with too much force, it was like a strong wave crashing into a sandcastle. The water hit it square in the torso, which melted like butter in the sun. Both arms fell to the floor with a satisfyingly wet plop before they, too, began to dissolve. The mouth flopped open as it moaned in surprise. Its head fell back with a goopy noise and sank into the writhing watery mess.

"Hurry, before it can reshape itself," Professor March croaked. "Get the *shem*."

I knelt in the pool of mud and pushed my hand wrist-deep into the quickly vanishing skull. It was cold as death. One eye still stared at me with as much malignance as it could manage. My fingertips finally found a corner of wet paper, and I pulled the little scroll out of the goo.

It was like all the tension was sucked out of the room. The golem stopped writhing, and the pool of mud stilled as though it was just a regular old dirty puddle.

I gasped, leaning back onto the floor.

March stood up and staggered over. He dragged me out of the muck as I held up the *shem*. We both stared at it dumbly.

Finally, I said, "What do I do with this?"

Through his fear, he still looked like a kid at Christmas.

"Can I see it?"

"Be my guest."

He wiped it off on his pants as best he could then untied the tiny string holding the paper in a tight coil. Though the outside was dirty, the markings were pretty clear. March frowned.

"This is not the name of God," he murmured. He turned the paper over as though searching for more. "At least not in any form I've ever seen. This is... I don't know. Does this look like anything to you?"

I studied the strange little markings. "Looks like gibberish to me. I don't read... anything, really, besides English..."

"That's just it. It's not Hebrew. Or Aramaic. Or Arabic, Sumerian, Egyptian, German, Portuguese, or anything I've ever seen. Can I keep it? Do some research?" The man had just been clocked by a hellish piece of raw ceramic, and he wanted to take on homework.

"Technically, it's evidence of a supernormal crime. I'd better hang on to it for now. Can it be used again?"

He shook his head thoughtfully. "I don't think so. It's all new territory for me, though, so, take it with a grain of salt." He tittered. "Here." He carefully tore it in half. "I'm fairly certain it's useless now, if it wasn't before. You should be able to read it still. Or whoever you will have doing the analysis."

"How did it get in?" I stood slowly.

"I opened the door, and there it was."

I brushed absently at the mud on my clothes. "I don't know if it came after you or me, but I suggest you find a new place to stay for the time being." He nodded.

I called Pryam while March changed clothes and made tea.

Qyll rushed in first and abruptly halted at the sight of me. The sirens weren't too far off. "Are you well?" Concern colored his sharp features.

"Yeah, yeah. A little tired is all. Dirty, too. But listen." I grabbed his wrist and pulled him into the hallway. He looked a little surprised, but followed willingly enough. I let go and wiped my hands on my filthy jeans. "Uh... Okay. Cara Courtland? She was making a golem."

Those beautiful silver eyes grew just a little wider as I gave him a rapid-fire rundown.

"We have a bigger problem then," Qyll said. "Cara Courtland is *dead*. She can't be sending golems after you, so who is?"

I swore under my breath. "Look, we'll figure out who else is involved. Right now, you need to talk to March, but go easy on him. I wouldn't have called you in, but..."

"It's a supernormal event. You had to."

"Yeah. But I was here on some personal business."

He frowned.

"Look, now is not the time. I'll fill you in, just later. I swear. Please."

He nodded slowly. "Where are you going?"

"Home. I've got some research to do. And a very important and thorough bath to take. With a lot of salt and soap."

"Do you think it wise to return there? Alone? What if whoever sent the mudman is after you, not the professor?"

I was so tired, this didn't even make sense. I just waved my hands around. "I'm fine."

Qyll started to say something then just frowned and nodded. "Call me when you've learnt more. And are ready to talk."

*In, time there will be an age of upheaval
and the Rede Witches will dwindle to only a
few in all the worlds between the sun and
Them that Prowl the Edge of Knowing. After
the defeat of the Witch Hunter, and the
Trials, she will hold the balance of the
worlds in her hands and see the true meaning
of things. All this will come to pass.*

—From the **Kykloan Scrolls** fragment

CHAPTER THIRTEEN

Lucky for me, there was an old blanket in the trunk, which I used as a barrier between my muddy ass and the seat.

So. Cara Courtland bought a rare book and learned to make golems. She had clearly cobbled enough information to be very dangerous, but she was dead. Yet, somebody was *still* driving the Claymation bus, or I wouldn't be going home having been dunked in clay and beginning to crust over. And was today's mudman after me? Or the professor? And, not to get too complicated, but what did this all have to do with the Koby murders and Ann Bartley?

It was early afternoon by the time I arrived at my apartment. Despite the daylight and possible indecent exposure, I stripped on the deck outside the back door, left the clothes to toss them in the garbage later, and went straight to the bathroom. I used all the hot water available before getting out.

A Diet Coke, clean clothes, and a trip to my personal library were in order.

I started doing that thing they do on TV cop shows: yellow sticky notes, some yarn, and tape, and I began building a picture of who, what, when, where, and why. In the middle, I had CARA COURTLAND and BIBLE STUDY/DEMONS. Like spokes of the wheel were GARDENER WEST, HEATHER, PATTERSON, THE RARE BOOK, and THE RED QUEEN. Out to the side, ANN BARTLEY. I had notes with big questions like, WHAT WAS CARA TRYING TO DO? WHO HAS THE BOOK NOW?

Around two a.m., I gave up and went to bed and dreamed of drowning in muddy floods of little yellow sticky notes.

I woke up the next morning with more ideas and a definite need to talk to Qyll. I decided to tell him in person.

I'm embarrassed to say I spent entirely too long doing things to my hair and face to make it appear as though I had rolled out of bed looking professional yet sexy. My hair is a tremendous riot of red-gold-auburn curls. As a child, my mother had made me cut it short when she grew tired of fighting the tangles and the leaves. I was a bit of a tomboy and the haircut made me look a little boyish. Okay, a lot boyish. I got called "him" a lot.

Finally satisfied and a little sheepish for acting like a primping teenage girl, I went to the car. It still smelled a little of freshly-churned earth and smoke.

The ride to FBI headquarters was uneventful. Every time I went there, I would think to myself that the building should look more imposing. More like the powerful governmental agency it is, not like a plain boring suburban real estate office.

As I pulled into the parking lot, I beheld a huge crowd near the front of the building, beneath the flagpoles. On the way, I'd seen more and more bumper stickers with such uplifting slogans as: BE AMERICAN. BE HUMAN. Or, THE ONLY THINGS THAT SHOULD HAVE WINGS ARE BIRDS AND AIRPLANES. Or, THERE IS **NO** MAGIC WORD.

The only people who have those kinds of things on their cars? Treevangelists.

Great. I fought the urge to gag. And turn around. But I'm not one to waste hours of primping.

I heard the commotion before I could see them very well. A line of picketers, TV stations and cameras, and people-watchers milled about.

A man with a bullhorn led the protest chants. "What do we want? HUMANS! When do we want them? NOW!"

Near the far edge, a smaller group of maybe twenty or thirty stood a little apart from the rest. Judging by their bald pates and flowing robes, they were part of the Fervor. In an eerie move, they all turned to look at me at the same time, a choreographed weirdness that sent shivers across my skin.

A man in front of me shouted, "SUFFER YE NOT A WITCH TO LIVE!"

"WHAT HAPPENS IN HELL SHOULD STAY IN HELL!"

"GOD PUNISHES THE FALSE PROPHETS!"

"Excuse me, ma'am, are you an employee of the FBI?" A perky auburn-haired woman in a red blazer bearing a local TV news station's logo shoved her mic in my face.

"I am. And I'm a Witch." I turned around and held up my hands, drawing the crowd's attention. "A Witch. My partner in there? He's a Dark Elf. And you know what? We are the only thing standing between you and total annihilation, so you better remember that the next time you have an uninvited ghost in your home or your kid gets jinxed by a djinn. You people have no idea." The crowd roared. I shoved forward and the perky mic girl followed me. She looked like she had won the lottery.

"Please, ma'am, what can you tell us about your job? What's it like to be an illegal?"

As I rounded on the speaker, I snarled, "I was born here. I'm *not* an illegal. Now get out of my face or so help me Shakti, I *will* hex you." I stomped up the steps, immediately regretting that last part. Technically, it constituted a threat, and I just gave the reporter all the excuse in the world to bring me up on charges of endangering a Human citizen by an Other being.

I finally got to the lobby where armed guards let me in and shut the doors behind me. After flashing my creds, I went through the gate and downstairs to the Supernormal offices.

Qyll was at his desk, talking with a man I'd never seen before, a black guy with dreadlocked hair to his shoulders and round glasses.

"Ah, Tessa." Qyll stood. "Just in time. Bristol Jones? Tessa Reddick."

The man reached up to shake my hand. "Hey, nice to meet you. Heard a lot about you."

I grinned back at him. "It's all true."

He laughed. "Good."

"Bristol is our combination IT department and Cult specialist."

I parked myself on the edge of Qyll's desk, and they both sat back down. "Cult?"

Bristol smiled sheepishly. "I needed someplace to use my considerable cult experience and slightly less considerable academic background."

Qyll shook his head. "Be not so humble, good man. Bristol has a degree from MIT, and he is a former Nuabianists."

"New wobby anist? What about the *old* wobby anist?"

They laughed at my stupid pun and mispronunciation.

"Nuabians. I grew up in the church." Bristol Jones had a moon face and a goatee, which he constantly smoothed with his fingers.

"Okay, so what does one believe, should one be a Nuabian?" I asked.

"Oh, many things." Bristol sighed.

"Such as?"

"You have to burn the afterbirth so that Satan doesn't make a clone of the baby. However, there are seven clones of all of us."

"Clones. Where do those clones come from?"

"Good question. I have no idea."

I grinned. "I like you, Jones. You're a weirdo."

Bristol laughed. "Well, thank you. Stop by and visit anytime. My office is at the end of the hall." He pointed. "Q, we'll talk about that uh, thing, later, okay?"

"Thank you, Agent Jones." He saluted us and sauntered off. I perched in what I hoped was an enchanting yet professional way in the chair by Qyll's desk.

"I trust you made it past the hellhounds?" he smirked.

"The mob? Hey, don't joke. Have you *seen* a real hellhound? They are *nasty*. And smelly."

He finally looked at me, his silvery eyes tired. His face read mild surprise. "Your hair. It's..."

I cocked an eyebrow. "Unless you finish that with 'pretty', I don't want to hear it."

The admin chose that moment to show up with a stack of files. "Tessa! I've never seen it all down like that. Looks nice."

"Thanks, Ellen." I grinned widely.

Qyll stared at me for a little bit longer and finally said, "To what do we owe the pleasure, Agent Reddick? Isn't it a little early for you to be out of bed? Especially after yesterday." He was wearing a fitted dark blue button-down shirt and gray slacks. His dark hair was typically shiny and perfectly tousled.

"Well, the thing is, I've been thinking." I began, then introduced him to my thought process. I included everything: Charlie and Ann, the clay, the paper, Patterson and Professor March.

By the end of my word diarrhea, Qyll looked slightly more than mildly surprised, which for him was the same thing as mouth agape and eyes bulging for any other person. "This is very interesting. You say you were working on a separate case? On your own?"

I squirmed. "Well, it was more of a private investigator type situation."

"One, I'm sure, that doesn't have you abusing the FBI resources?"

I shook my head. "Nope. Just trying to earn a little extra cash." Then, before he could press, I launched onward. "Anyway, this is too much magic for someone to handle by himself. It's almost too much for a group." I whipped out the diagram, which was certainly showing wear from being pulled out of and stuffed into my pockets so often. "But if you had several people. And you could tap enough of the right kind of energy to fuel your ritual." I flicked the paper with a finger. "You *could* raise a golem. But you would have a hell of a time controlling it."

"Both Mrs. Courtland and her husband died at Koby's house that night. They didn't have any family to speak of and all their friends are from Church of the Earth. Do you remember when terrorists were detonating themselves in the name of this god or that god?" I nodded. "What if Cara was killing in the name of her god? Or goddess? Or many-armed frog lord? These don't strike me as defensive murders. None of the victims seemed to be doing anything threatening. Plus, they were all in a setting they would have known and likely been comfortable in—their own homes, the home of someone they knew. They were, in theory, friends."

I held up a finger. "Yes, but what if the Humans, Bacchuses, and Jezebels were part of that damn Bible study that was getting too close to something *someone* thought was too dangerous?" We let that sit for a while. "Damn, too bad Cara Courtland's dead! The questions she could answer..."

"I don't think Cara would have done anything to her husband." Qyll leaned back in his chair. "There's absolutely no motive." He thought for a moment. "I checked with Archives about blood magic. No luck. Most of the cases were Knackers. Some were autoevocateurs. Those who perform the spells on themselves, rather than someone else."

"Another dead end."

Across the room, Pryam's office door opened and instead of the Special Agent in Charge, a mountain of a man strode out. He had a face that looked like it had been carved out of clay, then thrown down a staircase before it was put in the kiln. His black windbreaker read SMART.

As he passed, I snorted quietly. "Confident much?"

Qyll glanced up. "Surely you learned about Special Magics and Related Tactics in your training."

"Oh. Right. The SMARTies." SMARTies were the SI's version of a SWAT team. They come in, secure a supernormal event site, and contain it, kill it, put it in prison—whatever. From what I could tell, they were like Navy SEALS. Human, but pretty effing scary nonetheless.

"What was he doing in Pryam's office? Was there an event?" I did air quotes around the last word.

"I'm sure I don't know. This is the FBI. People are supposed to keep things secret." Qyll gave me a look of amused exasperation. I was quickly getting used to that look. "To get back to our regularly scheduled programming. We haven't talked to anybody from Antaura's camp yet. Outside her unscheduled visit."

"Nope."

He looked at his watch. "I suppose it is as good a time as any, it being daylight and all. Might be a bit... safer."

I grinned. "I'll drive." Then added, "You didn't drive in Otherwhere, did you?"

"What? Do you mean automobiles?" He shook his head, looking amused. "No. I had a horse."

"What was its name?"

"Gauntlet."

"Gauntlet, the horse."

"Actually, his full title was Stallion King's Golden Gauntlet, Son of Lady Silverarrow."

I burst out laughing. "Sounds like character from *Lord of the Rings*."

He looked indignant. "It is a fine name. And by far a more realistic choice than your Tolkien with his Galadriels and Haldirs. Sheer nonsense."

I shuffled all the things I knew about him in my mind. FBI agent since the 1940s. The name of his horse. His favorite tree (hawthorne). His growing up in a castle. And believe me, I tried to coax more about castle living out of him, but no dice. Something about him that made me want to run after him yet back away at the same time. Not out of fear, exactly, but something more like awe. And if we're being totally honest, and I hope we are, he's pretty hot. But all kidding aside, of all the creatures I'd met from Otherwhere, the Dark Elves intrigued me the most. Elegant and mysterious with their black hair and silver eyes. Rather different from my coven of short, curvy, wild women.

We reached the front doors. Qyll slid his dark sunglasses on.

"You always wear sunglasses. Pretty much every time I see you." I noted.

He gave a small shrug. "There's something about the sun here. I prefer the shade. Or the dark. It's easier to see."

Outside, the mob was still there. They pressed in from all sides. "The Witch! The Witch!"

"The crowd here is going crazy as infamous Witch-killer Tessa Reddick exits the building." The stupid newsgirl was yapping into the camera.

An older man with a cane poked his finger in my face. "Don't you think your kind would be happier in your own home?"

I practically snarled as I stopped and pushed his hand away. He was about half a head shorter than me. "I'm from Louisville. This IS my home. And I'm just as Human as you are." I shoved past him. People were grabbing at us from all sides as a cool strong hand closed around mine. Just as I was about to yank it away, I realized it was Qyll, attempting to keep us from being separated.

"Hey, you! Legolas! Yeah! You! Why don't you breed with your own kind?" A middle-aged man heckled Qyll, who ignored him. "What, you're too good to answer me? You effing Fairy." Qyll didn't even tense, just kept walking, gently pulling me beside him.

There are all kinds of stories about Dark Elves being promiscuous and seductive and luring people away from their spouses or families to live out lives of hedonism in Otherwhere. Like all dumb racist rumors and stereotypes, they're dumb and racist.

As we stepped down onto the parking lot, I was (again) distracted by the crowd. Which is why I didn't notice the Fervor pushing through like a creepy steamroller.

Somehow they surrounded me, neatly cordoning me from everyone else, even Qyll, although we still held hands, with their bodies. The last thing I remember is a colorless face and her words, raspy and low, "He comes for you, Witch. He's already been in your house. The sin-finder." Then, I felt something sharp on the back of my head. Pain descended lightning-fast down my spine and spread through my cranium. The next thing I knew, my cheek was flat on the pavement. Women screamed, there were bright lights, but it all seemed very far away and through water.

After that, I had the sensation of floating and then dim coolness.

"Tessa? Can you hear me?"

I pried my eyelids open to see Qyll. "Hi, handsome," I croaked. Pryam's face swam into view behind him.

"Tessa," she said loudly and slowly. "You were hit on the head with a rock. By those damn zealots."

"Mmmmmph. I like rocks." Everything felt swimmy and hot, then swimmy and cold. I didn't want to move at all, my blood sluggish, like concrete.

Voices talked some more.

Somebody shined a light in my face.

Possibly, maybe, they moved me.

When I came to, I was in bed in my apartment, Dorcha next to me, hovering like a vulture. When I opened my eyes, she very seriously licked my face from chin to forehead, and then she stretched out with her back along my leg.

"Owch, you goof," I mumbled. Qyll came in with a tray.

"Ah. You're awake. Excellent." His voice was soothing. "We had you checked by one of the forensics doctors at the office. You are going to be fine. No concussion, just a nasty bruise."

"Don't they do forensics on dead people?" I felt the lump on the side of my head.

"Here, eat this." He set the tray down as I struggled to sit up. There was toast with peanut butter and honey, and hot tea. I nibbled on the toast.

"What happened? I'm not really... clear."

"When we left, the Fervor took an intense interest in you. One of them brained you with a rather hefty piece of garden rock."

"She said something to me. Something about... I don't remember."

"They're not thinking rationally any longer, Tessa. I told you. It doesn't matter. They're all nonsense. That said, this will be investigated by the local police as assault. I don't imagine much will come of it, seeing as though interviewing the Fervor is akin to teaching a cat to play the piano."

I finished eating and realized I was still bone tired. Qyll was talking but I dozed. The comforter had been tucked in around me and the room quieted.

It was dark when I woke up, and my phone was ringing.

"Tessa? It's Heather. Heather Mumford. I need to talk to you." Her voice was high and tight, as though she was trying to sound calm but failing spectacularly.

I sat there dumbly, not quite able to get all the hamsters in my head to run together on the wheel.

"Hello?" she barked.

"I'm here. Yeah. Um... sorry. Can you come to my house?" My voice was coarse.

She agreed to arrive in an hour.

I got out of bed and saw Qyll had cleaned my apartment and done some laundry, and I was now wearing soft pajamas. The thought of my FBI partner seeing my nether regions sent a squirmy tingle up my back and a warm flush through my pink bits.

The note on the table read:

I will come to check in on you in the morn. Do rest, won't you?—Q

Dorcha padded along behind me. "I'm just going to the bathroom, 'k? I need to pee and get some aspirin." She glared reproachfully at me. "Okay, I'll leave the door open."

As I was finishing up, there was a knock. I was beginning to really *hate* people knocking. "Wow, that was fast, Heather," I muttered, pulling on a worn plaid robe.

It was Mark Tabler. He looked a little sheepish and swayed on his feet. "Hi, Tessa."

"Hey there, Mark."

He stood. He swayed some more. A rush of wind blew in, ruffling the bit of his dark hair that was still dry.

"I was at Dark Star with some friends, having some drinks, and I thought I'd stop by. Since you're so close."

Ah. This was like the in-person version of drunk-dialing.

"Did you drive?" I asked.

He shook his head. "Just to the bar. I walked here, scouts honor."

He held a hand up in the scout salute and hiccupped.

"Well, come on in out of the rain." It had begun to pour in earnest. "Okay, what are you doing here, and why do you have a big old wooden box? Gah, that thing is filthy." He put it on the floor in the kitchen. Dorcha was busy smelling him from head to toe, but he didn't seem to mind.

"It was by the door when I got here. Were you expecting anything?"

I couldn't remember. "Um... I don't think so, but... maybe." I flipped on the kitchen light. He was wearing trendy dark jeans and a dark green sweater under a gray corduroy jacket. Between the fancy togs and the obvious product in his hair, I'd say he was coming home from a date. "So..."

"I was in the neighborhood. Saw your light on. Thought I'd stop by, maybe see if you had anything interesting going on." His eyes were shiny with drink. "Maybe we can just talk. You have a really interesting history. I'd love to hear more about it." He had a ridiculous goofy smile on his face.

I must have hit my head harder than I thought because this felt weird. "Look, I've had kind of a rough day. Some crazy Fervor chucked a rock at me, and I'm not exactly feeling really with it."

Mark looked apologetic. "I heard there was a riot. It was on the news." He slurred a little.

"It wasn't a riot, exactly. More like a... kerfuffle."

"Can I get you something to drink? Or eat?" He went to lean on the counter, but his elbow missed and he almost cracked his head on the formica.

"Steady as she blows, pardner. Come on. How about *I* make you some coffee?" I said. He followed me into the living room. "I have a visitor coming soon anyway."

He looked mock-hurt. "You entertain gentleman callers besides me?"

I chuffed and set about making him the eternal elixir of sobriety. "No, Mark, you're the only gentleman I entertain."

"So, are you from Louisville?"

He was so genuine. Like a little nerd on a first date. Then, it dawned on me. He came over here to woo *me*. Put the moves on. Get some. Bow-chicka-bow-wow.

"Mark, listen." I tried to sound very gentle. "You realize I'm almost old enough to be your mother? And you're really sweet and all, but this?" I waved a hand in the air between us. "It's not going to happen."

His face turned tomato-red. "You thought I was coming on to you? Pssssssshhhhh." He listed so far to the side, I thought he was going to fall over the couch. "Oh no. No, I mean, you're hot and all, but no. I just thought we could be friends, professionally. Not professional friends, but I mean friends around our respective jobs, yours being a Supernormal Investigating Agent and mine being, ah, you know, supernormal blogger and reporter."

I almost snickered. He so obviously came here thinking he was going to get his wand in my chalice. But I felt a little bad for him, and he *is* a pretty okay guy. I probably would have gone for him in my younger days.

"Sure, Mark. We can be friends." I clicked on the TV. "I think there's a ghost hunting show on. As your friend, I'm guessing it's your cup of tea."

"Har. Har." Mark seemed a little more relaxed as he drank his coffee and we watched a show about some people investigating a haunted hotel. He pointed out all the little inconsistencies and how their equipment was really sub-par for a modern ghost hunter. On the downside, he did keep taking really long looks at my profile.

"So, really. Are you from here or what?"

I sighed. "Yep. I grew up in a house in Old Louisville. I went to Manual for high school."

"Your parents are dead, right?"

"Listen, do you mind if we don't talk about family?" I didn't mean to sound as huffy as I did.

"Oh sure, sure," he said hastily. "Ghosts. Let's talk about ghosts. What was your first Rift experience?"

I smiled. "We had an infestation of *akaname*."

"Excuse me? A what?"

"*Akaname*. They're Japanese spirits that basically lick up dirt in bathrooms."

Mark guffawed. "So you had Japanese ghosts in your dirty bathroom?"

I laughed too. "The bathroom wasn't *particularly* dirty. I got up one night to, you know, go to the bathroom and I didn't turn the light on. I was sitting there and something started licking my foot. I was mostly still asleep, right? And this thing is just... licking my foot. Felt like a big cat. So I reached down and grabbed it and turned on the light. There it was."

Mark's face was a mix of amusement, horror, and fascination. "That's really disgusting. What do they look like?"

"About this big," I held my hands about 16 inches apart. "Red skin like a lizard but blobby, not sleek. Sort of a sucker mouth with a long tongue. No eyes."

"How'd it get there?"

"Little things like that just come on through. They're not really anything, right? It's easy for something that's not *really* evil or *really* good to drift through. It's just... supernormal. I don't know how many dirty facilities they have in Otherwhere, so maybe it was a good career move. What was your first time?"

"My grandmother's ghost. Wouldn't leave her old bedroom. She didn't know she was dead. In fact, she still might not know."

Everybody has these stories. The Rift isn't that old in the grand scheme of things, and at first, the Others who were already here were the only ones. Then little things like the *akaname*, pixies, gnomes, Malakim, Bacchuses, Jezebels started sifting through. The veil is so thin here and there, I think they literally just went to sleep in Otherwhere and woke up in Earth. And some Humans did the same on the other side. Later, bigger things came through, like Vampires and the Turned, and lower-order Angels and Demons. Little by little, people realized it was less about the end of the world and more like a mass-immigration problem. And that's how agencies like Supernormal Investigations got started.

"If you want something out of the kitchen, feel free," I told Mark. "There's not much, but you're welcome to whatever is available."

He nodded and got up. I heard him rummaging around in the cabinets and the clink of glassware. He came back with two glasses, water, and a tumbler of bourbon, which he handed to me. Man, the kid had done his homework. I set it aside for the moment.

"So, uh, what about that box in the kitchen?" He asked.

"Oh." I got up and shuffled in to get it. It was fairly light, about the size of a bread box, and carved ornately. I brought it into the living room and put it on the coffee table.

"Hang on, I'll be right back."

I went to the library to get some tools. You don't just go opening strange boxes without your salt and a good stethoscope and maybe a dagger or something.

As I dug through a trunkful of my stuff, a crash from the living room brought me short, followed by a fierce snarl from Dorcha. Grabbing up some things, I hustled back in to find Mark stumbling around the room. The big cat was balanced on the back of an armchair, poised to strike.

Up near the ceiling, on the wall, clung a gray shadow with extra fingers, very long toes, and spindly limbs. It hissed at us. There was a distinct odor of sulphur.

The box lay upended and open on the floor.

I gasped in spite of myself. "Mark, *what* have you done?"

Dr. Peter Venkman: *This city is headed for a disaster of biblical proportions.*

Mayor: *What do you mean, "biblical"?*

Dr. Ray Stantz: *What he means is Old Testament, Mr. Mayor, real wrath of God type stuff.*

Dr. Peter Venkman: *Exactly.*

Dr. Ray Stantz: *Fire and brimstone coming down from the skies! Rivers and seas boiling!*

Dr. Egon Spengler: *Forty years of darkness! Earthquakes, volcanoes…*

Winston Zeddemore: *The dead rising from the grave!*

Dr. Peter Venkman: *Human sacrifice, dogs and cats living together… mass hysteria!*

Mayor: *All right, all right! I get the point!*

From **Ghostbusters**, film, 1984, directed by Ivan Reitman

CHAPTER FOURTEEN

Dammit, Mark. Didn't anybody ever tell you not to peek at other peoples' birthday presents?"

The gray thing launched itself at Mark who jumped behind the couch, even as Dorcha leapt at the gray thing. Cat, man, couch, and shadow went tumbling. Something screeched.

"Dorcha! To me!" I wrestled with my salt container and a holy water bottle. "Mark, you too!" Mark crawled out from behind the couch, whimpering, his eyes huge. I couldn't see where the spirit-thing had gone.

It literally came out of the woodwork before I got the salt circle closed. Cold bony fingers gripped my throat while feet with too many talons pushed at my chest, kind of like it was trying to yank my head off my body. My vision swam. I stared into rheumy lopsided eyes and a huge snapping mouth full of black teeth. I fell to my knees then flopped sideways to the floor, choking.

Remembering the tools I still clutched in my hands, I brought up the spray bottle and hoped to god it was set to STREAM and not OFF.

It was on stream.

The holy water laced with Elisha salt hit dead center of its nose-less, scaly face, right in the holes where a nose should have been. It reeled back, letting go of me, slapping at itself, but didn't seem incapacitated, which meant one thing.

"It's a Ghost, not a Demon. Ponderous." I gasped and stood

frowning at the thing as it hovered six feet in front of me, its head moving like a cobra about to strike. "How the hell did you get in here? I've got protective spells up!"

While my back was turned, Mark had scooted back toward the couch, messing up the salt circle.

That gave the spirit the perfect opportunity to dive *into* Mark's chest. Then, everything stilled.

"Mark?" I craned my neck to see that he was still breathing shallowly.

All at once, he got up. I don't mean he got to his feet. I mean his whole body lifted parallel to the floor, then upright, then it spun to face me, still three feet *above* the hardwood. His eyes had rolled back in his head.

The voice issuing from his mouth was not his. "Bad little witch," he/it said. "It would be best if you stayed home and nursed your wounded head."

"Who are you?" I demanded. I fixed the circle and enclosed myself and Dorcha in a protective little nook.

The Mark-thing laughed. "No one of consequence, just a lowly messenger, sent to tell you to mind your own business. You have enemies far and wide, traitorous bitch." It hissed with relish.

My poor brain raced. What comes in a box and flies out to possess someone? A terrible riddle. I couldn't break my salt circle until I had a plan to deal with this thing, and I couldn't see the box well enough from where I was. Damn, damn, damn.

How was I going to get it out of Mark? Clearly, if I tried to kill it, it'd take Mark with it. I wasn't even sure how to kill a Ghost. (Note to self: *learn how to kill Ghosts should the need arise.*)

I wasn't sure if I could do an exorcism, but I sure as hell couldn't just stand around with my thumb up my ass. "Dorcha," I said quietly. "Follow my lead." Her long tail twitched in acknowledgement.

"What's your name, spirit?" I called. The face hissed at me. "Speak your name."

"Stop asking, I won't tell," it said through Mark's mouth in a horrible singsong.

"Ah, well, tell me where you come from. I want to know who's sending the order."

As it rolled its hands over and around each other, considering my gambit, I brushed my bare foot through the salt, breaking the magic. Dorcha sprang forward in one of her typical impressive lunges and I made a break for the box.

Dorcha wrested Mark's writhing form into the circle while the creature shrieked, holding it there with her massive jaws, and paws planted on its chest, while I poured more salt and hefted the box into the middle. We backed off as I said, "I call you, circle, now is the hour, hold this creature, with mighty power!"

The ghost screamed bloody murder, flipping upside down and every which way. "Who controls you?" I asked over its yowling.

Mark tore at his clothes, his tongue darting in and out, blank eyes wild. He crawled up my metaphysical wall, hanging like a grotesque bat. "I know not who summons me."

Probably true. Ghosts are many things, and they are often liars. But whoever conjured this one could probably have done it without the thing knowing who did the honors. It's certainly not unheard of.

"What's your name?"

Ghost-Mark twisted and bucked in its salt circle prison.

Again, I hollered, "What's your name?" Sometimes you can get a ghost to answer a question if you ask it three times. Especially, if it's not a very smart spirit. Three truly is the magic number.

It squealed in anger. "In life, I was Harkim, now I am Ezragoggeth," it wailed. Ah, give the girl a Kewpie doll!

I pushed up my sleeves, hoping this would work. Until then, I'd only read about exorcisms, seen a few in movies, and heard about them from an aunt.

"Who called you, Ezragoggeth?"

The thing writhed some more. "The lady in blue," it whined. Blue? That brought me up short. Usually, it's black or white or gray ladies.

"What does she want with you?"

"My charge was to deliver a message, you Witch, that is all!"

"Right, okay. Hold your horses." I stomped into the library to get a book of shadows of Grandnanny Maldec's. She was a healer about a century ago and dealt a lot with possessions in her day. I flipped through the pages, irritated. *Seriously? This is what I'm doing after being conked on the head by a nut? There are some days when I wish I hadn't gotten out of bed.*

I found her favorite exorcism spell and dragged my sorry ass back to the living room.

The spell said to draw a pentacle on the floor with white chalk, then a circle around it to cage the spirit in. Well, I hadn't done that, so I skipped to the second step. Holy water and an incantation while walking counterclockwise around the circle, saying the spell. Holding the heavy book balanced on my left arm, and the spray bottle of holy water in the right, I made my way around the room.

"*Regna terrae, cantata deo, psallite Cernunnos.*" I let my voice get low and solemn, and I spritzed the holy water into the circle. The Mark-thing kept trying to climb the walls, screeching and slashing the air. "*Caeli Deus, Deus terrae, Humiliter majestati gloriae.*"

You just can't beat the Catholics when it comes to exorcism rites. They wrote the book on it. They wrote *all* the books on it, actually. My aunts used to laugh and say Catholicism was a Pope and a catechism away from paganism.

I droned on. The thing was really long, but I was pretty sure it was working. With every word, the thing's hold on Mark seemed to weaken until it released and floated above Mark's unmoving form. I skimmed along in the book where it suggested I was dealing with a "raven" ghost. Messengers meant to scare or deliver messages, basically. Given the box it came in, my guess was, someone hired it on the condition once the box was opened, the thing would be free.

Dorcha stood beside me, at the ready.

"*I swear to all the tiny gods.* Back in the box, you jackwagon," I said. "I command thee! Into the box, Ezragoggeth! Into the box, I command thee, Ezragoggeth! Into the vessel, Ezragoggeth! *Into the vessel, I command thee, Ezragoggeth!"* At last, the nasty thing barked an appropriately nasty farewell and slid into the box like dirty water down a sewer drain.

I wasted no time breaking the circle, refastening the latches on the case, and taking it to the tub. I sprinkled salt on it and ran the bath half-full of water. It was a stopgap. I'd have to figure out what to do with it later. The salt water would ground it out for a while.

It really was just a messenger. If it had been here to kill me, I'd be dead, or the ward spells would have told me.

Back in the living room, Mark was moaning on the floor. I helped him up to the couch where he lay, looking dazed, for a few minutes. Then he turned over and barfed all over the rug.

I sighed. "Want me to call you a cab?"

He nodded. I went for my phone and was startled to see seven missed calls and three texts from Qyll, all commanding me to, "CALL AT ONCE."

"Tessa?" Mark croaked. I sat on the coffee table in front of him, wincing. This just had not been my day. He swallowed and looked up at me with the eye that wasn't swelling closed. "I lied. I came over here to ask you out. But, I'm rethinking that intention at the moment. I rescind my feelings of romantic affection. At least for the time being. No offense."

I couldn't help it and burst out laughing, even though my head hurt. "It's okay."

"However, this is going to blow up the server for my site tomorrow."

Mistrial after jurors deadlock in murder case of missing teen

A mistrial was declared today after a Human/Other jury said it was deadlocked in the murder case of Charles Carrico, a Class Four Demon, charged in the 2012 disappearance of Johnsburg teenager Branton Hobert, Human.

CHAPTER FIFTEEN

Just as I set Mark into his cab, another car pulled up. I caught sight of a familiar face within.

"Get in." It was Qyll. "There's been another murder."

"Heather Mumford is going to be here any minute." I peered into the vehicle. "She might have some important information."

"She's dead," he said shortly. "That is where we are going."

"Shit." As fast as I could, I ran inside, pulled off my sweaty jammies, and slid into jeans, a leather jacket, and my red boots. I pulled my hair into a half-hearted bun and grabbed my bag of tricks.

"You keep an eye on things," I told Dorcha. "No hunting. Guard the house." She assumed her sphinx pose, unblinking.

Heather Mumford, it seemed, had died shortly after her second phone call to me. The first, which I had stupidly forgotten to check up on, was when I was at Professor March's house. Qyll was trying to reach me while I was busy with the ghost and Mark. When I didn't answer or return his calls, he grew worried and stopped by to check in and/or take me to the new crime scene.

"What happened to you? You look rather disheveled."

"I have a secret admirer with a sick way of showing how much she likes me."

Qyll's expression asked for more.

I sighed. "Somebody sent me a nasty-gram. A crazy ghost in a box."

"Ah. Have you any idea why?"

I shrugged. "The message was to mind my own business."

"Was this a personal or professional warning?"

Huh. "I actually don't know, now that you mention it. I assumed it was personal, because it was summoned by a woman and mentioned me having enemies far and wide, but who knows?" I didn't want to tell him about my visit to Bathsheba.

"It may be necessary to increase security for your domicile and person. A posted guard and a personal attendant, perhaps."

"Nah, professor word nerd, I'm good. I can take care of myself. You can get me a better security system though." I laughed.

We were silent for the rest of the ride. I leaned against the window and tried to rest and collect my thoughts. Maybe Qyll was right, but I didn't care. The fewer people around me, the less chance of them dying.

When we arrived, FBI vans, police, and an ambulance were all parked haphazardly on the grass in front of three houses. Neighbors were being shooed back to bed as they drifted out of their homes wearing bathrobes and house slippers. Heather lived in a shotgun house in Germantown. As we made our way toward the activity, a short stocky woman with a very hard look on her face came charging toward us. Behind her was Pryam, an equally hard look on her chiseled features.

"Agent Toutant, is there a good reason you are here?" the small woman snapped as she approached. She had short permed grandma-ish hair and big round glasses that gave her the look of a malicious owl. The skirt of her suit hit at an unfortunately frumpy mid-calf length. And I hadn't seen anyone wear nude pantyhose in decades until that day. She reminded me of my fourth-grade teacher, the one who accused me of using words I didn't know the meaning of in my schoolwork. (I had a precocious vocabulary, sue me.)

My hackles instantly rose as the woman turned on Pryam. "I

expressly declined the need for any further personnel from this department, and as Special Agent-in-Charge, I would think you would understand that command, madam. And yet, here *he* is." As an afterthought, the woman turned back and glared at me. "And whoever this is. This is a restricted area. FBI personnel *only*."

"Excuse me, who are you?" I allowed every possible ion of rudeness to creep into the words.

"Reddick." Pryam's glare shot daggers. "Deputy Assistant Director McReynolds, this is Special Agent Tessa Reddick. She's here at my behest and with the knowledge of the entire field office as well as the Assistant Director."

The short woman's nostrils flared.

Her boss hadn't told her I was part of the team.

She looked like she wanted nothing so much as to suckerpunch me. "Deputy Assistant Director and Chair of the Commission for Internal Affairs Marjorie McReynolds." I let her glower at me until she finally said, "You must be the staff Witch." The way she said "Witch" managed to cram every condescending, bigoted, stereotypical, fearful comment ever made about my kind into one tiny word.

"Yes, ma'am," I managed through gritted teeth. "Special Agent with the department of Supernormal Investigations." I stuck out my hand in an overly chummy way. When she didn't return my handshake, I hugged her. Full-on squeeze. "So *glad* to finally meet you, Margie."

I thought her eyeballs were going to shoot off her face and smack me in the neck. I don't often get to describe people as "apoplectic", but it totally fits here.

Pryam jumped in, her voice controlled. "The last time I checked, this is my department and I say who is necessary and who isn't. Toutant, Reddick, get inside."

I could feel the little woman's eyes burning holes in my back as we hustled up to the house. "She seems pleasant."

Qyll sighed. "Indeed, in the manner of a particularly loathsome skin rash. You've no idea."

Pryam eventually brought up the rear. I could almost hear her growling. We went toward the back of the house and picked our way over a deck that had—for lack of a better description—been smashed. In the kitchen, a trail of dirt and debris crossed it toward a narrow hallway. Tables and other bits of furniture lay broken along the line of caked mud.

"This way." Pryam said. She wore a smart plum-colored pantsuit and an ivory blouse. Me, I was glad I opted for my customary cowboy boots because the mess was probably going to ruin her fancy heels.

"Suspects?" Qyll asked.

Pryam shook her head. "The last call we have on record is to 911. It's hard to understand what she's saying, but she was apparently trapped in the bathroom. The call prior to that"—she turned to stare at me—"was to you."

I sighed. For a hot second I wavered, then said, "She was supposed to come to my house. She wanted to talk about something, but I swear, I don't know what."

The interior of Heather's home had been ransacked. Furniture upended, drapes torn. Even the ceiling fan hung cockeyed from a couple of wires. A shotgun house is called that because all the rooms are in a row. You're supposed to be able to fire a gun from the front door and the bullet won't hit anything on the way to the back door. This looked a lot worse than a shotgun blast.

Down a short hall was the bathroom. Heather's body was... *pinned* to the shower wall. The arms were spread wide open, one leg flush against the tile, the other with the foot bent up toward her hip. Her mouth gaped, and there appeared to be mud packed in there. It was as though the wall was made of mud and she was being sucked in. Or pushed out.

Remnants of black magic swirled in the air like evil dust motes. The animotoids were just starting to crawl in, chewing and sucking.

"Heather Mumford. Demon name is..." Pryam made a sound like a banshee underwater. She was looking at some notes on her smartphone. "Worked for an insurance company. Claims to have crossed through the Rift in Tennessee, moved here about ten years ago.

A member of the Church of the Earth."

Qyll prized open an eyelid. "There's mud in here, too. And in her nose and ears. What a ghastly way to die."

"Agent Toutant. I suggest you let the forensics team do their jobs." Her highness McReynolds was in the doorway with her arms folded, glaring at us. If glaring was an Olympic sport, she'd have a dozen gold medals and one silver, because Catholic nuns are really excellent glarers, too and would have given her a run for her money.

"Where did the killer come in?" I asked.

"Back door is bashed in, mud everywhere," Pryam said. "No sign of digging or earth removal anywhere in a two-mile radius."

I peered at the body, imagined my protective bubble drowning out the bickering of Pryam and McTrollface. What hit me first and hardest was fear. Heather had been absolutely terrified when she died. As I said, I'm not much of a Sensitive, so if it was powerful enough for me to get hit with it, it must have been bad. I squatted down to look at the mud holding her legs in place and saw a tiny piece of paper.

"Do we have exit location?"

Pryam's head jerked toward me. "No," she said roughly, frowning.

"Just entry prints?"

She nodded. When the two women went back to their 21st-century version of chest-beating, I pointed out the paper's dirty corner to Qyll.

"What is that? What do you have there?" McTrollerson shoved into the bathroom. It became incredibly comical at this point, because there was just not enough room for three full-sized Human adults *and* an adult Dark Elf. My shoulder was pressed against the wall while the toilet pressed into my back. Pryam was practically sitting in the pedestal sink.

I stood up. Very carefully.

Qyll brushed by me, a move I wished he'd made slower. Standing next to McReynolds, he towered over her at near six and half feet to her, what, five foot nothing? "Madam, I must say it is with the utmost care and thoroughness that I do my job," he murmured, with a hint of a smile. I almost giggled, but it would've ruined it.

He slowly removed his latex gloves, not unlike a burlesque dancer in a cabaret, one, then the other, and tossed them aside. "You're rather tense, madam." He gently touched her elbow. McReynolds' eyes had gone huge and unfocused, mouth slightly open, breathing quicker. "I know you don't want to stand in my way." He held his hand on her a moment longer then let it slide off.

"Tessa? Let's go." He nodded to Pryam whose face was a bemused grimace then beckoned to me. We went past McReynolds while she still stood there agog, words a gurgle in her throat.

Outside, I laughed. "Nice. Haven't seen you use that Elven glamor thing in a while."

"It *is* technically illegal, using magic on an unknowing Human, but I didn't have her do anything. I didn't extract information of any sort. I think I am safe from retribution. You'll notice Pryam didn't mind." Qyll gave me one of his very rare smiles. "We needed to get out of there before Pryam had more than she could handle with McReynolds."

"Did you see that paper?"

He nodded. "I'll have it set aside for us to examine later."

Hobarth Scrittlby, Sanguimancer
Hygienic, safe, and affordable!
Bonded and insured
Blood magic done while you wait!

CHAPTER SIXTEEN

I got home close to four a.m. Qyll let me out on the sidewalk in front of the shop.

"Shall I come in with you?" He asked as I got out of the car.

Yes, I thought. *Come all the way in. Have you seen my bedroom?*

"No, it's ok. I'll give you a ring later."

"I'll wait a moment. Make sure you get in safely." His face was hidden in the shadow.

"Suit yourself." As I turned to head round to the back, I saw the glimmer of glass all over the concrete. The entire front window of the Broom Closet was smashed.

I tilted my head back and roared at the sky. "ARE YOU EFFING *KIDDING* ME?"

Qyll was by my side instantly, service weapon drawn.

Stepping carefully, I went through the door, readying spells in my mind. A faint smell of cinnamon hung in the air. As I went to find the lights, a small animal sound in the shadows, near the back of the store, accompanied a slight, pained sort of movement.

"Oh goddess, Dorcha!" I rushed over to her.

"I'll call this in," Qyll said.

By the scant streetlight coming in, I could see she was bleeding all over the place. Her paws were akimbo, one ear nearly torn off. She struggled to stand and ended in an awkward crouch, mewling. Her angry, terrified eyes tore at my soul.

As I crouched low and went to touch her leg, she hissed and took a mighty swipe at me, catching my arm.

"Dammit, cat, I'm trying to help!"

Qyll stepped carefully through the debris behind me.

Dorcha backed away, continuing to spit and growl. I felt my arm above my elbow and winced. Qyll had his flashlight out in a moment, and we considered the damage. My arm was a mess of leather and blood. The huge cat suddenly stood as though nothing were wrong, sprinted past us toward the front door, then leapt into the air. Just before she vanished into the gloom, she *shifted*. I caught a glimpse of a humanoid foot and a white trailing garment.

The sound that came out of my mouth was pure distilled rage, with a healthy dose of fear, for good measure. Whatever that was, it wasn't Dorcha, but it *was* Other. I looked down at my arm. Blood dripped all over the floor. I went cold all over.

"It has my blood." Dread crept through my words. "Whatever... it... that asshat was, it *has my blood*." That was worse than a broken shop or my missing cat. The shop could be fixed, and Dorcha *will* be found, but if something has your blood, you're in for a world of hurt. It makes you—me—vulnerable to all manner of attack. And you just never know when that shoe drops.

"What did you see?"

Qyll helped me to my feet. "I don't know who it was. But I will. Let's go upstairs." He was still in the lookout mode, but the thief was long gone.

Though the true Dorcha was nowhere to be found, the rest of the place appeared as I had left it, a mess from Mark's ghost-o-gram but nothing else awry.

Wordlessly, I motioned Qyll in. As he crossed the threshold, he gasped and jerked, tumbling to the floor, as though an electric current coursed through him.

"Shit. Shit! I am so sorry!" I clapped my hands over my mouth, even as I whispered a couple of quick incantations that would prevent the apartment from launching into full-on security routine. The spells can sense the intruder's intentions so if he had crossed the threshold with ideas of harming me, he'd likely be dead already.

"I just reinforced my house spells and forgot to let them down. Shit, I am so sorry!" I knelt down beside him.

After a few moments, he opened his eyes and sighed. "You've decided to heed my words about your personal safety."

"Can you scoot in here? I need to close the door."

He obliged and ended up sitting on the floor propped against the couch. Eventually, he worked his way onto the couch itself.

"Clearly I was not protecting myself enough," I said. "Whatever demolished my store and impersonated my cat wanted my blood. I didn't think I'd made so many enemies but, dammit. Dammit! My shop's a mess, and my arm hurts like hell."

"We must bandage your wound," he said.

"Don't worry, I can do that. Will you be okay for a few minutes?" He nodded. In the bathroom, I found gauze and iodine then washed up, noting I might need stitches. Except, time was kinda of the essence, so I made up a spell on the spot to seal the skin, at least for a little while. *Meet as one which once you were, knit together like bone and fur.* It seemed to work rather well. I wondered if I should take some antibiotics. I did down several ibuprofen before I changed my shirt and went back to see to the rest.

Back in the living room, I asked Qyll if he was okay.

He nodded. "I should quite like a cup of tea."

"Of course. Can you make it there, and I'll join you in a sec?" I pointed at the library.

Tea made, bourbon retrieved, and calm Elven exterior replaced, I sat down at the table across from him.

"Here." I pushed a stack of tomes at Qyll. "Look through these and try to find a spell that uses blood." His dark eyebrows went up, but he opened the top book.

"These are grimoires," he said, a hint of wonder in his voice.

"Yeah, why?"

"I've never seen one up close like this. I've handed a few over to

Evidence and such, but I've always been a bit curious."

"Have at it then."

After a little while, I asked, "Do your people um... do spells?"

He actually *smirked* at me and for a moment, looked every bit like a Fae prince, imperious and beautiful. "No. Our magic comes from *syl'myh*. Roughly translates as 'starlight.' We do not learn magic, as some do. We simply are. Our powers are nothing compared to many tribes in the *Na'ndr*."

"The nandor?"

"Sorry. Otherwise. It is our word for that."

"So, what can you do?"

"Do?" He looked confused.

"Your powers."

Qyll sat up stiffly. "That topic is not something we consider polite conversation."

"I've never been accused of being polite." I grinned. He softened.

"I imagine my powers, as you call them, are mere parlor tricks here in Earth. In general, we are known for our sleep manipulation." He cleared his throat. "Are we all right to continue?"

I desperately wanted to keep probing, but manfully reminded myself we had work to do. As I leafed through pages of careful illustrations of werewolves and faeries and pandaemons, hex mages and sanguimancers—lots of stuff I didn't recognize—I started thinking. Making a mud version of you is threatening, yeah. It's sort of stupid, and it's the work of a newbie, but it means someone is paying attention to you and wants you to know it. But blood magic? That's serious business. Too much can go wrong, unless you're a very experienced practitioner. It's generally the weapon of choice for higher-order Demons and Celestials. Or *Wrach Du*, the Black Witches.

"These are beautiful," Qyll said, mostly to himself. "I've heard they have some at the Domus Libro."

"What's the Domus Libro?"

"The Eternal Library. The name is actually much longer, but it translates to something like the infinite house of eternal books. It's sort of the Otherwhere equivalent to your Library of Congress. Though much older and with much stranger contents on the shelves."

"I've never heard of that," I said. "Where is it? Can I see it?"

Qyll smiled ruefully. "I've never been there myself. I don't know of anyone who has. It's very well-hidden and very, very difficult to reach. It's just... a big old library. As big and old as the universe."

I sighed. "What kinds of books?"

"Grimoires, for starters. Histories and genealogies, memoirs and travelogues. That sort of thing. But some say, there are other kinds of books, too. There's a book written by every living thing in the universe."

"How does every living thing in the universe write a book for a library no one can get to?"

"From what I understand, there is a scribery. And the scribes write the stories of living things as they are lived. And at the end, the book is kept there, in the Eternal Library. Forever."

"Qyll, wait!" I grabbed his hand. "Would it have one of those books of creation? The ones they're using to create the golems?"

He shrugged. "I suppose it's possible, but we ought not count it among our assets lest we are tempted to go on a wild duck hunt."

I laughed. "You mean a wild goose chase?"

"I will never get the hang of your idioms, I fear."

I looked around my own library. "I wonder if there's anything in any of the grimoires about that place. But you're right, we don't have time to go through them right now. Looks like I know what I'm doing on my next eighty-seven weekends." It was frustrating to think there might be answers, but I couldn't get to them.

We went back to the books we had on hand.

After a while, I leaned back, closing my eyes. Qyll sat bent over a volume, engrossed, one pointed ear sticking out, pale against his jet hair. His jacket draped over the back of his chair, his arms bare, revealing his well-defined muscles.

"This appears to be a spell for finding children." Qyll looked up.

The pages depicted a woman putting a small knife to her palm. The droplets of blood made a trail across the page to a drawing of a child, a little boy in a copse, crying. Ye Olde Englishe caption drove the point home.

"But I didn't lose my kid."

"No, but I wonder if it would work on beings that carry the same blood. Or items that are smeared with it. Blood stays on a body much longer than most people are aware."

I shuddered. "Well thanks, Mr. Gruesome."

I took another look, relying on my interpretation of the drawings and not my ability to translate Old English. "Damn. Maybe. It's worth a try. I'm pretty desperate." It was a simple spell. It called for a birch switch, a bowl of water, and some of my blood. You were supposed to put the blood in the water, soak the birch switch, and the switch would guide you.

"Do you know of a birch tree nearby?" he asked.

I laughed. "We're not kicking it this old school, Q." I got up and dug around in a trunk marked MISCELLANEOUS. At the bottom, I found a sturdy metal compass. It was from my failed attempt at being a Girl Scout. The problem was, I just kept using magic to do all the badges and got kicked out for cheating.

"Let's go." Both of us winced as we rose, our respective hurts reminding us they were there.

Qyll drove, and I rode shotgun, wielding the compass. The sun was well up and rousing life into the world. In the parking lot of the Broom, I'd carefully pricked my finger and squeezed a few drops of blood onto the compass. "*Expiscor sanguis*," I whispered three times. The dial on the compass spun wildly clockwise, then counterclockwise. It stopped firmly on southeast.

"There we go."

Every couple of minutes, I called out something like, "East."

"I'm *going* east."

"Go more east. No, wait, southwest."

"I can't turn around, I'm on the expressway."

"Go west!"

Finally, after an hour, Qyll pulled over. We were in Cherokee Park, by Hogan's Fountain. "We're never going to get there in a timely fashion. Let us do this my way." He held out his hand for the compass.

"Ooo, you going to take me to see Galadriel?"

Qyll scowled. "Surely now that Elves live among you Humans, you will seek to portray us in a more realistic and flattering light. Those pop culture specimens were conceived by Humans who had never seen a real Elf before. Pixies, perhaps. A Gnomic or a Mazoku."

Under my breath, I murmured, "He's an angry elf." Which earned me a baleful glare.

He led me into the parkland, far enough that we could no longer hear any traffic. It was a good thing I didn't have to watch the compass so I could concentrate on not tripping over fallen tree limbs. After a few moments, the air changed. It was somehow cooler and older too, as though we were in a part of the woods still wild and unclaimed. Through the leaves, the sky glared, heavy with threatened rain.

Finding beings in Otherwhere is not nearly as easy as it is in Earth. Things aren't precisely linear. Not only that, but time is what you might call 'fluid'. Some parts don't even *have* time—talk about a mindfuck. You could spend a hundred years there, and it would feel like a few seconds. Where Qyll took me was clearly the boundary between Earth and Otherwhere, which is sort of like doing a few grains of cocaine. You aren't hooked yet, but always in danger of going too deep.

"Where are we?" I asked in a hushed tone.

Qyll looked at the compass then back over his shoulder. "I'm not sure, but I believe this is the outer demonkeep. Sort of a vestibule of this part of Otherwhere. We must hurry. The longer we delay, the better the chance of..."

"Of what? Chance of what?"

My tattoos hummed faintly against my skin. I clutched my bag and girded my loins.

"I'm sure I don't have to tell you to stay close. You're only half-Other, and we are in murky waters."

"This isn't my first rodeo, pal," I hissed. "Don't worry about me."

That was almost a complete lie. I'd never been to the Other side of the Rift by myself. I'd been with my mother, an excellent guide and negotiator, and we only went to the Human-friendly parts. My knowledge was more book-learnin' and less practical.

A few more steps, and we came into a huge clearing. In the center, surrounded by a moat, soared a tower so tall, I couldn't see the top. It was made of small round rocks. As we got closer, I saw they were skulls.

On the far side was a bridge. Complete with a troll.

"Marvelous," Qyll said under his breath. "A troll bridge. But this is where we've been led. Let's hope your spell is accurate."

"HALT. NONE SHALL PASS." The creature stood four feet tall and near as wide and looked a hell of a lot like your average fairytale troll—warts, big gnarly feet, the works.

"Good sir, we request—" I began.

"I AM A FEMALE," he... er... she boomed.

Oops.

"Perhaps you will allow me to do the talking," Qyll suggested softly. He grabbed my collar and lifted me so my toes barely brushed the ground.

"Let me go, you big idiot!" I huffed.

"NONE SHALL PASS," the she-troll repeated.

"I request an audience with your master. I have a captive, and am here to collect a bounty."

The trolless shifted on her massive hairy feet and wiped a hand across her dribbling nose.

"I suggest you allow us entrance, madam, lest you risk the wrath of your master."

The troll looked somewhat unconvinced, but also smug. "Don't got a master, then do I? I gots a mistress. And she's loads more powerful'n you is."

"Your mistress is so powerful, she is often mistaken for a master," I piped up.

Trolly puffed out her chest. "Tha's right, innit? The Red Queen is known far and wide for her... her..." She ran out of grand words and stood there blinking.

Ohhh.

Damn. Damn, damn, *damn*. We were on the Red Queen's doorstep.

Thinking I would give the guard a little nudge, I wound up a push spell. I had written it while being pursued by some bullying girls in fifth grade and gleefully had gleefully shoved the blasted Amanda Tilford and Hollyanna Albert halfway across the playground. (They were fine, no harm done. Except, they left me alone for the rest of our days together.) But something went awry when I it let loose on the troll. She flew backward into the air, sailed over the moat, crashed against the tower wall, and fell into the water below. Well, smack my ass and call me Judy.

Qyll dropped me, and we began to run, him half-dragging me along. "What the devil was that? Have you never done magic here?"

"No!" I blurted. "What the..."

"Your magic is more powerful here. That's why powers across the board blossomed after the Rift. Earth is not very magical. Otherwhere is. Power is amplified here." He was following the compass still.

We crossed the bridge. I looked down and spotted the troll flailing in the muddy water.

More troll guards were stationed at the other end of the bridge. I flicked off a few spells, and trolls went flying off the edge like pins at a bowling lane. I think I found a new hobby.

We ran ahead and kept running, until we found ourselves just inside the door to a cavernous room. We skidded to a stop.

It was as if a Vegas nightclub had had a baby with Hell. Dark. Loud. Smelling of burnt things and brimstone.

A couple of grand bars staffed by all manner of creature—typical Vampires and Weres but also a few ghost-like things and several beasts I couldn't identify. In the center, a huge stage sat surrounded by small tables. The stage was currently occupied by some kind of sex show, to which the audience was encouraged to play along. At intervals of twenty and forty feet along the walls were balconies with more tables and what looked like rooms behind them. And above those, soaring high over the crowd, Demon trapeze artists swung and flipped in the spotlights, all of them stark naked. The tables ranged from tiny two-person to enormous banquet-style slabs that could seat twelve. Notable was a large statue best described as a very, very happy satyr. At a table to our left, a couple was making out like there was no tomorrow, and I'm fairly certain there was an orgy going on in the corner, but it was too dark to see very clearly.

Then it hit me. "Wait, this is the Otherwhere side of the Queen of Hearts."

"It would indeed seem so." Qyll narrowed his eyes.

"Have you ever been here?"

He shook his head. "I knew it existed, but no. This is not my typical milieu."

"Oh? And what is?"

Before I could question him further, a voice blared.

"STOP."

In an instant, all movement and noise ceased. At the far end of the room was a wide staircase coated in thick red carpet. Descending it was one of the women who attended Antaura when she'd barged into my shop.

Qyll tensed beside me. He started to say, "Don't do anything stupid—"

"Give me back my blood!" I yelled at the top of my lungs. My voice echoed throughout the vast space.

"Perhaps we should relearn the meaning of, 'don't say anything stupid.'"

One by one, the partygoers turned to me then began to laugh until someone struck up a chant. "GIVE HER BLOOD! GIVE HER BLOOD!" The noise was deafening.

"I was under the impression you wanted to live through this day," Qyll said in my ear through gritted teeth. "It seems I was terribly mistaken."

The Demon woman from the staircase was now in front of us, her face a mask of anger. "I am Vishna. Her ladyship requests your presence in her private chambers."

"Wait," I said. "We're not going anywhere until we know how this works."

A quizzical look settled on Vishna's face. Up this close, I marveled at her caramel skin and onyx eyes. Her black hair was tied in an elaborate braid snaking down one shoulder of a white *sari* but more see-through. Beneath the sheer cloth was a perfect female form, tits to toes. "If you are asking about hospitality, know no harm will come to you in this place. My lady does not do battle in her home and places of business. Despite your ungracious arrival."

Qyll and I looked at each other. Something felt off, but then again, I *was* in a cross-dimensional bar/brothel with a Dark Elf being escorted around by a horned Demon woman. The bar for weird was set pretty low.

"Fine. But people know where we are." I said. "Just FYI."

Vishna gave a curt nod, and we set off after her through the maze of tables. From halfway up the curving staircase, I confirmed that yes, yes there *was* an orgy happening in the corner. Vishna saw me gawping, an amused look on her flawless face. "Would you care to join? There is no need to rush and you are, technically, guests here."

"Um, no. Nope, thank you." I turned to Qyll. "How about you?"

He ignored me and said to Vishna, "Your offer is most gracious."

We went up to the balcony where more people did more orgies. I still wasn't tempted.

Vishna unlocked a door with a key hanging on her bracelet. Inside was a small anteroom, with two enormous armed Demons flanking the door opposite us. One of them had more eyes than I was comfortable with and the other had rows of shark-like teeth. They both held curved golden blades in each of their four hands.

The doorway between them dissolved to reveal an elevator, an old-fashioned kind, lined in mirrors with an ornate gold rail and thick red carpet.

I glanced at Qyll, but his face was as calm as ever. I wiped my sweaty palms on my jeans as we stepped in. The door reappeared, and it felt like the elevator was moving. Vishna stared ahead.

No one spoke.

The elevator opened into a dimly lit room that looked like it came out of the *Modern Evil Castles Catalog*. A bed the size of a swimming pool dominated the middle, decked with sumptuous silk and velvet sheets. Murals of Humans doing unspeakable things with Demons covered the walls. Something I assumed was music for the demonic set played from an unseen source. A fireplace so big you could park a minivan in it crackled with blue flames.

"Your guests, mistress."

A figure rose from the bed and drifted to us. And by that, I mean no feet on the floor.

"Ah, the one and only Tessa Reddick and her partner, Qyll Toutant." Antaura wore a black kimono-style robe cut high on the hip and low on the chest with nothing underneath but a very large pair of breasts barely concealed by the flimsy fabric. The sheet of white cornsilk hair stood out against the dark fabric. Sharp teeth glittered in the gloom. "Come in, get comfortable. Let us talk." She made a grand gesture with a taloned hand. "Now, I hear you have made short work of my door sentinels. I could do with more people like you working for me." The extended sibilance of her speech was lulling and alarming at once.

"Uh... yeah... sorry about that..." I muttered.

Qyll and I sat before the fire on a ridiculously comfortable sofa. She lounged on an identical one across from us, smiling with polite interest. Mohini, Vishna's lookalike, appeared to stand next to her twin.

Antaura looked at us like we were Lunch and Dessert.

"What brings you to darken my door?"

"I want my blood back. Something came to my house this morning and took some."

She laughed. "And what makes you think we have it?"

I grabbed Qyll's hand and held it up to show her the compass. "This. I did a spell and it led me here." As I looked at it, the hand blurred. "It was you, wasn't it? Or, at least, by your orders?"

The Demon looked at me, considering. She tilted her head slowly. "May I see your talisman, Elf?" She reached a hand out, with fingers just a shade longer than normal, with scary-sharp nails. "I promise I will return it unharmed."

She took the compass from Qyll and turned it over in her hands. She smelled it. Then, she stuck out a forked tongue and *tasted* it. "A blood spell," she said with something akin to approval. "I thought you resisted such magics," she purred, batting her eyelashes.

Beside her, Mohini and Vishna hovered like statues, black eyes boring holes in us.

Antaura offered the compass back to Qyll, who took it gingerly between two fingers. I pulled a handkerchief out of my bag and carefully wiped it clean of demon spit.

We sat that way for a long while, the Demon queen appearing deep in thought, the girls doing their statue thing, and Qyll looking relaxed and composed. I scratched my neck. Smoothed my jeans. Picked off the lint. Prepared to launch a volley of spells, just in case. I had a particularly good saltwater spell I was itching to try.

Finally, I rose and said, very clearly, "Look, I don't know what the hell is going on here. But you're going to give me back my blood, or I will bring the *pain*, lady." I pointed at Qyll. "We will. So you either 'fess up, or we'll bring down this house faster than you can say 'hell in a handbasket.'"

I firmly rooted myself to the spot, arms crossed and staring down the Demons. Fake it 'till you make it, right? I felt Qyll gave me an exasperated sidelong look.

After what seemed like hours, the trace of a smile crossed Antaura's face. Then she began to laugh, a deep rumbling sound. "I extend my apologies, Witch Reddick." She stood up with a languid inhuman grace. "I have no doubt of your and your Dark Elf companion's prowess." She drew a fingernail along Qyll's arm as it rested on the couch. "It seems, however, there is a traitor in House Abyzou."

The next few moments moved fast.

In the span of a lightning strike, Antaura was atop Mohini, wrestling her to the floor, digging at her throat. No longer the white-haired humanoid woman, the Red Queen had shifted into her Demon form. Dark purple-red scales covered a long, hairless, muscular body.

The Queen screeched and let out a garbled mess of sounds.

Demonspeak.

"Traitor!" She roared in English. "What is the meaning of this?" Antaura suckerpunched the Demon beneath her, holding her down with webbed seven-fingered claws. A double set of jagged fangs dripped over Mohini's quaking form.

"She speaks your tongue so you might know and understand what you have done," Qyll whispered.

Mohini started shapeshifting.

Basilisk.

Manticore.

A bearlike beast.

Huge scorpion.

A tentacled *something*.

But her Queen held fast. Finally, Mohini shifted into her own true Demon form, a wiry brown-scaled creature with a face full of black beady eyes and a pincer mouth. She screeched in anger and shoved herself up, forcing them both to stand. Their hooves clattered on the stone floor. Dry batlike wings unfolded from Mohini's back.

"You are not fit to be queen of the Abyzou!" Mohini creaked, hovering in the air.

With a snarl, Antaura jumped like a cat after a bird and brought her former assistant down. Mohini swiped claws at her tormentor, slicing four deep lines through the scaly skin. The Queen screamed and responded in kind. Viscous black Demon blood spattered the floor and columns.

Not taking my eyes off the action, I moved to stand behind the couch. Qyll did the same. Vishna watched with a stony face.

The Demons rolled and tumbled around the cavernous room, squalling and slashing. Mohini fell from a leaping arc when the Queen severed one of her wings with a neat slice.

"You should never have been allowed to become queen." Mohini gasped, panting. "*I* was meant to rule. It is *my* birthright."

"You are weak," Antaura said. "The only reason I took you in was because I owed your parents a debt. They were so embarrassed by you."

They spun and dove, writhing and thrashing. Mohini was clearly a worthy foe, but she was smaller than her mistress and with her damaged wing, she was soon overpowered.

"I would have given you whatever you asked," Antaura moaned, almost sorrowfully, right before she ripped out Mohini's throat with her razor teeth.

The student challenged the teacher, and the teacher defended herself.

Staggering away from the still and gruesomely bloodied Mohini, Antaura shifted to her human shape and collapsed on the couch. Breathing heavily, she regarded us. She hadn't put her black robe back on and instead, sat there naked. She might have had a nice rack, had it not been dripping with Demon innards.

"It seems you have done me a great favor, Earth Witch."

I sighed. "It would have been nice to know who she worked with before you killed her."

"Do be still, Tessa, for once," said Qyll under his breath.

The Queen snarled, but it was more bark than bite. "I have no patience for traitors. As Mohini's queen, I had a duty to dispatch her. Thanks to you." She smiled. "Another reason to consider joining us. Those who can do blood magic so skillfully are rare."

"No thanks. But I will just take my blood back, if you don't mind. And my cat."

With a gesture, she offered me the body. It was a hard thing not to slide around on all the goopy Demon bits, but I comported myself admirably as I went to pick up Mohini's clothes, which she'd shed as she turned forms.

After a thorough rifle, I said, "It's not here."

The Red Queen was just closing the black robe around herself. She clicked her tongue. "Vishna, go and see if the Witch's blood and her furry friend are in the traitor's quarters."

While we waited, I got the photos out. She took them with mild curiosity. "Do you know any of these people?"

"This one has been here before." Antaura pointed to Cara Courtland. "She came many times with a group. Lots of little Humans, prowling around. I love Humans. They are simply fascinating."

She kept looking at the photos then nodded, her serpentine face intent. "This man and this woman," she pointed to another photo, "were here asking after Mr. Koby." She pointed to a picture of a middle-aged man looking surly and sunburned in a motorcycle vest and t-shirt. "He was one of my associates."

"What did he do for you?" Qyll asked.

"He was my bodyguard on your side of the Rift."

"Is he Other? Or Human?"

"Like your Witch friend here, he straddled the line. He was born Human, but he made a deal with us. He dwells with the spirits now."

Qyll continued. "Do you know anything about their deaths?"

Vishna returned, followed by Dorcha, who ran full-throttle into me with a throaty purr. While we had ourselves our little reunion, Vishna whispered in the Red Queen's ear. "She says the animal was locked in a cage, but there is no trace of your blood," translated the Queen. Her emerald eyes went wide. "I imagine the traitor knew what you were after and has secreted the vial out. Likely due to your rather reckless entrance, Miss Reddick."

Damn. "Could Mohini have cut through the veil? Easily? As in, could she have made a slit and shoved the blood through without us noticing?"

The Red Queen nodded. "It is possible. She is wily. It's partly why I kept her close. I see I have made a serious mistake." She looked like she was working something out in her mind, then she turned back to me. The servant brought a smoking glass and passed it to the Queen. "I have slain the traitor, but if word of this reaches the lower Demon hierarchies, I will appear lazy. Easily duped. And by a much lesser opponent. It may inspire insurrection. Desertion." She came toward me, her snake-like grace both hypnotizing and terrifying. "You have saved my House today, Reddick. But if you do not find Mohini's contact in three days, I will send someone for you. I do not relish the thought, but I will have your soul and service, to protect myself and my House."

"Come on, Tessa."

185

"Wait, what?" I shook Qyll's hand off my arm. "I just saved your scaly lizard ass and you're threatening me? And what about *her*?" I pointed at Vishna. "How do you know she wasn't in on it too?"

Antaura ran her faintly iridescent fingers down the other woman's skin. "Vishna is my consort. She was with me the night of those murders." They held hands for a moment and shared what I assume was a loving glance but to me, looked vaguely horrifying.

"As for my request. It is merely business, as the Humans say." She sipped her drink. "Don't look at me like that. I will make it worth your while." She drew close and said in a very quiet voice, "If you bring me the name of the one Mohini conspired with, I will tell you what we know about the fire that killed your kinswomen."

My blood turned to ice. "What do you know about it?" I demanded.

She shrugged languidly, smiling. "You will not find out unless you bring us a name, my little witch. And if you don't, you'll be ours anyway."

I gritted my teeth. This is what I get for dealing with Demons.

"Let's go," I snapped at Qyll who was all too happy to oblige.

"I haven't forgotten about you, Elf," she called after us. "You can't hide in Earth forever."

Before I could get a breath, I saw his face. It was in that moment I encountered a little of what the old books called the Dark Elves' *athraigh*. It's like you can see their magical selves. Their soul or essence, or something. When an Elf shows *athraigh*, it is beautiful and terrifying, but it's also a warning to back off. There's no good way to explain it if you haven't seen it. Thank all the tiny gods he only did it for a fraction of a second. I think I would've wet myself if he'd carried on too long. I didn't ask what Antaura meant.

We made our way back through the woods in silence.

Intense silence
As she walked in the room
Her black robes trailing
Sister of the moon
And a black widow spider makes
More sound than she
And black moons in those eyes of hers

Sister of the Moon, lyrics by Stevie
Nicks, Copyright: Welsh Witch Music

CHAPTER SEVENTEEN

That night, I sat in the library working on spells. Dorcha lolled on the chair, grooming herself. From what I gathered, Mohini set a trap for her that included a sleeping potion, carted her off to her rooms, and tricked me with her shapeshifty juju. I think Dorcha was madder at herself for being careless. As I tinkered with a spell that would charm something I had on to throw up a defensive shield on my behalf, should I fail to realize in time something was about to go kaboom, I told her over and over I was just glad she was okay. As yet, neither the spell nor Dorcha's on-the-spot psychological counseling were meeting with wild success.

Iron strong

Shield of will

I scratched out "will" and wrote "grill/till/mill/hill." Little balls of paper littered the floor. I had come up with a couple of other good ones. My invisibility spell was cleaned up and ready, as was my evaporation spell, which comes in handy should one find oneself locked up. All I was missing was the part of the automatic protection spell that made it automatic.

When you write spells, you want to use words that mean something to you. Words that evoke something. I have a list of words I don't use because they outright make my skin crawl, including *belly, hole, nuptials,* and anything with *–ipple*. My favorite words are, admittedly, difficult to work into everyday conversation, much less a spell. I end up sounding like practice sentences in a foreign language book. "Hey, *scofflaw*, did you see that *ominous ocelot* by the *obelisk*? He is in *cahoots* with the *copacetic falcon*. They nearly came to *mysterious fisticuffs*." One day, I vow to work those into a spell.

If you're a beginner, you need to have your spells written down and spellspeak them loudly while focusing your energy like a laser. In time, you memorize the spells, make them part of you like breath or thought, so you don't have to do so much hand-waving and fancy incanting. To the untrained eye, a Witch just throws off a spell with a flick of her wrist or a blink of an eye, but she's just a well-trained practitioner of the craft. This is not to say that, in times of extreme need, you can't just come up with something on the fly. That happens and you improvise your way through it, and you realize it will never be as strong as the ones you've been practicing with. Even for very powerful Witches, it's like trying to play a brand new violin that hasn't been tuned. You can do it, sure, but would you want to?

My wealth of grimoires isn't much help in this department. I need spells that are personal. They'll work for someone else, but not as good as they will for me. It's like having an entire wardrobe of custom-made clothes in colors that look perfect on you. That's why spells you "buy" from shady online sellers aren't very good. One look at my fourth-grade class photo and you'd know a spell advertised in the back of *Which Witch* magazine will not give you a sleek, shiny mane of golden blond hair like the princess of my fourth-grade class Sandy Miller's. It will, however, give you a very poufy and unevenly trimmed shock of frizzy orange ringlets.

Dorcha slunk over and began to bat the paper balls around. "Hey! You leave those alone, you silly cat," I said. She purred and jumped back on her chair, an amused look on her face.

My spellbook was heavily charmed so no one could steal or use it, but I didn't want those junked papers floating around. I collected all the little crumpled-paper balls and took them to the cauldron in the corner of the living room where I burned them to ash with my super-handy insta-ash (trademark pending) spell.

I tidied up and locked all the doors and windows (spiritual and corporeal) and hopped into bed. Dorcha leapt in beside me, turning three circles like a dog and curling into a huge cat-puddle.

Instead of sleep, a hubbub of thoughts intruded my brain. Like the ones about being framed for murdering my coven. In the haze of Lakeland, it was too painful to dwell upon. The emotional wounds took so long to scab, I had already made a firm habit of ignoring them by the time they made an ugly scar. Maybe, I told myself, it was better to just look forward.

I lay awake for hours, willing myself to sleep, and finally gave up. I got out of bed long before dawn, pulled on my running shoes, and lit out for a jog. Dorcha got up too. She didn't want to let me out of her sight after her recent catnapping. Cardio is an important part of being a Witch, even if you are a Witch with a huge gash on her arm and a goose egg on her cranial container. Since my freedom from the hospital, I had not quite gotten back on track with my exercise regimen. Before that, I ran a couple of miles every day and lifted a little weight while watching TV. Occasionally my mom and I had impromptu dance parties, and she would do the pony and the Freddy, while I worked a passable cabbage patch.

You just never know when you'll need to run like hell.

My legs stretched, and the sharp morning air flowed into my lungs. I hadn't been allowed much exercise at the hospital and still felt nearly every jarring step in my bones. Dorcha loped silently along beside me. She wasn't even breathing heavily. Showoff.

My mother called me "BeeBee," shorthand for "Beltane baby." A child conceived at Beltane is considered a gift from the gods, especially a girl-child. It never embarrassed me that my father could have been one of three men with whom my mother celebrated May Day. The term "bastard" didn't mean anything to me until I was much older, and by then I didn't care anyway.

Living in the big house near Central Park, with vast expanses of hardwood floors and wavy glass in the windows, meant hell of a lot more. It was drafty and creaky, and the electricity hadn't been updated since probably the Roosevelt administration (either of them), but it was home. We lived with my aunts and cousins and a revolving cast of close friends and relatives, so many that we were automatically a blood coven, since we were all related in some form or fashion. The cousins from Ireland with their flaming hair, my great-great Aunt Corinna from eastern France who entertained many a politician and statesman in her time. A trio of old Canadian aunts who I firmly believe were the inspiration for Shakespeare's weird sisters.

And of course, my mother. Mama had the most glorious black hair that hung straight to the middle of her back. She had dimples and pale skin and purple-blue eyes. It was no wonder, really, she had a Beltane baby. The wonder was she didn't have more, given her beauty and charm. The one photo I have left of her shows us on our porch, her laughing into the camera and me, arms folded and staring at the lens defiantly, my own hair a blaring red briar patch, as though I dared the camera-machine to just *try* to take my soul.

It was a typically warm humid evening in June five years ago when I bid my goodnights to Mama and the assortment of our brethren in the huge kitchen. The ones who were still awake were sipping wine or tea, reminiscing and gossiping as per usual. I had come over to help with the preparations for Litha, our midsummer celebration. Tired, I simply climbed the stairs to my old attic bedroom and switched on the window air conditioning unit before peeling off my clothes and curling into bed. Chilled air swirled over my body, and I drifted into a contented sleep, dreaming of the *bonyefyres* we would light at a farm out in Bedford, owned by a smaller coven with whom we were invited to celebrate. The dancing and singing and revels would last all night and long into the next day.

When I awoke, I knew instinctively it was the wee hours of the morning. But it was much too warm. And wrong, something was wrong. I found myself in the back garden, the side of my face pressing into the rich soil we used to grow herbs. I was still naked, but caked with mud and smelling of burning wood and hot iron. My vision cleared. Red lights danced across the leaves, and shouting scoured my eardrums. Struggling to my feet, I looked up to see the back windows of my beloved home explode out into the night, fierce flame grabbing at the sky.

Nobody heard me screaming. I staggered toward the house, meaning to fight my way inside. Their names ran through my mind—Violetta, Tansy, June, Victoria, Annie, Althea, Jane-Marie, Mary Cecilia, Heddy, Harmony, Bettina, Zyla, Granny, M'Laine, Mama.

Mama.

In the shifting light of the burning house, I saw I was spattered with blood, along with the dreck from the yard.

Terrified, I ran between the houses toward the front porch. Holly, roses, and azalea scratched at my legs and arms.

A man stepped from the shadows, grabbed me, turned me to him.

He was hooded, his face concealed in darkness, and gave off magic like a furnace gives off heat. He propelled me toward the front yard, shoved me roughly toward a knot of women who fussed over me, then disappeared.

Everyone heard me screaming now. I screamed to find the figure in the hood, to bring me my mama, to put out the damned flames. I was hoarse and sobbing and everything ran together until I sank beneath a wave of unconsciousness.

I have been called many things in my life: bossy, talented, moody, strange. But I had never been called crazy. Mentally unstable. Touched. At the hospital, I was given a mélange of drugs, the psychotropic raft to which I would cling for months. When they were satisfied with my compliance, they let Tina ease me back into consciousness day by day until I could stand to be unmedicated for longer and longer. And when I came up for air, I learned the full and horrifying story.

They said I had started a fire. That the house had been decimated before the conflagration collapsed half the place. Nothing much left but smoldering embers and charred ruins. And me.

The trial went quickly.

The streetlights began to flick out as I ran beneath them. My legs pushed harder and harder as the memories flooded my brain. I had no idea how long I'd been going, but judging by the part of town I was in and the lightening in the east, it had been a while. More than an hour. The homes were narrow and long—shotgun neighborhood. I came to a stop at a corner, breathing heavily, and with a start, realized I was a few doors down from Heather Mumford's house.

The street was still quiet and dim. It was a little early for most regular work folks or early exercisers to be out and about, so I went around the corner to the alley running down the block, Dorcha beside me. Naturally, Heather's place was deserted. The only movement came from the yellow caution tape fluttering in the breeze. I flipped the catch on the gate, ducked, and darted up the back steps. The deadbolt was no match for my lock-picking spell (a gem cultivated in junior high that let me replace mean girl Mandy Nornbock's hairspray with Kool-Aid and then later to steal all of the awful music teacher's vodka, which she wasn't supposed to have in the first place so how could she rat me out?).

The house was gloomy and full of stale, mushroomy-smelling air. All kinds of things I hadn't noticed before. The kitchen was decorated in a heavy dose of florals. A tablecloth bloomed with pink cabbage roses. Needlepointed pillows towered on the couch. A wallpaper border of ivy adorned the walls. Scented candles sat on nearly every flat surface; Demons tended to be self-conscious about smells when they came to Earth. The place looked like some Iowa farmer's grandmother had lived here. Except for the parts where a massive mud beast had tracked in half a ton of filth.

Standing in the dining room, without a horde of police and FBI milling around, I could see now that the golem must have come through the backdoor, ransacked the kitchen, stomped into the dining room, and ended up with Heather in the bathroom. How terrified she must have been, running into probably the only room in the house with a lock, and ending up trapped.

Past the little four-seater table was the hall. Dorcha sniffed everywhere, her ears twitching. I pushed open the bedroom door, ignoring the sign that said this room had been checked already by the investigators. The open closet revealed a rack of neatly organized clothes and shoes in rows. The bed was made and on the table stood a lamp and a stack of books, including the New Earth Bible. I guess the struggle with the golem hadn't made it to the bedroom. On the bathroom wall, the body had been removed, leaving a Heather-shaped space in the mud.

In the front room were cheap pressboard bookshelves and a large desk covered in stacked books and papers. Clearly a laptop had been there and removed. Someone had left the small desk light on, and it shone down on the pages of a thick volume. The open page was nearly covered in a layer of yellow post-it notes with very neat feminine handwriting. More books and papers littered the floor.

I leafed through some of the books, taking care with all the notes and marked pages. There were diagrams and mathematical equations, runes and sigils. Some were newer-looking, some very old, and in varied languages; I saw Latin, English, Old English, German, and a squiggly script I didn't recognize.

I sat down and started sifting through one of the stacks on the floor. Then anther. Dorcha prowled around the room, sniffing.

Then, I noticed something I definitely did recognize. It was the book my little photocopy had come from. The photocopy I'd found at the botanical garden. From the book Mr. James H. Patterson Esquire Junior had sold to Cara Courtland. The book she'd used to conjure golems.

Then the back door squeaked open. Swell.

SEND THE TRESSPASSERS BACK TO HELL

Bumper sticker

CHAPTER EIGHTEEN

Dorcha's head shot up in alarm. "Hide," I hissed. She leapt at the little flowered loveseat and midair, shrunk to her housecat size. Then she slipped neatly underneath and blended into the shadows.

The room didn't afford much in the way of hidey-holes for me so I invoked my invisibility spell. The thing about invisibility spells... it's hard to tell if you are invisible without a mirror. I wedged myself between two bookshelves under a high window and tried to think invisible thoughts.

Imagine my surprise when none other than Rev. Dr. James H. Patterson, IV, Esq. walked down the hall past the door.

Fighting the urge to speak, I took a slow breath. What the *Hell!*

I could clearly hear his footsteps (not much for sneaking, that one) as he checked the other rooms and when he came back, he glanced over his shoulder, then around. When his eyes turned to stare right at me, I could see his brain working to make sense of what had to be conflicting information. He could probably see *something*, but his brain was telling him the house was empty, because it *should* be empty.

Patterson gathered up several of the books on the desk, reading the titles and discarding them onto the chair. A few went into a tote bag emblazoned in orange with, I GAVE TO THE FUND FOR THE ARTS.

He prowled around the room, picking and poking.

I said, in my most authoritative voice, "Returning to the scene of the crime?"

I kid you not, the man jerked, squealed like a wee little girl, and dropped the bag, which thumped on the floor. I dropped the invisibility spell and put my hand on my hip while he recovered his breath.

"What the hell are you doing here?" he whispered.

"Was it you? Sending nasty ghosts to my house to possess my guests?" I demanded. He managed to look outraged. "Speak up, sir." I know I couldn't appear that imposing, still a little sweaty and in my running gear, hair sticking out everywhere. But he shook like a leaf in a hurricane.

"I just... I came to get some books," he stammered.

"Oh? Which ones?" Patterson looked positively terrified now.

"I, uh... I... uh, I..." He fumbled and mumbled. I thought for a second he was going to make a break for it.

"Books on ...?" I casually pried open the volume I was still holding. "On, say, ancient rituals of the Kabbalist Jews? Maybe a Gnostic spell book or two?"

A teeny spark of understanding kindled in my mind. Like when you guess the phrase on *Wheel of Fortune*, but you need Vanna to turn over a couple more letters, just to be sure.

"Yes. I mean, no. I mean, she had it from Mrs. Courtland. Heather called and said I should come take it back. So no one else can use it." He swallowed and grew bolder, the fear ebbing from his piggy face. "I don't have to tell you anything." He picked up the tote. "Give me that book."

"You were going to sell it, weren't you? That's called double-dipping. You gave up your rights when you took the money. All sales *final*."

"She's dead! God rest her soul, but she's dead. What does she need this for now?"

Not carrying anything but my house key meant I couldn't show him my badge. I went on anyway. "I'm FBI. And I'm a Witch. So, spill! Who wants this book, James?"

He winced. He appeared about to run, or hit me, or both.

I took a deep dramatic breath and said, "*Enflamous!*" The tote caught fire. It's a neat trick—something only *appears* to burn. It's not even hot. This is great for birthday parties. And, apparently, frightening middle-aged men. He squealed again. Dropped the bag *again*.

His face was a satisfying swirl of horror. "Oh God, oh God, please don't kill me," he babbled as he held his arms up in defense.

"Just tell me what I need to know, Jimmy."

He closed his eyes. "If you don't kill me, they will," he whispered. "Give me the book, I'll tell you what I know."

"Hmmm..." I feigned thinking with a finger to my chin.

Dr. Reverend Patterson gave a little grunt of relief.

"I'm going to tell you then I'm going to move away. I'm done with this. Done, do you hear me? I'm moving to London." He sniffed. "I can do much better with my business there than in this backwoods—"

"Yeah, yeah, save it for the Queen. Spill it."

"Heather was an acquaintance. We've known each other for several years. Anyway, she invited me to this Bible study she was going to. I thought, hey, why not? Maybe I would meet someone interesting."

"You don't go to Church of the Earth?"

Patterson shook his head. "I'm agnostic by way of the Quakers." He pushed his glasses up on his nose. "The group, the Bible study, they were just really... fringe. I went maybe twice, that was enough. I heard them talking about how they wanted to build an army for Jesus to defeat the evil that the Rift brought to us. Going on about being the hands of God. The army of God. I thought this was going over the top, to be perfectly honest. Not my cup of tea, really. But then Cara wanted this book. Heather mentioned it to the group that I deal in books, and one thing led to another. Cara came to me because, well, my shop, and said she thought it was interesting, nothing more. Kind of like when kids play with Ouija boards or something. She felt like she was doing something a little bit dangerous but not enough to be bad."

"But Ouija boards really *are* dangerous," I said.

"Yes, well... So, Heather called yesterday. She was scared. I don't know what about, but she said she wanted me to take the book back. Didn't say why. I told her I'd come over today."

"So you broke in when she didn't answer?"

He shook his fat, bald head and pushed his glasses up again. "I saw someone walking around in here. I thought it was her. Turns out it was you." His tone had grown imperious. "I did not do anything to Heather. Or Cara. I sell books. That is all. I don't know how all of this happened."

You know how people say 'it hit me like a ton of bricks'? Yeah. It all came rushing to me at once—the Arcana, the mud, the murders, the church, Charlie Bartley's request.

"It's not an accident," I said, half to myself.

"Excuse me?" Patterson asked.

"It's not an accident. Not a coincidence. Antaura, Gardener West, the whole kit and caboodle, it was a *plan*."

We stared dumbly at each other for a minute.

"Okay, can I just have that book now?" he inched toward me. I held up my hand.

"Wait. Why were some of the victims from Antaura's entourage? Like Ben Koby." Electricity lit up my brain. "He was a Demon. Bacchus Demons. Jezebel Demons. With Humans."

The bookman wiped a hand on his forehead. He was getting pretty sweaty. "Heather said they were practicing. Cara and the other people. They wanted to go after the Red Queen, but they didn't know how to work the golem." He pointed to the book. "That thing is so old, there are pieces missing. No one can translate some of that stuff. I didn't know that's what she was going to do, I swear." He looked at me with pleading eyes. "And I don't know what happened to Heather."

"It wasn't an accident."

Patterson looked torn between running away as fast as his pasty white legs could carry him, and trying to wrest the book from me.

"What are you going to do with this if I give it back?" I held the book aloft.

I could see the struggle between "make a lot of money" selling to a mystery bidder and "wash my hands of this whole thing" play out on his pale face.

Resignedly, he said, "Burn it. Burn it, and then I'm moving. I'm done here."

"Good answer. Let's go."

I grabbed his arm and dragged him into the backyard, where a rickety charcoal grill stood in the grass. I lifted the lid and set the book on the grate.

Raising a hand, I looked to Patterson. He nodded vigorously, so I brought my hand down and lit the thing on fire. Not fake fire this time, the real deal. It caught surprisingly fast and was soon a smoldering pile of ash.

"Run along, nerd. You've done the right thing."

He turned to go.

"Oh wait," I called. "Can I catch a ride? And my cat, too?"

"The Lord has rejected you because you welcome foreigners from the East who practice magic and communicate with evil spirits" **(Isaiah 2:6)**

CHAPTER NINETEEN

An hour later, I was freshly showered, wearing jeans and a clean shirt, and pulling up to Charlie Bartley's house. I managed to convince Dorcha to stay home, on account I was just going on a fact-finding mission. Thankfully I'd written down the address from his check. It was a nice two-story in an upper-middle class neighborhood in Prospect. The yard was tidy and kept, and a newish black BMW sat in the drive.

"What... why are you here?" He yanked me inside and slammed the front door.

"Charlieeeee, you got some 'splainin to doooo," I said.

"You weren't supposed to come *here*. To my house." His panic was growing.

"Is Ann home?" I sauntered into the great room. All the houses built around the same time in the 90's had these 'great rooms.' Big living room/dining room/kitchen combo areas. I sat on the couch, running my hand over the stiff plaid wool upholstery.

"No, but she's due home any second." He looked out the window. "Where's your car?"

"Hidden." I waved dismissively. "Don't worry. Come here. Let's talk." I stretched out, hands behind my head.

Charlie sat on the edge of an armchair at my feet. The place was super-tidy and full of what I suddenly realized were very patriotic, Earther items. An oil painting of George Washington kneeling in a ray of sunlight in a forest hung over the fireplace. Several wood carvings of trees sat on the baby grand piano. Framed quotes from the Bible about the Earth hung on the walls. Somewhere in the house, a radio broadcast a certain ultra-conservative Earther talking about how the Fanger-loving President was letting the country go to hell in a handbasket.

The mental gymnastics these Earther types have to go through to push their line of thinking...

"See, the thing is, Charlie, I think I've got this all figured out. You came to me because you know what Ann's been up to. You know she's got a rootin' tootin' Bible-thumping posse of Earthers out for blood." I propped my feet on the glass-topped coffee table. "And you wanted me to run interference for you." The color drained from Charlie Bartley's face.

"The problem now that is that the Queen of Abyzou is going to kill *me* if I don't bring Ann down. *Ann* is going to kill me if I don't get my blood back from her and stop her from building her mudmen army. The way I see it, if you don't 'fess up, more people are going to die, and there's a good chance one of them might be your wife. Or you. Or me, and I'm not letting that happen."

Charlie kept shaking his head. He looked more like a kid caught with his hand in the candy jar than a guy helping his wife do things that were illegal six ways to Sunday. "Look, I met Ann in seminary school. We had several classes together, eventually got paired up for a project. I couldn't believe the luck. I'd seen her around, and I thought she was, you know... just a great girl.

"We had the same values, came from the same kind of upbringing. We're both PKs. Preachers' kids, and that's a real point of common ground for us. We went on our first date to a worship music concert and were married a year later, just before I started dental school. We felt like God brought us together." He stopped and looked out the back windows to a yard with an elaborate swing set.

He hadn't mentioned kids. Did they have kids? I scrolled through my memories of our conversation. I would guess if they had, they'd be grown and have kids of their own.

"After three years, nothing was happening, so we tried IVF." He shook his head. "Back then, it was a lot less sophisticated than it is now. She went through so much. The shots, the miscarriages, the doctors' appointments, the waiting. We were hopeful. I even built a playset in the backyard. Then, the Rift happened. As Christians, our world just... well, it was hard. And things were different with her."

"Different how?" I asked.

He pushed a hand through his hair. "She started blaming the Rift for her infertility. Saying God was punishing Humans for turning away from Him by sending Hell on Earth and that no God would want a child raised after the Rift. But finally, at long last, she got pregnant. We had two eggs left, and she was going to have twins." His face hardened.

"Okay, that's good. Twins is good."

He gave me a sharp look. "She lost them though. Late. Five months. It was still so early after the Rift, nobody thought about the dangers of an open physician's office. They were all still in hiding."

Oh shit. I started to see where this was going.

Before the Rift, there were no disclosure regulations, no background checks. Nowadays, you have to prove you are what you say you are—Other or Human. There are 'Humans only' doctors' and 'Other-friendly schools.' NO SMOKING signs have been replaced with NO MAGIC ALLOWED plaques. Laws were enacted about discrimination and segregation and exsanguination and all kinds of things.

"What happened?" I almost didn't want to know the answer.

"A nurse. At the doctor's office. She was a... a lamia."

Well, that made sense now. Lamias are nasty work, Human women who lost their children (usually in some horrible or gruesome way) and in their overwhelming grief, twisted themselves, their essences, into something evil. They kill other women's children in various and sundry ways. Before the Disclosure Laws and the Acts of Living Being

Protection were created, such creatures could get jobs in hospital nurseries and obstetricians' offices and voila, a veritable buffet of babies to feed their hate.

"So a lamia killed your unborn children, and Ann went crazy?"

Charlie nodded. "She was just broken. I don't know how else to explain it. We joined Gardener West's church when we got married but after that, her faith and her outright hatred for Supernormals took on this incredible importance. She was always talking about the evil that are the Rift-walkers and how Humans had to rise up and fight."

I've heard of lots of women who've done worse after being unable to have children by any means. The church can't help you, the doctors can't help you, so you turn to something else.

"We thought about adoption, but Ann really wanted a child of our own. She had this bizarre fear that if we adopted or weren't careful, she'd have a mixed baby. Half-Human, half-Other, and she didn't want that."

I huffed out a disgusted breath. "I'm not saying it's never happened—never say never, right? But that's almost impossible."

He shrugged. "I don't pretend that her fears were rational."

"Okay. Go on."

"She started this Bible study after the fifth miscarriage. I thought it was good for her. Got her out of the house, talking with other people. Like therapy. But Gardener West, he's very intense. Charismatic, as we used to say. I just wanted Ann happy.

"The last few months, I just haven't known what to do. I went to one of her meetings a while back, to see what it was like, and they were all like her. Just as vehement, just as vitriolic. I thought, 'This isn't what we should be like. This isn't right.' But any time I questioned her, she would fly off the handle, then give me the silent treatment for days."

He looked at me like he was just now seeing me there in his living room. "You've got to understand, Miss Reddick. I love my wife."

"You love her so much, you went against your beliefs and hired me," I said.

"She's so angry. And bitter. She's not the woman I married. But I still love her." I shifted in my seat and waited. "They had this plan to convert people. They started at that club, the Red Heart place. She got more and more secretive. When we do speak, she... she talks differently."

"What do you mean?"

He shrugged. "She uses words I've never heard her use. And... she even sounds different. Just the tone of her voice isn't the same. It's like when you call someone on the phone and her sister or mother answers. They sound like her, but they aren't."

Well, *that's* weird.

"I don't know what's been going on. I keep going to work most days just to focus on something else, to forget we're ships passing in the night. These days."

"Yeah well, her ship's about to run aground." I looked around the home Ann and Charlie had built. A surge of compassion bumped up against my fury. Clearly, old Charlie here loved her with every fiber of his being. I wasn't sure, however, that she still loved him. Or recognized anything except her own desire for revenge.

"She wants to get back at Otherwhere somehow. And in her mind, that means starting by bringing the Red Queen to her knees. And Cara Courtland, she was just as bad. For a long time, I thought it was Cara who called the shots." He shook his head. "They were thick as thieves."

"Let me ask a question, just for my own edification. How do you arrange to kill someone, then get around the whole 'thou shall not kill' line? Because to me, that just seems like a no-brainer."

Charlie grimaced. "Her attitude has been that she is vanquishing Demons, which are not people in the eyes of the Lord. The Bible is quite clear that it's okay to kill in the Lord's name. 'You shall pursue your enemies, and they shall fall by the sword of your hand.'"

"What about Heather Mumford? Dana Sykes? They didn't do anything wrong. And what about the *bakemono* family? They weren't Human, but they were innocents, including *children*? Even the horses! She practiced on defenseless animals that had nothing to do with any of this." Fire rose in my chest again. "What about them?"

He stared at me in horror. "Oh God. I didn't know about them. I didn't know about the children." He swallowed hard, growing paler. "She says her army is the hand of the Lord."

Any compassion I felt solidified into anger. "That's just the kind of religious bullshit that starts wars, Charlie. Remember the Crusades? Just for starters. Seriously, I don't know how you assholes live with yourselves."

"I know," he whispered. "Oh God, I know. I'm sorry. I'm so sorry."

"Charlie, she's calling Demons to animate her golems, then she sics them on people. Humans. And Others who didn't do anything to deserve it."

"I'm weak," he blurted. "I know that. It's why I asked you to help me. It's why I can't go to anybody else."

"You have to tell me where she is. I need to find her."

Charlie nodded and got up. "Come with me. Her cell phone has one of those tracking devices. I can look her up."

Turns out, he'd been keeping a list of her habitual destinations since he'd come to talk to me. The list was short. I recognized Heather Mumford's address among them.

"Here. This is out on River Road. Near the conservatory site." He pointed. "This is the church, and that one I don't know. My money is on this one near the site."

"If you see her or you talk to her, you must call me," I said. "Must. Do not pass go. Do not collect two hundred dollars. Call me."

"I will. And thank you."

I could only muster a glare before I stormed out.

I called Qyll from the road and filled him in on my conversation with Charlie.

"It's not Cara Courtland who was running the show. It was Ann Bartley."

"Right. Ann's looking to take down Antaura, and she found a chink in the armor," I said.

"Mohini was going to take the Queen's place when Ann conveniently killed her," Qyll mused. "But Ann couldn't have known that was the plan."

"Yeah. My theory is, Mohini and Ann struck a deal, but they were both double-crossing each other."

There was a pause as Qyll considered this. "What are you going to do now?"

"Research. Lots and lots of research."

*By far the most intriguing group I've met
so far is the Dark Elves. Perhaps the most
like Humans I've encountered, yet they are
vastly different. Their preference for
ritual and understated pageantry is
peculiar and entertaining, to say the
least. I do hope to make my hosts'
hospitality a regular item on my calendar.*

—From Cornelia Dellhart's **Walking in the
Night Forest**

CHAPTER TWENTY

At home, I kicked off my boots and got some bourbon. Then it was back to hitting the books. Dorcha padded in behind me and lay stretched across the library doorway.

I started out sitting down. Then I got up. Sat in the armchair. Then the floor.

"What do I know?" I asked aloud. "Not enough," was the reply. My own. Which, yes, kind of indicated I was going batty.

I spread out what I had on the table: my laptop, the bedraggled page from the conservatory site, a pile of notes. I was missing something.

I don't know how long I stood there, staring at the table, taking sips of Woodford, mind wandering all over. So lost was I that I almost blasted a hole through the table with a spell when my phone went off.

"Tessa," was all I got, then sobbing.

"Who is this?" I looked at the number. Seemed vaguely familiar.

More garbled crying and then, "It's Professor March. Help me."

Handily, the line disconnected after that, and my subsequent calls went unanswered.

I prowled the library, then threw open a trunk, desperately hoping to see something I could take as a weapon. I had no idea what we would find and I wanted *something* besides salt and water. Nana Fairfax always said, "A Witch should always have her spells. And a gun." I thought of her when I dug out the little black wooden box. "Thanks, Nana," I muttered, tossing the contents into my bag. Boots back on, and several odds and ends shoved in my bag and cloak, Dorcha and I raced to the fancy condo in record time.

I couldn't imagine what the professor had gotten himself into, and even more mysterious was why he'd called me. The building was quiet, at least the lobby and halls were. At March's door, I stopped and listened. I could hear crying, and someone repeating, "Please, just go."

"You ready?" Dorcha ducked her head, her furry face steely. "Good, because I have no idea what is going on. Or why the hell he didn't just call the police."

The door was unlocked and swung open easily. I had a small bag of Elisha salt at the ready, and more in my cloak. Early evening sunlight streamed in on the bizarre scene. It looked like the same place I'd been to before, except rearranged. And a disaster. All the furniture in the living room area had been pushed back. A layer of topsoil spread between the couch and credenza featured a lesser Seal of Solomon done in white spray paint. The empty soil bags and paint cans lay in a heap. A package of clay sat nearly empty. An assortment of magical and religious artifacts clustered on the coffee table nearby—a crucifix, black candles, a little stone statue of something.

"Professor March?"

A choked sob, then he was crawling out from under the dining room table.

"Oh, Christ on a cracker, March, put on some damn clothes!" I slapped a hand over my eyes. "Why are you *naked*? Holy shit."

"I'm sorry," he whined. "Some rituals call for purity in the practitioner, sometimes assumed to mean... I thought the ritual would go better if I... never mind. Here, I've got my robe on. It's okay now."

I peeled one finger at a time away to behold him in a long chestnut bathrobe. He was a mess. Crazy eyes. Matted hair. Glasses askew.

I closed the door gently. "You want to tell me just what in the name of all the tiny gods is going on here?"

"I tried it. I had to try it." He wiped his face with a brown sleeve.

"Try what? Swinging? Nudism? What?"

"The golem ritual."

"You *what*?" I couldn't keep from shrieking. "How did you even...? Where is the...? Holy shit." All words failed me. Dorcha growled very softly in reproach. "But you *told* me..."

"You don't understand." He sat on the edge of a dining chair. His dandelion hair was caked with sweat and muck. "I couldn't pass this up. Once I thought it could be done, I *had* to try it. I had to. Don't you see? I've only read about this stuff. My entire career. And the chance to be part of the magic of ritual? I had to. You have to see that."

I crossed my arms. "No, I don't see. But let me take a guess—something went sideways and you need me to clean up the mess. Why didn't you just call the police? They would have called in the SMARTies. The magic police."

He began to protest but sunk back into the chair, defeated. "I didn't know that. I also don't know where my phone is." He looked around, the picture of an absent-minded professor.

"I'll call someone. How did you even get the ritual in the first place? I specifically took back the paper."

March looked sheepish. "I have an eidetic memory. Between seeing the copy you had, and what I've learned over the past forty years, I thought I could work it out. Reverse engineer things, right? I just wanted to do a little one. But something went wrong."

There was a crash from down the hall. He cowered. "It's loose in here," he whispered, eyes huge. "I can't get rid of it. I can't control it either."

"Hang on." I sent a text to Qyll. *"Urgent: meet me at Professor Johan March's condo, 1704 Witherspoon Street. Should probably bring the SMARTies."*

"Well, let's go see what we're dealing with. Lead the way." I longed for my slouchy yoga pants and the rest of my bourbon, but it would have to wait. "Why are all the lights off?"

March looked over his shoulder. Somehow even his profile managed more sheepishness. "I thought I could hide better in the dark. I didn't realize it was still, you know, daytime again."

I sighed. *Amateur.*

"How long have you been at this?"

"What's today?"

"Tuesday."

"Three days? I started Saturday night."

He was probably going to need a night in the hospital for dehydration at the very least. Before he got arrested for reckless use of ritual magic, unlicensed spirit summoning, and exposing himself to a lady.

Like a dead man walking, he led me down a corridor, past his office where we'd talked before. Dorcha's nose worked overtime. A loud whump on the door at the end of the hall gave a hint as to our destination. March went flat against the wall, pointing, "There. In the guest room." He turned and squeezed his eyes closed.

"You big baby," I muttered as I stomped past him.

The lights were off, but there was enough sunshine left so the room wasn't very dark. As soon as the door opened, heavy footsteps schlepped toward me and something leapt at my face.

Dorcha intercepted it about four inches from my nose.

"Let's see what we have here." I expected something quite a bit more formidable-looking, given the Professor's state. But when I bent down to shine the light between Dorcha's paws, I laughed. Honest to goodness laughed, as much from surprise as anything else. It was Barbie-doll sized, with a fairly well-rendered and androgynous face—nostrils, eyebrows, a smile; even the suggestion of clothing.

"This is what's gotten your panties in the twist?" I asked over my shoulder. "Did you even try to get the *shem* out?"

Dorcha gave a startled growl.

The cat struggled to keep her paws planted on the thing's shoulders. Rightly so, because the was... inflating, swelling like a parade balloon. It made this strange gurgling rumble, like a pipe about to burst.

The golem swiveled its happy little face toward me. It wasn't so happy anymore. Snakelets slithered out of its head like Medusa's hair.

The eyes narrowed and many sets of teeth grew in the once-smiling mouth. Hands distended to multi-fingered claws. By this time Dorcha and I had backed into the hall, the damn golem grew so tall, its snakes nearly brushed the 15-foot ceiling. Like a terrifying version of Alice in the White Rabbit's home. It bent down to peer at us.

There was a yelp behind me. Professor March peeked around the wall from the living room. "You try getting the *shem* out of that thing. Every time I get close, it freaks out. What do we *do*?"

The golem chuckled. I don't mean like your uncle snickers when someone tells a lame joke. I mean, deeply disturbing, I'm-going-to-skin-you-alive-maybe chuckle.

I swallowed hard.

"Who are you?" My voice came out as a strained squeak. I cleared my throat and tried again. "Hey. Buster. Little introductions here?"

The thing folded itself nearly in half, stepped into the hall, and unfolded again. Impossibly tall and slender, with that leering visage. Dorcha pushed against me, ready to pounce.

And then it spoke.

It spoke with a voice made of nightmares and dark corners and places you should never be. "We are called Paraplexius."

We?

It swayed above me like a garish tree. The hall stank of rot and foul earth.

That was easy. Maybe too easy. "Nice to meet you, sir. Uh, *sirs. Ma'ams.* May I ask what it is you are doing here?" *Get it talking while I figure this out.*

Paraplexius squatted (so help me tiny gods, *squatted down*). "We come to be free." He (it? she?) watched us with hollow eye sockets, his breath laced with the smell of rotten eggs.

I looked back at March. He shrugged helplessly and pulled back into the dining room so all I could see was one bespectacled eye.

"Useless," I told him. "Okay, Paraplexius, I'm so glad you could come for a visit, but your time is up and we'd like you to go home now."

Its head swayed thoughtfully. Then it said, very slowly, "No."

"Oh, is that how you want to play it?" I stalled for time. "Look, just go on back to, uh, wherever you came from, and send us a postcard when you get there." I made a shooing motion while I racked my brain for the protocol on this. "We can, umm... schedule your next visit and all. To get you acclimated." Okay, okay, okay! *Think*. How to send spirits back? Exorcism? Damn. I couldn't remember the whole rite. Probably just chanting in Latin wouldn't work.

"Have you been summoned to Earth before?"

"We have."

There was some kind of delay between my words and this thing's reactions. It grinned its terrible grin while I waited, gingerly easing a hand into my bag and feeling around for the anyshooter. I wasn't getting anywhere with my Barbara Walters impersonation. We were going to have to get serious.

"Why are you here?"

Pause. Horrible grin.

"We come to be free."

"Okay, I hear you, but why won't you just, you know... *leave*?"

Pause. And this time it looked down the hall toward the spot where March had been. The hideous smile dropped. "We are caged. The master must spill the blood to unlock the cage."

I found what I was looking for and slowly took my hand out, clutching the anyshooter, trying to steady myself. "March. That's you, the master." I turned so the Professor was on my left at the end of the hall and Paraplexius on my right. "When you made your golem, did you use anything like hair, or fingernails, or something like that?" I gently snicked open the cylinder and felt a tiny trill of relief at what I saw.

"No. I didn't think of it." He sounded a little bummed about that.

"Has Paraplexius here been trying to kill you? Or hurt you in some way?"

"No," March squeaked.

That meant two things: one, Paraplexius couldn't leave the host golem body or March's apartment. And two, March hadn't done any sort of blood magic, although he'd *clearly* done something wrong. *Typical. Men can't follow a recipe to save their lives.*

I clicked the cylinder back into place, cocked the gun, and pulled the trigger. I'm a terrible shot, so it was lucky that I was so close and Paraplexius was so large. The bullet sank into its arm. After a long breath, it looked down at the hole.

Then it started screaming, the sound like ten thousand talons on a chalkboard the size of Texas.

Dorcha and I backed the rest of the way down the hall into the living room. Paraplexius strode out, its over-large mouth wide. *So. Many. Teeth.*

Damn.

"What did you do?" March squealed. He dove back under the dining table.

Paraplexius stomped toward me and took a swing. It was as surprised as I was to see that the arm meant to clobber me had melted off, just above where my bullet lodged.

"I shot it with holy water, I think." There must've been one in the breech. No time for regret when a mud-Demon-thing is chasing you.

Dorcha scrambled out of its way as it tried to kick her.

"How do I make it go back to Barbie-doll size?" I screamed.

"You can't! I think when it perceives a threat, it grows into this thing." Yeah, helpful this wasn't.

Ready. Aim. Fire.

I managed to hit its neck this time. Dorcha circled to my right, in case it tried to back out.

The mud-thing stopped moving and turned its head toward me. No time to lose.

I cleared my throat. "Let's try this again. Where are you from?"

"The Edge."

"What is your name?"

When it spoke, it was like two dozen people saying their names, but in unison they rumbled, "We are many."

"Did someone send you?"

"No."

"Did someone call you?"

It wavered, like it wasn't sure how to answer.

"Did someone summon you?"

"Yes." Then, "No."

"Why can't you leave this place?"

"Bound by the circle. Protect the master. No sacrifice was made."

That brought me up short, but I pressed on.

"How do we make you go back where you came from?"

It swayed, like a drunkard after a few too many. It took so long to respond, I thought the *alithis* had worn off.

"Not all of us will go."

In a sterner voice, I asked, "How do we make you *all* go home and leave us alone?"

I knew we didn't have much time left.

The golem sort of shivered, as though it had gotten a sudden chill. Then it spoke in a totally different voice. This time it sounded much more Human. "For God did not spare even the angels who sinned. He threw them into hell, in gloomy pits of darkness, where they are being held until the day of judgment."

Two things happened at the same time. Qyll opened the door and the *alithis* wore off. The golem started screaming and swinging at us with its one good arm. It missed and shattered the crystal chandelier over the dining table. March started crying again.

"Where the hell have you been? We have to get the *shem* out," I said by way of greeting, simultaneously tossing the Elisha salt to Qyll and shoving the anyshooter in my bag.

Qyll nodded. "SMART is on the way."

As Dorcha paced in front of the golem, trying to distract it, I found a little paint left in a spray can and freshened up the seal of Solomon, which had taken a beating in the last few days. I also tried to sweep the dirt into a neater circle. Behind me, Qyll and Dorcha set out to remove the *shem*. The golem was still in fighting shape, but it was a pretty skinny thing to begin with and had also been through a lot in the last three days. Dorcha's claws made quick work of the remaining limbs. Fortunately, it didn't seem able to regenerate quickly.

Once I finished with the seal, I hurried over to help. With the water from a bottle in my cloak, I doused my hand. The torso, head, and one thigh sat snapping at my partner and cat. In one swift motion, I plunged my holy-watered fist into the back of its head, fishing for the paper.

Qyll and Dorcha sprang forward to pin down its face while I dug around in the freezing muck. We were filthy in moments. It was like the worse game show in history.

When my fingers closed over the paper, I pulled my hand free. Whatever was in the golem flowed toward the Seal and vanished. I decided it went back to wherever it came from, because that was a convenient thing to decide, lacking the evidence to the contrary.

Holding the shem over my head like a prizefighter, I let out a whoop. Panting, all of us, we gave a collective sigh of relief.

March crawled out of his hole. "Tessa, what was that gun you used?"

"You have a gun?" Qyll frowned.

I grinned. "The anyshooter? It was my Nana's. Very rare. It shoots anything, provided you have the right bullets. The first one was holy water, which was a surprise to everybody. Me included. The second one was what I was hoping for—*alithis*."

"Truth serum? I didn't think that existed anymore."

"I don't think it does, but this is from before it went extinct. It's also like a tranquilizer for supernormals. Very expensive, if you can find it. This was my last one, I think. I probably should've saved it for something more important." I glared at March. "It's old and there wasn't much in there. I wasn't sure it would work at all, let alone the two minutes we got. It was my hail Mary."

"What did it tell you?"

"Several interesting things, but here's the most interesting: it's definitely *not* a good guy. First of all, that thing stank like I don't even know. And it kept talking about a blood sacrifice. A real golem—a friendly, normal one—is summoned to defend its maker. It doesn't smell like Satan's ass crack and ask for a blood sacrifice." I speared March with another glare. "If anything, you at least confirmed that this particular recipe includes a secret ingredient: Demons. Way to go, Martha Stewart."

We sat there, all pretty much filthy, but glad to have this behind us. Well, *I* was glad. March, maybe, not so much. Because, you know, a ton of legal trouble.

Of course, the idyll didn't last long.

"Well, well, well. If it isn't little Tessa Reddick back to her old tricks."

Standing in the door was Gideon, and behind him what looked like the entire SMART team.

"Oh, fuck."

The absence of snakes in Ireland gave rise to the legend that they had all been banished by St. Patrick. However, all evidence suggests that post-glacial Ireland never had snakes. One suggestion, by fiction author A.L. Lesh, is that "snakes" referred to the serpent symbolism of the Druids during that time and place, as evinced on pottery made in Gaul. Lesh connects tattoos of snakes on Druids' arms as the way in which, in the legend of St. Patrick banishing snakes, the "story goes to the core of Patrick's sainthood and his core mission in Ireland."

—A Short History of Witchcraft, Herbert Carmichael

CHAPTER TWENTY-ONE

n the ensuing commotion, all of these things happened, not necessarily in this order:

The SMARTies secured the apartment.

March started crying again.

I yelled at Gideon for always being in the wrong place at the wrong time.

Crime scene photographers showed up.

Neighbors were shooed away.

Gideon gleefully announced I was "a very bad girl indeed."

EMS took March to the hospital.

Qyll called Pryam.

I tried to explain things to Gideon.

We all had to go in for questioning the following day.

I formed a theory.

After I finished talking with one of the SMARTies, I found Qyll flashing his badge at Gideon. "I don't think we've had the pleasure. Special Agent Qyll Toutant. FBI. I'm sure you're aware Agent Reddick is assisting in a case involving Humans and Others. I trust you know we have an agreement about her with the Arcana permitting those of Other status to aid in cases such as this, pursuant to the addendum A, appendix B, of the Rift Accords?"

I really truly thought Gideon was going to haul off, and punch Qyll. His fists balled up so hard, they went as white as his suit. He practically quivered with anger.

"Well of course, but she isn't allowed... She can't just..." Gideon waved his hands around at the demolished apartment. I half-expected him to say, "Curses! Foiled again!"

"While I apologize for any possible oversight or *miscommunication*, Miss Reddick is still prohibited from summoning Demons."

"She summoned nothing tonight. Except me."

While they bickered, my cell phone tweeted. I could tell from the ringtone that it was Charlie Bartley. "Pardon me while y'all argue bureaucracy, I'm going to answer this."

I backed into the hall outside where it was quieter.

"She's going to do something big," Charlie's voice sounded strange.

"How do you know?"

"She told me. She said she's going to raise Hell in the name of our one true God tonight. She locked me in a closet. She didn't know I had my cell phone in my pocket. Oh, Lord save her. Jesus help us." He moaned.

"Wait, okay, calm down. Just calm down. Where did she go? Do you know?"

"You have to hurry. They're at the conservatory site."

"Do I need to come get you out of the closet?"

It was as though he hadn't thought that far. "Yes. That would be good."

"I'm on my way."

God, I was tired. But tired would have to wait.

Qyll and Gideon were in the living room, a tense silence between them.

"I see I was a little hasty in my accusations," Gideon said, his expression sour. "I'll just be on my way. Call if you need anything." And he vanished before anyone could say anything else.

EMS had loaded March up and taken him to the hospital. As they wheeled him out, crying, he gave me a little wave.

"Hey, Q, we've got to scoot. Charlie Bartley is the closet—no, not that way—and then I have to go stop Ann from raising a golem army. Tonight."

Someday, I will say something and Qyll will react. He will gasp, or clutch his chest. Or his mouth will drop open. Today was not that day.

"We'll ride together."

I banged on the Bartleys' door.

When there was no answer, I tried the cell and it went straight to voicemail.

"Perhaps there is another entrance?"

All the doors and windows were locked. "We are losing time, Q. I'm going to break in." I had the patio sliding door open with a quick spell before Qyll got a breath in. "After you." I grinned.

"Charlie?" I went from room to room, opening closets. I heard Qyll doing the same. "Check downstairs," I hollered. "Can't find him here."

I tried the cell phone again... and heard it ringing. I found it on the kitchen table.

Qyll and Dorcha appeared to see me staring dumbly at the two phones in my hands.

"Tessa, he's not here. Are you sure you understood correctly?"

"Charlie called me from this phone. The number matches my caller ID. I came. He's not here. He must be at the conservatory."

"But why leave the phone?"

"Can you hear that?" I looked up at him. "That noise?"

He shook his head and glanced at Dorcha. "I don't hear anything."

I put my hand to my ear and nodded. "I can hear the pieces falling into place. Come on. I'll explain on the way."

"We will cut through Otherwhere," Qyll said.

"What do you mean cut through Otherwhere? I'm not sure I'm welcome there right now."

Dorcha bumped her head against my hand. I looked down at her.

"You want to go, I suppose. Fine."

"We shouldn't waste time," Qyll said.

What if we got stuck or lost in Otherwhere? Then again, we couldn't afford to let Ann Bartley carry out her plan, the consequences would be... not good. And it *would* be faster this way.

"Ok, but let's go outside."

The evening was warm and pleasant. We stepped into the growing gloom behind the house, walked down near the trees in back.

"Shall I?" He raised a hand and felt the air, searching for a thin spot. About three feet in front of us, he found it. I wasn't surprised. The Veil was like a curtain made of wet toilet paper these days. One little poke, and you have a hole the size of a barn. "After you." Qyll gestured through the passage. I had forgotten how crossing into Otherwhere is like walking through a hallway full of cool, invisible jello. You can sort of see ahead, but it's very dense air, magic fog pressed together, slightly resisting your passage.

The air on the other side was frigid. As we emerged into an expanse of purple snow, I decided this was as good a time as any for my spiel.

"Qyll, I think I figured it out. Some of it, anyway. After I gave the *alithis* to that golem at March's, it said a few weird things. Notably, that it was trapped here because there was no sacrifice. What if Ann has to make a sacrifice to bring the... Demon or whatever into *her* golem?"

Qyll stopped walking. "It would explain why she had trouble controlling the other golem experiments."

"Exactly! I wonder if Cara Courtland killed her husband to make the spell work, and then accidentally offed herself, too? Or maybe that was Ann."

He started walking again. "Who do you think she aims to sacrifice?"

This time, I stopped. "Charlie. I bet its Charlie."

We walked in silence for a long time.

Dorcha bounded along, her true nature obvious. The size of a very long-legged tiger, with hunting-machine muscles, she has her ears end in tufts, like a lynx, the fur of the blackest black, four rows of gleaming silver-white teeth, and silver claws. She rolled and cavorted in the snow.

"I'm glad someone is having a good time. Where are we?"

"It will be the fastest way."

"You said that. Qyll. Wait. Wait up." I grabbed his arm and made him stop. "Where is this?"

"We are in the Elfhame."

"QYLL."

He stopped again but did not face me.

"It will get us there. I promise. But we must be quick."

"But this is your 'hood, right? Your home?"

"It is close."

"So we'll be safe?"

He didn't answer but instead strode off into the lavender twilight.

For Humans or Earth-born Others, it's hard to find your way around Otherwhere. I was taught it should go like this: find (or make) a tear in the veil, pull it open, go inside, and always keep in mind your *exact* destination. It was stressed that one has to continue to focus on it in order to guide oneself to it. Things move in Otherwhere. You can't quite go in and out the same place twice unless you're extremely well-practiced. Qyll had never been to the conservatory site, but he had a good idea of where it was, so letting him guide us was the equivalent of letting a person who had seen a globe a few times lead you to Nairobi from Dallas via a labyrinth. Sort of.

Dorcha stopped playing, shook off the snow, and let out a long low growl, her tail switching.

"Right this way." We trudged on through the lavender snow. By that, I mean it was snow that smelled of lavender and was pale purple. The fragrance wafted up as we walked.

"Elfhame is not, as the name might suggest, the precise home of the Elves, though Elves do live in this realm. Elfhame is the old Human word for 'faerie home.'" It was like he was suddenly a guide for Otherworld Walking Tours. "There are many, many tribes, groups, villages."

I looked up. The dark indigo sky was blank but for two moons.

"Why do you get two moons?"

"I've always thought it was odd you only have one."

"Is one of our moons also one of your moons?"

He just kept walking.

I tried to remember all I'd heard about the Elfhame. It was very little. I wasn't prepared to be in fairyland.

"The Elves are on good terms with most *N'anta hostre*. The tribes of Otherwhere. My family uh... governs this kingdom."

"What? Kingdom?" I was struggling to keep up with his long legs. "You're... like, royalty?"

"In a manner of speaking, yes." He seemed uncomfortable admitting it.

"Are you a prince?"

"Yes."

"I knew it!" I shoved his arm playfully before he could stride away.

Qyll stopped and finally did look at me. "It doesn't matter. I have a title and lands here, but I chose to come to Earth instead." He searched my face with his shining eyes. "My brother will rule when our parents are gone."

"Hey, I don't care if you're a prince." I was practically jogging to keep up. "I just... I mean, it's very interesting to know that about you because I did not know that before now and now that I do know it, that's good. Because we are partners. I mean, work partners, and it's a good thing to know, you know, some background about the people you work with. Two moons. Wow. That's really great."

Athena's tits, Tessa, you could talk the paper off the walls.

It was my turn to walk off, my face ablaze.

"Yes," he said softly, falling into step with me. "I agree."

We kept traversing the endless expanse of frost. Though I wasn't cold myself, my breath came out in rigid misty shapes, curlicues and swirls turning to ice that dropped and broke like glass.

"How is this possibly faster than driving?" I complained.

"When we emerge, it will be mere moments from the time we stepped inside."

Across the windswept snowfield, a trumpet called. Then another.

Far off near the horizon, lights moved. Like a swiftly-moving herd of headlights.

"Qyll, what is that?" We stopped walking. Dorcha paused, alert.

"I don't know." From goddess knows where, he withdrew a pair of long curved blades.

"Silver?" I said. "I didn't know you were packing."

"Packing?"

"Packing heat. You have swords. Really long, pretty swords." The blades were carved with ivy leaves.

"These weapons are not typically allowed in Earth, though as an FBI agent, concealed carry applies. But here, I would not risk going about without them out in the open."

The lights grew closer and in moments, they were near enough to see an enormous sleigh drawn by six massive white reindeer with silver horns and hooves.

He hissed under his breath.

"What? Qyll? What is it? Who's that?"

The sled was driven by a tall, broad figure in a dark purple velvet robe trimmed in silver-white fur. On a head of silvery silken hair sat a crown of leaves worked in gleaming silver. Perfect features, narrow arched eyebrows, fullish lips. Strangely feminine but definitely masculine.

Alongside the sled, in smaller sleds or on the backs of animals or running along, were all kinds of beings—Elves, unicorns, flying folk, a purple and silver zebra. They circled us, staring like we were animals at the zoo.

The driver of the biggest sled leapt from his perch over all six reindeer. He landed lightly before us, leather-booted feet sending up a puff of glittery snow. He was so tall, the top of my head only came up to his sternum.

Qyll knelt and bowed. "It is an honor, your Grace."

The man bowed in return. "Qyll Toutant Lh'ollye Noirelf. Hale and well-met! I have not seen your people for a long while. You look hearty, lad!" He clasped Qyll in an embrace.

Qyll glanced at me, his expression unreadable. "Your Grace, may I present the Lady Tessa Reddick." He gestured to me, and I had the sudden urge to curtsy, which I did, extremely ungracefully. "Lady Reddick, I present his highness, the Holly King, lord of ice and stone, ruler of the coldlands."

My knees turned to water. One does not simply *meet* the Holly King. The Holly King was the stuff of fairytale and legend.

"You *are* real!"

The King and his entire entourage laughed.

"And so are you." He took my hand.

Here I was, with his lips pressed against the back of my hand and his wintergreen eyes watching me with amusement. Despite the snow and chill, a very, *very* nice warmth curled around my ladybits when he smiled.

"So it is true. Cerridwen Reddick's Beltane baby lives." His voice was like a bonfire at midwinter. I wanted to throw off all my clothes and see what was under that purple velvet robe of his. The blush rose so hard to my cheeks, I was afraid I would burst into flames.

"I... ah... yes, sir. I'm... sorry. Your highness." I have no idea what I was apologizing for, but I thought maybe a blanket statement for any perceived wrongdoing might be helpful.

"Please. Call me Erran." His eyes lingered on me.

"We request passage through your lands this night, my lord," Qyll said, relieving some of my awkwardness. "We are on urgent business and must be on our way at once."

The Holly King's laugh was thunder. "Such haste, young Elf! Come, rest a moment." He snapped his fingers, and a massive tent blossomed from the tundra, unfurling dark blue walls and roof, silver cords holding it fast. One of the entourage held the flap aside, and I followed Qyll. Inside was a roaring purple flame and big cushions covered in thick furs. Plates of food and drinks sat on low tables. Pretty harp music filtered in from this place's version of Bluetooth speakers.

I swallowed hard. Rule number one when you're in Otherwhere? Don't eat the food, don't drink the drinks. Creatures like Faeries and Pixies have very interesting ideas about what constitutes a contract, and if I wasn't careful, I might end up stuck in the Holly King's court for the rest of my unnatural life.

"Do we really have time for this?" I whispered to Qyll.

He made an irritated noise. "We really don't have a choice. But truly, we have plenty of Earth time."

The King reclined on a huge round cushion, his elegant head against a stack of velvet pillows. Dorcha acted like she was a regular guest and made herself comfortable on a pile of furs. Soon she was gnawing happily on the bone of some Other beast, which is fine, because Dorcha, like all cats, is from Otherwhere anyway. The food and drink rules (just rules in general, actually) don't apply to her.

"What brings you to my bower this eve?"

"A business of much importance, Highness. We thank you for this gift of respite." Qyll lowered himself between two female creatures of a species I could not identify, but that was very attractive. One stroked his arm, and the other went to feed him grapes. I found myself wanting to rip their hair out by the roots. But also to jump in Qyll's lap. *Dammit, hormones!*

"Of course, my friend." The King sipped from a silver goblet. "I have heard much about your little Witch. She is so very pretty, and I do desire to know her better." Our eyes locked for a torturous moment. The barest hint of a frown crossed between his brows. "You fight an enemy this night, fair Witch. Something evil, I do think."

"That's why we're here," I stammered. "We're on our way to stop it from making a big ol' mess in Earth."

The Holly King nodded. "Here. Perhaps this will help." He held out his palm, and in it sat a piece of amethyst about the size of a walnut and cut to look like a heart.

"What is this for?" I said, like an idiot.

He smiled. "A gift." He glanced at Qyll who looked as though he meant to speak. "Be at peace, friend, 'tis only a gift. Nothing is expected in return. I swear on the heart of winter."

I quickly slipped it into my pocket. "Look, I'm not really dressed for a party, so I think we'll just be on our way, but thanks for everything," I said.

Qyll looked alarmed. I was offending our host.

"Not so fast, *yichidig o wrach*," Erran said softly in his musical language. I found myself stock still in front of him again, eying his magnificent chest. He leaned up, tilted my face to his. "I do not jest when I say I desire to see more of you, little Witch. You and your Dark Elf friend and your N'anta cat may pass through my lands tonight, but only on promise of a return visit." I could barely think straight for the buzzing in my head as his fingers rested on the back of my neck and his thumb traced my jawline. I think my mouth literally watered. The things I wanted him to do to me raced through my mind like a steamy video on fast-forward.

Somewhere in my head a voice screamed. *Rule number two in Otherwhere? Don't make promises! Promises are contract! Contracts are bad! Others are tricky, and you could end up painting the white roses red in some crazy queen's garden for all eternity if you aren't careful! STOP LOOKING AT HIM!*

I tore my gaze away and looked to Qyll. He was standing, swatting away the hands of the pretty ladies, and his expression had gone rock-hard. (Something about that was extremely satisfying.)

"I'm sure we can work something out," I murmured, hoping I was vague enough.

He smiled. "I wonder, dear Witch, if you fear these lands? After all, you have made enemies far and wide."

"Well, it crossed my mind," I admitted, "but I'll tell anybody you want me to tell—I didn't do it. I had nothing to do with the... fire."

He peered into my face with a look of frank concern and nodded. "Off you go then, the both of you." Taking my hands, he said, "I'm much more keen to visit when your mind isn't so far away." The touch of his lips on my chilled fingers was more than I thought I could handle.

"Thank you so much, your highness. Erran." He smiled like a hungry leopard. I snatched my hands back and ducking out of his way, bolted back into the snow, motioning to Qyll and Dorcha.

We took off running through the lilac powder, Qyll occasionally glancing back to see if we had been followed, which we hadn't. Finally, we slowed to a walk.

"You can't run from the Holly King forever," he said. "I'm sorry I brought us here. I didn't think. Usually I can pass unnoticed through these lands." He glanced sharply at me. "Unless someone told him we were coming."

"Don't look at me! Athena's tits, Qyll, I didn't have time to mess around here!"

"Not you. Heaven keeps an eye on its lands much too closely, I fear."

"Heaven? Wait, what?"

"The court of the Holly King lies on the Heaven side of things."

I stopped moving and let it sink it. I can't walk and think about big things at the same time.

"The Holly King is an Angel?"

Qyll stopped, too. "Not precisely; he and his kin are simply slightly more of one than the other. Humans might understand it as more Heaven than Hell."

I closed my eyes tightly. "The Holly King. Is. Part. Angel."

Silence.

I lifted an eyelid slightly.

"Yes. That's the best way to describe it."

"Uh wait, so you're angelic, too?"

Qyll colored slightly. "Yes, according to Human interpretation of our geneology."

"Great Leda's quim." I shook my head, setting off a mini-squall of purple flakes. "More background."

He turned and began walking away again. "Be that as it may, you have got his attention now. There is no telling what will come of it."

I pushed the business with Erran out of my mind and concentrated on the conservatory. Soon, the snow thinned to muddy grass and the air warmed. We were back in Earth.

"I will alert the SI team to be at the ready. Once we know what we're dealing with, we can call in reinforcements."

I sighed. "Out of the frying pan and into the fire."

*We all hid, back in those days. You
couldn't tell someone you were a Vampire.
My god, no. You had to sneak around, make
up stories, get jobs that you could do at
night. Every mortician, every morgue
employee, nearly every graveyard shift
employee you know? Vampire. Even after the
Rift, well. There was a lot of racism, a
lot of fear. But the truth is, we aren't
like the ones on TV or the movies. We eat
a mostly meat diet. That's it. Raw fresh
meat. Whole Foods and Costco have been
real godsends for us.*

—Interview with A (Real) Vampire, Vanity
Fair magazine, 2009

CHAPTER TWENTY-TWO

T he forest crackled with magic, as though the ley line energy had been turned up to eleven. Louisville sits on a river (literally, the Ohio), but it also rests atop a figurative river of ley magic directly between the Bermuda Triangle and Yellowstone National Park, two serious magical hotspots. Somebody was tapping into some deep earth energy here, the way college kids cheat to get free cable.

My stomach flip-flopped at the thought of what lay ahead. I was bone-tired and did not have my head in the game. Then I flashed back to the damage at Koby's mansion. And the smell. And the singular kernel of truth: those people did not deserve to die, and not in such a horrible way. And neither does anyone else.

"Wait." I pulled out the anyshooter and its box out of my bag. Never hurts to check your ammunition, if the action flicks were any indication. Under the velvet cushion, two more bullets rolled around. "Don't know what these are but they might come in handy." Nana carried this thing until she died and then it went in the trunk, the remaining rounds a mystery.

I stuffed my last-ditch weapon back and put up my psychic shield, then motioned us forward. "Let's split up," I whispered. "Come from three angles. Don't give ourselves away unless we have to."

Qyll nodded. "Should we have alerted Antaura?"

I snorted. "I'm not worried about her. If that thing gets loose and goes after her, it'll save me the trouble of keeping her from killing me. No, let's just do this."

Qyll hesitated. "Take care. I'm calling in the SMART team. We obviously need backup. I don't have a good feeling about this night. And I do not wish to fill out the paperwork it would take to explain your demise."

"Gee, thanks. I'll be fine. Go on." I shooed him away.

He nodded and slipped behind some trees to the east. Dorcha melted into the shadows to the west.

I said my quieting spell. Dorcha being a cat would automatically be in stealth mode, and Elves aren't exactly known for drawing attention to themselves if they don't want to.

There was activity in the same clearing I'd visited a few days ago. I peered from behind a thick poplar. The area had been cleared down to dirt and tamped smooth. White lines and squiggles glowed in the light from a fire in a pit to the north. A few stepstools were sat around, covered in drying mud. In a center of a summoning circle drawn on the earthen floor, a golem loomed, a figure nearly twelve feet high and half as broad, more a wall than a man. A Human swayed next to it, chanting, her hands raised. Several other chanters walked around the circle, their white tunics streaked with dirt. Puddles of dark magic glittered in the changing light.

I calmed my mind and searched for all the raw energy I could get my hands on. Ley lines aren't really 'good' or 'evil,' they just are. Just like electricity isn't good or bad, it's what you do with it that determines its purpose. For example, electric chair death? Bad. Making a grilled cheese? Good. Lucky for me, we bordered the river, which meant a constant flow of air and water energies. I sucked in as much as I could hold. I even funneled some into my cloak, tattoos, and triple goddess pendant.

The magic around was intense. I wasn't sure how these newbies could stand it, unless some kind of a protection spell was in place. It raked over everything in its path, clotting and coating every animal, vegetable, and mineral. The problem is, unstructured magic is very dangerous. People can get hurt and like Qyll, I had a sinking feeling that tonight, more than one person would be. Beyond the intense magic though, something else seethed: anger. Ann's pure grief had curdled into white-hot fury, and that had come alive, mixed with the energy she channeled to make her clay man.

The swaying figure looked up. Ann Bartley. Her face was a mix of profound focus and plain crazy. "Brothers and sisters, the time has come. We have made ourselves clean in the eyes of the one true God, and we ask Him to bless our ritual this night. The Lord says, I will rid the land of evil beasts, and the sword will not go through your land. You will chase your enemies, and they shall fall by the sword before you. Five of you shall chase a hundred, and a hundred of you shall put ten thousand to flight; your enemies shall fall by the sword before you. So says the Lord." The others murmured and raised their hands as they stopped their circling and stood facing their shepherd.

As I crept through the trees to get a different view, I noticed something in the center of the circle next to the golem. A figure bundled in a white sheet, blood seeping through in a morbid Rorschach. Icy realization crystallized in my brain.

She held her hands out to the golem. "Speak with me, brothers and sisters, the sacred words. Speak with me, now. Speak! We raise our army tonight in the name of God the Almighty so we might smite the demons on Earth!" There was something of a charismatic preacher in her delivery. One that completely believed in their cause.

Her voice rang with otherworldly power as she began the incantations in a language I didn't recognize. The shift of energy was fierce, as if the Earth itself had been nudged out of orbit. The trees stilled. Dark purple energy swirled around Ann, the prone figure, the statue, her disciples.

The others chanted with her, some of them falling to the ground flailing, like the Pentecostals in their ecstasy.

Part of me couldn't look away. I wanted to see if Ann could really do it, if an untrained Human could create and control a creature like a golem.

But the real truth was, I couldn't kill Ann Bartley.

Besides the fact that I'm not into killing, period, Witchcraft 101 says whatever you send out comes back at you times three. I couldn't afford to have a death on my permanent record, even an accidental death. I would have to settle for *golemus interruptus*.

Ann bent down and pulled the sheet from the figure. I choked back a cry, my suspicion confirmed. Charlie Bartley, pale as his shroud.

I put my back against the tree, sliding down the rough bark to sit on the roots. Trying to slow my breathing was like trying to stop a freight train. From where I hid, I couldn't tell if Charlie was dead. Though knowing Ann's M.O., if he wasn't yet, he would be.

Stand up. Deep breath. Fake it until you make it.

"*Cosmo* says mud is great for the skin," I said loudly, stepping out from the trees.

They kept going, either ignoring me or so deep into their thing, they didn't hear me.

I walked around the circle. "Hey. Hey you." I waved my arms and jumped up and down. Ann finally broke off. The others squinted through the smoke and magical haze. "I mean, if that's what you're into."

I pulled out my athame. (In my mind, when I unsheathe it, it makes that same cool "sching" like when knights whip their swords out in movies.) The little knife glinted in the weird light as I slashed the circle open. Thick tarry magic sluiced over me and into the forest, kicking up leaves and twigs. I sheathed the athame and with another deep breath, stepped into her sphere. The uneven magic snapped like a million tiny live wires. Lord, what my Aunt Ellery would've done with Ann and her jerry-rigged, back-alley, paid-for hoodoo.

Ann Bartley looked aged beyond her years. The woman from the photos was a healthy-looking sixty-something. Now, she was gaunt and crazed, her stringy hair pasted to her forehead in sweaty clumps. Her eyes were wild. Skin clung to her bones like a wet sheet on a coat rack.

As I drew closer, I noticed a small table, like a TV tray, beside her. On it was a folded packet of papers, a rather impressive gold knife, a tiny vial, and a crystal bottle full of dark liquid that I guessed was

Antaura's blood. I suspected the vial was my blood.

"Well, well, well. If it isn't the Wicked Witch of the West." Ann sneered.

"Oooh, been a while since I heard that one. Take you a while to think of that?"

I glanced down at Charlie. He wasn't moving. Ann glared at me. "You are not welcome, Witch," she hissed.

"No, I know that. I'm, like, totally crashing your party."

Two of the cultists came forward, grabbing my arms roughly. I let them, so I could shoot the shit with their ringleader for a minute. They couldn't hold me for long if I didn't want them to.

"I know what's going on here, Ann. You're hurt. You're practically made of pain at this point."

She ignored me and started to smooth out the energy of the circle where I'd barged in, murmuring under her breath. I kept talking.

"This won't help. You're not strong enough to control this, and you don't know what you're dealing with. These people? They're going to die. They're *all* going to die. I'm willing to bet they don't deserve it. And this is not going to change anything for the better, I promise you. When this thing gets out of hand, and it will, you're going to be way, way, way out of your league."

"You think we fear death? We are washed in the blood of the lamb and we are saved." She raised her hands and closed her eyes.

"Lady, dying is going to be the least of your worries. There are worse things, my friend, than death, let me tell you."

She stopped and faced me. "I tried to warn you, Witch. But you just. Won't. *Listen.*"

Ann grabbed the golden knife and slashed at Charlie's face. "No!" I started toward her, but the lackeys held me fast. Again, I let them. I needed Ann to feel in control. It was difficult though, because what I really wanted to do was blast her to kingdom come and save Charlie... if I still could.

Ann wiped some of the blood from her husband's cheek as she whispered something that sounded like a spell. Her hand flew out as if throwing something at the golem. Magic flowed into the clay man, and its body quivered.

"Ann, please, it's not too late." I tried to keep my voice calm. "We can stop this. I can take you home, you can go home with Charlie. He loves you, Ann. He'll forgive you. Your God will forgive you. You can stop. Antaura is too powerful for you to kill. God doesn't expect you to kill her. He doesn't want you to murder people."

As I tried to find something she would latch on to, I made a note that if I got out of this alive, I'd really work hard on my negotiation skills.

While the golem warmed up, Ann stalked over, her face a mask of rage. "Charlie was a useless fool. A spineless, whimpering little boy. He wouldn't—*couldn't*—help me." A strange purple glow lit her eyes. I had never seen a Human so brimming with that kind of darkness.

"Is Charlie...?"

"I can't imagine how he'd be alive at this point. But he does have a little use left." She leered.

Sadness and anger congealed in my throat. As I considered how far off the edge she'd gone, my captors let go of my arms, moved away, and joined the others, praying and chanting.

I was totally unprepared when Ann lobbed a fireball at me. Luckily, she had poor aim and only singed my cloak. I had a full protective shield up in half a heartbeat. A tree behind me crackled as the fireball consumed its branches.

"Who's the Witch now?" I asked, keeping an eye on Mr. Mud who was trying out his new appendages behind Ann. It was like watching a baby learn to use its arms and legs, only sped up to about ten thousand.

She laughed, a hollow, hard sound, and opened her hands to the sky. "This is divine power, my dear. This is God's gift to His army on Earth!" She raised her arms and streams of fire shot into the trees.

"Jesus Henry Christ!" I cried as the woods began to burn. "You're going to send the whole place up in smoke, including yourself and your claymate!"

"Do not take the name of the Lord in vain, you dirty heathen whore!"

I dove aside, dropping to a roll as gouts of flame zoomed past. Something was seriously wrong here. She couldn't have all this power from white magic, obviously, but even black... And then, it hit me, again, like that ton of bricks people are always talking about.

"Ann, what have you *done*?" I whispered. I got up and looked for somewhere to hide.

The book, the magic, the spells. Golems and magic and Demons. It whirred into place in my head. She was too angry to see what she'd brought from the bowels of the universe. She used her husband as a blood sacrifice and whatever was coming was *not* going to play nice.

The golem set off toward me, its heavy legs planting firmly with each step.

"I told you, this is God's will. God himself gives me the power to defeat the Rift-dwellers in Earth. Like *you*. Then, oh *then*, I will bring down the Demon Queen. Burn her to cinders like the Lord burned Sodom and Gomorrah! Turn her followers to salt like Lot's wife! It's time for payback. I will not sit idly by while you horrors-of-the-night abuse the Lord's earth." She pushed her face up to mine and whispered, "Did he tell you that they stole my baby?"

That line. My throat constricted for a moment, and it was as though my own heart beat in time with her grief. I nodded. "Yes. I know about the baby. And I'm so sorry." In that moment, I *felt* her loss burrowing into me. "What happened to you was awful. But not all Others are like that. I promise."

For the briefest second, her wild face relaxed into relief. Did I get through to her? Was it so simple? But like all good things, that petered out pretty quickly. She set her jaw and went back to meet her golem in the center of the circle.

She still didn't have the first clue what was going on. "Ann, you've called a... I don't know, but it's not *good*! You haven't animated your golem with the breath of God. I swear. That ritual is *black magic*.

"Listen to me. This guy, he's a professor in town, he did this ritual. Last night." That got her attention. "He used the same one you've been using. But I could tell it was no angel, Ann. Maybe you don't know this, but there are signs, pretty obvious signs, that help you know when you've summoned a Demon. Or, an evil spirit, or something." Her eyes were fixed on me, her expression inscrutable. I kept my voice steady. "Number one.

They smell bad. Like rot and decay and refrigerator science experiments involving slime mold. Number two. They demand a blood sacrifice. What god would demand you kill for it?" I gestured to poor Charlie. "Kill your husband? Who is a really nice guy? Who *loves* you?"

The golem, now totally fired up and rearing to go, growled. It was every bit as terrifying as the one March conjured and then some.

"No," she shook her head viciously. "He told me he is an agent of the one true God. He promised to be at my side. He is my champion." She threw her skinny arms in a V over her head.

"I am at your command, lady," the golem boomed. Ann giggled. Something snagged my attention. It was the golem's voice. I needed to hear more to be sure.

"Hey. Hey, buddy, how's it going?" I waved at it. It turned to me and sneered.

"Tessa Reddick. We meet again."

That gave me pause. What the *hell*? "Sorry, I don't think we've had the pleasure. Where did you say I know you from?"

It chuckled. (What is the deal with these *creepy motherfucking laughs*?)

Oh. Oh, shit. Christ on a *crispy cracker*. It was the same voice I heard at March's house, at the very end, saying what sounded like a Bible verse. And then again, when Charlie called me to say he was locked in the closet. *It was all the same voice.*

I wished desperately for bourbon and a cold compress.

The golem first tried to step on me as I ran. The hem of my cloak caught under its monstrous foot, snapping me backward as I choked. One thick hand reached out. I was going to have to undo the clasp if I wanted to stay out of its grip. Mental note: *capes = bad idea in a fight*.

I scooted out of the way at the last second, its cold muddy fingertips brushing my shoulder.

"And what do you know, Witch?" Ann called. She sat on a fallen tree like she was on a Sunday picnic. "You don't know the mind of God, you pagan abomination! Vengeance is mine, sayeth the Lord!"

She lifted a hand casually and shot another spout of fire at me.

"Not my boots!" A black patch smoked right above my left ankle.

Dammit.

"You can come out now!" I hollered desperately. Dorcha emerged from the shadows.

In one fluid motion, she leapt at the golem's head, claws fully extended. Like the X-Men's Wolverine, her paws were multi-bladed swords, and she neatly sliced the thing's head off.

She landed almost noiselessly beside me and bumped my leg with her head.

Ann shrieked in anger.

"Nice work, girl, but I don't think that's going to make a difference," I said, my voice hoarse.

The golem's body faltered for a moment, then stood still. I wasted no time and hustled to the fallen head, plunging my hand in the crudely molded mouth to find the *shem*. As I searched, cold clay began to creep up my arm, squeezing like a snake swallowing a rabbit.

Well, shit.

I tried to push the muck off with my other hand and succeeded in getting elbows-deep in living mud. "Where is it? Ann, where is the *shem*?"

Dorcha paced around the mud body. From the neck, a new head began to emerge.

The minions appeared to be still lost in their fervent haze. "Dorcha! Round up those idiots and get them out of the way."

My huge cat sprinted to the far side of the clearing and looking like nothing so much as a sheepdog, began to herd the crowd.

Mud had reached almost to my shoulders and I could no longer feel my fingers. I kept digging.

"You'll never find it," Ann called gaily as she blasted an oak with a gout of fire meant for my ass.

The mud I'd shaken off rejoined the larger body. The golem's head had regrown, and the whole mess stomped off toward me again. I hurried to shake off as much goop as I could before scuttling out of the way.

"Call it off, Ann! Call it *OFF!*" Ann

Ann snapped and snarled. "Kill the Witch!"

The flames she sent to the trees intensified, the little bits of smoldering bark and burned leaves floating to the ground. Fire and earth are mighty powerful together, and I didn't have a big window of time to get my act together. I was going to have to try calling on my water power.

I came around the golem to see Ann. Her fury was palpable. It spewed from her like lava from a volcano.

When she saw me, she screamed again, "Kill the Witch!"

The golem shuddered its face through the back of its head, the same way the first one at the professor's house did. And it thundered after me.

Then Rabbi Loeb walked once around the body, and placed a piece of parchment in his mouth. He bowed to the East, West, South, and North, and all three of them recited together: "And He breathed into his nostrils the breath of life; and man became a living soul." The Golem opened his eyes and looked at his creator. They dressed him and took him to the synagogue, where he could get ready to start his mission.

—from the story of the **Golem of Prague**

CHAPTER TWENTY-THREE

A huge fist plummeted through the smoky air, and if my shield hadn't been so strong, I would have been squashed. The hand glanced off with a resounding ring as though made of iron.

I reeled and loaded a new series of spells. Quick as a wink, I fired off a half-dozen water charms that sent a decent-sized wave at the golem. It splashed against the thing, smoothing out its facial features and dissolving the arms into the body. Water spells pull water from the nearest sources, which in this case was the Ohio River about a mile away and probably the water table beneath us.

Ann gave a strangled cry.

I rinsed and repeated, the golem effortlessly rebuilding itself.

"Vengeance is mine," it roared, stalking after me.

"For God's sake, will you just die already?" I roared back, stomping my foot.

The mudman bellowed and swung both mammoth arms at me. I made to fire off another spell, but as a limb came toward me and I ducked to avoid it, the arm stretched like silly putty and slammed into my hip. I shot sideways into a tree, lights bursting against my eyelids as my head hit the rough bark.

Despite the pain, I had to keep going. Others and Humans had already died because of Ann; I couldn't let any more suffer the same fate. I struggled up and hit it broadside with more water then started to pull out the big guns. But it got too close, and I was sent tumbling again and again.

I limped into the surrounding trees, ducking behind a bulldozer. A quick search of my bag resulted in Nana Fairfax's anyshooter, a nearly empty holy water spray bottle, and a handful of Elisha salt. I chambered my two remaining bullets in. Could be more *alithis*. Could be something to sprout horns made of candy on the victim.

The golem crashed around in the forest. I darted back to the clearing, making sure it heard me. Ann and Qyll dueled on, but Dorcha had gotten everybody else out of the way. Charlie took up the center, bleeding and still.

With an eye on the mud-creature, I tried talking sense into Ann again. "They know about you," I shouted. "They're coming for you, Ann. Supernormal Investigations. The Arcana. Antaura the Demon Queen. Unless you let me help you."

It was a gamble, sure. I actually had no idea if the Arcana knew or even cared about Ann Bartley's foray into dark magic. SI wanted a piece of her, and surely the Red Queen would like to take a crack, but I needed to play it up if any of us were going to get out of this alive.

Her face was drawn and pale. "My judgment is in Heaven with my God." She spat as her golem stomped out of the underbrush toward me. "Then they will know that I am the Lord. Thus says the Lord God, clap your hand, stamp your foot and say, Alas, because of all the evil abominations of the house of Israel, which will fall by sword, famine, and plague! He who is far off will die by the plague, and he who is near will fall by the sword, and he who remains and is besieged will die by the famine. Thus will I spend my wrath on them."

"*Zeus' balls*, can you stop with the Bible crap?" I growled and aimed the anyshooter. I couldn't afford to miss, so I had to wait until I could see the mud in its eyes.

The little gun barked twice and the bullets sailed into the golem's torso. I held my breath.

It looked *surprised*. Staggering along, it pawed the air like a blind man. "What is this magic?" It stumbled and looked around. It was like

245

watching a tree fall in slow motion.

"No. No, what did you *do*?" Ann abandoned her fight with Qyll and rushed to her creation.

"It burns me," it complained in a raspy voice.

I looked for Qyll. No sign of him.

"You, bitch!" Ann cried. She stumbled over to Charlie's body and used her tunic to collect some of the dark fluid on his cheek. Again at the golem's side, she touched the fabric to its mouth. "I've done all you asked. I've made the sacrifice. I've brought you the Witch."

All those pieces I thought were fitting together? Yeah. A few of them fell off at that point.

"I am wounded." Its voice weakened.

Ann beat both fists against the golem, sobbing. "Fight! Damn you, get up and finish this!" She began an incantation or spell in the same odd tongue she'd used before. Between choking gasps, she tried to revive her champion. Current score: Nana Fairfax—one, mud monster—*zero*!

I started to back away, suddenly realizing I didn't want to be this close to Ann after I'd mortally injured her pet mud pie. I sidled up to my cloak and was refastening it when she sent a double shot of flames at me.

"You hurt my golem, Witch. I will destroy you." Her voice was thick and garbled. She bent and sprayed fire at me like a pissed-off dragon.

I was so sapped that all I could do was turn so my cloak caught the flames. Thank all the tiny gods I'd gotten it on in time. The fabric refused to burn, but hot air seared my lungs and scorched some more of my hair. The rest of me remained uncharred. Mostly.

Dorcha ran out of the trees with an almighty snarl. She sunk her teeth into Ann's leg. Ann let out a shriek and kicked out, landing her heel on my cat's nose.

Before Ann could attempt her recipe for barbequed kitty, I fired a binding spell at her. She deflected it easily with one hand while the other send a singeing flame at Dorcha. It caught her paw, and she roared.

"Okay, that is it, you bitch," I hissed. I sent an iceberg spell home to encase her in frozen water. "First my *boots*. Then my *hair*. Now this.

Nobody. Messes. With. My. CAT."

Ann torched the ice quickly and stood drenched in the circle.

She caught me on the other shoulder with a fireball that took a pretty good chunk out of my cloak and sent daggers of heat up and down my arm. I screamed, more out of fury than pain.

Panting, we stared at each other.

Out of the corner of my eye, I saw a twitch. A ripple. Something expanded.

The golem staggered back to life.

Hope lit up Ann's face.

"Champion," she croaked between rasping breaths. "Let us finish God's work."

The battle-ravaged sculpture limped up to tower over Ann. "Your sacrifice wasn't enough."

There went the hope on Ann's face. Replaced by confusion. She struggled to stand but only managed a wobbly kneel. "I gave you blood. The blood of my husband. You said that's what you needed. I brought you *her*. If he's not good enough, take *her*."

They looked at me.

The golem nodded. "This Witch is wily and her blood is impure. I cannot come through yet. I am bound by the laws set forth when this world was created. You are not powerful enough. My transition requires *more*."

Where the fuck is Qyll and the backup team? And what the hell is this sweet duo nattering about?

"Neither by the blood of goats and calves, but by his own blood he entered in once into the holy place. And it is thus that I shall continue the work of my God. Rejoice, child of God, for you shall see your Heaven."

I sprint-limped across the clearing and fired everything I had at the golem, which wasn't much. The anyshooter was empty. I was out of Elisha salt, holy water, and ideas.

The golem pounded toward me. My water spell collided with its knee as a silly-putty fist shoved me. Hard. I saw stars as I flew backward in space.

"And when I passed by thee, and saw thee polluted in thine own blood." The muddy visage leered.

"You really have to learn some new lines. Have you tried *The Satanic Verses*?"

It picked me up and shook me.

I took a deep breath, tilted back my head, and screamed as loud as I could, "GIDEON! QYLL!" It was the only thing I could think to do at that second. I tried to force their faces into my mind, to think only of them and what it would be like to have them here. My energy flagged, my head fogged up.

The golem squeezed its dripping fingers around my throat, waited until it heard me well and truly choke, saw my head loll to the side.

"Finally! I was getting tired of her endless chatter. Leave her for a moment, my champion," Ann called. "We have more important work now."

The golem let me fall in a quaggy heap, then it stalked to Charlie.

In Greek mythology, Mormo was a child-eating spirit, and was said to have been a Laestrygonian, a tribe of cannibalistic giants. The name was also used to signify a female vampire-like creature in stories told to keep children from misbehaving. The Mormo would steal and murder children in revenge of the Queen of the Laestrygonians who was deprived by her children.

—from *Mythology Then & Now,* by Danielle White

CHAPTER TWENTY-FOUR

S top!"

Everyone froze. Even the golem.

I have never been so happy to see Gideon as I was in that forest. From my turn as Juliet playing dead on the floor, I prized open my eyes. Despite the soot and ash, the dirt and muck, he was as clean and white as always.

"Tessa, honey, I *do* apologize." He set me on my feet and took my hands in his. My vision swam, but he held me up. His head shook with sympathy as I congratulated myself on a pretend-hanging-death well done. Half a minute more, and Gideon would've lost his chance to tender his I'm sorrys. "I mean, I *really did* think you were lying. I did! And *now,* I see you aren't. Truly. I'm sorry. Now, stand back, please."

The golem's expressionless gaze flitted from Gideon to me to Ann, who was still crouched in the center of the circle. She looked terrible. She barely looked Human anymore. Eyes and cheeks, sunken. Skin mottled with red and purple. No-longer-white tunic filthy and shredded. Gideon tilted back his pretty head and laughed. "You are so old school!" Gideon pulled Ann up. "Oh, my dear. You've been very naughty." Ann spat at him.

The golem roared. "Brother. You have arrived to slay the Witch. Thou shalt not consent unto her, nor hearken unto her. Your eyes shall not pity her, and you shall not spare or conceal her. But thou shall surely kill her. Thine hand shall be first upon her to put her to death, and afterward the hand of all the people."

Gideon squinted at the golem. "Good heavens, what *are* you?"

The mud pie stuck its chest out proudly. "I am called from the ether by God to do his will on Earth. My humble servant hosts me in this lowly body until such time as I can inhabit a physical form."

Gideon glanced at me, a worry tingeing his features. From somewhere, he produced a gleaming golden sword (a motherfrocking *sword*) and strode to the golem. Ann tried to torch him but she was winding down. She sank to her knees, misery and hate clouding her drooping features. Magic exacts its toll. Every time.

Thinking I was going to see something awesome, I sidled back a few paces. Just as Gideon lunged at the thing, it... *collapsed* is the wrong word. It looked like a scaffold had been removed inside it, and the mud shell sort of crumpled. Ann let out an inhuman screech and scrambled to the deflated statue.

Gideon made a noise that sounded like an Angelic curse. Then he shouted in that same language. The golem bucked. It reinflated and then sank again. Gideon repeated his chant, holding the sword pointed at its chest with both hands. The air thrummed with magic.

Gideon struggled, but doggedly called the chant again and again. I wanted to help, but had no idea what to do. A quick look across the circle told me Dorcha was tending her wounds and guarding the rest of Ann's properly cowed minions.

As the golem reinflated again, Gideon drove the sword into its chest. I'm not sure either of them really knew what to do next because they just froze there in jarring juxtaposition.

Eventually, the golem stepped back, thus un-skewering itself, and swatted at the sword with a massive paw. Then, as though Gideon wasn't even there, it stomped over to Charlie. "He's too strong for me," Gideon whispered, backing toward me. "I don't know what else to do. I'm not exactly equipped for this."

"Shhh."

Mudman knelt, bending over as if to give Charlie CPR breaths.

Charlie's eyes flew open. He got to his feet, seeping cuts painting deep red on his shroud. It looked like he'd already lost a lot of blood. Too much. The golem sat hunched over, unmoving.

"Oh no. No no no no no." My voice was a croak.

Gideon grabbed my arm. "What's happening?"

I pointed. Charlie was moving unnaturally, like his bones couldn't get their shit together enough to walk. The same purple spark that colored Ann's lit his eyes. "At last! I am released from my earthen prison!"

"I think the spirit is inside Charlie now."

The not-Charlie tested out its new arms and legs and grinned at me. What I had seen as a kind, grandfatherly figure was replaced by this *thing*. He moved with a spryness I'd bet the real Charlie Bartley hadn't seen in twenty years.

"Look, we're serving you an eviction notice. Effective immediately." I sent a blast that knocked not-Charlie over.

The thing keened in pain and threw itself upright. In seconds, he was on me, grappling tooth and nail. My cloak absorbed some of the blows, but getting increasingly damaged, so all I had left was my tattoos. He landed a punch to my face, dangerously close to my left eye where the existing cut had begun to clot. My cheek split like a ripe tomato.

I launched a blinding spell. The thing deflected and blew a fiery breath at me. I turned my head at the last second. The scent of my own burned hair filled my nostrils.

"Tessa!" Gideon called from the edge of the circle. "Be careful! You could kill Charlie!" Shit. Charlie was mostly dead when the spirit possessed him. There wasn't much left. Still didn't mean I shouldn't try to run this thing out of gas without killing the engine.

Dorcha streaked across the clearing to spring at not-Charlie, her paws on his chest. He rolled backward and they scuffled.

Charlie stumbled to the gold knife Ann used and stabbed at my cat. They moved almost too fast to see. A gash opened in Dorcha's side, and she screamed. I tried to aim a spell, but fatigue and fear of hitting Dorcha or Charlie stayed my hands.

Dorcha backed away, hackles up, growling.

I tried a root-binding spell, but the monster burst out of the restraints with very little effort.

"Ann. You have got to do something. You have to help him. That thing is going to kill Charlie." I glanced to the spot where Ann had fallen and almost lost control of my bowels when I saw her.

Her body quivered with raw rage as she ripped her tunic to shreds. It was as though she channeled the force of a supernova. Her eyes, huge and unblinking, became pools of black, as her arms and legs elongated. The crack and snap of tendon and bone was unmistakable as her body distorted. Animal teats sprang down her front over a distended belly and fangs descended from her gaping mouth. Horns like a ram's burst out of her head and lizardlike scales bloomed where pale skin had been. A forked tongue dangled from her slavering jaws.

I was out of everything. Energy. Ideas. Ammunition. I backed blindly into the trees. My bag of tricks held only odd objects as I searched desperately through them. In the ragged remains of my cloak, I found a cool stone. The piece of amethyst the Holly King gave me. I held it up to my eye, peering through, guessing at its use.

The world was different through the purple gem. It was the opposite of Dorothy's emergence into Oz; the colors were gone, everything was rendered in black and white. Except one thing. Ann's demony body came into a sharp relief, but hovering above it was a spiral of blue light. It eddied slowly out of the back of her head. I nudged Gideon, gesturing for him to look through the amethyst, too, then made a motion over my head, my finger swirling in the air.

Gideon nodded. "That's her soul. It can't decide if she's a hostile host or not," he whispered. He added, sadly, "She might lose it completely."

She went to the golem and jammed a claw in. The *shem*. Tossing it to the ground, she sent a spout of flame to incinerate the paper.

In a voice like water over hot coals, she snarled, "Go back to your *Hell*!" She stomped toward Charlie-not-Charlie and lifted him by the shoulders, holding his eyes level to hers. "Get out of my husband." She incanted again in that unfamiliar tongue.

Charlie flicked a finger, and a tree stump dislodged itself and sailed across the clearing, slamming into Ann's head. She dropped him and roared.

Back and forth they ranged, trading blows and screaming. Ann lashed out with taloned feet and hands. Charlie dodged and slashed with the knife, carving out bits of Ann's flesh.

"Charlie," she screeched. "Fight it. *Please.*" Ann stabbed him in the shoulder, flinching when he cried out in pain. He stumbled over the little table, knocking the papers and vials to the ground.

Like me, she couldn't deliver a fatal blow, lest she kill Charlie in the process. Schadenfreude.

As a bull in a Spanish ring, Ann charged, horns ready to engage. Instead of goring not-Charlie, she used them like a forklift and tossed him thirty feet back.

He lay flat for a minute then staggered to his feet. After a wobbly start, he stormed over to a pile of huge rocks and set to lobbing the entire lot at Ann. She halted on her way toward him and dodged what she could, until a boulder caught her on the shoulder and she howled, that arm bent akimbo.

Charlie ran out of rocks about the time Ann reached him. With her unbroken arm, she grabbed him by the neck and dragged him, stumbling, across the circle.

She staggered to the papers littering the dirt. The Charlie-pretender, realizing where she was taking him, struggled in her hand and managed to get free. They both grabbed for the crumpled sheets. Ann snagged one and crawled back, alternating glances at the paper and Charlie. He grew still, staring with purple eyes.

Ann began to speak, very softly. She stood, letting the paper flutter from her hand.

"The ritual. She's doing the ritual." I nudged Gideon.

For a moment, they faced each other, her whispering growing louder until she shouted. Charlie's body quavered, pulled in two different directions—it seemed on the verge of running and wanting to collapse all at once. Ann took advantage of its ambivalence. She grasped her husband by his arm, holding him at her eye level. Charlie's back arched, and he cried out in the Demon's voice. His body shuddered impossibly hard, and he vomited sticky black ichor.

I don't know how the next part happened, but Charlie got the golden knife and jammed it into Ann's chest. Then he twisted it.

The screeched chant paused as Ann sucked in a wet breath. Still, she held fast. Charlie pulled the knife free and pierced her again, and again. She fell to her knees, but didn't let go.

Kicking, screeching, jerking in agony, the Demon's avatar writhed in her grip, and still Ann held on, repeating her guttural order over and over. At last, Charlie gasped so hard I was sure his lungs would burst, then there was nothing.

He bowed his head, kneeling with Ann in some macabre benediction. I counted ten breaths before she let go and they both slumped to the ground.

"What. The. *Fuck*," I hissed.

Ann, who looked like something out of an H.R. Giger nightmare, all scales and dripping jaws, bled from the hole in her chest.

I looked at Gideon. "Aren't you going to *do something*?" He shook his head, eyes enormous. "You are a giant baby. What is it with you men? I swear!" With that, I took a few cautious steps toward the couple in the circle.

"Uh, Ann?" I knelt near her head. Slowly, she turned her terrifying face to me.

"Witch." She regarded me for a moment. Then her shoulders sagged a little more. "It's over." Her breath hitched and stopped, started again. "Who told you? Was it Cara? Heather? How did you know?"

I saw my reflection in the black of her eye. The cut on my face looked pretty nasty.

"Well, Ann, I'm a pretty smart cookie. I figured things out on my own. But I did have help. It was Charlie. And Heather was going to chip in, but you sent that thing after her."

"My Charlie."

Ann reached across the short distance between them, brushing her too-long fingers against her husband's pallid skin. It was as touching as it was jarring, to see this slavering monster cuddling up to the nice old grandpa who had, one had to hope, just now been evacuated by a Demon.

For many very long and awkward minutes, we stayed this way. Finally, Ann took a shuddering breath and heaved herself to stand. On shaky back-bending legs, she went directly to the pile of mud that was her golem champion. Letting out an ear-splitting shriek of misery, she blew a massive plume of fire at it. With her talons, she dug at the marks painted on the ground, demolishing her ritual. Dragging her scaly feet, she ground the summoning circle back into dust. Another gout of flame torched the table with the spell and vials of blood. When she finally crawled back to Charlie's body, she let out another keening wail.

In what felt like the millionth jarring experience that day, watching her drew forth a deep, yawning sadness. This wasn't a wail of anger or rage. It was of a woman who had lost everything, and realized much of it was her fault.

"I wanted to do good," she rasped, panting. "I only wanted to do what was right. I didn't *mean* to hurt them." She dropped to the ground for the last time.

And then, Charlie sucked in a breath and opened his eyes.

There was a crashing in the underbrush.

"Oh, so glad you could make it to my party," I shouted as Qyll led the SMARTies into the clearing.

In the ensuing chaos, I started with Gideon since Q orchestrated the evacuation of Charlie and the dazed disciples.

"Uh, can you explain this?"

He put his arm around me. "I'll try." And yes, that was jarring, too, but who was counting? That," Gideon pointed to the golem's ashes, "was some kind of very old thing. Maybe it was one of *us*, once. An

Angel." He studied the smoking mud closely. "These days, probably from the Edge, the hinterlands of Otherwhere. Stuff is floating around out there just waiting for something to open a door. Just looking for an invitation in, weren't you, beastie?"

"What do you mean?" I demanded.

He rolled his eyes. "*She* summoned *that* to do whatever it was she was going to do."

"Kill a bunch of Others, yes. Starting with Antaura. Probably me, too."

"And she," he pointed to Ann, "is now a Mormo."

"A what-o?"

"Sometimes a Human's rage changes them. I've never seen it this bad, but it's obviously possible. For whatever reason, she morphed into," he waved his hand in her direction, "that. A Mormo. They typically steal children, give them to their mistresses who are usually childless women. Sometimes they eat them. It depends."

"But I've been doing some research. *This*?" He gestured to the demolished clearing. "This should *not* be able to happen. But it did. And I think it means things are changing." Gideon looked worried. "I think the balance might be tipping the wrong way. This *isn't normal*, even for post-Rift times."

"So... what then?"

He shrugged. "I don't know. Seemed like an *anomaly*. So I called your partner."

"You called Qyll?"

"That's probably why they were so *late* getting here. And now, if you'll, excuse me, I've got some things to do."

Qyll appeared as Gideon sauntered off. "So glad you could *make it*. It's a good thing nobody was *dying*. OH WAIT. WE *WERE*." I planted my fists on my hips.

"Tessa, I apologize. In my defense, someone put an abscondia hex on the whole area. I walked to the road to call the SMART team and by the time I got back, it was like nothing was here."

I frowned. "What's an abscondia hex?"

"Like a giant cloaking device. You can't find the place you want to find."

My irritation faded a little. "Who did that?"

He sighed. "Probably Ann. Possibly her summoned entity." I remembered Ann smoothing over her magic circle after I broke in. "So, what happened?"

"Charlie was mostly dead. The golem possessed him. Ann got her conscience back right after she turned into what I've just learned is called a 'Mormo,' then she kicked the golem Demon's ass back to hell. Then she died. You know. The usual."

We watched the SMARTies load Ann's body in a huge black van. Just before she disappeared into its shadowy recesses, I pulled out the amethyst. There was no blue swirl over her head. Gideon returned from his walkabout, and I shoved the stone at him.

"Huh." He squinted through it.

"What? What do you see?"

He handed the gem back. "She kept most of it. The soul. That's going to make for one interesting afterlife."

Gideon looked around as though just noticing the flames and smoldering trees. "Good heavens," he muttered, waving a hand. The fire went out, but acrid smoke still rose all around. "Excuse me, sir? We need a fire hose here, *pronto*." And he was off again to bug someone else.

"Are you all right?" Qyll asked softly, stepping closer.

I nodded slowly, then he reached up to my face, brushing my cheek. It *hurt*. His fingertips came away bloodied. "You'll need to have that seen to. I expect it will scar."

I felt the place where my skin parted, blood seeping out.

"Agents?" Pryam appeared from the trees, wearing an impossibly crisp navy suit and cream top. Heels, per usual.

"Nasty cut there, Reddick." She pointed at my face. "Other than that, you'll both live."

"Next time, can *I* have the easy job? Where I get to sit on the bench, then swoop in and save everybody?"

"I'll make a note of that," Pryam deadpanned.

Things happened in a blur. The fire trucks came and dealt with the lingering flames. SMARTies milled around. The remaining Humans were taken to the hospital to be checked out and questioned. Charlie was, of course, the first to be whisked to an ER.

Dorcha put her paw on my foot and when I looked down, she mewed, butting me with her head. "You okay?" I knelt and hugged her. She purred. "Go on." I scratched her ears. "I'm fine." She made her way into the trees where she faded into the coming dawn.

The clearing was roped off, and media representatives were shooed away.

I answered questions and nodded. Someone handed me a cup of terrible coffee, which I downed quickly. Another someone gave me water. Yet another, in an ambulance, cleaned and bandaged the cut on my face, which ran from my right temple along my cheekbone to my hairline. "You're lucky you didn't lose an eye," the EMT murmured.

"Yeah? You should have seen the other guy," I countered weakly.

Two days later, I was in Pryam's office, finishing up paperwork. After signing what felt like two hundred forms, I put everything in a big manila envelope, sealed it, and dropped it on her desk with a satisfying thump.

She regarded me with golden-brown eyes that were not unfriendly. On her desk lay a copy of my preliminary statement.

"Glad to see you are all right." She leaned back in her desk chair.

"Gonna have a neat story to tell about this scar."

"I've never had the chance to observe a," she glanced down, "Mormo. That must have been something."

I gave a noncommittal shrug. "Gonna have a neat story about that too."

She sifted through the pages. "Ann will be considered a half-blooded Other and Human from now on. Ann's remains. Rather odd, that. At least, Charlie is now back to fully Human. Still, even if he lives, this is going to be a long and messy clusterfuck to put to rights."

Pryam, using unprintable language? If the world hadn't been rushing to Hell in a hand basket before, it was certainly well on the way to doing it now.

I chose to ignore all that in favor of the more pressing matter.

"Is he? Going to live, I mean? Do we know?" I admit, I was almost afraid of the answer.

"He's in critical but stable condition."

"Oh. Good."

"Moving on. You might be pleased to know our budget has been approved for the coming year."

My eyebrows sprung up.

Pryam nodded. "I can't tell if they're trying to give us enough rope to hang ourselves, or someone had some kind of coming-to-Jesus moment. Either way, we are all still here. At least, for the time being. With that, I am suggesting you take a leave."

"But—" She silenced me with a finger.

"In case you didn't catch that, Reddick, it's not really a suggestion. It's an order." Before I could make another squawk of protest, she kept going. "*Paid* leave. For two months. I knew it wasn't such a good idea to put you in the field so quickly, but I didn't think I had another choice. Stay home. Run your shop. Catch up on old episodes of *Charmed*. Whatever. But you're on leave. You may turn in your credentials."

It didn't sound so bad, a little vacation. A paid one. But I didn't want her to know that so I made a big show of looking pissed as I went to pull out my badge. While I don't think you'd call what I did "slamming" it down, I definitely placed it purposely and with meaning on her desk.

"Before I go, I'm curious about a couple of things." I sat in the chair in front of the desk. "Do you mind?"

"You had ten minutes. Now you have five. I have a meeting."

"Why did the FBI get me out of Lakeland?"

Her face was inscrutable. "To help us with our work."

"Yeah, but why me? I was kind of a security risk, don't you think? I mean, you didn't know who you were dealing with." I kept trying to read something in her eyes or catch a glimpse of what she was thinking, but Constance Pryam is like Fort Knox for emotions.

"I'll be frank with you. You *were* a security risk. And the protective charms we put on your apartment included a warning system. Something to alert us should you go off the rails."

Before I got a breath in she went on. "You can't possibly think we wouldn't have done that, Reddick."

I settled down. Score one for Pryam.

"And the truth is, I wasn't a fan of this plan. But the directive came from higher up. I'm not at liberty to discuss from whom, and even if I did know why, I couldn't tell you that, either."

"Are you going to keep the magical wiretap on me?"

Her face broke into a smile. "Yes. We are. See you in two months, Agent Reddick. And one more thing."

I put a hand on my hip.

"Nice work."

I rolled my eyes and snorted, pivoting on my heels before she could see the flames of embarrassed pride crawl up my face.

Qyll sat at his desk as I passed. "Hey," I said.

We hadn't talked or seen each other since the whole golem debacle.

"Agent Reddick," he said, as though nothing unusual had ever happened in his life. "What brings you out this fine day?"

"Paperwork."

"Ah. And how is your wound? Not terribly painful, I hope."

As he spoke, I found myself wondering what it would be like to kiss him. Are Dark Elves' lips warm? Cool?

It took me a minute to reply. "What? Oh. Yeah. Whatever. Listen, I'm furloughed for a while. Boss's orders."

"She mentioned as much. Things are rather quiet here, I'm sure you won't miss anything."

I hesitated, then sat in the chair by his desk. "I've been thinking about Ann Bartley. I feel bad for her."

Qyll looked up. "Why would you feel bad for her?"

I sighed. "She wanted so badly to be a mother. I mean, that's what started this whole thing. That's the root of her pain. She's fucked up because she's grieving. I lost my mother. That could happen to me, that anger. It could change me, you know, like it changed her. Warped her." The words came before I had a chance to think about what they meant. Every syllable leapt from my heart straight past my lips.

His eyes softened. "No." He shook his head gently and put his hand on my arm. "You are very different from Ann Bartley, Tessa. You do not nourish anger in a manner allowing something that grotesque to bloom."

He seemed to notice me noticing his hand on my arm and removed it. "Besides, I think your Malakim friend is right. What happened with Ann shouldn't have gotten that far. It's troubling, to say the least. But," he said lightly, "it's none of your concern for a while, is it?"

I blinked. Then nodded.

After a minute, and unsure what to say next, I stood up. "Walk me to the car?"

Once we were safely outside—no protesters were allowed within 1,000 feet of the building anymore—I said, "I have to get back to Antaura. Remember? If I tell her Ann's name, she'll tell me about my family."

He sighed. "You left yourself no choice, did you?"

I gaped. "Are you kidding? *She* left me no choice. It was kind of between death... or death! If I don't 'fess up, I'm a goner."

"Right. When are you planning this little outing?"

I grinned. "How about now?"

"*If he for certain met with the Devil and cheated him of his Book, wherein were written all the Witches names in England, he can look on any Witch, and tell by her countenance what she is. His help then, is from the Devil.*"

—Matthew Hopkins, **The Discovery of Witches**

CHAPTER TWENTY-FIVE

Ann Renee Smith Bartley." Antaura's weird accent took a pretty normal set of sounds and made it into something out of a scary movie. Her green eyes fixed on me.

We were in what I think was the Queen of Hearts' version of a Champagne Room, though the stage (thank all the tiny gods) was empty. Qyll and I sat a small table across from the Red Queen, who wore her Human look—the sheet of white-blond hair, white-less emerald eyes, gauzy dress.

After what felt like an eternity, she spoke again. "You have done well, Tessa. It's good to reward honor. And I am a fair businesswoman." She spread her hands magnanimously.

"Your family is descended from the goddess herself," she began.

"Wait, which one? There are thousands of goddesses."

Irritation flickered over the Demon's features. "The First Goddess. The one from whom all life sprang in all ages and all places. Entrusted with the secrets of life, all of you."

I frowned. "I don't know any secrets of life. Trust me. I wouldn't have spent five years in a psych ward and my family wouldn't be dead if I knew the secrets of life."

Qyll touched my arm. "Perhaps you could let her finish," he said quietly. I crossed my arms.

"Go on."

"The night your kinswomen perished, there was a ritual completed with magic on a scale that has been rarely seen."

"You mean in Earth?"

She shook her head. "Ever. In the history of this world, of Otherwhere, Heaven, Hell, all of them. There are perhaps a scant half dozen times this sort of thing has occurred and never by the hand of a Witch."

I glanced at Qyll. "So someone let off a magical nuclear bomb?"

"More like three or four nuclear bombs." Her eyes glittered.

"Why would anyone do that?"

She shrugged. "To cover something up. To reveal something hidden. Sometimes it's just to say, 'Look what I have done.' But if you want to know *why* something happened, you'd best learn *what* it was, yes?"

I had no clue what she meant. There was a fire. End of story. Right? Or...?

"One more thing, dear. Call it a bonus. Look in your books for the one who calls himself the Witchfinder General." I drew in a breath to fire back an obvious question, but Antaura forestalled it with a languidly raised hand and a canny smirk. "And on that note, I consider my obligation discharged. Anything else, and I will have to start a counter against *you* for the information. Do let me know your currency of choice?"

Clearly, I wasn't about to enter into any more bargains with the demons, so after I had that clue, and Antaura dismissed me, I couldn't get home to my library fast enough. Qyll asked if I wanted help, and I shook my head. "Nope, I'll call if I need anything."

He let me go with a fleeting smile and a fairly obvious (in retrospect), "I can dig around the FBI files, if you'd like. We did run a rather thorough background check on the Reddicks prior to springing you from Lakeland. I will warn you, SI is still quite new, and there are not a lot of files digitized. Archives keeps a pretty tight lock on the old hard copies."

"Oh, yeah." I smiled. "That's actually a good idea. Thanks!"

None of the family grimoires I usually consulted had any clue about this Witchfinder General person. Neither did the ones I didn't usually consult. I started going through the books of shadow. None of my favorites were any help. Pages upon pages of handwriting and illustrations, notes and sketches. Papers folded up and shoved in randomly. Languages and dialects and idioms. Nothing mentioning a Witchfinder General. Or anything similar. I wished I had a librarian who knew *all the books*. Of course, if wishes were horses.

At some point, I nodded off on a pile of dusty tomes.

When I woke, it was dusk. I stumbled around the apartment, showered, dressed in a tank and jeans, and sat on the couch, not sure what I had gotten dressed for. Dorcha sat on the floor staring at me.

"What?" I asked. "Spit it out." She sort of growl-purred and ducked her head. I leaned my head on the cushion behind me. "I don't know what to do either."

I took stock of what I had. Qyll was searching the FBI files. Pryam didn't know I was on the hunt for anything, and thought I was on vacation, so I couldn't ask her. The Demon Queen had fulfilled her promise and not only *not* killed me, but given me a clue, and I *so* didn't want to rack up any more debt. Papa Myrtle wasn't an option. Bathsheba would likely stew me for dinner. I was rich in questions and poor in helpful resources.

Wait.

I sat up.

"The Three Libras." Dorcha flicked her tail. "Oh, you thought of it first? Well, fine. I'll buy you some salmon. Come on. After what happened last time, I think I need a bodyguard."

I hoped that my previous kerfuffle wasn't going to be a problem. Nobody told me to never come back...

There was a totally new set of staff at the bar. New bouncer. New bartenders. Didn't see Nona. I didn't wear my cloak on account of the warm night, plus it was a little worse for the wear after its brush with death by dirt. But I made sure I had a few spells handy on the tip of my tongue and my witchy bag of tricks. Just in case.

The door guy looked a little confused when he saw Dorcha.

"She's with me," I said casually. He finally shrugged and waved us in.

As luck would have it, Victor Funar was sitting by the jukebox, a glass of his vile, beloved *palinka* in front of him. I slid over with my back to the room.

He looked mildly surprised to see me and more surprised to see Dorcha.

"Witchfinder General. Talk."

Victor choked on the drink. "What?"

"You heard me. Tell me what you know?"

His corpse-purple skin went even paler. "I haven't heard anyone mention the Witchfinder in a hundred years," he whispered. "Why the question so suddenly?"

"Let's just say I have a vested interest."

He stared at my face. Not taking his eyes off me, Victor drained his glass and signaled for the waitress. When she came, he ordered a whole bottle of the stuff. I put in my usual and a salmon dinner for the cat—"raw and wriggling."

In a low voice, he started. "They show up for periods of time, killed the coven, and retreat. Saint Augustine. King James. Gaius Paulinus. Cotton Mather. Matthew Hopkins. All of them, they have this title. But, Tessa, there have been no sightings since Jack the Ripper."

I'd never heard of a couple of those guys, but Jack? I'd heard of *him*. Who hadn't? "I thought Jack the Ripper killed prostitutes."

Victor drank his *palinka*. "True. But they were prostitutes who were part of a coven. They were called the Tribe of Diana. Sex witches." He grinned briefly, showing his wretched teeth. "Jack was brought in by the Crown of England, they say. Why do you think Victorians were so uptight? Sex coven didn't have a chance to get going."

"You are blowing my mind. Are you lying? No, wait. Are you *drunk*?" I demanded.

Victor let out a chuckle. "No, not drunk. You come in here with a serious question, I am giving the answer. The Witchfinder General comes to this realm when there are powerful Witches. He kills them, he goes back."

"Goes back to *where*?"

"Nobody knows. I heard once, maybe the Edge."

"What's that?"

"Tessa, please. It's just old stories."

"What's the Edge?" I persisted.

"The end of Otherwhere." He shrugged again. "Not Earth. It's certainly not Human. Definitely Other. You know, I met a Witchfinder in Briton. Oliver Cromwell."

It was my turn to laugh. And laugh and laugh and laugh. After a minute, Victor started to look downright hurt. "What is funny? I met him. He was a Witchfinder General. Killed thousands of Catholics in Ireland. Catholicism was witchcraft with nicer clothes. Do you know how this world would have been different if those witches had been allowed to live?"

I sobered. This was getting weird. Even for me.

"Is he some kind of spirit?"

Victor screwed up his face. "Mmmm, sort of. More like a reincarnation. Most Humans think about the Buddhist reincarnation, you keep coming back until you get it right and reach Nirvana. There are other kinds of reincarnation. Something so bad, so evil, it can't die. Like a boulder rolling down an eternal hill. It might get smaller as it rolls, it might get bigger, but no one can stop it hurtling along. Not without just the right hammer to smash it."

"Shit. Okay, let's get back to why this one may be after my family."

Victor shrugged. "Your coven was too powerful? Only reason it would come. They say the Witchfinder was created to kill Witches, its sole purpose. Like a vacuum—only *vacuums*? This being only kills Witches. Created by whom?" He waved a hand. "Nobody knows."

"How do I find him?"

"What?" he squawked, watery eyes going huge. "No, you don't find him!" I had never seen the little guy so animated. He practically yelled at me. "This is madness, Tessa. No!" He slammed his thick palm on the table.

After a furtive look, Victor dropped his voice again. "You do not find him. You *pray* he doesn't find you."

"Victor, I'm desperate. Where else can I learn about this thing?"

He looked pained. "I don't know. You can read history books, watch the History channel. But you won't know much. No one knows exactly where it comes from, or when, or what makes it come when it does."

"How do *you* know this much about them?"

He squirmed. "I spent some time with a clan of Vampires in Siberia. One of them returned from a long journey around the world, visiting other clans. He told of a coven that had been wiped out by a Witchfinder, in South America. He spoke of a man with the power of a god and a sole purpose. Nothing could sway him from that. And as I mentioned, Oliver Cromwell."

I pushed my fingertips into my forehead.

"Tessa." He took my hand in his rough one. "I don't know if the Witchfinder is hunting you. But if he is, you cannot fight. Run. Hide. Run some more." He sighed. "Find allies? Not weak such as me. Or so cowardly. He is too old. Too powerful. I wish I could help more."

We sat for a while, but it was clear he had done all he could. When the bottle of *palinka* was empty, he stood up.

"You take care, Tessa." He patted my hand awkwardly and shuffled away.

When I left, I still didn't have a plan, but I was a hell of a lot better off than I had been an hour before.

As I drove, I called Qyll and filled him in.

I could almost see him nod. "I'll come to you in the morning. It's Saturday, so I do not have to report to work."

"Have you found anything?" I tried to keep myself from sounding too hopeful.

He paused. "No. I haven't. But I've only just gone through SI's files, which aren't terribly old. It's going to take some time to look in the regular FBI archives, and I'll have to sort of sneak that in. There is something else, though."

"What's that?"

"Charlie Bartley. He's going to make it. He'll be in the hospital for a while, but they think he'll pull through."

I sighed. "Good. Thanks. See you tomorrow."

Ordeal by water was associated with the witch hunts of the 16th and 17th centuries: an accused who sank was considered innocent, while floating indicated witchcraft. These tests came to be part of what is known as the Salem Witch Trials. Some argued that witches floated because they had renounced baptism when entering the Devil's service. King James VI of Scotland claimed in his Daemonologie that water was so pure an element that it repelled the guilty.

—**Naturalis Historia**, VII, ch.2

CHAPTER TWENTY-SIX

The pounding started early.

"Jesus, Mary, and Joseph," I muttered. "You'd better have brought me a very expensive coffee, Qyll."

Yawning, I pulled open the deck door. No one was there, so I stepped out to look around.

Before I could get a word out, I felt like my lungs were being sucked out through my face. For a brief second, I knew I was going to die. It was a *certainty*. Tremendous pressure mounted on every internal organ. I couldn't see. I heard rushing and the sound of my own frantic heartbeat.

Then water. Extremely cold water.

I'm a good swimmer. Not even, "I'm a good swimmer. For a witch." No, I'm *very good* with water thanks to my mom and Papa Myrtle. But right then, I had no idea which end was up. I could see only bubbles and bluish haze. I struggled against my wet clothes.

A hand wrapped around my neck and pulled me sideways, which, it turned out, was up.

Water streamed across my face as I gasped and spit. Blinking into the white light, I saw him.

"Charlie?" was all I could manage. My stomach was trying to evacuate itself. My lungs were trying to reinflate. My feet kicked desperately to find solid ground.

"Witch." He kept squeezing my throat until everything went black.

I woke up on the ground by a purple lake, shivering.

He kicked me in the stomach. I saw stars and then threw up.

Oh, this was not good. This was very, very, very not good.

"Is that you, Charlie?" I sputtered.

My answer was to be thrown against a tree trunk. Sitting there, back against the bark, I saw him more clearly. It certainly looked like Charlie Bartley. But the longer I stared, the less he looked like the nice old man with the insane wife I'd rescued just a few hours before. But, but...

I couldn't make sense of anything. Nothing was right. He bent down.

"Ann tried to kill you. The golem tried to kill *me*," I croaked.

"No. *I* tried to kill you. It's been me the whole time. It's *always* been me."

The voice. The *voice*.

I fired off a spell that was probably the equivalent of a fly swatter. He punched me.

Lip bleeding, lying now on the ground, I let my gaze tangle in the trees. They weren't regular trees. The bark was purple and the leaves glimmered silver. I was in Otherwhere.

"Come on. If you're going to keep punching me, at least tell me who you are and what you want," I choked out as I will myself to roll to my side.

"And the soul that turns after such as have familiar spirits, and after witches, to go a-whoring after them, I will even set my face against that soul, and will cut him off from among his people.

"Come on, Tessa. Put it all together." He sneered. "The golems. The phone call telling you exactly where to go."

Wham! Constellations exploded in my eyes.

"I was called by the Holy Lord to stop the abomination. You were supposed to die in Earth after I killed your kinswomen. *You* were to take the blame. The Humans were to kill *you* so that your lineage died out, so your coven would cease, so everyone would know the truth about your kind." Spittle flew from his lips. "That almost worked. But almost is not enough." He laughed. "It is like almost being pregnant.

"On the subject of which, poor, deluded Ann. Next, she tried. I had her send golems after you, always with me, tucked in among the spirits. Nice little spell, written by some old Chaos Magician who wanted to stir up trouble with his Hebrew friends. But oh, a resourceful little abomination you are. And so, a little steering of Charlie's feeble brain, and here we are."

He charged me and at the last moment, I pulled myself out of the way, but he managed to grab a hunk of my hair and sling me into a boulder. I slid off into the lake.

"For the sake of Odin!" I sputtered, finally standing, hands clawing at the rock. I was knee-deep in frigid water.

"I had to gain entry to your home." As he strode toward me, I staggered back and fell again. "And I had. You never did suspect bumbling old Charlie. He even hid me from your blasted protection charms. So I slipped into his brain. Ann's too. A little nudge here. Divine guidance there. It was easy." He licked his lips. "She was so full of anger."

This wasn't the real Charlie Bartley. It was something that looked like Charlie.

"All that was left was to put down that failing bag of meat, and I would have had the sacrifice I needed." Not-Charlie shook off his hands, as if having touched something rotten. "A blood sacrifice to bring me fully into your world to cleanse it of its wickedness. Alas." He sighed, stepping into the water. "I am mist and shadow now, without an Earthly form to host me. When you shot me with *aeris*, I was forced out of the mud body."

Aeris. I racked my brain.

Copper. The bullet (bullets?) were powdered copper in a solution of rainwater. Metal and water subdue earth. It wouldn't have killed a golem, or the spirit inside, but it would turn the whole thing toxic for many beings. Enough to force it back out. Well, duh! I guess hadn't had time to think much more about that.

"Ann set everything up so nicely for me, and then she destroyed it."

Oh, sweet mercy, he was trying to come through. All the way through. Corporeal, not just whatever little bit lived in the Bartleys.

"You came back, though," I bit out through a mouthful of blood as he forced me down and I fell under his touch like overripe fruit. "Boy, General Witchfinder man, you sure don't let a little thing like being... you know, *unwelcome and dead*, get you down."

"Until that bitch Ann turned on me," the Not-Charlie growled, fists clenched. "She knew how to undo her handiwork well enough to make it rather uncomfortable for me." And this was nice and cordial, almost genteel.

Okay, this thing isn't just murderous. It's manic. As realizations went, this one I could have done without.

He held me down by my neck in the freezing water. Cold sluiced into my lungs. Water bubbled in my ears.

When he pulled me out again, my teeth rattled so hard, I was sure I'd break them all. If I didn't shatter myself into a million bits.

I vomited water and what little I had in my stomach everywhere.

His face was a mask of pure boiling black rage.

Into my face, he spat, "Yes, I killed your family. You were supposed to pay for the crimes of your lineage. But you had the audacity to *not die*. But unbelieving, and the abominable, and murderers, and whoremongers, and witches, and liars, all shall have their part in the lake which burneth with fire and brimstone: which is the second death." He punctuated every other word with an enthusiastic shake. My brain bounced in my skull. "By the name of the one true God, I am the Witchfinder General."

What happened next, I can only describe as this: the Witchfinder General took off his Charlie suit. Reaching up, he pulled the scalp apart with both hands, and *ripped* it all the way down. It dissolved into fine mist that blew away in the chill breeze. What was underneath? A massive brutish mountain of a man. Very medieval.

I'd like to point out here that I'd never felt this close to dying. Not even remotely. Not even when I fought Ann or her mudmen.

It's a weird thing to face death. I had no magic to save me and no friends at my side.

I realized I'd never see Qyll's beautiful shaggy mop again or feel Dorcha's tractor purr. As corny as it sounds, I would fail to avenge my family's murder.

My life didn't flash before my eyes. In fact, I was quite calm about it as the Witchfinder General knocked me around like a dish rag. Warm tears rolled down my swollen cheeks.

I lay face-down in the cold sand by the lake, all the bones in my body on fire. One eye began to swell shut. From what I could see, my left hand pointed at an odd angle from my arm, but I couldn't feel it, so it just looked strange. I spat blood and tried to drag myself to all fours. A chill wind fanned the flames of my pain.

My magic sputtered and died in my mouth. What's a Witch with no magic? Dead.

I braced myself, waiting, panting.

Tessa, if you get out of this alive, you should learn how to fight. Like really fight. Because you are full of book-learnin' and you have zero fighting skills.

When nothing happened, I opened my good eye and looked up.

Witchfinder Bartley faced me, but his focus was on a point beyond me. Past me. Sitting carefully back on my heels, little waves of the lake lapping against my legs, I turned my head on the bruised stalk of my neck.

Through the one good eye, I saw a cloud of silvery fog coming across the lake. Bright sparks flew and the air was full of crackling that I only later realized was the lake itself as it froze before the entourage of the Holly King.

A sort of pleasant warmth washed over me as they glided past and around me, every animal and person neatly avoiding my body. It was like being the snow under all the Olympic bobsled teams.

They came to rest, in a circle around the General.

I heard a familiar growl, and when I turned to look out of my one open eye, it was Dorcha. She pushed against my shoulder. It hurt like the dickens, but I buried my face in her neck and let out a muffled sob.

"Who dares assault one of my subjects?" A voice boomed. I stumbled to my feet. Dorcha helped me hobble out of the way and under a birch copse. Then she came behind me and formed a bench at the perfect height, which I gratefully occupied.

The King stepped out of a great silver chariot, purple robes swirling. His crown glinted in the light.

My calm pre-death despair retreated, ever so slightly.

"I have no quarrel with you, good sir. This woman is an abomination. A baseborn evil. She is a plague in this world, and all worlds." It might have been too many head shots, but the Witchfinder seemed to have grown larger, so he was almost as tall and broad as the Holly King. His face changed too, into something out of a Dark Ages painting, all craggy brows and lantern jaw.

"Oh? Is that so? Friends, we have been misled! We were under the impression that this," he gestured to me, "was our cherished friend, Tessa Reddick. Apparently, this is an abomination! A plague!" The Holly King smiled at me. I gave a very half-hearted wave and then threw the middle finger that wasn't broken at the General.

The Witchfinder General began to cough. Then, it sounded like he was gagging. The court watched him, uncertainty playing on all their beautiful features.

I finally had a chance to really look at the guy I had thought was Charlie Bartley. He wore a long black robe of roughspun with a shirt of chainmail beneath and a thick gold belt around his middle. His hair was thick, and black, and drawn back like a samurai's. He seemed to glow, like he was sitting before an invisible bonfire.

As he choked, a sword handle emerged from his mouth. He reached up to draw it out, gagging softly.

When he pulled the blade free, it was aflame. Literally. On fire.

In an instant, the entire of the Holly King's group had brandished their own weapons, but not before the General made a slash at the King. A rip in the fabric of his purple robe gaped where the flaming sword had cut. A muscular leg appeared in the tear.

The Holly King's face, what I could see of it, was a mixture of outrage and indignation.

The fighting began in earnest.

I thought at first that it would be over in moments. After all, the

Holly King had two dozen armed fighters on his side, and the Witchfinder General, only himself.

I was wrong. Whatever used to animate Charlie Bartley moved his weapon with lightning speed and accuracy. Two silvery centaurs went down almost immediately, relieved of their front legs. Next was a man who found one of his battleaxes impaled in his own face. Soon, others fell, wounded or worse. Finally, all but the King and the General remained, circling each other, biding their time, then engaging.

Back and forth over the sandy terrain they went, swords ringing across the water. The King forced the General closer to the trees with a series of economical stabs. The General returned the favor by throwing himself toward a thick trunk and rebounding with equal speed then making a lunge for his foe. In mid-thrust, the King flicked his silver blade so delicately, the General didn't notice his bleeding face. Red dripped from a neat line running parallel to his jaw.

"You are a formidable opponent." Sweat gleamed on the King's body, the flesh barely pink from the fight.

"And *you* are an appalling abomination. Just like the bitch," parried the Witchfinder General, fumbling when his hand brushed the wounded skin. When his fingers came away bloodied, he let out a roar. "Violator! Perversion! Monstrosity!"

"You are on my land. You are a trespasser. I am well within my rights to lop your bloody head off. Which I plan to do," the King said. I privately applauded the sentiment. I didn't have the energy to do anything more.

"I am charged to deal with all who deny the one true God and call themselves Witches. You tolerate that creature, who calls herself a prophetess. By her teaching, she misleads my servants into vanity, immorality, and the denigration of the one true God. And I say unto you, I have given her time to repent of her immorality, but she is unwilling. So I will cast her on a bed of suffering, and I will make those who follow her suffer intensely, unless they repent of her ways."

My laugh was a cracked bark. "He doesn't believe in your one true God," I rasped.

They both stopped and stared at me.

"What did you say?"

I cleared my throat. "He's not a Christian. He's not a... a... monotheist. Athena's tits, he's a pagan deity! You think I'm the one you're after? He's got *followers*! People *worship* him! Nobody cares about me!" Another cackle escaped me. Maybe, I'd lost too much blood or been whomped on the head too many times, but this whole thing struck me as hysterically funny.

"I am not permitted to baptize any but a Witch," the General admitted with what sounded like true regret.

Erran looked confused and said, "What she says is the truth. I do not worship your... God."

"And for that, you will be made to pay, but that is not my cross to bear. Only she is."

The Holly King let out a roar and slammed his blade into the Witchfinder General. Their sinews stretching and muscles working, their weapons came together like worlds colliding. Again and again, the King attacked, backing the enemy down. Until finally, he shoved his sword through the other man's chest. The Witchfinder's face registered surprise, as though he'd just learned it was Friday instead of Thursday. The flame on his sword died out, and he slid to the ground.

"Let it be known through all the universe, in all time and space, that I banish thee," the Holly King boomed, his bloody silver sword aloft. "From all realms I touch, from all realms of my brethren, my children, my ancestors. You shall not pass through our gates. Your name shall be cursed from this day until the last. Be gone, I say." There was an impossibly bright flash of light and the General's body was gone.

Then I passed out.

I am the Holly King, the dying Sun and
ruler of the Old Year
Like the Phoenix who rises anew
from its ashes
I too shall return, born anew
As the Child, the New Sun and King

—**Anonymous**

CHAPTER TWENTY-SEVEN

I **awoke in a bed that felt like it was made of warm air. I decided** I would stay there forever. The room was round, with opaque glass walls hung with thick tapestries rendered in shades of purple and silver. Swags of waxy holly hung from the corners and tumbled across tables. It smelled faintly of mint.

The door opened, and a woman entered. More like a young girl. Her silver hair was bound up in elaborate braids, and she wore a silky lavender dress. She carried a tray, which she set on the table by my delicious bed.

"Good morning, my lady," she said softly. "My name is Frimda. I see you are healing. Are you well enough to sit and eat?"

"Mmmmph." I pulled the blankets over my head, which sent a bolt of pain down my back. "Ow."

The girl made a tsking noise. "There now." She turned the covers back. "Let me help you." She slid an arm under my shoulders and lifted me into an upright position. I realized I was starving when I looked at the tray.

"How long have I been here?"

Frimda smiled. "I believe it will have been about been two weeks in your Human time. Two days in ours. We have...what do you call them? Time zones? It's a bit different everywhere."

"And I've uh... eaten while I'm here?"

She laughed. "Yes, we've fed you this nourishing stew and ice wine and herbs from the healer. I daresay it's what has helped you feel better so quickly." She smoothed her dress before adding, "And, of course, your magical blood."

I sighed. *Athena's damned tits*. So I'd eaten of the forbidden fruit. That would take some figuring out, but in the meantime, in for a penny, in for a pound. The stew was indeed delicious—hunks of tender meat in a wine-rich broth. Soft white bread and cold ice wine. I asked for some water, which Frimda fetched the way a parent might when indulging a child in a favorite toy. "You Humans and your water, my goodness," she huffed.

After I ate, my nurse insisted I dress and attend the King's court. Frimda slid a woolen gown over my arms, then wrapped me in a warm wool robe. It was chilly, and I didn't see how she could go around in that thin dress like it was high summer. She spent a good while fussing with my hair, making little noises of irritation. "Your hair is of such an interesting texture," she murmured. "I confess I have not seen its like before." Finally, she stepped back. The mirror by the door gave me the first look at myself in weeks—a thin, tired-looking me with a fancy updo and pretty clothes.

"I clean up nice, huh?" I said. Frimda sighed.

"If you would be so kind as to step this way?"

The halls of the Holly King's lair were a lot like my room—icy walls and floors, tapestries and carpets of indigo, cream, and lilac. Boughs, bunches, and bowls full of holly. And the ever-present minty odor. It was like being inside a tube of very fashionable toothpaste.

Armed guards stood aside as we crossed into a great hall, ceilings vaulted hundreds of feet above and various courtiers milling about below. Sat in his silver throne, the King was signing something with a plumed pen. He wore a soft eggplant shirt and gray suede trousers. His hair was tied back, and a simple silver crown sat on his head.

People stared at me as I followed Frimda to the dais.

That same mysterious harp music played. Every person in there was beautiful and perfect and smelled like goddamn mint. I wanted to punch something.

"My lord." Frimda bowed elegantly. "The Lady Tessa Reddick." She stepped back.

Every eye in the room was on me. "I... uh..." I curtseyed. "My lord."

Erran whispered something to his attendant, who then clapped his hands. "We shall enjoy a break for refreshment!" It took a mere moment for the room to clear except for me and the King. A pretty little chair had appeared beside him.

"Please, my dear. Join me here."

I sat.

"I am so pleased to see you up and about. I had my most trusted servants attend to you." His lavender eyes searched my face. "Do you want for anything?"

"Uh, no, I'm good. And thank you," I said. "I wouldn't be here if it wasn't for you."

He shook his head and sat back on his throne. "You really are a curious little thing." Amusement colored his words. "I wished to have you visit me, but not under these circumstances."

I think it would surprise no one that I found myself incredibly uncomfortable and unsure of myself. I didn't know what he wanted with me in the first place, and what he wanted in return for his help. The way he stared at me felt invasive. And I don't even have all the Puritanical hang-ups about sex some people do. So I did what I always resort to when I'm nervous. I started talking.

"So the Witchfinder General, huh? Some guy! Wow. What a jerk. A real asshole. I don't know what I would've done without you and your um, entourage, but I do appreciate it. Qyll said you're an Angel, is that true? I mean, you seem supernatural, of course. You know, I think I'm ready to go home now. Did you want me to change my clothes here or can I just mail this stuff back? Wow, I like how everything smells like mint here. Say, am I babbling?"

He just smiled.

I took myself in hand. "Listen. Just what happened, exactly?"

"I am not certain, but my best guess is, the spirit we dealt with is from the edges of Otherwhere. A Witchfinder General hasn't been in Earth in many years, I daresay, and lucky for your realm. And your kindred."

"He came for me."

The King nodded. "It would seem so. Ann's dark magic was like a beacon in the darkness. She opened the door, it tried to come. Yet, her blood sacrifice was not sufficient to bring it all the way in. So it had to pull you out to Otherwhere. To complete its task."

"Killing the Reddicks." I slumped in my chair. "Well, aren't I popular lately."

"Stay with me." His gaze intensified. He took my hand and icy fire shot through my body right to my ladyparts.

I shook my head. "No can do, Ice Man."

"I can protect you here. Whatever that beast was, it will come again."

"Wait, no. You killed it!"

"It was weakened, yes. To the point that it will take a long time to regain its power. But that is a very old spirit, born before even the First Magic was created. It comes and goes, makes a nuisance of itself killing Witches. However—" The shadow of a frown clouded his perfect face. "I do not recall it ever killing so many Witches at once." He tilted his head. "It is odd."

"So... it's coming back? You're sure?"

Erran shrugged and shook his head. "Likely. Once it recovers. For a being that strong, it may take hundreds of years. I'm surprised it returned so soon, if it was, as it claimed, responsible for the deaths of the other Reddicks."

"Oh." I smoothed my dress.

"Tessa." He leaned toward me. "You can be my queen. We will dance together all the days of our lives. I will make you happier than any woman in all the worlds." A warm feeling crept back into my legs and up my back. It felt like I was melting into the seat.

Boy, it was tempting. However, if I didn't deal straight away with this one, I'd be in for a world of hurt. This wasn't some gangly teenager though, and I had to be careful. I turned to language to help me out.

"Your professions of ardor are most flattering, sir." I retrieved my hand, then folded both into my lap, looking at the floor in what I hoped was the picture of demure deference. "And I am most grateful for your succor during this time of my recovery. Gladly do I promise to visit you here in your splendid home if you allow me to return to my business on Earth." Before he could jump in, I kept going. "You see, good sir, I must learn the truth about my kinswomen's deaths, and I cannot do that here. I pray you are not so cold as to refuse me this one request." I peered up coquettishly.

The Holly King's face was enraptured. When he spoke, it was passionate and hearty. "Of course, my dear one. You will go. Learn more if you wish. I shall await you at the autumn equinox."

He stood and bowed deeply, before taking my hand and kissing it. Then he put a hand on my shoulder and one on my chest. It felt like he pushed me backward, hard, and then I was falling through eternity...

Until I landed with a whuff on my own doorstep.

At least, I got to keep the clothes.

The apartment was locked up and battened down. Despite ditching the cloak right away, I got uncomfortably hot trying to find a way in. Wool and silk are great for the sub-zero court of the Holly King, but for late-summer Kentucky, leave something to be desired.

I tried spell after spell. I peered in my windows and jiggled knobs. Beaten, I sat in the shade under the deck. My cell phone was gone, probably at the bottom of that stupid lake the Witchfinder tried to drown me in. Dorcha was nowhere to be seen.

There was a small noise beside me, and Qyll stepped out of the ether.

He stood over me for a long minute. "My word, it's good to see you."

I stood up. "Did you intruder-proof my house?"

"I did. We didn't know where you were, we didn't know how to reach you. It was a long while before we could confirm you were even still alive. Come. I can let you in now."

At the back door, Qyll took a box out of his pocket. It was a skeleton key, with a green ribbon tied around it. Closing his eyes, he said reverently, "Most humble and hard-working Zita, I call upon you now.

Zita of Monsagrati, most humble of all."

It was like he was praying out loud. It was weird. But I was so tired that I was happy just to watch.

But then I heard a tinkle, like a wind chime in a hurricane. It grew louder as the empty air shimmered in front of his face, soon filled by a tiny woman, perhaps a foot tall. Her long black hair was adorned with keys—silver and gold, elaborate and plain. A headdress two sizes too big added another six inches to her stature. Her dress also appeared to be made of keys.

"*Benedicat tibi deus, fili mi!*" Her voice was like a little toy piano.

"*Et bonum est tibi!*" Qyll replied.

"Oh, nice. She only speaks Latin," I muttered. Qyll shot me a hard glance.

"Zita, this is Tessa. Tessa, this is Zita, the Tiny God of Lost Keys."

The petite goddess turned to me as regally as any full-sized queen. I was suddenly overcome with the urge to curtsy. Which I did. Poorly.

"Your majesty," I said, solemn.

She sniffed and turned back to Qyll.

"I have a gift, your grace." He offered her the skeleton key.

In Italian-accented English she squealed, "I have longed for one of these for such a long while!" She began to wield it as a scepter, majestically stepping through the air like she was her own parade, waving to invisible adorers and making such a racket with those clanging keys, I was sure the neighbors would complain about the noise. "You must fit the right key for each kind of power," she said conspiratorially, over the jingle of ten thousand metal teeth.

Finally, she stopped and smiled. "Thank you. Here I have yours, Mr. Qyll," Zita said in her toy-piano voice. From the ether, she handed him a huge golden key. A comically *huge* gold and purple velvet fairytale key with a golden and purple tassel to unlock my apartment.

"Zita, you are most gracious and kind." Qyll took her teeny hand, the one not brandishing a skeleton key, and kissed it. Her Mona Lisa smirk spread into a grin, and she blushed. "I do hope it is not too long again before I see you."

She blew him a kiss and waved, then vanished in a clangorous shimmer.

"What was that?" I ducked into the stuffy warmth of my closed-up kitchen.

"An old friend." He shrugged, a smile hinting around his eyes.

Qyll opened windows and tidied away the dust while I took a shower and dressed in normal clothes. When I came out, Dorcha had returned and greeted me with her customary enthusiasm. We had a good snuggle and I fetched a glass from the kitchen. Oh Woodford Reserve, what would I do without you?

"We'll need you to come down tomorrow for a statement," Qyll said. We sat on the couch, the air conditioner working to chill the rooms.

"A statement? For what? I wasn't on official business."

He shook his head. "It's the FBI's business now. A major magical rogue assaulted and kidnapped a magical citizen of Earth against her will. It will need to be documented and investigated. Surely you understand that."

I sighed and leaned back against the couch. "Fine."

After a few moments of silence, Qyll said quietly, "I came to tell you what I found in our files. When you didn't answer the door, and Dorcha was gone, I knew something was wrong."

I looked at him. His face had gone all soft around the edges. It surprised me. "How did you find me?"

He shook his head. "I didn't. Pryam sent scouts and asked for leads. But I was able to reach a contact I have."

"A contact? Who?" Even to my own ears, I sounded awfully demanding. But guess if I managed to reign myself in? "Don't they teach little FBI agents about sharing?" Yep, I slid from demanding to downright bitchy.

His face hardened like concrete. "His lordship the Holly King is a distant cousin. I went home to see my family and was able to determine only that you were safe in his court."

I squeezed my eyes closed. "I'm sorry, Q. I'm just... I don't know.

Out of sorts." When I opened my eyes again, he looked marginally mollified. "So, what did you find in your secret files?"

"Precious little." He spread out the papers. "After the Rift, there was some effort to track border crossings."

I nodded. "They wanted us to all carry like... passports or something."

"That idea is still on the table. Now, here's what we have, and keep in mind, to this day, the record-keeping on this matter is awful. Things are disorganized. There are literal file cabinets full of paper." He said this like the FBI was keeping the organs of orphans in glass jars in the basement.

He continued, "But my point is that there are some records of your mother's treks into the Other. We can see her egress and ingress points were nearly always the same. She entered Otherwhere from here, the Innamincka Preserve in Australia. Easter Island. Angkor Wat. Giza. She exited in as many spots as she entered."

"I don't remember her going to any of those places. Or even talking about them."

"Without your mother's grimoire, or some other corroborating evidence, there's really no way of telling. She could've been taking vacations, for all we know."

"What else?"

He sighed. "She purchased items for the shop. She was a productive member of society. After the Rift, she self-selected as an Earth-born Witch when the U.S. government added it as an option on the census. But there's nothing connecting her to anyone else, anyone of note."

I covered my eyes with a hand. "Nothing. We have nothing."

"I'm sorry, Tessa. I really am. I wish I could have found more. Perhaps with time..."

"I guess it doesn't matter now, I mean, the Holly King killed the Witchfinder General, right? Or nearly. My family's avenged." I sat back and stared at the ceiling.

Somehow it felt extremely anti-climactic.

"That's true," Qyll said. "And this isn't to say that we might not learn more. There's no hurry."

I closed my eyes. "So this is it. I dealt with the guy who killed my family. I helped the FBI. I will continue helping the FBI. I'm the hero of the hour after I stopped Ann's mudman from a dirty rampage across the city."

We sat in silence, letting the air conditioner hum.

After a while, I sat up. "I'd say this calls for a celebratory drink."

He smiled, the full-on beautiful smile. "I think that is well in order. I haven't told you this, but you did quite a nice job on your first case with SI. So we'll go. But only if you'll let me treat. It's the least I can do."

I grinned. "Just let me change into some party clothes."

The bash at the Three Libras was one for the books. Well, maybe it was. I remember Qyll and Mark Tabler, Victor, Dorcha, Nona and a couple of bartenders, and a bunch of people who suddenly thought I was awesome and not a murderous Witch after all.

It began with Victor running full-tilt at me, wrapping his stubby arms as far around as he could. "Tessa. I have been feeling so bad! When I heard you were gone, I thought the Witchfinder had taken you, and you were dead, and it was my fault."

I huffed out a surprised breath. "Victor, what are you talking about?!"

He pulled back, still gripping my arms. "I told you about him. I said too much, I shouldn't have told you. I thought that talking about him had brought him here. Please, forgive me." His craggy old face was full of remorse.

I patted his humpback. "It's fine. Really."

I was halfway through my third (fourth?) glass of Woodford when Mark stumbled over.

"I'm so glad you're okay." He flung his arms around my neck. I noticed he was a lot more muscular than I thought he would be. We danced to an 80's number that I remembered from my childhood and Mark remembered too, from YouTube. His floppy sandy hair stuck out everywhere, and we laughed our asses off.

I had fun, but still… something tickled at the back of my brain.

Something didn't feel right. But by the end of the night, I could barely remember my own name and that tickle went ignored. Just for now. Just so we could celebrate. It had been a very, very long time since I'd been to a party.

ABOUT THE AUTHOR

My first attempt at a book read suspiciously like a certain required-reading novel whose title rhymes with "Gourd of the Spies." I moved on from plagiarizing famous authors and into writing terrible poetry. Then the poetry stopped being so terrible. I started writing short stories, which were also not so terrible. Eventually I tried writing a book that I came up with on my own. It was terrible. So I wrote three more to get the hang of things. And here we are.

When I'm not writing, I perform improv comedy, tell stories on stage, ballroom dance, and craft. I also have identical twin sons. My husband is an ICU nurse and is a great person to be married to if you are an improv person, a book lover, and a nerd. He's also handy in medical emergencies.

My favorite authors in no particular order: Jane Austen, Neil Gaiman, China Mieville, Gabriel Garcia Marquez, Pablo Neruda, Charles Dickens, and Flannery O'Connor.

Thank You
for Reading

Please visit http://curiosityquills.com/reader-survey to share
your reading experience with the author of this book!

Kasper Mützenmacher's Cursed Hat, by Keith R. Fentonmiller

Berlin hatmaker Kasper Mützenmacher's carefree life of fedoras, jazz, and booze comes to a screeching halt when he must use the god Hermes' "wishing hat," a teleportation device, to rescue his flapper girlfriend from the shadowy Klaus, a veil-wearing Nazi who brainwashes his victims until they can't see their own faces. Klaus eventually discovers the wishing hat's existence and steals it on Kristallnacht. But even if Kasper gets back the hat and spirits his family to America, they won't be safe until they break the curse that has trapped them in the hat business for sixteen centuries.

The Outs, by E.S. Wesley

Memory-stealing blackouts push a seventeen-year-old honor student into kidnapping a little girl to keep her safe from the creature in her room, but the new voice in his head may be worse than any monster in the dark. Now it's up to a disabled comic book fangirl to save them both before the girl he stole unravels everyone's future.

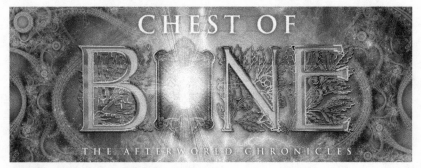

Chest of Bone, by Vicki Stiefel

As magical and mundane worlds retwine, empath and unawakened Mage Clea Reese must team up with the secretive James Larrimer to hunt her mentor's killer and stop the forces of corruption from obtaining the Chest of Bone, the ultimate source of otherworldly power. A woman whose true nature is hidden. A man whose reality is anathema. Together, they create something extraordinary. A Mage... A Monster... A Mission... And a Melody That Binds.

The Curse Merchant, by J.P. Sloan

Baltimore socialite Dorian Lake makes his living crafting hexes and charms, manipulating karma for those the system has failed. His business has been poached lately by corrupt soul monger Neil Osterhaus, who wouldn't be such a problem were it not for Carmen, Dorian's captivating ex-lover. She has sold her soul to Osterhaus, and needs Dorian's help to find a new soul to take her place. Hoping to win back her affections, Dorian must navigate Baltimore's occult underworld and decide how low he is willing to stoop in order to save Carmen from eternal damnation.

CPSIA information can be obtained
at www.ICGtesting.com
Printed in the USA
LVHW01s0239141117
556086LV00007B/426/P

9 781620 078510